With love & blessings,
DKH +

HEART

OF

REGULUS

THE SKULL CHRONICLES
BOOK VI

D. K. HENDERSON

Published by Lyra Publishing, 2020

Lyra Publishing
Wiltshire, England

Cover design by EBook Launch
www.ebooklaunch.com

www.dkhenderson.com

ISBN: 978-0-9934125-6-1

AUTHOR'S NOTE

It's been a while since Khalia's Tomb, (Book IV) was published, so for those readers who will find it helpful to have a reminder of the key characters and events that relate to this book, I have included some 'Catch-up Notes' as an appendix on Page 363.

New to the series? I've set a 'Spoiler alert' before the relevant section so you can choose whether or not to dive in.

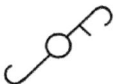

OTHER BOOKS IN THIS SERIES

HEART
OF
REGULUS

MUU-NAN

PART 1

THE GRAND COUNCIL OF GALACTIC ALLIANCES

(APPROX 250,000 BCE)

Chapter 1

'So, it is agreed? We proceed to the next stage?'

'Aye.' The response was unanimous.

'Good. Then we move forward without delay. Yes, Thoros?' Graklin, leader of the Council, frowned at the young administrator who had appeared at his side. 'What is it? I gave clear instructions that we were not to be disturbed under any circumstances.'

'My apologies, Councillor Graklin. Councillor Salan of Regulus is calling, demanding an immediate audience with the Grand Council. I explained that I could not interrupt the proceedings in this chamber but...,' he licked his lips nervously, 'she refused to listen to me. She was – um – most insistent.'

Graklin swallowed a smile. He knew Salan well, and he also knew that she did not like to be refused. She rarely was. Few would chance their arm – perhaps literally – by doing so. It was unsurprising that the young and inexperienced Thoros had crumbled in the face of her insistence.

Why though was she interrupting the Council session? The Regulans had only recently mastered interstellar travel; they were a long way from possessing – or even understanding – the technology they would need to participate in this ambitious project. And if indeed that was her purpose in coming here today, and he was certain that it was, how had she learned of it? Because the plan was so unique and unprecedented, those member races of the Grand Council involved had been asked to maintain the strictest secrecy. All, he believed, had honoured that directive. He turned to the twelve representatives present; whether to allow Salan audience was not solely his decision.

'What say you, Councillors, shall Salan be admitted?'

A chorus of 'Aye's replied. They were all curious as to the reason for her visit.

'Let her speak,' the Metulian Councillor, Qzed, called. 'I would know what she has to say that is so important that she wishes to gate-crash our deliberations.'

'She is most insistent, Councillor,' Thoros repeated.

'Very well, Thoros. Show her in.'

Instantly, the hologram of Salan appeared beside Graklin. She was magnificent. Her tawny coat glinted golden under the lights, sweeping smoothly over the strong, muscled shoulders and haunches of her sleek body, and her eyes flashed amber and fire in her proud feline head.

'Good day, Councillors.' Salan's voice was as rich and smooth as her coat and held a power that few could equal. 'My gratitude to you all in allowing me to come before you today. My request is simple. We, the races of Regulus, wish to be part of your great undertaking.'

'How have you learned of this, Salan?' Graklin was disturbed. 'All members of this Council who are participating, those here today, took an oath to keep it secret.'

She shrugged, and the tawny-gold coat rippled like ripe corn in the breeze. 'We learned of it. How is not important, Councillor. Whispers in the wind. I can, however, reassure you that we pose no threat to your endeavour.' Her eyes swept through the Chamber, her gaze settling for a brief yet potent moment on each of those seated there. 'I make my request again, Councillors.' Now she addressed the assembly. 'We, the races of the star system of Regulus, wish to be part of this great undertaking. Will you agree?'

'Salan, you do not have the capability. If you have truly learned what we intend, then you already know this.'

'We know. We also know that there will come a time when our great star Regulus will come to prominence on this blue and green planet that is your focus. When it does, the energy of Regulus must speak through one of the Skulls of Light.'

'How have you come by such information?'

'Your technology is beyond anything we can at this time dream of. That is true. You will recognise, however, that our astrologers and sages are incomparable in their skills. They have seen it, and they foretell that when this time comes, when our star's energy falls upon this world known to all as Tera, we will walk amongst its people. We must be involved in this endeavour. It is written in our destiny, and in theirs.'

The truth in the she-lion's words was felt by all, yet how could it be? The thirteen Skulls of Light were being forged from pure consciousness using abilities and technology that Salan herself had admitted were not just beyond her races' capabilities but were also – at that time and for millennia to come – beyond their capacity to comprehend.

'We have the twelve contributors, all of whom have been chosen after long and thorough consideration. Surely there is nothing to be done.' Graklin turned to his peers, questioning.

Atheol, the Pleiadean representative, rose to her feet. 'I am with Salan. She speaks with wisdom. There is a solution to be found, if we have the will.'

'It's ridiculous. The plan has been set out in every detail and is already under way. I acknowledge Salan's wishes, but to even attempt what she asks would mean delay, and we are all in agreement that the process cannot be interrupted.' The Eleusian representative bowed to Salan as he spoke.

Views in favour of and against her request echoed around the Council Chamber until Graklin held up his hand for silence.

'Salan, we have heard you. Your words carry great truth and wisdom; nonetheless, there are other, critical, factors to consider. This Council must now discuss your request. Leave us while we do so. We will send for you when we have reached our decision.'

Salan bowed her sleek head to the floor. 'Thank you, Councillors, for permitting me to present my plea to you. I ask only that you look into your hearts. As our sister Atheol has asserted, there is a way to be found, if the will is there.' She withdrew, the grace and elegance of her movements reflecting her absolute certainty that the Council would give her exactly what she had asked for.

* * * * *

Salan padded up and down in her living quarters, her ears twitching and her whiskers bristling. Usually, she would luxuriate in the silken wall hangings and the thick furs that covered her bed; today, she saw none of it. She was restless, impatient for the Council's call.

The council would agree to her request, of that she had no trace of a doubt. So, if she was so certain of the outcome – and she was – why was she this unsettled? It was a feeling she wasn't familiar with, and she didn't like it.

She lifted her head and drew in a lungful of air, following its cool path down her throat into her lungs and from there into the blood that carried it to every cell of her sleek, strong body. She took in another breath, long and slow and deep, then another. The tension in her muscles eased. Eager as she was to move on to the next step, the Council would summon her when they had come to their decision and not before. Her impatience would not hasten it.

'Why this restlessness?' she asked herself, settling on the furs and closing her eyes. Waiting for the answer that would soon float up from her deepest core, from that sacred place within where every answer could be found for those who knew where to look. Salan knew. Behind her eyelids, misty silver-violet shapes formed, dissolved, and reformed, ever changing, flowing constantly in and out of her vision. She was drifting in a nowhere time and a nowhere place.

An image crystallised around her: blue oceans and green forests, so alien to her home world. A single sun. She was looking down on Tera. She watched closely; this was the answer she sought. High above Tera, a star – her star, Regulus – glittered, its light falling on the planet's verdant surface; a civilisation rising in the shadow of a great stone lion, falling and rising again, a civilisation that would influence the Teran race for millennia; its people, diverse in skin colour and language, yet who beneath these superficial differences were the one and the same. The same blood in their veins, the same flesh on their bones. The same heartbeat. The same sorrows and the same joys. And lying dormant within every one of them, the same power.

Walking amongst the Teran people were her brothers and sisters from the Regulan worlds. Together with Muu-Nan, Skull of Arcturus, they would teach the Terans, help them to awaken and embody the power, the self-sovereignty, the courage, and the strength that were the essence of Salan and her races. They would become masters of their own destiny, slaves to no-one. If they chose to open their hearts and minds to the opportunity.

Salan trembled violently. This was the cause of her restlessness, the one element that, no matter how much the Council planned and prepared, would forever be beyond their control. The people of Tera had free will that no-one – no race, however advanced – could violate. It would be their choice alone whether to wake up or to stay sleeping. Awakening, all the gifts of Muu-Nan, of Arcturus and Regulus, and of the other twelve skulls and star races would be theirs. If they chose to remain asleep, they would live in ignorance of their birth-right, controlled by all the outside forces that assailed them, for another ten thousand years and more.

* * * * *

It was shortly before noon the following day that Thoros called, his disembodied face floating in the air. Graklin had requested her return to the Council Chamber; the Council had reached its decision.

Salan hurried to the Communications suite, her soft padded paws silent on the smooth, cool floor, greeting those she met with a nod. An automatic response, not really seeing them; her thoughts were elsewhere. With a low click, the door slid open and she entered the pure white, domed room, stopping in the centre.

'Are you ready, Commissioner Salan?' The disembodied voice of the communications technician echoed around the stark, empty hemisphere.

She nodded her reply. Moments later, the white around her vanished and she was standing once again next to Graklin in the centre of the Chamber, facing the twelve representatives.

For a moment she stood silent and unmoving struck, as always, by the real-ness of her surroundings. Logically, she knew she was still standing in the centre of the snow-white holo-chamber. Yet at the same time, here she was, with the Grand Council who had convened on the edge of the Andromeda Galaxy, millions of light years from the star system of Regulus. No matter how often she was transported in this way to a far-off location – and it had happened hundreds of times – she never stopped being amazed by the real-ness and solidity of the worlds that materialised around her. Her expression and stance gave away none of this.

She brushed off the familiar sense of wonder. She was here for a reason. Her gaze swept confidently across each face.

'You have come to a decision.' It was statement, not a question.

'We have.'

'There was lengthy debate?'

'Very lengthy. Though not as to whether to agree to your request or not. Everyone here holds the astrologers, sages, and oracles of Regulus in the highest regard, and no-one doubts the accuracy of their words. No, Salan, that was quickly decided. However, once it had been, the debate was no longer whether to include Regulus in our endeavour but how to do it. The creation of such skulls as those we are taking to Tera is unprecedented. We are not creating simple inanimate objects. These are sentient beings with their own will and consciousness. The process of bringing a new and – forgive me, Salan, if I speak bluntly – less evolved energy into that is not as straightforward as it may appear. We had to find a solution before delivering our answer to you for without it, no matter what our wish, we would have had to refuse you. The initiative is already underway. The creation of the skulls has begun and must proceed without interruption. We could not delay in order to come up with a solution.'

'But you did find a way.' Salan's voice was calm, level, self-assured; her heart, however, was racing.

The Council leader's eyes twinkled. 'Indeed we did, Salan. Welcome to the initiative.'

Before she could prevent it, a low purr of triumph had escaped her lips. 'That is wonderful news, Graklin. We, of Regulus, thank you. I thank you.'

'You will contribute much, Councillor.'

She inclined her head to the tall, bronze-skinned Sirian who had spoken, then turned back to Graklin. 'What happens now?'

'The Arcturans have agreed that you will add your energies to their skull, Muu-Nan. The skull is of rose amethyst and will carry a dominant male energy. He will be a perfect combination of the energies and essences of Arcturus and Regulus. To speak truly, and all present are in agreement, our Arcturan sisters and brothers are perhaps the only ones amongst us capable of accomplishing this fusion without threatening the integrity of the skull. Councillor Olzek?'

The slightly built Arcturan rose to his feet. 'It is our honour to welcome you, Councillor Salan. As Councillor Graklin has stated, the creation process is already underway, therefore we must act quickly if we are to successfully incorporate the Regulan energy and essence into the skull. In addition, I have spoken with those overseeing the process and we are all in agreement. The skull's name will remain Muu-Nan. However, I am delighted to advise you that it will also be known as the Heart of Regulus, in your honour.'

Salan bowed her forehead briefly to the floor in appreciation of the gesture, then lifted her head. There was no time for further courtesies. 'How long do we have?'

'An interstellar craft is even now on its way to you. It will arrive at dawn, your time, the day after tomorrow, to leave later that same day. We require you to send one member of each of the qualifying Regulan races – those whose technology and spiritual evolution is sufficiently advanced – to join us in the diffusion process.'

'That isn't long to find such ambassadors.'

'No, but it is all the time there is. The process has its own timetable and, as I have already explained, this cannot be halted nor delayed. Consult your oracles. They will find those you seek.'

Salan lowered her head in acknowledgement. 'We will be ready. And after, when the skull has been created?'

'We ask that one representative remain with us to travel with us to Tera as we place and activate the skulls. The others, we will return to their homes.'

'Very well. Is there anything else?'

'We of Arcturus will hold full responsibility for Muu-Nan and his guardians until such time as Regulus takes the ascendant energy over Tera. During that period, when its influence holds sway, we will step back and the energy and wisdom of Regulus that is carried within the skull will prevail. I wish to reassure you that this energy will always be present, always play a crucial role, always be accessible to those who seek it; however, except for that period, it will not be predominant.'

'That is reasonable. Let it be so. We await your craft with eagerness, Councillor Olzek. Councillors, Councillor Graklin, I have much to do and very little time to do it. I take my leave of you with my thanks.'

The comfortable Council Chamber dissolved around her into the white dome of the holo-chamber. Quickly, she crossed to the door. As she had just told the Council, there was a lot to do in a very short time. It was down to her to make sure it happened.

* * * * *

The first rays of the great suns of Regulus had touched the lilac waters of the vast lake that edged the star-port on Salan's home world, turning the sky rapidly from deepest black to rich mossy green to pale emerald as the light strengthened. Salan stared out over the landing field, a chaos of nervousness and excitement churning through her veins. She had travelled many times between the worlds of the Regulus system. Today, for the first time, she would travel far beyond those boundaries, out into the distant stars.

The representatives had been chosen and to her lasting surprise, the sages had called her name first. Two others waited with her. On her right was Kylx, a male from the closest neighbouring planet. He was well-built, muscular, and almost human in form, except for the thick, golden fur that covered his skin and the retractable claws that took the place of finger- and toenails. A thick mane of tawny gold hair settled like a halo around his shoulders and his eyes flashed orange-gold. Normally naked, today he wore a short sarong around his hips.

The second companion, Exxa, had none of the others' leonine features. Exxa was tall, twig thin, and completely androgynous, with a soft, gentle manner. Not one hair grew on his smooth, white skin and her eyes were the palest blue. Most of the sages and oracles were drawn from Exxa's people, who for generations had been the mystics and sensitives of this solar system. All three were strangers to each other, and not for the first time Salan wondered at the mix and how they would get along in the days to come.

She peered at the black speck she had initially dismissed as some flying creature. It was approaching rapidly, growing ever larger until it filled half the sky, revealing itself as an intergalactic ship comprising two flat discs, spinning in opposite directions, linked by a central core. This had to be the vessel they were waiting for. She held it fast in her gaze as it loomed overhead, blocking the suns, dropping slowly, so slowly, to the ground as if it weighed no more than a helias leaf.

It was time to welcome her guests. She turned from the window, outwardly as dignified, graceful, and elegant as always. Inside, however, she was skipping with the joy and excitement of a cub. Flanked by her two companions, Salan walked into the greatest adventure of her life.

PRESENT DAY: WILTSHIRE, ENGLAND

GEMMA, 1

Chapter 2

I jerked back, startled.

'Easy, Gemma,' Duncan soothed. He had only pressed a glass of brandy into my hand, and I had nearly hit the ceiling. I had been a long way away, back in the car an hour before, reliving and re-reliving those ghastly moments over and over again. Joe was sitting opposite me, as white as paper and still shaking so much that the glass of Jack Daniels Duncan had given him threatened to spill over the carpet.

At last Joe spoke, a hoarse whisper. 'What the fuck just happened?'

'It appears that someone tried to kill you both.' Duncan was remarkably matter of fact.

We were in his living room, having turned up around ten minutes earlier looking like ghosts and gabbling like lunatics the moment he'd opened the door. One look at us and he'd hurried us inside, sat us down, and somehow made sense of what we were saying. As soon as he had, he'd raced down to the road and pulled his Mercedes into his garage, out of sight of curious glances. Now he was back, looking anxious and pouring us all, including himself, a stiff drink.

'You really think it was the same car that turned up at Callum's squat while you were there?' he asked. Joe had already voiced his suspicions.

I leaned back against the soft cushions. I had a fearsome headache coming on and wanted nothing more than to forget the whole ghastly incident. Which, of course, was never going to happen.

'I don't know, Duncan. Joe believes it was and he had it in his rear-view mirror all the time it was chasing us. I hardly saw it. I had my eyes shut most of the time.'

'I'm convinced of it.' Joe rubbed his eyes wearily. 'Although it's only a niggling prodding at the back of my mind. I've nothing else to base it on other than that both cars were the same colour. Dark metallic grey. Gunmetal. It's a common colour. There was something else about it too, only I can't work out what it is.'

'Then stop trying. The more you chase it, the more it'll run away from you. Let it go and it may come to you.'

Joe switched his focus. 'So, what do we do now? The police will be searching for us. We just caused a fatal accident and ran away. Even if the other driver isn't dead…' He paused swallowing hard. Remembering the mangled wreckage of the Range Rover, neither of us believed in that possibility. '…failing to stop after an accident, or whatever the phrase is, is still a crime. And what about any injuries in the other cars involved?'

'More likely to be dangerous driving.'

'Duncan!'

'Sorry.' He turned to his laptop, hit a series of keys, and studied the screen for a few minutes before turning back. 'OK. The initial police report states one fatality. In the Range Rover. No surprise there from what you've told me. Half a dozen minor injuries from the ensuing shunts. The casualties were taken to the Great Western Hospital in Swindon, none serious.'

'Thank God.' Joe slumped back, the tension in his eyes easing a little.

'How do you know that?' I frowned. Then it clicked. Duncan, I recalled, had – um – ways of accessing information that perhaps he shouldn't. 'Anything else? Do they have a description of your car?'

'Nothing definite. A large, dark – possible black – saloon. The lorry driver thinks it might have been a Lexus or a Mercedes or some other high end make but he isn't certain. They don't have a registration number or model. Nothing there to trace it to you. Or to me.' Of course. It was Duncan's car. Any leads the police did have would end up here.

'If they do, they'll have all the evidence they need.' Tense, Joe ran his hand through his hair. 'The Range Rover's paint is all over the back bumper and wing where he rammed us. Which means your Merc's paint will be on the wreckage of the Range Rover. It won't take them long to fit the puzzle together.'

'I've dealt with that. I've one or two contacts, all legit, not on any police files. One of them is already on his way to pick up the Merc. By tomorrow evening every trace of this evening's events will be gone and my car will be safely back in my garage.'

I stared at Duncan, dumbfounded: top class (and apparently undetected) hacker, network of secret, skilled contacts. Was this pleasant, unassuming man actually a real-life undercover James Bond or what?

'What about CCTV? I've watched enough TV crime dramas to know that could have caught us.' Joe was still worried.

'In those lanes? No, there won't have been any out in the sticks. And we're not in the city here, so yes, there are a few cameras dotted about in the town centre but not much elsewhere. You'd have had to be really unlucky to have been caught on your way here. I can find out though.'

Reassured – slightly – by Duncan's confidence, Joe relaxed back into his chair. 'Again, what do we do now?'

'You get some rest. Both of you. You're badly shaken up. Tomorrow, you'll be better able to think more clearly. Gemma, you've got the spare room.' He rummaged in a cupboard and dragged out a duvet and a pillow which he tossed to Joe. 'Joe, you've got the sofa.'

I hauled myself to my feet. With a start, I realised that after the nightmare of the evening, Callum's funeral and the mysterious Pieter van Broek were no more than hazy shadows. For now, at least. My mind was a chaotic mush, and my body was lead. Duncan was right. Curling up in a cosy bed would be heaven, though I doubted very much I'd get any sleep.

I was wrong. My head had hardly touched the pillow before sleep claimed me. It was not, however, a restful sleep. Chilling dreams haunted me endlessly, no doubt brought on by the events of the day. I was running down endless corridors chased by unknown figures with blank spaces where their faces should have been; I was deafened by the screeching of brakes and metal and tyres, and the screams of injured and dying people, trapped in twisted, unrecognisable wreckage; Callum's coffin, disappearing behind the crematorium's curtain on its way to the oven; the lid flying open, Callum's brutalised and decaying corpse jerking up to stare directly at me, grey skin and clouded eyes almost touching mine, mouthing words I couldn't hear; his mottled, rotting fingers reaching out, clutching at my clothes. I was screaming and yet no sound issued from my mouth. No-one could hear me. No-one could come and rescue me. Screaming and screaming as what was left of Callum dragged relentlessly at me, and the oven flames blazed and roared ever closer behind him.

'Gemma. GEMMA!' I thought I heard my name, coming from a long way off. Still those rotting hands gripped at my arms and still I fought to get free.

'Gemma.' The voice was closer now, breaking through the nightmare like the sun's rays break through clouds. Slowly at first, then ever stronger. Callum was fading. The coffin, the flames were fading.

'Gemma! Wake up.' Joe's voice, gentle and soothing. Worried. But those hands still gripped me. Still held me prisoner. 'Wake up, Gemma, it's a nightmare. You're dreaming.'

My eyelids flickered open. Joe was sitting on the bed, Duncan standing behind him looking concerned. Hands still held me, only now they were Joe's hands, firmly gentle and reassuring on my shoulders. Shaking me lightly, pulling me up out of the dark depths of my dreams.

I was shivering violently, my heart pounding as if I had run a marathon, my breath coming in rapid, shallow gasps.

'It was just a nightmare,' Joe repeated, shifting his hold to take my hands.

Duncan disappeared, returning a minute later carrying a glass of water. 'Are you OK now?' he asked, passing it to me.

'I think so.' Only I wasn't sure I was. The hideous scenes still burned vividly in my memory.

'Good. Then I'm off back to bed.'

'Duncan, what time is it?'

'Just after two.'

Two in the morning? I'd only been asleep for a couple of hours. There was still most of the night to go. Would I be able to go back to sleep? In truth, did I want to? What if the nightmare returned?

'Shift over.'

I had been lost so deep in thought that I hadn't noticed Joe leave the room. Now he was back carrying his duvet and pillow, which he dropped on the bed.

'I'm going to stand watch,' he explained. 'See off any bad dreams that think they can show up again.'

Dear, precious Joe. Always watching my back. Always knowing exactly what I needed. I snuggled down next to him, my head on his shoulder, feeling safe for the first time in hours within the refuge of the arm he had wrapped around my shoulders. It wasn't long before I had drifted away into the warm darkness of a deep and dream-free sleep.

Chapter 3

Joe was gone when I woke the following morning; I could hear him chatting to Duncan in the living room. I stretched, feeling rested and surprisingly relaxed and back to being myself given the events of the evening before. I quickly dressed and went to join them.

A short while later, we were seated around the table tucking into a hearty breakfast.

'So, to repeat my question from last night – what do we do now?' Joe asked between mouthfuls of sausage and mushrooms.

'Like I said, I've checked again this morning and the police have no more leads on the car involved.' Duncan was repeating his earlier conversation with Joe for my benefit. 'It looks like you – we – are in the clear from that direction, at least for now. As for whoever was driving the Range Rover and who employed him…'

'Why try to kill us?'

'To tie up any loose ends? I know you said you got away from Callum's squat unseen but what if you were spotted? The car anyway? They may well have been at the crematorium watching the guests, seen you and the car there and put two and two together. If they believe you have Callum's notes…'

'Which raises another question,' I put in. 'If that's the case, who came here and forced you to hand it all over? It can't be the same people. They'd already have what they wanted.'

'Unless they believed we knew what the notes contained and wanted to ensure we wouldn't either share it or follow it up ourselves.' Joe let his fork drop with a clatter onto his empty plate.

'No.' That didn't feel right. 'It has to be two separate groups.' I turned to Duncan. 'The ones who came here were professional but didn't use any violence, right?' He nodded. 'It seems the people who grabbed Callum have no qualms about it. They can't be the same group.'

'That's plausible.' Duncan fell silent for a moment, thinking. 'Maybe he wasn't trying to kill you. Maybe he was planning to run you off the road and kidnap you, like they did Callum. To find out what you do know and force you to hand over the notes. One man could do that, if he had a gun in his hand.'

I got up and walked to the window, looking out over the oh-so-normal street where everyone was going about their oh-so-normal everyday lives. This was all speculation and guesswork; the painful truth was that we didn't have a clue, and to be honest, that was the worst part of it. Not knowing who was after us or why, other than that it had something to do with the skulls and – maybe – the stories I was writing about them. Not knowing when they might try again.

'Maybe we should forget all about this, Gemma. Just walk away. Go to Chamberlain, tell him everything we know and let him deal with it. These people, whoever they are, aren't playing games. They nearly killed us last night and they won't stop until they have what they want.' However well he was hiding it this morning, Joe was clearly still very shaken.

I wanted nothing more than for it all to stop. To go back to my safe, comfortable, uneventful life (at least, most of me did. There was a tiny bit that, I'm embarrassed to admit, revelled in all the excitement) but…

'I don't think we can, Joe. They aren't going to let me. They think I – we – know something, even though we don't, and they want to find out what it is. I'm in this too far to turn back now.' A sudden flash of understanding did little to ease my anxiety. They – whoever they were – also wanted me for my connection to the skulls. I said as much. 'And then there was Gal-Athiel's message,' I added quietly.

'What message?' Duncan was looking curious. Joe, baffled. I'd forgotten I hadn't told them. It was as crystal clear in my mind as the day she had shared it with me and as I repeated her words to Joe and Duncan that morning, that same sense of calm I'd experienced then washed through me again.

'My dearest Child, from the day the Skulls came into your life and you accepted their invitation, you always knew, in some secret place deep within your soul, that this was the way it would go. That the road would not be an easy one. That it would demand of you more than you believed you were able to give. Even so, you said Yes. And you are still saying Yes.

'Make no mistake, there is more, much more, to come, Little One. You, and those who walk with you, will be challenged again and again. Again and again, you will want to give up, yet you will not do so. Even now, when your head tells you No, your soul is saying Yes. You will find the courage to go on, and in doing so, you will prevail. Do not give up hope. Do not give up your quest. It is too important.'

'You see, I can't give up now.' Though I may have known little else, I did know with utter certainty that I couldn't even if I tried. The Skulls of Light wouldn't let me. I squeezed Joe's hand. 'I'm so sorry for dragging you into this.'

'Hey, what else has a man to do with his life? Besides, this is all down to Callum, not you. He got himself killed when he started snooping in places certain people didn't want him to go. We simply got caught up in the fall-out. The police won't be too interested in re-opening his case without further compelling evidence so we can't expect much help from them. There's not a lot of sympathy for him in that circle. They're convinced he's a murderer, and a vicious one at that, even if we know otherwise. He was a friend. We owe it to him to get to the bottom of this.'

'One will lead to the other,' Duncan stated. 'Solve one mystery and you'll solve all of them.'

'How?' That was the answer none of us could give.

MUU-NAN

PART 2

HANNA

Chapter 4

The thirteen men had gathered in a small natural amphitheatre measuring no more than fifty paces across, with gently sloping, grassy banks that formed a green and peaceful cradle in the land. Small standing stones of granite, speckled pink and black amongst the white quartz and none of them more than waist high, encircled the outer perimeter, set close together with barely five paces separating each one from its neighbour. At the northernmost edge, the arc of the shallow bowl was cut off by a wall of dark rock that, over the ages, had been scoured clean of soil and plants by the elements. It rose up out of the ground to the height of two, maybe two and a half, men and dropped gradually down to ground level at the rear in rough, natural pillows and steps formed over aeons by the wind, ice, and rain. The front was a near vertical face in the centre of which a small alcove measuring from waist to shoulder high and the same wide, and as deep as a man's arm to his elbow, had been carved out by the men's long dead ancestors.

The group had spent the previous night camped out in the hollow. In the centre, the fire pit embers still glowed amber and crimson, and the supple, hide bed-mats were scattered over the close-cropped turf. They had travelled here from all over the land for this night's ceremony and were already preparing for the moon rise. It would be a full moon, the largest and brightest of the year, the most propitious for this contact with their god.

Hanna watched the activity from behind one of the standing stones that encircled the rim. She had been sent from the inner cove only a short while before; at the onset of the preparations, it had become a sacred space that no female was permitted to enter until dawn had come once more and the sun heralded a new day. Her father, a strong, upright, and commanding figure, was sprinkling fragrant herbs on the sweet grass directly below the alcove in the rock face, looking every inch the clan leader that he was. As were the twelve who busied themselves alongside him.

Her presence here was unusual. Though not unheard of, it was rare for anyone else to attend these rituals, even more so a female. But she had had her first woman's bleed at the dark moon and suspected that was why her father had brought her along. Now that she had come of age to be a wife, his intention was to marry her off to one of the other clan leaders, creating for himself tighter alliances, and in doing so strengthening and protecting his position as head of the clan council.

Hanna had no desire to marry at all, and certainly not to any of those here, all of whom were far older than even her father and, without exception, were rough, hairy, and decidedly unattractive. Today, at least, that distaste had been eclipsed by excitement at the wonders she might witness. No, she could not take part or be present within the circle itself; nonetheless, her father had permitted that she watch, in silence and hidden from sight, behind the standing stone where she now waited, wide-eyed and fidgeting with impatience.

Since their arrival, she had fulfilled her woman's role well, serving food and drink to the men, staying mute and out of the way as they sometimes heatedly discussed clan business. She had seen the moment her father had offered her hand; they had all turned to stare at her, appraising her suitability as a wife and heir-bearer. Hanna was on the verge of womanhood, tall and lithe with long limbs and a grace in her movements, and the promise of a voluptuous if slender figure to come as she matured. A mane of golden curls cascaded to her shoulders and huge amber eyes, flecked with gold and shadowed by long, dark lashes, flashed evidence of her stubbornness and wilful temper. She was aware that her appearance would not appeal to them; she was too unusual in her looks. She had been criticised for being different too often to ignore and understood now that she was odd and deeply unattractive. The men of this land much preferred the short, wide-hipped, and full-breasted women who birthed babies easily and often. Hanna had never been given a second glance.

Seeing the girl's pain, Grandmother had often told her that she should be proud of her looks, that they were a gift from the gods. Hanna didn't believe her; from the bullying and insults of the other children and the frowns and cold shoulders of their parents, none of them believed it either. She was a freak. She didn't fit in. If her looks had been a gift from the gods, they had bestowed upon her the gift of a curse and not a blessing. No, it would be her other qualities, not to mention the large dowry her father was offering, that would seal the matter. She had been relieved when the men had stood, talking over, and her father had sent her from the hollow with a wave of his hand, away from their less than flattering scrutiny.

The men moved quickly and efficiently. Within a very short time, the bed-mats had been rolled up and set to one side, the fire built up, and torches rammed into the ground between the standing stones in readiness for the ritual to come.

The day came to a close in a blaze of red, gold and violet. The fire burned brighter, fiery orange sparks glittering in a darkening world. When the last dazzling arc of the sun dropped beyond the distant treetops, the torches were lit; immediately the whole arena was illuminated as brightly as midday. In the flickering light, the men took up their position in a semi-circle with the fire at their backs, facing the recess in the cliff face. Her father, who had been waiting at the rear, now moved forward and stopped forward of the others, two paces back from the centre of the rock face. He was carrying a square box that she had never seen before, even on the two-day journey they had made here from their village. It wasn't large, perhaps twice the length of her father's hand on each side, and it gleamed like metal in the dancing flames. She peered through the twilight, enthralled and curious.

Her father set the box on the short, cropped grass and reached into his tunic. Hanna stifled a gasp. Gold. Whatever he now held in his hand, and from where she crouched she couldn't see clearly, it was made of gold for it shone like the sun where the torchlight brushed it. She had no time to dwell further. Her father had bent over the box and was pressing the object against its side. A soft click reached her across the still night. He reached in and...

What was he holding? It was roughly round and a pale pinkish-purple colour, like the star flowers that bloomed in early spring, covering the hillsides in a soft blanket of scented blossoms. Her mouth fell open. She had never seen such a treasure, had not known it had existed. Where had her father kept it that she had never come across it? She watched spellbound as he set it on the ledge in the cliff face and stepped back until he was only a pace or two in front of the others gathered there.

*　*　*　*　*

The man at each end of the row began to drum, the steady, deep resonating rhythm of a heartbeat that reverberated through the still night. Building. Building. Creeping deep into Hanna's bones, her blood, her skull, until it became part of her, every cell vibrating to its rhythm. The world around her vanished and she clutched at the stone by her side, eyes wide, barely breathing, seeing nothing but the scene unfolding in the hollow, captured within the circle of stones.

Two shimmering columns of sparkling white light twisted and swirled in the night, one each side of the alcove, and within the alcove itself, a dazzling silvery sphere was spinning rapidly. She shut her eyes to protect them from its radiance. The drumbeat grew louder, faster, until she feared her head would explode and she clasped her hands to her ears and squeezed her eyes even more tightly shut, trying to block it out. Still it went on, louder and louder, faster and faster, until the air itself hummed and quivered.

Just as it reached a level where Hanna couldn't endure it any longer, it stopped. Suddenly and completely. She peeked through her fingers; her eyes widened, and her mouth fell open. Whereas only a short while before the alcove had been filled with light too bright to look on, now that light was a gentle pinkish lavender glow that pulsed with life.

If what she had witnessed up until now had stunned her to her core, it was nothing compared to what was to come. In front of her disbelieving eyes, the two columns of light were crystallising into human-like forms. No, not human. If, at the beginning, she believed them to be so, she soon realised that they were far from it. They were roughly human-shaped, certainly, of upright stance with one head, two arms and two legs each, but there any resemblance to the human form ended. They were no bigger than children of perhaps ten summers, slight of build with silver skin brushed with a soft green hue. Their heads were disproportionately large; domed craniums tapered to a pointed chin in triangular faces from which huge, midnight-black eyes peered inscrutably. Who... *what...* were they?

The clan leaders stood firm; they must have experienced this many times before, she reasoned, for none of them seemed surprised or bewildered by the experience. On the contrary, the men paid no attention to the two guardian figures – for surely that was what they had to be. The group's focus was solely on the alcove and its contents, which filled the area with a soft, eerie light. The men were chanting quietly, a sequence of phrases and notes that harmonised, split and flowed back together again in a river of mesmerising sound.

Her father dropped to his knees, now barely only a step away from the rock face, his head bowed in veneration. He spoke, and this time Hanna heard his words clearly.

'Blessed Muu-Nan, bringer of light and peace, we welcome you. Bless us with your wisdom. Guide us in moving forward in harmony and co-operation. Send harvests and meat to fill our stores. Bestow on us your love.'

The light within the alcove flared; tendrils of light twisted out from its centre, reaching out towards every man present, twining around them, enveloping them until they too shone as brightly as the midday sun. Hanna couldn't have said how long they stayed like that; it felt like an eternity before the glow softened and the glittering tendrils pulled back.

'It is done. We thank you.' Her father's voice was strained, as it was those times when he returned exhausted from the hunt. He was slumped forward, as if the weight of his head and shoulders were too much to carry, remaining upright through force of will alone.

The light within the alcove dimmed and then vanished, leaving only darkness. The not-quite-human guardians were shimmering now too, losing solidity with every second that passed until they too dissolved into nothingness. Only then did her father lower himself to the ground and close his eyes. The others did the same.

'Father?' Was he dead? Had what had just occurred drained his life from him? She had to know he was safe. 'Father?'

Heedless of his order that she should stay out of the circle until daybreak, Hanna raced across the soft turf to his side. She breathed again. No, he wasn't dead, he was snoring gently in a deep sleep just like all the others, every one of them exhausted by the events that had taken place. Relieved, she lay back on the cool, dew-damp grass and stared up at the night sky, a soft velvet-black expanse thickly dusted with glittering pinpricks of light, in which the plump sphere of the full moon was dipping close to the far horizon.

'Hanna.' The whisper drifted gently in the still night air. Her eyes flew open. She had fallen asleep and dreamed that someone was calling to her. It had sounded so real. Except... She was wide awake now and there it was again.

'Hanna.'

She *was* awake, wasn't she? She pinched the flesh of her forearm hard and yelped in pain. Yes, she was awake. Beside her, her father still slept soundly. It hadn't been him. Who was calling her name?

'Come, Hanna.' The alcove. It was shining once more with a soft, inviting light. And within the light... She rose and stepped across to look more closely, immediately drawing back in alarm. The luminescence surrounded a large carved skull of clear, pale lavender crystal. No, that wasn't right. The light wasn't around it; it was coming from *inside* it. Was this what her father had spoken with earlier? Instinctively, she knew that it was. Why then had it woken again now? Why had it called her name? And where were the guardians who had appeared before?

Barely had they formed than the questions evaporated. They didn't matter. All that mattered was the skull in the alcove. It was drawing her in, commanding every bit of her consciousness to it, and she was unable to resist. Her arm, her hand, lifted and moved to it, driven by a power outside of her will.

'Do not be afraid, child.' Words whispering in her mind. 'This is your destiny. It has been so forever.'

But she *was* afraid. She was terrified! What was happening? Is this why her father had ordered her to remain outside the circle? She had disobeyed through fear for his life and now...

'Peace, child.' The voice came again. 'You are safe. You will come to no harm. This is your destiny. Come now and fulfil it.'

No. No, she wouldn't. She didn't want it, this destiny, whatever it was. She wanted to stay here with her father and mother and brothers and sisters. She'd even willingly marry one of those hoary old men if she could escape this.

'Hanna!' Her father's desperate and terrible cry reached her through her fear and the compelling magnetism of the skull.

'Father,' she screamed, 'help me!'

Her hand was brushing the crown of the skull; it flashed and crackled like captive lightning at her touch. Her fingers, her palm, her wrist tingled like nettle stings. Try as she might, she couldn't move it. It was glued to the stone.

She screamed again. 'Father!'

'Hold on, Hanna. I'm coming.'

Her arm was tingling now too, the sensation moving rapidly up to her shoulder and across her back, growing sharper and fiercer as it did so, expanding until it filled her body. The world around her was vanishing, engulfed little by little in an ever-thickening mist. She could just make out figures running towards her, calling her name – but they were moving so slowly, as if they were fighting through thick, claggy mud at every step. They wouldn't reach her in time.

'Father...' It was a last, desperate cry for help before the mist enveloped her completely in its white shroud and obscured their shadowed forms. The shouts faded away and were gone. From a great distance, she heard the voice again, only this time it wasn't talking to her. It was speaking to her father.

'She is safe, and she will be well looked after. Do not mourn her. She is alive and well and will remain so. You knew that this day must come. You knew she had a greater purpose. Let her go now. Let her fulfil that purpose. She is safe.'

Then that too was gone and there was only the skull, aflame with crackling light. Although... No. No, that wasn't all... Behind the skull, an opening had formed, pulsing to the rhythm of her heart, expanding with every beat. Its edges were indistinct, concealed by a swirling, ever-changing curtain of mist and light. She was being drawn into it. With surprise, she realised that she was no longer afraid. A warm, deep peace had wrapped itself around her, the terror of only a moment before extinguished and forgotten. Had she ever known anything but this feeling and this place? She tried to remember her name and it eluded her. She tried to remember how she had come here. Fragments of images, sounds, words, floated through her consciousness and melted away as soon as she turned to them, too ephemeral to grasp.

She was moving forward ever more quickly now, faster and faster, until she had to close her eyes, unable to keep up with the motion. Her stomach lurched and churned. She fought down the urge to vomit. Still the speed increased. Her senses were in overload. They shut down. The tiny space that enveloped her went dark and she dropped into unconsciousness.

Chapter 5

Hanna lay sleepily on the stone ledge, her legs dangling in the cool, tumbling waters of the cascade that spilled into a crystal-clear pool far below. She was surrounded by lush foliage – ferns, trees and shrubs of all sizes, flowers of every colour and scent – that formed a leafy haven of peace high above the dry plains floor below. This oasis of vibrant life, created by the river that flowed through here all year, continued from the pool, stretching across the landscape to the horizon in a verdant green ribbon cut through by a silver glittering thread.

She was glad of these waters, of the shade of these trees. This season of the year was hot, very hot, and beyond the narrow strip of vegetation, the parched land baked under an unforgiving sun. It would remain so until the autumn rains. In that vast dusty emptiness, there was little food or shelter. It was only here, beside these waters, that the land teemed with life. The herbivores found a feast in the lush leaves, roots, and fruits; the predators who stalked these docile creatures, an equally abundant larder.

Hanna daydreamed as she half-dozed in the warmth of the afternoon, nebulous half-formed images drifting through her mind...

That first morning she had been woken by light flickering through her eyelids. Bright light. Sunlight. Soft grass had tickled her bare legs and arms and the earth beneath her had been soft and yielding. She had lain there for a long time, confused and disoriented, soothed by the warm sunshine that had bathed her face and the gentle breeze that had played with her hair. She could have been no more than twelve or thirteen sun cycles in age she guessed now, looking back, though she had no way of knowing for sure.

In that still, restful place, elusive, hazy images had teased her, only to vanish when she reached out to grasp them. Perhaps, after all, they had simply been the shadows of dreams. Except that, alongside those images, sat a subtle but persistent certainty that some momentous event had occurred and that she had been part of it. More than that remained a mystery, her past a slate wiped clean of all traces of what had once been written there.

On one hand, she had had the sense that this had always been her home, and that she had simply forgotten what had happened prior to that day. It certainly felt that way and, in truth, she couldn't remember ever *not* having been here. And yet those vague shadows refused to leave her alone; they hovered even now, so many seasons later. She couldn't remember who she was or how she had come here, although sometimes, when she was on the edge of sleep, the whisper of memories from another place, another life, nudged her from the fringes of her consciousness. Ghosts that dissolved into nothingness as soon as she looked at them.

Her home was a small, sturdy cabin of interlocking logs. An enclosed area served as her sleeping space, welcome shelter when winter came and its icy blasts raced down from the north. It was on the lush grass next to this small hut, in a clearing amongst the towering trees, that she had awoken on that first morning when the sunbeams had kissed her eyelids and drawn her from the depths of her sleep. Adjoining the cabin was a larger covered area, open to the side and front, its roof supported by a massive tree trunk whose canopy stretched so far into the sky that she couldn't see the top.

She had been a child back then, and she had watched the cycle of the stars a dozen times since as the seasons passed. Now she was a woman, the promise of her pubescent body come to fruition, full-breasted and wide-hipped with strong, lithe limbs. Her most remarkable feature however were her eyes, which were rich, deep amber flecked with gold, and which flashed with fire.

And beside her when she had woken on that first morning, as on every morning since, had been the strange and eerily beautiful crystal skull. It was as clear as the ice that transformed the waters of the cascade into solid sculptures when the cold times came, its colour a delicate lavender-pink, and was filled with rainbow flashes and ethereal veils formed by the delicate internal fractures in the crystal. The crystal seemed alive, flowing as slowly as liquid ice; within its frozen core, images formed and shifted constantly, fading and reforming before her eyes, merging into another, and another, in an endless stream.

* * * * *

In all her time here, she had never felt afraid or alone. At first, and always, there had been the skull, a constant comforting presence, and the birds and animals of this sanctuary that had shown no fear, coming close and warming her heart with their trust and companionship. Later, people had come for her help and healing. At first, the occasional traveller in need had chanced upon her and benefitted from her gifts. Word of her 'miracles' had spread, and soon more and more sought her out until today, she had people arrive at the cascade every few days. She gave to them freely.

Her eyes sparkled with amusement. The first time the skull had spoken to her! Well, not exactly spoken. Perhaps a better description was that he (and to her surprise, it was a 'he', for there was no doubt that the skull held a strong male energy) had 'thought' to her, his words carried on rich, mellow tones that had resonated in her mind, not in her ears.

She had been in that beautiful place for only a few days and had been collecting water from one of the small streams that led into the main river when he called to her.

'Hanna, come. It is time.'

With a yelp, surprised and not a little scared, she lost her balance on the uneven bank and sat down with a bump and a splash into the cold water, staring round nervously to see who was there, even as she understood that the voice had come from inside her mind and not the external world.

A soft chuckle echoed in her head. 'I apologise for startling you, Child. It was not my intent. Come, now. It is time for your learning to begin.'

'What... what learning?' Hanna's question hung in the still, warm air. Who was speaking to her as kindly and lovingly, and as demanding of obedience, as a father?

'I am Muu-Nan, Skull of Arcturus, Heart of Regulus. You are here to learn what we have to teach.'

Slowly, bewildered and uncertain, Hanna scrambled to her feet and returned to the clearing. The skull – Muu-Nan – was where he always was. Now though, he shone with a brilliant white light.

That afternoon, she sat spellbound as he told her how he had been created in the distant star system of Arcturus and how the races of Regulus had participated in his creation. When day darkened into night, he guided her to find those worlds amongst the millions of others that glittered in the velvet-black sky, told how he had been brought to her world in an immense craft that had travelled between those stars and how, with twelve other skulls, all of them created by beings from across the galaxies, they had been set in place at key points around that world.

She listened wide-eyed to his words, growing wider-eyed still when he informed her, very clearly, that she was now his Guardian. She was not of this world, he said, even though she had been born here. She had been a gift to her mother and father from her people, that same people who had helped to forge Muu-Nan with hand and mind and soul, imbued him with his consciousness and love and sent him here to help those of Tera. Her origins were in the constellation of the Great Lion, and this had always been her destiny. She had been chosen for this role long, long ago, long before the birth of even her father's father's father. Her father? Who was he? She must have had one, that much she understood, a mother too, and yet their faces, their touch, their voices, were lost to her.

At first, she refused to listen, refused to believe. She was Hanna, nothing more, and she had no great purpose or destiny. She had not come from another world halfway across the cosmos and, whoever her mother and father were, she was of their blood and no other.

It was an utter rejection born of fear. She was a child still and it was all too much to accept. Yet, somewhere in her soul, the truth of the skull's words stirred. It was pushed down, yes. Refused, yes. Killed... No! It lived, biding its time.

In spite of her resistance, she let Muu-Nan teach her, and although so much was new and complex and unbelievable, she understood clearly all he taught as if the knowledge was already there in her consciousness, simply waiting to be re-awakened. How could she know of such strange things?

He had taught her healing and, as she called it, 'magic' although Muu-Nan would have none of it, explaining that she was simply learning to use her natural abilities to sense, mould, and control energy. He taught her to access the infinite dimensions that existed for the most part unseen, unheard, and unfelt alongside the physical one she lived in, and to seek out the ones she needed for each purpose, whether to learn, find answers, bring healing, or simply for guidance.

Chapter 6

Returning to the present, Hanna gazed out over the world at her feet. It was the height of the dry season; little rain had fallen for over five moons. Beyond the rich green ribbon that followed the river's course, the land was parched and barren, baked by the relentless sun that beat mercilessly down all day, every day. Even the trees and bushes at the edge of the slender oasis, those farthest from the river, could not escape. Although still green, they looked weary and worn-down, their leaves dull and lacking the vibrancy of those closer to the flow. The river itself was an ever-diminishing thread winding lazily between boulders that, at a different time of year, it would engulf completely in its torrent. Left behind were pools and inlets that shrank by the day. In their deeper parts, blue-scaled fish crowded for space and at times, when the light caught them just right, usually towards sunset when the heat of the day eased and the fish came to the surface, the water turned into a rippling, ever-moving sapphire blanket of glittering scales.

Yet even now, in these furnace temperatures, those in most need would make the arduous and perilous journey to seek her help. As they would come at all times of the year, from the unbearable heat of this dry season, through the deluges of the rainy times when the river swelled and the desert sprouted green for a brief moment in time, to the icy cold and snows of winter when, blue and shaking with cold, they would pick their way up the rocky face of the waterfall, thick and treacherous with ice. Most came in the gentle season, that brief period just after the snows had melted and their thaw had receded from the river, and before the sun had reached its full power. Only those who, in their desperation, had no choice but to risk all made the journey in the harshest of times.

Today was no different. Squinting through the blinding sunlight, she made out two tiny distant figures crawling across the scorched landscape, no more than black ants from her vantage point. As soon as they reached the river and its shade, their burden would ease a little. Before that relief, they faced at least a half day's trek. It was past midday now and, assaulted by the heat and rays, they had had no chance of rest or respite. For a long time, she watched them until, at last, they vanished into the lush green canopy of the river's oasis. She had plenty of time to prepare. They would not reach her before nightfall.

She stiffened. Her skin was tingling and the hairs on her arm were standing on end, the way they did when there was thunder in the air. Except that there was no thunderstorm threatening. The sky was clear and the air light and fragrant. Bolts of energy shot up and down her spine. Someone – something – was standing behind her. Something unfamiliar. She knew the energy signature of every bird and beast in this place. This was one she did not recognise. It made her wary, though not afraid; Muu-Nan would have warned of any real danger long before. Slowly she turned... and froze. Two beings stood watching her, small, childlike beings with large heads and huge dark almond-shaped eyes. They were unlike any creature she had ever encountered, and yet... There was an unsettling sense of recognition and a half-formed memory that remained stubbornly elusive.

Uncertain, she glanced at Muu-Nan. He glowed from within, a sure sign that he was involved in what was unfolding. She knelt and laid her hand on top of the skull, seeking guidance.

'It is time for you to leave here.' The familiar deep, resonant voice filled her mind.

'Leave? Where should I go? I have nowhere else.'

'They will show you.'

'These... people? How?' Sensing his affirmation, she pulled her hand away sharply. She didn't want to leave. This place was home, and she was safe here. Besides...

'I can't. I won't. There are travellers coming to me, seeking my help. They've come a long way and they've endured much to get here. I will not abandon them now. I won't have them come and find me gone.'

'You must go. You have no choice. It is time for you to return.'

'Return? Where?' This time her question remained unanswered. Huge, dark almond-shaped eyes watched her steadily, silently, certain of the outcome. In that moment, under their unwavering gaze, Hanna understood that, indeed, she had no choice. Very well, if she must leave then she would. But not now, not today. Not until she had helped those who were approaching in the welcome shelter of the forest.

'It will be so, child.' Muu-Nan agreed. 'You have until this hour tomorrow. Then you will leave. It cannot be delayed further.' The strange beings nodded, shimmered, and disappeared.

Time was short. Her visitors must be near; she had to prepare for what was to come. Stripping off her tunic, she bathed in the cascade, rubbing her body with fragrant herbs that would cleanse and purify her physical form, which she then anointed with oil scented with those same herbs. She simmered more herbs, drank the hot liquid, and sat naked on the earth in front of Muu-Nan. She began to breathe slowly and deeply, stilling her thoughts.

Gradually the world around her dissolved and she entered a different place, a place where time had no meaning – indeed, where time did not exist – and where she was no longer just a flesh and blood creature but so much more. She had returned to the true essence of who she was, a swirling cloud of light and energy that embraced the entire cosmos. She was infinite, all time and all space. In a thought, she could travel any place she chose; after all, she was already there. She was everywhere at once, with no beginning and no end.

She loved this place. It was freedom. Total freedom. She often dreamed of staying here forever, but she couldn't. She had made the choice to incarnate into physical form for a reason and she would return to that form soon. For now, though, just for a little while, she would bathe in the peace and wholeness of this heaven.

Chapter 7

Those coming to see her were nearing the top of the steep path that led up the side of the waterfall, she sensed it. She must be there to greet them. She pulled some of her consciousness back into her body and the physical realm, leaving the rest in the infinity of the universe where it would guide her actions as she worked. Rising unsteadily, for as always after this reconnection she was a little light-headed, she slipped into her robe and went to meet them. She had been mistaken. They were three, not two – a woman and a man carrying a child who had seen no more than three sun-cycles. His parents were exhausted to the point of collapse. They had borne him all the way; three days walk in blistering heat.

Gently she took the child from them and laid him on a bed of soft furs, bidding them to rest and giving them water and fruit for their parched, hungry bodies before she turned her attention back to the little boy. He was very sick indeed. A heavy, dark energy was draining him of his life force – the energy of the disease that consumed him. His skin was pallid, clammy, and chill to touch despite the fever that raged within his tiny frame. They had reached her just in time. Another half day and he would have been beyond even her healing skills.

She stripped him of his clothes, which she threw on the fire to burn, purifying any lingering miasmas. His tiny, naked body lay frail, vulnerable, and trembling despite the warmth of the late afternoon, and for a moment her heart beat more quickly and tears filled her eyes. It was always the children who affected her the most. Tonight's work would demand much of her but there was no time to dwell on that now. He needed her help, and quickly.

Taking up a long, slender milky quartz crystal, as long as her hand though no thicker than her finger, she laid it on his abdomen with the point towards his feet. His body jerked at its touch, a clear signal that she had chosen well. At the other end she laid a small, river-smoothed pebble of pale, smoky quartz and set nine fist-sized chunks of black tourmaline around his body, allowing the guidance received from the nowhere place where most of her consciousness still roamed to lead her actions.

His parents slumped where they had dropped, hopeful and fearful in equal measure. Hanna's skills and magic were renowned for many days' walk in every direction. Hanna herself, confident that her first actions had contained the immediate danger to the child and were – for now – holding death at bay, quickly gathered the herbs she needed and set them over the fire to simmer. When the draught had cooled, she knelt at his side and trickled a spoonful between his blue, chill lips. Resting her right hand lightly on his forehead, her left on his ice-clammy toes, she closed her eyes and set her consciousness to travel again, seeking the source of the disease that was sucking this baby's life from his body.

* * * * *

The walls pressed in around her, dark and claustrophobic. She couldn't breathe. The air was stale and foul, and each step sucked at her feet as if she was struggling through thick, sticky mud. Every movement demanded an energy-sapping effort that became harder and harder as she forced her way forwards. She had to fight this. She had to gather her strength to carry on. Whatever was ahead, waiting, wanted her to give up and turn back, just as it did every time she made a journey like this. Well, it would be disappointed. She wasn't going to give up. She never had, and she never would.

The air closed in, thicker and fouler, until she was fighting for every breath. 'I'm not going away so you might as well show yourself,' she muttered through clenched teeth. 'Muu-Nan, I could do with some help.'

Immediately, she could breathe a little more easily, though each lungful was still an effort. Looking at her hands, she saw they were sheathed in a pale mauve glow that moved up her arms to envelop her whole body. Muu-Nan had heard her call and had come to her.

'Thank you,' she whispered.

With the skull's support, her progress, though still painfully slow and draining, was just that little bit easier. She had no idea how far she would have to travel before she reached her destination and she was already fatigued. Now that Muu-Nan was with her, however, she was certain that she would succeed.

She clutched at her throat, gasping. The air was being squeezed from her lungs. Coughing and stumbling, she forced her way onward. This, however frightening it was, was a positive sign. She was there, wherever there was. She had reached the energy that was killing the child, in which it was determined to succeed. This attack was to prevent her intervention; after all, its survival depended on the child's death. Well, it hadn't reckoned on her! There was no way she was going to let that happen.

She planted her feet firmly, straightened her back and squared her shoulders. Feeling Muu-Nan's energy surging to help, she drew their combined power into every cell of her body, expanding it, watching it grow with each breath until it pushed through her skin to surround her in an aura of glowing golden light. Expanding and expanding, until the once-dark tunnel around her glowed with her radiance.

She felt the dark energy pushing back, fighting her, unseen tentacles seeking a way past her defences. This was a battle of will and power, neither for now gaining the upper hand and neither retreating. It was stronger than she had expected, fired with a desperation to survive. Yet its survival meant the child's death and, while she understood the impulse that drove it, she would not let it win. She focussed more intensely than ever, pushing her golden light towards the dark entity, searching out a weakness she could use, summoning every bit of her power to overcome its attack. Muu-Nan was with her still, lending her his strength. Was it yielding? Yes, just a little. The force was not as strong as it had been. She pushed harder, focussed even more intently, and felt it drop back further. She was winning.

Hanna's hand flew to her throat, clawing at the band that had seized her and was tightening, tightening, around her windpipe. She was choking. She couldn't breathe. Somewhere she had left a chink open in her defences and the energy form had spotted the weak point, exploiting it brutally. Tendrils wrapped around her throat, strangling the life from her.

'Muu-Nan...' There was no response. He wasn't with her. Horrified, she realised the link to the skull had been broken in the attack. She had to keep her other defences strong, to keep this entity from overwhelming her but it was gaining ground. She felt herself weakening, fighting for every lungful of air. No, it couldn't win. It mustn't. The child...

Panic surged uninvited and she battled with every bit of willpower she had to keep it from taking her over, forcing her mind to calm even as her body was assaulted. Summoning every last shred of her resources, she drove it back. Her fierce retaliation took the assailing energy by surprise; for just a split second, its grip loosened before it tightened again. Her head was swimming, flashes of colour sparked in her vision, but it was the opening she had been waiting for. In that fragment of time, she had reconnected with Muu-Nan.

The entity was no match for both of them, Hanna and the skull. Its power faltered just a fraction. It was enough. Lifting her hands to face the invisible attacker, she sent light and power streaming through her palms towards it. She could still see nothing, but she felt – sensed – it writhing and shaking under the assault. Muu-Nan's light joined with hers and the beams strengthened until they were blinding in their intensity. A shrill, piercing shriek filled her head, louder and louder, unbearable in its stridency. Still she did not yield, even though it was agony to her ears, for she recognised the sound. It was the death scream of the entity. She gritted her teeth against the pain and went on. She would not stop until it had been silenced forever.

Within the space of a heartbeat, silence – blessed silence – filled the space and the darkness that surrounded her began to dissolve. Ahead, a soft white glow beckoned. Drained, shaking, she walked towards it and into daylight.

Hanna opened her eyes, swaying with fatigue, so exhausted that she could barely stand. In front of her the child stirred. He was sleeping peacefully, the fever broken; beneath her trembling hand, his brow was a healthy temperature and colour. It took a concerted focus and effort of will to examine him further without collapsing. His heartbeat was strong and steady, his breathing regular. On his chest, the quartz crystal point had at some point in the process shattered into three jagged pieces. It had borne the force of the entity's demise, a force that would otherwise have killed the child. Looking up, she saw the faces of his mother and father, drawn and haggard, scarcely daring to hope.

'He is out of danger. He will be well very soon. He sleeps now. When he wakes, give half a beaker of the herbal draught, and let him eat and drink as much as he wishes.' She indicated the water and fruit she had set out earlier. 'He will be hungry.' She stumbled and fell to the ground, unable to hold herself upright any longer. 'I must rest,' she whispered.

The father was instantly at her side, supporting her as he helped her into her cabin where she fell onto her bed and was asleep in moments.

Chapter 8

Muu-Nan let her sleep until long past noon before breaking into her dreams to wake her.

'Hanna,' the resonant whisper called to her, 'it is time. Come. We must wait no longer.'

Hanna's eyelids flickered and blinked open. No, they would wait no longer. Wherever Muu-Nan was taking her, it was time to go. She rose and walked out into the afternoon sunshine.

The child and his parents were gone, having left as soon as he had awoken and eaten. She felt their thanks carried on the breeze. The gratitude of those she had helped over the years was strongly imbued here. This afternoon, with her heart full of sorrow at leaving the place that had been her home for so long – had, indeed, been the only home she could remember – she felt it more strongly than ever. The air fizzed with its energy. This forest clearing would be held sacred for a long time to come.

On the lip of the cascade, the two silver-skinned beings awaited her. In front of them, on a flat slab of rock lapped by the current, sat Muu-Nan and between, where the ground gave way to air as it fell away into nothingness, a vortex of light swirled and danced, awakening the ghost of a distant memory.

'Come closer Child and lay your hand on me,' the skull commanded, softly but with an authority that allowed no refusal. Hanna knelt in the water and did as she was bid. Instantly the forest, the stream, the cascade, vanished; she was floating in a soft white mist that caressed her skin and her soul. How long she drifted, she couldn't have said. Time no longer existed. There was only the one, endless moment in the embrace of the clouds that held her.

* * * * *

Sunlight tickled her closed eyelids, calling her back from her dreams, and they had been such strange dreams. Of a life in another time and place. Of towering trees where neon-feathered birds flitted through the branches. Of tumbling waters full of music. And of people – so many people – coming to her. She lay still, enjoying the warm sun on her skin and the soft grass beneath her bare arms and legs.

'Hanna? Is it you?' The voice held an overwhelming disbelief and incredulity, and not a little fear. 'Is it really you?'

She woke fully, her father's voice chasing away the last vestiges of drowsiness. He stood over her, staring down at her as wide-eyed and white-faced as if he had seen a ghost. Behind him, a sea of faces peered over his shoulder, all equally struck dumb. Why? Why were they all so bewildered and frightened?

'Father?' She sat up slowly, still a little dazed and decidedly wobbly. She was lying on the cropped, sweet grass of the amphitheatre next the rock face with the alcove that rose above her. Why was she there? What had happened? Slowly, the memories returned. There had been a light and two strange looking people. She had been afraid for her father and had come to check that he was safe, fearing for his life. She couldn't remember what had happened next… Why though was he now looking so shocked and fearful?

'Hanna. It *is* you. Where have you been all this time? We thought you were dead, lost to us forever.'

She didn't understand. What did he mean? It had been only yesterday... She looked at him closely, searching for answers in his eyes, only to draw back in surprise. What had happened to him? He was still the same, and yet... He was also different. There was white in his hair and his face was etched with furrows. Shock ran through her. Overnight, he had grown old.

'What do you mean, father, all this time?' she asked slowly, unwilling to let the truth in and yet knowing she must. The evidence was irrefutable. Looking down at herself, her own body was the proof she needed. It was no longer that of a child. She was a full-grown woman now; the mounds of her full breasts and the curve of her hips pushed against the fabric of her tunic.

'Twelve times the stars have circled our land, twelve harvests have come and gone since you disappeared from our lives,' he faltered, tears flowing down his lined cheeks. 'We have mourned you every day since then, believing we had lost you forever. Now, by a miracle, you return to us, safe and well.' His emotions would no longer be held in check; he threw his arms around his daughter and sobbed uncontrollably, clutching her as if terrified she would vanish again. 'Where have you been, child?'

'I don't know. I was dreaming of trees and streams and birdsong before I woke up...' In that moment, her glance fell on Muu-Nan who sat still and silent in the alcove, glittering as the early morning light fell on his glass-smooth surface. And she remembered. She remembered where she had been and what she had done.

She remembered all that she had learned and all that she had given. Muu-Nan had taken her into the vortex that night, so long ago, and Muu-Nan had brought her back to her home and her family this morning. What she didn't know was why. Would she ever?

'Yes, I do.' Her voice was suddenly clear, strong, and confident, the voice of a woman certain of herself and her power. 'I'll answer all your questions, soon, I promise. If I can. First though, tell me, how is mother?' A blade of fear twisted in her heart. Did her mother, never strong in her health, still live or – she could scarcely bear to consider the possibility – had she died in the time she had been away?

'She is in the village with your sisters. She has not been at all well since you vanished from our lives.' He smiled warmly. 'Pray the gods this will change that.' He hugged her close and the tears fell once more, tears that he had held back inside for so long. 'Come. Let's give her the gift she wants more than the world.'

Accompanied by the others, some of whom she recognised – long-time clan leaders present the night she had left, though older now – others new, who had taken the place of those elders who had moved on to the Land of Light, they set out for the village and a future that held... What? Only time would reveal that story.

Chapter 9

The village was peaceful this morning, its folk going about their daily activities with smiling faces and a song on their lips. It had been that way for many years now. Hanna leaned stiffly back against the door post of her hut, her aged bones and muscles protesting both at the movement and at the hardness of the ground beneath her wasted buttocks. She rested her head against the rough timber and closed her eyes, soaking in the welcome warmth of the early spring sunshine. It had been a hard winter; day after day, relentless, bone-chilling wind and morale-sapping rain had battered the land and its people, dull grey clouds stretching from horizon to horizon with only rare and precious glimpses of washed-out blue skies and a pale, impotent sun.

Now though, the weather had changed for the better. Spring had crept in. For almost a full moon cycle, blue skies had greeted them when they rose each morning, the rain-sodden land had dried quickly in the strengthening sun and seasonal breezes, and the first tender green shoots were already poking cautiously up through the soil.

Despite the rigours of the darker months, no-one had succumbed to their grip. No fresh mounds marked the burial ground; even the eldest of the elders had made it through. That was to rejoice in. A low chuckle escaped Hanna's wrinkled lips as she caught the thought. After all, wasn't she herself one of those eldest elders? On her lap, Muu-Nan glowed a little brighter. He too was amused.

Muu-Nan. Her constant companion, guide, and teacher since he had taken her to the Other Place. That was all she could call it. She still didn't know where she had been during those years. On her return, she had refused to allow the clan leaders to take back the skull and keep him a secret, hidden, as they had once done for so long. Instead, she set Muu-Nan outside her hut on an altar of pink and black granite, accessible to all.

They had not pressed the matter. After all, who were they to argue with her? She had appeared from nowhere, a grown woman in place of the child who had vanished so many seasons before, returned from another world with a connection to the skull that had never been seen before and holding within her untold wisdom, power, and the gift of healing. She had been sharply aware that from the moment of her reappearance they had treated her differently, had spoken to her with a deep reverence and respect, and looked to her for advice and guidance. And, on the death of her beloved father, they had unanimously agreed to grant her his place, not just as leader of her clan, but also as head of the Council of the Clans. As a woman, it was simply not possible, and yet it had happened.

She had lived through nearly ninety-five summers, bid a tearful farewell and blessed so many of her friends who had passed before her beyond the veil. Now, her time too was at an end. She had sensed its approach for several moons and did not fear it. She was tired, as only those who have carried responsibility for the welfare of others for a lifetime can be tired, and she would welcome the sleep that would refresh her in preparation for her new life beyond the veil. As for those who she and Muu-Nan watched over, they would be in the safe hands of her successor, Aliana. Muu-Nan had chosen Aliana when she was still only a baby and Hanna had trained her well, teaching her all she knew of the healing skills and the wisdom of the plants. Muu-Nan, too, had shared with her his knowledge and wisdom. Aliana had been an eager pupil, learning quickly. Now, as a grown woman, she was ready to take Hanna's place. In her hands, the village would continue to thrive.

With a soft sigh, and a smile playing on her lips, Hanna took her last breath and slipped into the darkness of the blessed sleep that preceded her next adventure.

Chapter 10

The clan encircled the bier, solemn and silent, their heads bowed in grief, pierced through with the sharp pain of loss. They had gathered on that misty, chill morning to say their final goodbye to the woman who had been their leader, their rock, and their inspiration for over seventy cycles of the sun. This evening, as the sun set, Hanna would be laid to rest. Until then, they would stand in vigil over her body, watching over her as she had watched over them for so long.

Hanna's frail form had been wrapped in the softest of cloth, woven from the fine fleeces of the long-haired goats that provided for so many of their needs. Dyed a brilliant blue with the roots of the tall, yellow-flowered plant that grew on the banks of the nearby stream, it shone a blaze of colour into the dull morning. Her hair, as long and as thick as it had always been, though silver now rather than the gold of her youth, radiated from her head in a halo of starlight. Her face, deeply lined through age and life, and as pale as milk under the cloak of death, still carried its strength and softness in its features and had not, in death, lost the serenity that had graced it in life.

They had built for her a magnificent burial chamber. The four vertical walls were individual slabs of pink and black granite, identical to the rock wall in the amphitheatre, laboriously cut from the bedrock on its far side where it tumbled down the hillside. The floor was of the finest sand gathered from the bed of the stream that provided the clan with its fresh water, laid thickly, smooth and level. In the centre, filling most of the space, they had piled a thick bed of the softest furs where she would lie in comfort.

Having no children or grandchildren of her own, it was her sister's two grandsons who, when dusk fell, gently lifted Hanna's body from the bier and laid it in the chamber, nestled in the bed of fur, and set around it her most treasured possessions. They were few, most of them of little intrinsic value for she had cared nothing for such things. She had found her treasures in the natural world and its progression: a crimson-streaked sunrise, the song of the wind in the trees, the first flowers of spring, a new-born baby's cry. They laid her medicine pouch at her head, together with the few items she owned, mostly shards of crystal, pebbles and feathers she had gathered from the land as she wandered.

The most important and beloved treasure was set last of all at her feet, resting on its own cushion: the skull, Muu-Nan, which had become as much a part of Hanna as her flesh and bone. To leave it here, buried and unreachable, was the greatest sacrifice the clan could offer; it was a sacrifice they made willingly and joyfully.

When it was done, a fifth massive slab of granite, so heavy it took thirty men to raise it, was carefully, and with great difficulty, manoeuvred to lower onto the four wall slabs, sealing Hanna's body safely within, far from the reach of predators and grave thieves. The entire tomb was then covered with a thick layer of earth – every clan member from the youngest toddler to the eldest elder taking part – and sown with the seeds of the fragrant herbs Hanna had loved and treasured.

* * * * *

In the generations that followed, the clans flourished, declined, and flourished again, as is the way of the world. They moved into new territories and Hanna's tomb was left behind and forgotten. She rested in peace in the warm darkness of the Earth's womb as the centuries passed. Grasses, bushes, trees, and other lush vegetation grew over the mound, hiding it from sight until it was just another bump in the landscape, its meaning lost and forgotten.

Not forgotten to all, though. There were still those, in far distant places, who remembered.

One morning, when Hanna's bones had long since turned to dust, and just at the moment that the sun peeked over the distant hilltops, two figures emerged out of the early morning mists of autumn, one male and one female. They were human-bodied, though there the similarity ended. They were small and delicately formed with silver skin brushed with soft green, and huge, dark, almond-shaped eyes. Certain of their destination, they moved purposefully to the base of the shallow dome, thickly shrouded in thorns and undergrowth, that was Hanna's tomb.

The female carried with her a small, square casket, dull silver in colour and measuring no more than two handspans along any axis, its sides and top etched with strange, exotic symbols. They knelt and she set it on the ground between them and opened the lid. It was empty. Closing their eyes, their arms at their sides, palms facing the mound, they began to chant; within moments the air hummed with a low, throaty resonance that rose and fell in pitch and volume. The air vibrated with sound, shimmering around the barrow and the two figures kneeling reverently in front of it.

Within the box, sparks of pale lavender and pink crackled and danced around the sides, the light intensifying, expanding, until it spilled over the edges in a dazzling cascade. As one, the voices broke off. The box was no longer empty; it held Muu-Nan, Skull of Arcturus, Heart of Regulus. With great care, the visitors closed the lid, rose to their feet, and left in the direction from which they had come.

Chapter 11

The Pyramid Temple in Yo'tlàn was nearing completion, the final gold cladding all that remained to be put in place. The Skull Chamber was already finished. The curving walls, lined with rich, purple amethyst, cast an otherworldly glow over the twelve glistening crystal plinths that glittered in the light, awaiting the arrival of the sacred Skulls of Light that would very soon be set upon them. In the centre of the circular chamber, a massive snow quartz crystal plinth held a giant cluster of ice-clear quartz, many of its points as long and as thick as a man's arm, and above them hung another immense quartz point, shot through with rainbows and sparkling veils that pulsed and twinkled. It was on this centre bed that the Master would one day sit, surrounded by the other twelve skulls. For now though, only one plinth was occupied. That skull was Maat-su.

An exotic procession entered the Chamber led by a tall, strongly built man in robes of electric blue and cream shot through with gold. This was Almukh-tar, High Priest designate of the emerging Pyramid Temple, in whose hands lay the responsibility for the safe-keeping of the Skulls of Light. Behind him, the two small silver-skinned Arcturans carried the box containing Muu-Nan. They were flanked by two tall, powerful Regulans, feline-like in grace and features, their bodies covered in tawny fur that gleamed like polished gold. The group walked with reverence, aware of the significance of both the moment and the location. This was a special place, a place of power, where the thirteen Skulls would watch over the infant realm of Atlantis and guide its people wisely.

At the appointed plinth, they set the box on the ground. The female Regulan lifted the skull and held it high above her head, offering it to the Temple. In her outstretched hands, Muu-Nan's unusual hue was enriched and deepened to a vibrant plum by the dark violet-purple of the walls. Almukh-tar nodded. Carefully, she set the skull on its plinth and drew back. Now, it was the turn of the Arcturans to step forward. They rested their hands on the crown of the skull and closed their huge, black eyes, connecting psychically with Muu-Nan. He flashed brilliant for a split-second, claiming his place in the chamber. It would not be long now before the eleven remaining skulls joined him and Maat-su, and the thirteen Skulls of Light would be reunited for the first time since they had been brought to this world aeons before. This sacred continent of Atlantis was at last ready to welcome them with an open heart.

GEMMA, 2

Chapter 12

No matter how I looked at it, I couldn't see how any of the pieces of the puzzle fitted together. I was sitting at Duncan's table in front of a large sheet of paper that I'd covered in names, dates, and events – all the confusing and scary stuff that had gone on since I'd returned from Arizona. I'd hoped that putting everything down in one place might bring up some clues. It hadn't. Despite the maze of lines I'd drawn in a vain attempt to link them together, it was still an impenetrable muddle. Joe and I were caught up in a lethal game where we didn't know our opponents and we sure as hell didn't know the rules.

My phone rang, interrupting my frustration.

'Mrs Mason? It's Pieter.' Pieter? Pieter who? He must have sensed my lack of comprehension. 'Pieter van Broek. We met yesterday at Callum Davis' funeral.'

Of course. After the drama and stress of the previous evening, I'd totally forgotten about him. Had it really only been yesterday that we'd said goodbye to Callum? I shook my head in an attempt to clear it.

'Mr van Broek. Yes, I'm sorry. My head's a bit all over the place this morning. Yes, I do remember you. You told us you've found the hiding place of one of the skulls.'

'The black one. Gileada, you call it in your book. Yes, I'm certain I have.' Did I believe him? I wanted to, only…

'Where is it?' I blurted out. There was no way on earth he was going to tell me, but I asked anyway. I was right.

'Not here and not on the phone. We must meet. Tomorrow. Somewhere where we can't be overheard.' He sounded as jittery as he had looked the previous day.

'Ok,' I agreed. 'Where do you suggest?'

'Do you know West Kennet long barrow?'

Know it? It had been my go-to place for years to soothe my too often over-active mind. It was a huge Neolithic burial mound frequently used by the spiritual community for drumming, meditations, and other similar activities. I went there often to sit on its grassy structure and soak up the energies.

'Yes, I know it,' I told him.

'Then I'll meet you there at eleven tomorrow.' He rang off, leaving me in whirl of thoughts and unanswered questions.

* * * * *

'That must be van Broek's car.' We'd pulled into the lay-by at the bottom of the track that led up to the long barrow. The only other vehicle there was a ropey Suzuki Grand Vitara. I turned to Joe, who was next to me in the passenger seat.

'Do you think he's for real? Could he have actually found it? Or is he some crazy *'Skull Inheritance'* fan who's lost track of reality?'

'Or a pal of the thug who got squashed last night?'

Not what I wanted to hear! I was well aware of the possibility that this could go badly for us if I had misjudged the mysterious Pieter van Broek. My feeling though was that he was genuine, and I wanted to hear what he had to say. So did Joe.

'Well, we'll soon find out.' I got out of the car, pulling my coat tighter around me, and grabbed my scarf from the back seat. It was a cold, dank morning with a bitterly cold wind blowing across the exposed downs, unusually cold for this time of year and a stark contrast to the balmy sunshine that had bathed Callum's funeral two days earlier. Curious – and more than a bit apprehensive – we pushed through the gate and made our way up the half mile long track. Pieter had wanted a location where we wouldn't be overheard or taken by surprise; he had chosen the perfect spot. The burial mound lay at the top of a long slope, surrounded by open fields and little cover. No-one would be able to get anywhere near us without being seen.

Cresting the hill, the long barrow appeared in front of us like a sleeping giant. Standing on top, scanning the landscape, was a rotund, bespectacled figure bundled up in a dark green duffle coat and knitted pull-on hat. Pieter van Broek. He waved enthusiastically when he saw us.

'I know where it is,' he called out as we approached. 'The skull. It – Gileada – showed me. Five years ago.' The words tumbled out over themselves, carrying only the faintest trace of a northern European accent.

I stared at him wide-eyed, lost for words. The skull had showed him? Of course. Why should – why *would* – I be the only one the Skulls of Light were contacting? I just hadn't ever considered the possibility. But… five years ago?

'So why only come forward now? Why haven't you gone to find it before?'

'The skull came to me in my dreams.' Just like it had for me. 'But I didn't know what they meant. To be honest, at first I didn't really think they meant anything at all. There was a black skull and a location. Well, the image of a location. Nothing more. I thought it might be important but because it stopped coming and I received no more information, I set it aside. In fact, I'd all but forgotten about it until I read '*The Skull Inheritance*' a couple of months ago. That was when I understood what it was all about. It was absolute confirmation that I was the one who was to find it and bring it back into the world.' This was a very different Pieter van Broek to the man who had introduced himself in the café and phoned me yesterday. Excited, eager, confident.

'You didn't bring us out here just to tell me this though. Why are you being so cautious? Are you afraid that someone will get there before you?'

'No, I firmly believe that I'm the only one that holds this information. Even you have no idea where the skull may be, other than within a circle of hundreds if not thousands of miles somewhere in northern Scandinavia.' His voice hardened. 'No, I'll tell you why I'm scared. Because of what happened to Davis.' Which made complete sense.

'How well did you know Callum?' I asked.

'Not well. I'd met him a couple of times at conferences and we corresponded once or twice. His area of interest and mine overlapped. When I heard he had died, I felt compelled to attend his funeral – and as soon as I saw you, Mrs Mason, the reason became crystal clear. Like I said, I'd read your book and I recognised you straight away from your photo on the back cover.' He swallowed. 'I'm afraid because I don't want to be next on the mortuary slab. And I could be, if they learned I know where the skull is.'

I held back from telling him he would have to join the queue. It seems we were all lining up to become the next dead body.

'They?' Would we at last find out who our adversaries were?

'Those people who want the Skulls' power for themselves, just as there have been throughout history. I believe they are seeking to acquire all thirteen skulls, to reunite them and use their power for their own, somewhat less than humanitarian, purposes.'

'So where is it?' Joe wasn't going to be stalled any longer.

'I can't tell you.'

'What? You said that if we met you here, you'd tell us where Gileada is hidden. Now you say you can't. What the hell is your game?' Joe didn't try to hide his annoyance.

Understanding dawned, bringing with it crushing disappointment. 'He can't tell us because he doesn't know,' I said. 'Not exactly. Do you, Mr van Broek?'

'No,' he admitted. 'Not exactly, although when I said I knew where it is, I wasn't actually lying either. I do know. I've seen it, I know what the place looks like. Gileada showed me, if you remember what I told you. I've spent the last six months investigating areas that match that image and I've narrowed down the possible sites to one area of around one hundred and fifty square kilometres. As soon as spring comes and I can get back up there, I'll spend as much time as it takes searching until I find the exact location. I'll know it as soon as I see it.'

'In which case, why did you ask us to meet you here?'

'I need the key to open the cave entrance. The one described in your book. Will you let me have it?'

If my jaw could have hit the ground, it would have done. Of all the requests he could have made, that was the last one I had expected. How the hell did he know I had the key? I didn't trust myself to speak. Fortunately, Joe had no such problem.

'What on earth makes you think Gemma has this 'key'?'

Van Broek's bespectacled eyed bored into mine. Not threatening, simply certain. 'Mrs Mason is the Skulls' mouthpiece. If she doesn't have it, she knows where it is. I ask you again. Will you let me have the key?'

I wanted to trust him, but I wasn't anywhere near ready to. 'I'm sorry, Mr van Broek .You're mistaken.' My voice came out carrying a lot more confidence than I was feeling. 'I have no idea where it is. Assuming it exists at all.'

He nodded, accepting my answer though clearly not believing it.

'Alright, Mrs Mason. I understand where you're coming from and I understand your caution. I'd be the same.' He pulled his hat down tighter. 'The next time I contact you, I'll have the proof you want. Hard evidence that I've found Gileada's sanctuary. In real life. Then you'll let me take the key. Until then...' He shook my hand, then Joe's, and slithered down from the roof of the long barrow. Lost for words, we watched him march away through the drizzle, back down the hill to his car, and drive off.

Standing on the top of the massive burial mound that had been the resting place for the bones of so many for so long, I suddenly had the sense that we had stepped out of time and out of place into some other, as yet unknown, dimension where the 'real' world was out of reach on the other side. Just Joe and me, waiting. But waiting for what?

The sensation passed as quickly as it had come. We were back on the deserted barrow, alone but for the whistle of the wind gusting across this ancient, mystical landscape. Only then did I become aware of how cold I was. The chill, gusting wind cut through my coat, settling in my bones, and I could no longer feel my fingers. Shivering, we made our way back to the car and warmth.

'How does he know we have the key?' I burst out.

'God knows. Do you believe him?'

'It's a bizarre story. Though, honestly, it's no more bizarre than mine. Or yours,' I added, remembering his adventures in the Himalayas. 'I actually do believe him. It's a gut feeling, no more, and I'm certainly not prepared to gamble our lives on it. We have no evidence to prove that van Broek is who he says he is, and after everything that's been thrown at us, I'm going to stay suspicious of everyone until – unless – they can convince us otherwise.'

'Like you, I'm inclined to trust him.' Joe rubbed his fingers in the blast of air from the heater, massaging feeling back into them. 'It still doesn't explain how he knows you the key though and that worries me. Because if he knows, who else does?'

'What do you think he'll do now?'

'What he said. Keep looking. Either discover he's wrong and we won't hear from him again. Or he'll come back with the proof he promised. In which case, you'll have a big decision to make.'

'We, Joe. *We'll* have a big decision to make. We're in this together, remember?'

MUU-NAN

PART 3

FAREWELL TO ATLANTIS

Chapter 13

The high polish of the silver mirror reflected back the anxious face of a tired, middle-aged woman. Cleantha stared sadly at her image, usually so confident, so certain. The events of the past ten days had relentlessly robbed her of those qualities; she wasn't sure they would ever return. She was about to embark on the most perilous mission imaginable, with little certainty that she would succeed. Maybe, a few years ago, she would have felt more capable, more excited even, in a perverse way. Now she simply felt terrified. And yet she had not refused. How could she have done, after Muu-Nan had expressly chosen her? Still, she wondered, why had the skull settled on her, when there were so many younger, fitter, stronger – and much more suitable – candidates for the task that lay ahead?

Her fingers caressed the mirror's rim, beaten and worked into delicate filigree swirls by the hand of some long-forgotten craftsman. Within this frame, a perfect oval had been smoothed and polished to such a degree that it reproduced in every tiny detail the face that stared into it. This morning, Cleantha wished that it was a little less brutally honest in its representation.

Her heart constricted in a sudden wave of sadness. The mirror had belonged to her mother, and her mother's mother before her, and so on back through the generations. She had given it to Cleantha on her initiation as a Priestess of the Light. It was the most precious object Cleantha owned and had become even more so since her mother's recent passing. Now she was leaving it behind. Leaving it all behind.

Her gaze swept across her small bedroom, taking in the treasured mementoes of her life. A spray of wildflowers, carefully pressed and dried, from the posy Kua'tzal had given her so many years earlier when she had believed they would become man and wife. That was before... No. She shook the memory away, irritated that it had escaped to pinch at her heart. No, she would not let her thoughts go back there. Kua'tzal had been lost to her a long time ago. She breathed a prayer of thanks that their paths would not cross again. She saw him rarely these days; he was always busy cosying up to the Shadow Chasers' hierarchy, although from time to time she did bump into him hurrying along one of the Temple's corridors. And while she did not live in the past, wishing for what might have been, at those moments she could not prevent a stab of sorrow for the man he had become, so different from the one she had fallen in love with. Again, she shook away the thoughts.

There was the little carved wooden chest her grandfather had given her when she had first entered the Temple. She had been still only a child then, not quite twelve years of age, and although excited that she had been chosen to train as a Priestess, she had also been heartbroken at leaving her family. Grandfather had made her the chest so that she could take a memento of everyone with her. Every time she felt sad or homesick, he had told her, she could take them out and know that those she loved were with her. Her little sister, Aria, had given a ribbon from her hair, her brother a glistening white pebble from the stream that ran through their farm. He had written his name on one side and hers on the other. Father and mother's gift had been a long, love-filled letter in which they told her how much they loved and cherished her, and how proud and excited they were that she was going to be a Priestess of the Light. She had kept the gifts in the chest ever since and still took them out occasionally, connecting with the deep love they held.

Now it was all at an end. She was abandoning everything – nearly forty years of her life – for the unknown. To embark on a perilous and possibly deadly journey to... She had no idea, only that it would be a very long way from the peaceful corridors and light-filled gardens of the Pyramid Temple. She must take nothing other than the bare essentials, certainly nothing that would reveal her real identity. And yet... On impulse, she plucked a dried flowerhead from the pressed spray and slipped it into the pocket of her robe. Why, she had no idea but she had felt a strong pull to do it, and so she had. She did not ever question her intuition.

With a heavy heart, she picked up the small travelling bag that lay on the bed and, with a final, lingering look at the little house that had been her home for so long, she slipped out and pulled the door closed behind her. When the latch dropped into place with a dull clunk, she could no longer hold back the tears. She was already missing her life in the Temple. Annoyed, she wiped a hand across her face and brushed them away. She couldn't draw attention to her desolation. It had to seem to the world that everything was as it always was; she had to keep up the appearance of a Priestess going about her usual daily duties.

*   *   *   *   *

That had been three days ago. On the morning she had said goodbye to her home for the last time, Cleantha had travelled south from Yo'tlàn to the Temple of Sonika in Muahatan to meet with its elders. In her bag she had carried only those basic necessities. Muu-Nan was not with her. The skull had been exchanged for a replica several weeks earlier and was already hidden in the Temple of Sonika, although those who worked and served there had no notion of the priceless treasure sitting patiently in their vaults. Haa'nu and Regus had travelled to Muahatan only days before with a large, heavily wrapped bundle that they had placed in the Temple vaults with strict orders that only Cleantha was to retrieve it. In that bundle was Muu-Nan.

Cleantha had seen the replica. It had been magnificent, a virtually undetectable copy skilfully recreated by a master craftsman. Even she, as the genuine skull's long-time Guardian, would have had difficulty detecting the imposter purely from its appearance. Only its energy gave it away, the output a fraction of that of the real Muu-Nan. It would not be noticed; she was the only one who would have contact with the skull, and with most of the other skulls remaining in the Chamber until the night of the exodus, the shift in the overall energy signature would be negligible.

Everything possible had been done to deflect suspicion that anything untoward was happening. Muahatan had been a stop mid-way through a tour that Regis and Haa'nu had made of the principal temples of Atlantis, under the pretext of reassuring the elders of those temples that the Shadow Chasers were not strong enough yet to act. It was an important, if false, reassurance that served as cover for the real reason for the visits – the night spent at the Temple of Sonika, where they had left the real Muu-Nan. A direct journey, and the skull's disappearance only a little while later, would leave too clear a trail, so they had travelled the length and breadth of the continent with their priceless treasure until they had reached Muahatan, ten days before Cleantha's arrival. To those who were curious, they had spread the tale that the bundle contained ancient documents and relics that the scholars in Yo'tlàn wished to study. Regis and Haa'nu had then continued their journey south, leaving the bundle for Cleantha to transport back to the Pyramid Temple. Or so everyone believed.

* * * * *

This morning, with unhurried steps and still wearing her robes of office, Cleantha left the Temple of Sonika and made her way through the crowds that thronged the main thoroughfare of Muahatan. In sharp contrast to the previous days of rain and biting winds, it was a beautiful morning of blue skies and warm sunshine, and it seemed that the whole town had come out to enjoy the fine weather. Cleantha was glad. In the busy streets it was easier to pass unnoticed and should, by chance, the Shadow Chasers be watching her – for no other reason than that she was a Priestess and therefore an enemy – they would be hard-pressed to keep her in their sights.

Casually she headed towards the shuttle terminus from where the next transport to Yo'tlàn would soon leave. The large square was busy with shuttles from all corners of the land arriving and departing at frequent intervals and she had no problem staying lost in the hustle and bustle. Fighting an urge to look behind, she increased her speed and walked briskly into the square, past the waiting rows of shuttles and out the other side. Darting into a deserted alleyway, she stepped out of her robes of office and shoved them down a culvert opening, out of sight. Along with her robes, she left behind her name. From now on she would be known as Calista. Anonymous now in the simple clothing she had been wearing beneath her robes, she stepped back onto the street, an ordinary townswoman going about her day.

An hour later, she stood on an ancient, crumbling jetty staring in dismay at the vessel that was to carry her across the ocean. It was a small boat – surely too small for the voyage it was to undertake – ugly and ungainly in appearance. Its beam was wide and squat, the mid-section covered in a wooden shell from which rose up a thick, stumpy mast carrying a patched sail that flapped dejectedly in the light wind. At the front and rear of the cabin section was a small section of deck, and at the very back a square wooden box served as shelter for the helmsman.

'She may not look much but there's none better for the seas we'll meet.' A cheery male voice broke through her misgivings. 'You must be Calista.' A tall, thick-set man – no longer young but not yet old either – unfolded from the cabin. A moment's hesitation, then she nodded.

'Good.' He shoved out his hand. It was strong and knotted, burned brown by the sun and wind. 'I'm Ruarth. Come on. Come aboard. We can't afford to miss the tide, not from this beach, or we'll be here until tomorrow.'

She hesitated. 'Is this it?'

'This is it.' A huge grin split her new companion's face. 'Just you, me and Amphitrite. Oh, and the great waters of course.'

'Amphitrite?'

He waved his arm proudly at the little craft. 'My one true love.' The grin was back, dazzling white teeth in a bronzed, weather-beaten face. He saw her expression and chuckled. 'Don't worry. She won't let us down. She'll take everything these seas can throw at us and more. The cabin is completely sealed when the doors are shut. Unless the water gets into the hull – and it won't, once it's sealed – there's no way on earth she can sink. Come on.'

Chapter 14

Cleantha – Calista as she now called herself – lay back on the cabin roof and let the warm sun caress her face. They had set sail three days previously and the weather had so far been kind, with sunshine and blue skies through which the occasional cloud drifted lazily past, and gentle, balmy winds that combined with favourable ocean currents to blow them steadily eastward. She had spent most of her time here relaxing, letting the mental and emotional strain of the past – how many? Ten? Fifteen? She'd lost count – days float away with the clouds. There would be difficult times ahead and many of them, but for now she could rest and be at peace. She refused to think of what might be; it was a complete unknown. She could make no plans, because to make plans you had to have some idea of what you were planning, and she was travelling blindly with no idea of what she might encounter. They – she – would deal with any problems as they arose. There was no need to tie herself in mental knots trying to anticipate the un-anticipatable.

She sat up suddenly, remembering. They had been at sea for three days. Which meant that the 'exodus' – the removal of the remaining skulls from the Skull Chamber – was due to have taken place two days ago. Had it all gone according to plan? Or had the Dark Ones somehow discovered the plot? She had no way of knowing and she could do nothing in any case. Whatever the scenario, she had the comfort of knowing that Muu-Nan was safe with her. Even if the Dark Ones had seized the remaining skulls, they could not fully complete their ambitions without him. She lay back down, soothed by the lapping of the waves against the hull, and reflected on her situation.

Ruarth was a pleasant companion and she had taken to him immediately. He was a few years younger than she was, she guessed, an amiable, gentle giant of a man. Eyes the colour of the sea on a sunny day peered out from under heavy, dark eyebrows, and a mass of unruly wavy jet black hair that was only just beginning to show a few silver threads framed a smiling, weather-beaten face darkened almost to mahogany by the sea, wind and sun. He had told her that he had asked no questions when he had been approached to take her across the ocean, eager for the opportunity to escape the Dark Ones' deepening oppression. An offer to cover all costs incurred in making his boat seaworthy for the long ocean voyage was all it had taken. As a marked opponent of the Shadow Chasers, he had first-hand experience of their 'persuasive' tactics. It was an experience he had no wish to repeat and he had leapt at the opportunity to leave Atlantis.

He had asked no questions of her, simply helped her aboard, stowed the few bits of luggage she carried – the small bag she had brought from Yo'tlàn and the bundle containing Muu-Nan – in the cabin, and cast off.

* * * * *

She had spent little time in the cabin since their departure. It was cramped and offered nothing in the way of privacy. Two bunks – one for her, one for Ruarth – lay either side of a walkway that led to a tiny, partitioned-off rear storage area. At least there she could wash and perform other personal activities in private. They cooked on the open foredeck on a small stove that was stored in one of the lockers that lined its sides, as was most of their food supply. Ruarth was easy company and the days had passed pleasantly enough.

Muu-Nan remained dormant. Active, the Shadow Chasers could still have picked up his energy signal – the boat was not yet out of range of their instruments, or their trained sensitives. There was also a high possibility that his active presence would have been picked up by Ruarth, awakening his curiosity. In any case, the skull's help was not needed, not right now.

Their route lay east across the ocean. Although Ruarth had never travelled these seas before, he had studied the charts in detail, committing to memory the position of favourable currents, land masses and islands, and had determined that they would travel in a southerly arc, sailing from island to island. While a more northerly route may have been quicker, their small craft could not carry the provisions needed for a long, unbroken voyage. They would have to make landfall every few days to replenish their fresh water supplies and provisions with any fruit, berries and other plants they could find, and Ruarth would hunt for meat to supplement the fish he caught as they sailed.

A day later, the sunshine and calm seas were only a memory. Overnight, a storm drove in from the north, raising towering waves that battered the little boat, time and time again threatening to tip it over. Ruarth had assured Calista that they would be safe, that Amphitrite was perfectly balanced, designed to be self-righting. Nonetheless, fear stiffened her limbs as she lay in her bunk, strapped in so that she wouldn't be hurled around the tiny cabin. Ruarth stayed outside, hauling on the tiller in a desperate attempt to keep them on course, roped to the stern timbers so that he wouldn't get swept away as the tiny craft leapt and plummeted through the mountains of water.

*   *   *   *   *

How long the storm lasted, she couldn't have said, only that it felt like an eternity. The pounding seas turned her stomach upside-down and she vomited until her guts were empty, and still she retched and strained. Strapped into her bunk so that she wouldn't be tossed around like a ragdoll and seriously injured, all she could do was lie there in a lake of her own vomit and suffer. Nothing had prepared her for this.

Ruarth was unable to help her. He remained at the helm, battling this relentless force of nature, until even he could not continue and slumped exhausted to the streaming deck, still lashed to the stern.

In the last – how long? Only a very short while – there had been a change in the movement of the boat. Calista sensed it even as she couldn't say what it was. Choppier perhaps, rather than the deep, lurching rise and fall that it had been.

'Ruarth?' she rasped through a parched throat raw from stomach acid and bile.

'There's an island ahead,' he shouted back. 'The wind is pushing us towards it. If there's a beach, I may be able to bring us up onto it. It might be a bit rough.' She couldn't hold back a blast of dry, hoarse laughter. Rough, he said. What then had they just come through?

Amphitrite lurched and bucked as she caught the breakers, their thunder crashing around her as they broke on the shore. A few moments later, a harsh crunching announced that the boat had grounded. When at last the cabin door opened, she saw the bedraggled, exhausted Ruarth for the first time since the storm had unleashed its fury on them. How many days had he been at the helm without a break?

'I've fastened up to one of the big rocks. It should hold. It looks like the storm is blowing itself out at last. Come on, let's get you ashore.'

Still sick, weak and dehydrated, shivering with cold and nausea, Calista struggled up from the bunk, swaying perilously as she pulled herself upright. Once outside the shelter of the cabin, the blast of the gale knocked her off her feet. Ruarth picked her up as if she weighed no more than a child and carried her to shore, the breakers tugging at his legs with every step, seeking to drag them both under. He battled up the steep shoreline with her in his arms and didn't put her down until they reached the shelter of a shallow recess in the cliffside.

'Here.' He held out a small water bottle. Gratefully she put it to her lips and swallowed the clear, sweet water.

'Enough.' He took it from her hand. 'Little and often. Too much at once will make you ill again. Now rest.'

Now that she was no longer being tossed like a cork, the nausea was rapidly easing. Beside her, Ruarth was already fast asleep, exhausted from his days of struggle through the storm. She lay down on the hard stone floor, shivering in her damp, soiled clothing, and huddled up against him for warmth. Despite the deafening crash of surf on the shingle and the roar of the wind as it howled around the rocks, within moments she too slept soundly.

Chapter 15

When she awoke, a pale sun was peeking out of a washed-out sky. The storm had blown itself out, just as Ruarth had predicted. The beach was littered with branches and leaves torn from the island's forests, and at the waterline lay the bloated carcass of some large sea mammal, the species no longer identifiable, that had been blown up onto the shore by the gales.

Where was Ruarth? The little rock shelter was empty. He was gone. Panic gripped her. A shadow fell across the entrance and there he was, bedraggled and still haggard with fatigue though even now, after all they had endured, his habitual grin spread from ear to ear.

'Good morning.' He tossed a bundle into her lap. 'I thought you might like a change of clothes.' His nose wrinkled. 'Those smell a bit ripe.' His grin robbed the words of any malice.

She looked down at herself. What a mess. Her tunic and trousers were stained and stinking, her limbs – and no doubt her torso as well, she grimaced – were a mass of livid bruises where the safety straps had bitten into her flesh. She felt as if she had been thrown down a cliff. On top of all that, her throat was raw from vomit and salt water and she was ravenously hungry.

She stared out at the bleak shoreline. 'I'm not sure there's too much that's good about it.'

'One, we're still alive, which in itself is a miracle. Two, it's going to be a beautiful day. And three... I have food.' She saw now that he was carrying a small crate.

'The last of our rations and fresh water,' he explained. He gazed around at the island. 'I'm certain we'll be able to find plenty to restock with here. As for water, there's a small stream flowing out onto the beach just over there.'

Nuts, dried fruits and overripe fresh, hard cheese. Simple fare that to their hungry bellies was a feast. Eventually, the final crumbs devoured, Calista sat back and looked at Ruarth questioningly.

'What now?'

'Fresh water has to be our priority, and food. Berries, nuts, roots, seeds. Whatever you can find that's edible, and plenty of it. There may be some animal life on this island too, in which case we'll have meat. I'll see if I can find any.' He pointed across the cove to where a small stream broke out of the forest and trickled over a rocky bed onto the beach. 'Take the water bottles and follow the water upstream until you find the spring.'

'Why can't I get it from there?'

'It'll have been fouled by the storm, probably heavy with sea water and salt. The gods alone know what else was dumped in it. Chances are, it will poison us – and I'm not willing to take that chance. Follow it upstream until you find the spring if you can. The water will be safest where it comes out of the ground. I'm going to check the boat for damage then I'll get my crossbow and follow you up. See what else we come across.'

Revived by the fresh water, and with her hunger temporarily satisfied, Calista grabbed the bundle of clean clothes and headed towards the stream. At first, the terrain was easy to negotiate; the sandy, rough soil beneath her feet was generally barren, dotted only here and there with wiry grasses and stunted shrubs. She hadn't gone a few steps beyond the forest edge, however, before progress became a lot harder. Thick growing undergrowth covered the ground in tangled, thorny brambles so that she struggled to find anywhere to put her feet. Ahead the land rose steeply; every precarious step would be a challenge. She stopped, pulled off her boots and stepped into the stream, gasping as its icy grip closed around her ankles. Stripping off her filthy tunic and trousers she splashed her body clean with the frigid water then pulled on the clean garments.

The riverbed was uneven, a jumble of rocks of all sizes, some sharp edged and newly torn from the surrounding land by the storm, most worn smooth by the passage of time and current. It was still difficult going but the way was much clearer, other than for the occasional low growing branch or trailing briar. Of a spring, there was no sign; the stream stretched ahead as far as she could see. Where was it? Where was she? She could see nothing but the tunnel of green forest around her and hear nothing but the splash of her footsteps and the rush of the water as it tumbled down the mountainside.

Sunlight glittered up ahead, a bright contrast to the shadowy forest world that enclosed her. She pushed out of the vegetation onto a small open ledge no more than six paces wide. To her right, a low cliff rose up to perhaps three times her height over which the stream spilled in a pretty waterfall into a small pool edged with lush ferns that reflected the blue of the sky, from which it overflowed to continue its journey down to the sea. Although she was still not at its source, surely she could stop here to collect the water they needed.

'No,' a voice inside her urged. 'Not here. Go on.' Go on? How?

When she looked more closely, however, the task showed itself to be a little less impossible. The exposed stone had weathered into layers creating a series of somewhat tricky hand and foot holds, and in places had formed into rough, natural stairs. Cautiously, unsure whether the rock would crumble beneath her weight, Calista began to climb. It was easier than she expected and only a short while later she hauled herself over the top. Stretching out in front of her was a wide plateau of bare stone gashed through with deep, narrow crevices, some only as wide as her hand, others too wide to jump across. At the far side, the mountain slopes rose as steeply as before.

From her vantage point, far above the densely packed trees, brambles, and creepers that covered the lower slopes, Calista had a bird's eye view of this entire side of the island. She had come further than she had thought. The beach was far below; the boat, now well above the waterline, lay like a toy on the shingle, leaning over at a forty-five degree angle on its keel. The waves had tossed it way up on the beach the previous night and now it sat high and dry like a stranded whale. It would take all their strength to haul it back into the water.

She could see Ruarth, still inspecting the hull, walking around it, kneeling and peering under it to check more closely. Their lives depended on its integrity and he was taking no chances. At last, he scrambled across the slanted deck and into the cabin, reappearing seconds later with what she assumed was his crossbow slung over his shoulder. She shouted and waved a hello but he didn't look up. She was too far away for him to hear.

Calista turned her gaze out to sea and froze, staring dumbly, a cold hand gripping her heart. Unsure of exactly what it was she was seeing. The horizon had reared up into a thick, dull green wall of water and even from such a distance, she could see it was colossal. Had Ruarth seen it too? She glanced back down at the beach and a cry cracked in her throat. Whereas only moments before the waves had been gently lapping at the rocks that pushed out into the waves on each side of the little inlet, the water had now vanished, laying bare the sea floor. An eerie, uncanny silence settled over the island.

What was happening? Whatever it was, it wasn't good. The wall of water was moving closer, slowly and relentlessly, towards them. In front of it, the sea was dead, dark and menacing. No sunlight glittered on its surface. Seabirds, that only moments before had been circling and wheeling noisily, had vanished, their cries fallen silent.

No, it had been an illusion. It wasn't moving slowly. It was racing towards them at a terrifying speed. It was going to hit the island. Ruarth was on the beach. The boat was on the beach. And Muu-Nan was in the boat. At last Calista was galvanised into action.

'Ruarth. RUARTH! RUN!' she screamed over and over until she believed her lungs would burst. 'RUARTH!'

He couldn't hear her. He hadn't noticed the horror bearing down on them. He was kneeling on the shingle under the bow, his back to the waterline. She wouldn't be able to reach him in time, and even if she did, they wouldn't be able to escape a crushing death under the mountain of water. Frantically she leaped up and down, waving her arms in a desperate attempt to attract his attention. It was no good. It was only when he stood up to leave the beach that he noticed her, a tiny figure jumping up and down on the hillside high up above him. He waved, and she flung her arm towards the sea, pointing in desperation. He must have picked up the urgency in her action for he turned to look. His knees buckled, just for a split-second, then he turned and raced up the beach at breakneck speed towards the vegetation, heading inland.

He had no chance. The wave towered above them, racing silently and remorselessly towards the island, the complete absence of any sound making its approach even more terrifying. Calista stared, transfixed; although it was still some way from shore, she already had to lift her head to see its crest. She couldn't move. Her legs wouldn't obey her screaming mind. So she stood and watched in awe-filled dread as the monster bore down on them. This was the end then. She had left Yo'tlàn only to die here on this forsaken lump of land in the middle of the ocean. She had failed. The water would swallow the island whole and sweep them all to a watery grave.

It loomed over her. Mesmerised, transfixed by its awfulness, she watched it race ever closer. A silent apocalypse. Just in time, self-preservation overrode her paralysis and she fled, stumbling and tripping, across the bare, fissured rock of the plateau and up the far slope towards the mountain's summit, oblivious to the branches and thorns that tore at her clothes and skin. She scrabbled and scrambled to get as high as possible, even as part of her whispered the futility of the attempt. Surely she could not escape this monstrosity, even if she reached the highest point of the peak?

The tsunami hit the island with a roar that shook the ground beneath her feet, sweeping away everything in its path. Calista lost her balance as the shock wave rippled through the rock she stood on and she tumbled down, her arms scrabbling to find an anchor. With a thud, they smacked against a tree trunk and she flung them around it, holding on for her life, closing her eyes against the inevitable.

Chapter 16

It never came. The tree trembled and shook from its highest twigs to its deepest roots. A torrent of salt water rained down, drenching everything, including Calista. Her world shrank to the roar of the water exploding in her ears as it swept across the mountainside. But somehow the tree stood firm, and Calista kept her hold on it, and death never came.

The world was silent once more, only this time it was a different silence. The calm after the storm. The danger had moved on. She pushed herself up and dragged the hair from her eyes, barely able to believe she was still alive. Dazed, shaking, she turned to look down the mountainside – and lost the ability to breathe for a few moments. Only a couple of paces below where she had fallen, the hillside had been stripped bare. There was nothing left. No trees. No shrubs. No vegetation of any kind. Even the boulders that had littered the slopes were gone. Only a few shattered tree stumps remained, snapped off where they emerged from the ground. The water had swallowed everything in its path, carrying it away across the land and who knew how far across the ocean on the other side. She sat back down abruptly, suddenly brutally and painfully aware how close she had come to the same fate.

A fierce sob burst from her throat unannounced, robbing her of breath. Terrifying, hopeless realisation hit. She was alone here. Everything was gone. Ruarth. Amphitrite. Muu-Nan. Her heart cracked and tears rolled down her face. Her beloved Muu-Nan. He had been entrusted to her, and she had failed him. Why hadn't she taken him with her when she left the boat? No matter that she had been so weak and ill that she had been barely conscious. She should have taken him. He should have been her first thought. He was the reason she had come all this way and now he was lying somewhere on the ocean floor, possibly half a world away.

Self-pity mixed with despair and heartbreak. She was under no illusion; she would die here, and before many days had passed. She had water – *if* she could find the spring, and *if* it hadn't been contaminated with salt water – but there was nothing to eat. Virtually all the vegetation had gone along with any animal life that might have provided meat. She would starve – if she didn't freeze to death first, for she had only the clothes she stood up in and no shelter. If the temperature fell, so would she. Ruarth, who would have had the survival skills she so desperately needed, had gone. He could have barely reached the forest's edge when the wave had hit. Like everything else, he had been crushed by its force and swept away.

Her mind numb, hardly seeing the broken terrain, she tripped and stumbled down the mountainside, overtaken with shock, fear, and exhaustion. The few hours of sleep the previous night had not wiped away the nights when she had lain awake in her bunk at the mercy of the storm, and any amazement that she had survived was eclipsed by the knowledge that it meant nothing. Her future was non-existent unless she could get off the island. And that was impossible.

Her eyes to the ground, she picked her way downwards through the shredded remains of the forest, now just an occasional jagged tree stump poking up from the ground. Devastation lay all around her. The newly naked slopes seemed steeper and more uneven than they had when she had trudged up and she moved slowly to avoid falling. If she missed her footing, there was little to stop her until she hit the beach.

At the low cliff over which the little waterfall had tumbled, the cascade had vanished, spread out into a thousand tiny rivulets that squirmed down the rock face seeking new routes to the ocean far below. She paused, staring out at the horizon with hopeless, dead eyes. Why bother? What did she hope to find down there on the beach? Why not simply sit there on the cliff, staring out over the once more calm, green blue of the ocean, waiting for death. No, she couldn't give up. She wouldn't. She had to do something, no matter how futile the action.

She blinked, and blinked again, drew her hand across her tired, aching eyes and rubbed them hard. She had to be hallucinating, exhaustion playing tricks on her mind, for there, beyond the far side of the cove, perched high up on the near vertical slope of the cliff and clinging onto it at an impossible angle, she swore she could see a boat. It was resting stern down, as if it had simply sailed up the cliff and dropped anchor. Impossible, she told herself sternly; she was imagining it. The boat was long gone. Even if by some miracle it was still afloat, it would have been carried far away. She rubbed her eyes and looked again, squinting and the first shoots of new hope took hold in her heart. She wasn't imagining it. There *was* a boat, dangling from the rock. Their boat, Amphitrite. By rights it should be lying on the bottom of the ocean and yet there it was, plain as day. And if the boat was there, then so was Muu-Nan.

Her elation was short-lived. There was no way she could reach the little vessel. Even if she could somehow climb the near vertical rock face, the boat was so precariously balanced that the tiniest of movements would send it plummeting to the sea below, taking Calista with it. Nevertheless, she had to try. With more haste, and a lot less caution, she scrambled, slipping and stumbling, ever downwards, determination defeating fear. By some miracle, she reached the shore without injury.

The beach had been devastated. The shoreline was piled high with branches and boulders and the remains of grotesque sea creatures sucked up from deeper waters, churned up in the tsunami's crest and deposited on the waterline as the sea had receded. The sand and shingle that had once covered the seabed had been sucked away, leaving the wetly shining black bedrock exposed all the way up to where the forest's fringes had once been. Skirting the waterline, she clambered across to the far side of the cove.

The cliffs rose almost vertically here, demarcated by a narrow ravine she had not noticed the previous day when she had been too ill and too exhausted to take in her surroundings, or do anything except sleep. The ravine effectively divided the gentler slopes – the ones she had climbed – from the steeper outcrops. She would have to make her way inland until she found an accessible route to the top. How far that would be, she couldn't begin to guess.

Before she had gone a dozen paces, a faint creaking, cracking sound stopped her in her tracks. It had come from high above her and she looked up anxiously. Was an imminent landslide giving out a warning? She studied the ground. She could see nothing that appeared unstable.

She set off again. It came again. Another creak, another scraping crack. Louder this time. Again she halted, unsure of its origin, staring intently at the direction from which it had come. Over there, where Amphitrite dangled precariously.

Slowly, very slowly, so imperceptibly that at first Calista thought she was imagining it, the boat moved, at first slipping fraction by tiny fraction down the cliff face, then gathering momentum until the movement became unmistakable. Her heart was pounding. Had she found it, only to lose it again? Surely it would shatter on the reef at the base of the cliff. Or when it hit the water. It could never survive the drop, and neither would Muu-Nan. She held her breath; the stern of the boat edged sluggishly downwards until, with a grinding crunch, whatever had been holding onto it gave way. Calista couldn't hold back a cry of dismay as the little craft hurtled stern first towards certain destruction.

Except… it didn't. The keel swept over a protruding lip of rock that launched it outwards away from the cliff so that the boat missed the rocks guarding its base and plunged into the sea, disappearing below the surface in a massive plume of spray. She stared at the point at which it vanished, hope shattered for a second time that morning. This couldn't be the end, not when the boat had so miraculously been saved from the tsunami. She threw herself down onto the ground in frustration.

'Muu-Nan.' She reached out in desperation to the skull, convinced there would be no answer. Surely he was nothing now but splinters of crystal. 'Muu-Nan,' she called again. Silently. Reaching out to him with her mind. 'Are you still here? Is this to be our final destination? If so, then so be it. But if not, if our path lies far from here, I need your help. There is nothing more I can do.'

A warm wave of reassurance washed through her.

'Have faith, dearest child,' the whisper came, as soothing as sweetened milk. 'All is not lost. Your destiny will take you further. Much further. This will not end here.' Muu-Nan! He had survived the fall. He was still with her.

In a rush of bubbles and spray, the little boat surfaced, bobbing up from the depths like a cork in the water. It was as Ruarth had promised; Amphitrite was indeed unsinkable. The watertight hull was still intact, and the air trapped inside had given sufficient buoyancy to lift it back to the daylight from the deep reaches of the underwater chasm into which it had plunged. Now it sat floating happily on a mirror flat sea. A warm sun shone from a clear, deep blue sky and wavelets lapped gently against the shore. It was calm, benign, serene, a surreal image against the carnage on the island where the devastation wreaked on the land betrayed the cataclysm that had so recently occurred.

The boat was drifting slowly away from the shore. She had to get to it before the currents carried it out of reach. She could swim out to it if she acted quickly, but what then? Ruarth had been the seafarer; helmsman and navigator, he had possessed all the skills needed to travel the seas. She had no knowledge at all of boats or the oceans. If she ran into another storm...

'Trust me.' The words fell like soft rain onto her turbulent emotions, soothing and reassuring. 'The storms have passed. I will guide your hand now. What happened was a tragedy that could not have been prevented. It was the consequence of events that have occurred in Atlantis since the exodus. In times to come there will be more, and greater, repercussions. Do not trouble yourself with those; they are far in the future and you will play a part in mitigating their effects. For now, precious one, be untroubled. All is well.'

Chapter 17

She had misjudged her strength. Drained by lack of food and the events of the past days, by the time she reached the little boat Calista's arms and legs were leaden and her breath ragged. Gasping, she clutched at a small piece of rope that hung over the side and rested for a moment. She had nothing left in her, but she could not stay there; the chill waters were already numbing her limbs. With a final, monumental effort, she hauled her aching body up and over the gunwales, landing hard on the small foredeck where she lay panting and spent. She allowed herself to relax, just a little. She had made it. She was back on board the boat. And Muu-Nan had assured her that everything would be alright. Lulled by the gentle rocking of the waves and the soft lap-lap-lap as they caressed the hull, she slept.

When she woke, night had fallen and a huge full moon bathed the boat in a silvery light. She could see as clearly as if it were day. Quickly, she took stock. Amphitrite appeared to be floating level and high in the water. That must mean there was no damage to the hull, she reasoned. The gargantuan wave had swept the foredeck clean, including the storage lockers whose doors – and contents – had vanished. She scrambled over the roof to the stern; the tiller and rudder looked intact and moved under her touch but the little wooden hut that had covered it, providing shelter to the helmsman, had gone, as had the mast. She unsealed the cabin doors, anxious at what she would find. Although everything inside should be dry, the damage could be immense. The boat had not only been hurled around like a child's toy by the tsunami, it had then plunged from the heights of the cliff top deep into the ocean. Muu-Nan could have been smashed against the bulkhead or any of the other fittings.

Nervously, she peered in. The cabin was in darkness. She fumbled around for her bag and pulled out a small candle stub. In the flickering light of its flame, she looked around. The cabin was dry, which meant Ruarth had spoken the truth about the boat's soundness. It was also a chaotic heap of blankets, mattresses, and personal belongings, somewhere under which Muu-Nan had to be buried. She found him lying face down on one of the bunks beneath a mattress, wrapped in a tunic that had tangled itself around the skull. She swept him up with tears in her eyes and examined him closely. He was completely undamaged. Not a scratch, not a chip, marred his perfect surface. He was safe. She lay down on the bunk, cradling him to her chest like a baby. What should she do now? What could she do now?

'Nothing,' the whisper came. 'There is nothing you need to do. All is well.'

How could all be well? She had survived, Muu-Nan had survived, and the boat had survived. Ruarth had not, and Ruarth was the mariner. How would she find land – how would she sail this boat – without his skills and knowledge?

'All is well, dearest One. Do you not trust me?'

The warm glow of the skull's reassurance enveloped her, the words seeping into her soul like sweet honey. She did trust him, implicitly. Even if she didn't, what choice was there? Her destiny was now in the hands of the winds and the tides. And Muu-Nan. She was under no illusion.

Although she was now on the boat instead of the island, the gravity of her situation had not changed. She had no food and no fresh water. If she did not make landfall within a few days, she would die a lingering and very unpleasant death.

She slept the rest of the day and into the following night when the lustrous disc of the moon woke her, shining through the open hatch onto her face. The island was merely a faint shadow on the horizon, a dark mound standing against a dark sky. The tide and the brisk breeze that had sprung up while she slept had carried the little craft away from shore and into the grip of an ocean current that flowed steadily eastwards. Stiffly – although she was not yet old, she was no longer in her youth and her joints were complaining fiercely after the unaccustomed exertions of the previous days – she crawled out onto the deck.

The breeze had dropped again and the night was still. The boat drifted easily on the current, although where it was taking her, she had no idea. Eastwards still, she guessed, looking up at the stars. No doubt the Temple astronomers would have snorted in amusement at her attempts to make sense of the constellations amid the cloud of starlight, and she would be the first to admit that she was no expert. She had never had cause to use the knowledge she had learned during her training. Maybe, though, she had remembered enough. Not that it made any difference. She couldn't change the boat's course if her life depended on it. While the rudder and tiller were intact, the boat had lost its mast and sail. It had no power of its own, its progress controlled solely by the forces of nature – and completely at their mercy.

Calista lay on the deck, her head resting on her hands, gazing up at the velvet dark sky. Whoever had said night was dark? she wondered. Above her and to all sides stretched a giant hemisphere of the deepest inky black almost hidden by twinkling points of light that glittered like gemstones. When she focussed on individual flecks, she could make out their colours – pale pinks and yellows and blues, deep reds, and rich golds – amongst the brilliant diamond sparkle. Rivers of gem-dust came together in a glowing, glittering ribbon that snaked across the sky. And the silence, warm and all-embracing. Even the lapping of water against the hull had stopped as the boat drifted on the flat, unmoving ocean surface. It was as if time – and the world – had stopped, frozen into one eternal, elemental moment. She remained there, motionless, while the moon imperceptibly but steadily traced its habitual arc across the sky and sank towards the far horizon, and a pale glow in the east heralded the arrival of a new day.

It was a hot one, still without a trace of wind, and by midday Calista's thirst had become unbearable. Her tongue felt huge and was sticking to the top of her mouth. She had no saliva to soothe it. Although hunger knotted her belly, food was not her priority. She could survive many more days without eating. Without fresh water, especially in this heat, she would be lucky to last until tomorrow.

It took every ounce of effort to rig a canopy from an oiled jacket she had found amongst Ruarth's possessions. Under it she placed a baling scoop filled with sea water. She hoped that the seawater would evaporate and condense as fresh water on the underside of the oiled cloth, leaving the salt behind.

She spent the day in the cabin. Stifling hot though it was, at least it provided some shelter from the burning rays of the sun. When sunset fell over the ocean, she ventured out onto the deck. Her heart sank. The experiment had not been a success. Only a thin mist of moisture lay on the underside of the oilskin. Nonetheless, she licked at it thirstily, ignoring the brackish, oily taste. It barely moistened her mouth. Calista lay awake all night, gripped by fear, wondering how she would survive.

The following day was the same…

On the third day, it rained.

* * * * *

'Wake up, dearest Child. Wake up.'

By now, Calista was unconscious a lot of the time and dangerously dehydrated. It was a long, long time before Muu-Nan's gentle promptings filtered through the fog of her mind.

'Wake up, dear Child. Wake up.' Slowly she stirred, clawing her way back up from the murky depths to a hazy consciousness. 'It's raining. You must get up.'

Her arms and legs had turned to stone. They didn't want to move. It took every ounce of her willpower to get to her knees. It was raining, Muu-Nan had said. That meant water.

A thick, heavy drizzle was falling, rapidly soaking everything it touched. Calista dragged her protesting body from the cabin and fell to the deck, her face skywards, mouth open to the precious liquid, letting it soak her clothing and wash over her limbs. Gradually the water replenished her cells, and her mind and body began to function again. She crawled back into the cabin, searching for anything that would catch the precious droplets. There wasn't much. She grabbed the baling scoop, tipping out the salt water it still held, and fashioned the oilskin into a crude bucket. Next, she pulled out the two thick woollen blankets that had covered the bunks and laid them on the decks. The rain would soak them and she could ring the water out later. It wouldn't be particularly clean or sweet, but in her position, she reasoned, she couldn't be fussy. The containers were already filling and Calista drank until her thirst was relieved. Slowly, little by little, so as not to become ill, just as Ruarth had taught her.

There was still no wind, and it was still blisteringly hot. With the rain, humidity levels were sky high and it was hard to breathe in the thick, moist air. Calista went back into the cabin and lay on her bunk. It too was damp, the moist air seeping into everything, finding its way into all the nooks and crannies in the cabin. She didn't care. She had water now, and if she was careful it would last a good few days. Holding Muu-Nan tightly, she prayed that this miserable voyage would soon be at an end.

By late afternoon, the heavy blanket of cloud had begun to lift, slender fingers of hazy sunlight pushing through the clouds to brush the dull, grey surface of the sea with patches of shimmering silver. The air began to move, rapidly becoming a light breeze that hastened the clouds' dispersal. Calista hurried to store the water she had collected before the returning sun stole it from her again.

She had water now but still no food. She would have to try and catch fish as Ruarth had done. With what though? All the lines and hooks had been on the deck. Revived both physically and mentally, she ripped an old cotton cloth into strips and tied them together to create a crude rope, and she found a cloak pin for the hook. There was nothing to use as bait. She tossed the line over the side and waited. And waited. It had to be a hopeless exercise, but it was all she had. By the time darkness fell, she had caught nothing. Dejectedly, she stared at the empty hook. Leaving the line dangling over the gunwale, she lay down to sleep, hunger cramping her belly.

The wind had changed direction and was now at the stern; Amphitrite was travelling faster, still heading east according to Calista's crude calculations. Though the ocean was vast, she had been travelling for days now. Surely she had to reach land soon? Unless, of course, her calculations and estimates were completely wrong and she was sailing around in circles. It was a possibility she refused to consider.

Though the water kept her alive, hunger was taking its toll. She lay listless on the deck, crawling with difficulty to the shelter of the cabin when the sun grew too fierce. Time was running out for Calista. She would not survive more than a day or two more.

Chapter 18

Land. She could see land. It had been the suspicion of a shadow on the horizon for the past day and a half and if, initially, she had dismissed it as clouds or maybe even an illusion created by desperation combined with near starvation and refused to allow herself to hope, she could deny it no longer. Low rounded hills, dark green with forest, rolled up to the sky. Only... the boat had changed course. It was no longer heading for the coast; it was now drifting parallel to it. She eyed the distance to the shore with dismay. It would have been too far to swim even if she had been in good health and strength. In her weakened state she wouldn't manage more than a few strokes. And who knew what lethal currents or creatures lay in wait beneath the surface. Not forgetting Muu-Nan. He was heavy; he would drag them both down to the seabed.

'Muu-Nan,' she begged, 'help me.' The skull did not reply.

* * * * *

A shadow fell across her face; she opened her eyes – and screamed. Staring down at her were a pair of gleaming coal black eyes set in a face as dark as nebo wood. They wore a curious, if somewhat confused, expression. Gently, with no hint of aggression, her visitor reached out a hand – pale pink palm in vivid contrast to the dark brown, virtually black skin that covered the rest of his body – and brushed her cheek. His expression was friendly. In fact, there was nothing hostile about him at all. With difficulty, Calista pushed herself onto her elbows.

There were five of them, all with the same dark skin and all wearing nothing but a woven belt holding a vicious looking knife, staring at her as if she had arrived from a different planet. A wave of dizziness and nausea washed over Calista, forcing her to lie back down onto the deck. Concern replaced curiosity in the first man's expression. He turned and spoke to his companions; it was a strange language, unlike anything she had ever encountered, even though ancient languages had been her field of study in the Temple. Three of his four companions nodded in agreement. The fourth did not. He glowered at her, not attempting to hide his animosity, his voice raised in a very vocal and impassioned dissent that was quickly and firmly overruled.

The man standing over her pointed to his chest. 'Kal.' He repeated the gesture. 'Kal.' He was telling her his name.

Calista lowered her head in acknowledgement and did the same. 'Calista,' she croaked.

He nodded, satisfied, and reached out his hand to help her to her feet. She was desperately weak and swayed perilously as she stood; Kal grabbed both her arms and held her firm until she was steady. In the water, bobbing against Amphitrite's hull, were three strange little craft, held together by a sixth man who had remained in the prow of the centre one. They appeared to be the hollowed-out trunks of large trees. She didn't have the opportunity to wonder much; her companion was speaking again, waving his arms in the direction of the distant beach. While she didn't understand his words, she grasped their meaning from his gestures. They were going to take her to shore.

She nodded to show she had understood and, being careful not to do anything that would worsen her queasiness, turned to retrieve Muu-Nan from under the blanket at her feet. As the skull came into view, she heard a sharp intake of breath from the men who surrounded her, followed by a murmur of amazement and awe. And, she sensed, not a little fear. The one who had argued against her was more vocal. At first sight of the skull he began to shout and wave his hand, a rapid stream of incomprehensible words pouring from his lips. To her dismay, a couple of the other men were also now looking less sure of themselves and nowhere near as welcoming as they had. Kal was having none of it. With one short, fierce syllable he silenced the dissent. He was the leader, she reasoned through the fog that had taken the place of her brain, for they bowed – three reluctantly, one resentfully – to his authority and helped her, still clutching Muu-Nan, into the nearest of the three little dug-out craft. It wobbled perilously as she stepped into it and felt extremely unstable, lurching worryingly at the least movement. She had been put in the centre of the middle boat and she sat stiffly with Muu-Nan in her lap not daring to move. Kal sat in front, deftly wielding his paddle; another of the men did the same behind.

With a few swift strokes, the men turned the craft and headed for the shore, the boat rocking so alarmingly from side to side that she gripped the rough wood tightly with her free hand. Kal turned and grinned, and dropped a large, oval fruit into her lap. Its skin was smooth and golden, flushed with pink, and spicy sweetness assailed her nose. Hunger won. Hesitantly, she let go of the boat and lifted the fruit to her mouth, sinking her teeth deep into the flesh. Its sweet fragrance filled her mouth and her senses, luscious juices dribbled down her chin onto her tunic and, with the honeyed flesh, trickled into her cramped, starving stomach. Kal watched her, grinning at her delight, his white teeth dazzling against his pitch-dark skin. She was acutely aware, however, that another was watching her with far less goodwill and amusement. She tucked Muu-Nan into her tunic out of sight while the malevolent stare burned into her back from the following canoe. She had made an enemy already, it seemed.

Chapter 19

The village lay just back from the shoreline, a cluster of small huts scattered over the sandy ground amongst tall tufts of coarse grass. Kal led her to one on the far side of the settlement, furthest from the beach, and indicated that she should enter. It was cool inside after the searing heat of the sun, and the floor was strewn with soft grasses and leaves that whispered as she walked on it. It gave off a faint fresh scent that reminded her of the new mown hay that filled the fields around Yo'tlàn in summer. She had always loved the smell, spending hours enveloped in it on those long, warm days when she could take time away from her duties to simply sit and be. Sadness washed over her. That had been in another time and place, a long way from this sun-baked coastline, and a lifetime ago.

She sank to the floor, exhaustion and despair threatening to overwhelm her, and her head sank into her hands. She had no idea of where she was or where she was going. Or how to get there. Ruarth had been skilled, capable. He would have seen her through this trial. But Ruarth was dead, drowned, and she was alone with people with whom she could not communicate and, she was under no illusion, who could turn on her at any moment. She had seen the fear in the men's faces when they had seen the skull, and fear frequently led to violence. She shivered, seeing again the malevolence in that stare. Why had she agreed to do this? Why?

Someone was coming. She drew a hand across her face, wiping away the tears, as a young woman entered, rustling the leaves of the doorway as she brushed through them. Like the men, her skin was dark and her eyes like coal. Her only clothing, if it could be called that, was a string of shells draped around her hips.

All this Calista noted without being aware of it. Her focus, wholly and solely, was on the woven dish the woman carried in her slender fingers, and the irresistible aroma of – what? Something delicious, that was certain – that issued from it. Her visitor placed the bowl on the floor, peering with concern at the older woman's tear-stained face. Very gently, she reached out a hand and brushed the last of the tears away, then smiled and nodded at the bowl before she turned and left. Calista eagerly picked up the dish.

There was fish that had been wrapped in leaves and baked. That was the source of the mouth-watering savoury aroma. There were ripe, luscious fruits; some pink-gold and oval like the one Kal had given her, others that were knobbly, crimson and scented. And there was a water skin. She held it to her lips, tasting the contents. Water. Pure, sweet, clear water. After the brackish liquid she had survived on for the past however many days it had been, it tasted as good as the finest wine.

When she had eaten her fill, Calista lay back and gazed around the hut, idly noting that the whole structure had been constructed from slender, pliable branches overlaid with large smooth leaves, many of them longer than her arm and twice the width of her outstretched hand. Soon her eyelids grew heavy. The leaves and branches blurred and melted into one another. With a full belly and her thirst properly quenched for the first time in days, and with solid ground beneath her instead of the constant rocking of the boat, Calista gave herself up to sleep.

She was woken by raised voices outside the hut, close to where she lay. She shook the sleep fog from her brain and crawled across to the doorway, peeking out. It seemed that the entire village had gathered to watch an argument that was taking place between Kal and the man who, earlier, had challenged him. It was loud and angry, punctuated by a series of abrupt, angry gestures. No-one was looking in her direction. Everyone was focussed on the argument which, at this point, Kal appeared to be losing. The expression on most faces was one of fear, heads nodding their agreement as his opponent raged. He had the support of maybe three quarters of those present, who numbered forty or so, she would guess. Even so, Kal was not yet defeated. His bearing held a firm authority which, at present, no-one but his opponent was openly daring to question. Who was he, Calista wondered? King? Shaman? Spiritual leader? All three?

She spotted the young woman who had brought her food standing on the edge of the crowd nearest the hut. She must have sensed Calista watching, for she turned to look directly at her, gesturing urgently and anxiously that she should keep out of sight. If Kal was defeated, it would not go well for her. Calista ducked back inside just as Kal's adversary hissed a phrase and pointed directly towards her hut. She shrank back into the shadows, suddenly very scared. In that brief second she had seen in his eyes a deeply rooted fear, one that demanded action.

A moment later, he burst into the hut, grabbed her arm, and dragged her out into the sunlight. Holding her firmly with one strong hand, with the other he reached into her tunic and pulled out Muu-Nan. Cries of fear ran through the crowd, several villagers falling to their knees, terrified. Even Kal's supporters were looking nervously at each other, backing away as, letting her go, the man lifted the skull above his head and paraded it through the crowd.

Stunned into inaction for no more than a second, Calista darted forward to seize it, only to be stopped by a hand that clutched at her arm and held her back. She turned to meet the soft dark eyes of the young woman, which were filled with fear for Calista and pleading silently with her not to move. Calista stepped back, watching anxiously the people recoil when Muu-Nan drew near them. They feared the skull and that fear was being fanned by the man who brandished it ominously in their faces. They were becoming restless. There was real danger for her here. She pushed back further against the walls of her hut, wishing they would close up around her and hide her from their suspicious glances. Evidently, Kal noticed it too. Moving with the speed of a striking cobra, he seized the man's upraised arm and barked out what could only have been a warning.

For a split second, Calista thought the man would refuse to obey, overtly challenging Kal's authority. He thought better of it. Scowling, he handed over the skull and stalked out of the clearing, followed by at least a dozen of the villagers. Under the decidedly unfriendly gaze of those who remained, Calista took the skull gratefully from Kal and allowed the young woman to hustle her hastily into the flimsy sanctuary of the hut. She did not need the frantic gestures urging her to remain out of sight. It was starkly obvious that she was not welcome here and neither was Muu-Nan. Kal could not ignore the unrest of the entire village. How long before he ceded to its demands? His authority had already been challenged. He would not be prepared to lose it on her account.

Chapter 20

Startled, her eyes flew open. A soft hand was pressed against her mouth. Who was it? Was there one, or more? What did they want? She could see nothing in the night-black interior of the hut. She relaxed a little. There was nothing rough or threatening in the touch. More like it was warning her to silence. The hand lifted from her face and closed on her arm, pulling her up. Whoever it was wanted her to follow. She scrambled to her feet, picking up Muu-Nan as she did so, and felt her way out through the door.

Outside was almost as dark as inside had been. The moon was nothing but a hair-fine silver crescent, too new to shed light, and the starlight too was dimmed, as if sucked up and drained by the night's heavy cloak. She could just make out the silhouette of the young woman who had helped her earlier in the day. Where were they going, and why? With no means of communicating, Calista could only follow. Sensing that danger prowled amongst the leaf-covered dwellings of the village, she crept as quietly as she could in the woman's footsteps, out of the village and onto the plains beyond.

The grass here grew as high as her shoulder. It brushed at her arms as they wound their way through its forest along paths invisible to her. The tribeswoman had to have the nocturnal senses of a bat. Not once did she hesitate or pause to consider the direction but pressed on rapidly and unerringly, leading Calista by the hand. A couple of steps in the wrong direction and Calista would have become hopelessly lost in the rustling green sea that enveloped them.

They walked for a long time, not stopping until the first rays of dawn lightened the horizon. A thunderous roar echoed through the still air. Below them, in monochrome shades that little by little brightened into the vibrant colours of day in the light of the awakening sun, lay a shallow depression; beyond it, two great rivers came together, each battling in vain for supremacy, neither one winning, neither losing, as they merged into one vast thick brown torrent that roiled and churned towards the sea. Her companion led the way into the base of the depression and stopped, looking at the lightening sky. She was waiting for something – or someone.

As the first rays of the sun tipped the rim of the basin, he came. Kal. At first, she did not recognise him. This morning, the ordinary man in his simple shell waistlet of the previous day had been transformed, adorned as the great tribal chief that he was. On his shoulders he bore the tawny gold skin of a huge he-lion, the paws reaching down to his chest, the powerful jaw and massive teeth resting on his forehead while the mane, glittering like flame in the early light, had been brushed and teased into a halo of fire around his head. The moment the sun touched him, he turned to greet it. Lifting his arms to the sky, he opened his mouth and roared.

A water pouch and a large bundle, tightly wrapped in leaves with woven grass carrying straps was lying on the floor of the hollow. Her companion picked up the bundle and strapped it to Calista's back, tying the straps tightly and wedging the water-skin underneath. Calista stood compliant and confused. What was happening?

Kal approached her, a fearsome figure in the lion pelt, his bearing that of a man of absolute power and authority. He placed his hands on her temples and began to chant – steady, rhythmic, melodic – hypnotic in its timbre, until she was aware of nothing but its echo resonating through her flesh and bones. When, at last, is stopped, his hands left her face and he dropped to all fours in the stance of a prowling beast. It was uncannily and scarily life-like. Throwing back his head, he opened his mouth once more and roared. Once, twice, three times, the sound echoing off the sides of the hollow until it came at her from every direction. Barely had it died away when an answering roar echoed across the plains. Then another, and another, building roar upon roar that rolled like thunder in the cloudless sky. When it faded, Kal rose and pointed to the east, at the fiercer of the two rivers that met below their feet – the torrent that flowed from the distant range of blue-violet mountain peaks. A gentle push on her shoulder left her in no doubt. He was telling her to follow the river.

Wait. Did that mean...? Were they going to leave her here to go on alone? They couldn't. Muu-Nan was not offering any guidance; indeed, he was as dormant as the day she had left Atlantis with him. She had no idea what or where this land was, or the dangers it might hold. She wouldn't stand a chance. She stared at them wildly, refusing to believe what she knew in her heart to be true. The woman looked at her sympathetically and gestured again, smiling encouragement and reassurance. Kal merely bowed. Then they turned and walked away. Neither looked back.

Chapter 21

She watched until long after the grass forest had swallowed them, hoping until the last that they would take pity on her and return. It was not to be. She was alone once more. Alone and abandoned in a stark, unknown land.

Finally, after having endured so much, the last vestiges of Calista's courage deserted her; she sank to the ground, unable to repel the overwhelming despair that robbed her muscles of strength and her heart of hope. They had been kind to her, Kal and the young woman whose name she hadn't learned. Why then would they bring her out into this wilderness and leave her? She didn't stand a chance. She might as well stay where she was and wait to die. It was all too much. The sequence of nightmares she had lived through since sailing away from the coast of Atlantis continued, and she no longer had the strength or will to fight them. She curled up on the hot sand, closed her eyes and gave herself up to her fate.

'Courage, precious Child. Courage. Rise to your feet and go on.' Muu-Nan? She didn't need to ask. His love, as soft and gentle as starlight, embraced her. 'It is not your destiny to die here. You have much yet to live for, much to accomplish. Come, rise. It is not over.'

'I can't, Muu-Nan. I am tired. So tired. I can't do this any longer.'

'I know, Child. I feel it in you. You have been through much. Yet you are stronger than you believe. You will succeed. I would not have chosen you otherwise. Come, rise,' the skull insisted. 'It is not over.'

It was true. Muu-Nan had chosen her, out of all the younger, stronger, more suitable candidates in the Pyramid Temple. Surely he wouldn't have done so if she wasn't capable of fulfilling the responsibility.

'Rise.' Muu-Nan encouraged gently but firmly, accepting no refusal. 'Rise and go on. There is one who will come to walk beside you. He will come soon.'

'I don't know the way.'

'I will guide you. Trust in me and follow where I lead.'

Of course he would. Her faith in the skull, so recently waned, returned and with it came a renewed determination that gave her strength. She had a mission to fulfil and Muu-Nan was relying on her to accomplish it. She would not fail him. She would not end it here in this lonely, desolate place, giving up with a whimper. If death did claim her, it would only be after a fierce battle, and after she had done everything possible to finish the task she had started. She may not know her final destination but of one thing she was certain – it would not be here.

'Which way, Muu-Nan? Where do I go?' No reply. He had fallen silent once more. Only the shriek of the eagles that circled high overhead answered her.

The skull had promised to guide her, and she trusted his word, so the answer had to be there, in front of her. But where? How?

Of course. Kal. Before he had walked away, he had pointed in the direction of the rising sun where the silhouette of a distant mountain range shadowed the horizon and from where the mud-brown waters of the larger river roiled and bucked. Calista hoisted the small, leaf-wrapped bundle higher on her back and wrapped the skull tightly in the front folds of her tunic. Squaring her shoulders, ready to take on all that was to come, she crested the far rim of the shallow depression and strode down to the river.

Day after day, on and on, she walked, finding shade where she could when the sun was at its highest. It was hot. So hot. Hotter than Yo'tlàn had ever been. Muu-Nan had promised to guide her and she trusted in that. She was less sure that he could protect her from the many predators that snuffled and growled unseen in the darkness, and she slept only fitfully under the stars, yet night after night she remained undisturbed and unharmed.

She kept close to the river as Kal had signalled, watching it change character as she followed its banks. Before she had gone far, the turbulent silt-laden waters calmed, flowing serenely and smoothly through deep, crumbling banks. Instinctively, she kept her distance, for although all appeared peaceful and innocent enough, occasional sinister ripples suggested unseen terrors lying in wait beneath the glassy surface. She refilled her water skin at the occasional small streams that crossed her path on their way to the main watercourse. The water seemed fresh, though she couldn't be certain, and each time, Ruarth's warning rang in her ears.

Ruarth would have known if it was tainted, as he had known then, but Ruarth was not here. How she wished he was. A sharp pang of loneliness pierced her, so suddenly and unexpectedly that she gasped. No, he wasn't here. No-one was here except her and Muu-Nan, and the skull had not spoken since the day she had descended to the riverbank and set out on this endless trek. She wasn't accustomed to the unremitting solitude. Though solitary reflection had been an important practice during her life in the temple, there she had always been surrounded by the other Priests and Priestesses; after, there had been Ruarth's genial company. Since the island and his death, however, she had been almost constantly alone. It was hard. Impatiently, she shook off the memories and the melancholy. Dwelling on them would do no good at all.

She had no choice but to take her chances, filling her waterskin whenever she could. The sun's relentless heat sucked the moisture from her skin and her throat, and her thirst often raged. Yet she remained well, although she was constantly hungry. She had carefully rationed the food in the bundle she had been given, eating sparingly of the tough strips of dried fish and seaweed and the hard flatbreads, supplementing them by whatever she could find as she walked. Those supplies were all but exhausted. There was, at least for now, a plentiful supply of the small crimson fruits that hung in clusters from the bushes that grew abundantly along the edge of the riverbank. They reminded her of the day berries she used to gather as a child, sweet yet at the same time tart and intensely refreshing. Collecting them was a hazardous process for the bushes bristled with thorns as long as her thumb and as sharp as a sailmaker's needle. She wouldn't fool herself. With her other supplies gone, she had to find other food urgently. She couldn't live on day berries alone.

Except... there was nothing else. Few other shrubs and plants grew up from the coarse grasslands and sandy soil, even at the water's edge where any tender shoots were quickly trampled by the wildlife that came to drink. With the passing days, hunger gnawed ever more sharply in her belly and she stumbled with increasing frequency as her body weakened. With it, her will weakened too. She fought it fiercely. She would not let despair take hold again. She couldn't. If it did... It was a battle that, little by little, she was losing.

Where was the guide Muu-Nan had promised? Or had his words simply been a ploy to trick her into going on. No, he wouldn't have done that. Maybe the guide had had an accident? Each morning when she woke it was harder to stand up and continue yet day after day, step after step, stumble after stumble, she forced herself on. One question assailed her mercilessly, filling her thoughts: why was she doing this? It was utterly futile. She was going nowhere because there was nowhere for her to go. She had done what had been asked of her. She had taken Muu-Nan from the Temple and kept him from the clutches of the Shadow Chasers. What else was there to do? Why go on? And yet go on she did.

With every sunrise and every sunset, the mountains drew a little closer. Their once hazy outline now stood out sharp and vivid against the sky, grey and silver with white caps on the highest peaks. The sweeping plains were giving way with increasing frequency to rocky outcrops that stuck up out of the flat lands like warts on the back of a hand, precursors to the foothills beyond. The terrain was rougher, harder to negotiate. The river too, had changed again. It was faster, wilder, the water clear, tumbling over a rocky bed.

Calista tripped constantly, too weak and exhausted to lift her feet over the stones that littered the ground. Still she kept walking, moving like an automaton, more through habit than intention.

Please, no. The crag loomed up like a sinister beast preparing to strike. From steep slopes of sandy gold soil, jagged slabs of dark grey stone thrust up out of the earth promising pitfalls to the unwary – or the exhausted. Under different circumstances, possessed of her full health and strength, it would have been a minor inconvenience. In her current condition, it would be an almost impossible hurdle. Was there an alternative route? There appeared not. On one side the river tumbled through a deep gulley, its current too fierce to attempt a crossing; she would be swept away in moments. On the other, the ground rose sharply to vanish in a cluster of jagged pinnacles. It appeared that this was, in spite of everything, the easiest route, unless she risked a very lengthy detour that would take her a long way away from the river. If she could find one. And Kal had been clear that she should follow the river. She came to a decision. She would rest, and tackle the climb in the morning.

Chapter 22

It was as difficult as she had feared. Although a natural pathway of sorts – maybe an animal track? – snaked up the hillside avoiding the worst of the jutting slabs, it was steep and treacherous. Loose soil slipped under her feet at every step. She didn't look down, keeping her eyes firmly fixed on the ridge above, which drew steadily, if painfully slowly, closer.

Her leg muscles were screaming in protest, already at their limit of endurance, her lungs gasped for air and her heart thumped as it if would burst from her chest with the effort, but she had made it. It had taken her all day; the sun was already dipping rapidly towards the horizon. It didn't matter. Against all the odds, she had made it. She slumped down against a tongue of dark rock that thrust up out of the hilltop and within seconds was sleeping soundly in the leaden, numb sleep of those who have nothing left to give.

Calista woke with a start to a roar like a thousand thunderclaps that echoed through the chill dawn light, reverberating around the ridges and valleys, vibrating through every cell of her body. Her heart hammered against her ribcage and her fingers clutched at the unyielding ground in terror. What was it? Where was it coming from? It was everywhere, surrounding her, exploding through the clear morning air.

'Muu-Nan?' Her tremulous whisper went unanswered.

She shivered. Icy fingers plucked at her skin. The sound had been unearthly, supernatural even. Were the spirits of this land, irritated by her intrusion, announcing their displeasure? Why now though when she had been travelling these lands for so long? Those spirits surrounded her in every moment of every day. They could never not, for they were the soul of the rocks, the river, the soil beneath her feet. Over those long days that she had walked amongst them she had ceased to be merely a traveller on this land, she had become part of it, and she felt its heartbeat. If that was truly so, she reasoned, then she had nothing to fear.

In any case, she would continue despite the anger of the spirits because she could do nothing else. Ahead, she might find the answers she was looking for. Behind her, she would not. There was nothing for her back there. She stood and moved to the far side of the ridge, across ground that shook with the barrage of sound, too curious as to what awaited her to hold back.

Lifting her head, her fear and confusion vanished and her bone-deep weariness was forgotten, at least momentarily, at the vista that lay spread out before her. The world was waiting, holding its breath for the birth of a new day. At the exact moment when the sun crested the furthest mountains, a dazzling gold-silver disc that balanced on the summit of the highest peak like an acrobat teetering on top of a pole, and the clear, new light brought the landscape into sharp focus, the thunderous roar fell away.

In the sudden silence, the beauty of the new day wrapped around her and she caught her breath, spellbound. Distant purple-hued mountains thrust up high into the pale blue, new morning sky, standing guard over a huge lake whose still waters reflected the cloudless hemisphere overhead. The lake filled the bowl created by the steep slopes of the foothills she had so recently crossed through, which curved around on either side as far as she could see, from the ridge where she stood to the base of those far-off mountains. Here and there the sun's rays glanced off a ripple on the water's surface, sending splinters of dazzling light dancing across its mirror.

It would not be easy to find a route around the lake. The slopes were steep and rugged and would test her remaining strength to its limits. But there was no alternative. In spite of herself, Calista smiled. After so much arid desert, the sight of the lake was as unexpected as it was welcome to her parched throat. The change in landscape and the sparkling, calm blue waters revived her spirits and her courage.

The thunderous uproar had not resumed. Pushing away all thought of what had caused it – worrying about it would not serve her at all – Calista swallowed her last mouthfuls of water. Chewing on a handful of her precious supply of day berries, she clambered stiffly to her feet and made her way to the far side of the ridge where she surveyed the descent. It appeared to be easier than the previous day's climb had been, not too steep and relatively free of loose stones and rocky traverses. Some way below, a cliff edge cut across the slope in a sheer drop all the way to the shoreline, but it stretched for only a short distance across the hillside. If she headed down diagonally to the left, following a faint animal path etched into the ground, she would stay well away from its dangers.

* * * * *

She had been too optimistic. Though the path was indeed less steep on this side of the ridge, the sandy soil was much less stable than it had appeared from above. She slipped and slid unsteadily down the slope, more than once having to grab at the stem of a straggling shrub to slow her descent. She wasn't safe yet; the cliff edge and the danger it posed waited below for one wrong move.

Calista's terrified scream echoed around the empty hillside. A misjudged step had put her on a section of loose soil that had given way under her weight. Scrabbling for a handhold, a foothold, anything that would stop her fall, she plunged down towards the edge, hands scrabbling in vain for a lifeline. High above, the eagle that had startled her flapped lazily back up into the sky, not knowing – not caring – that it had sent Calista to her death.

'Muu-Nan!' she screamed. 'Help me.' The skull did not respond. She was going to die, and Muu-Nan was doing nothing.

She slithered and skidded downwards while the world around her spun in slow motion. There was nothing she could do. After all that she'd been through, she was going to die. Here. On this hillside. Alone. Hope surged for a split second when her hand gripped the spiky stem of a low-growing shrub, only to vanish as the roots ripped from the ground. Her feet were over the edge of the drop, her hips… She was in free fall, tumbling head over heels through empty space. She prayed she would not feel the end. Moments later she hit the ground. Agony flared as her body shattered, then was gone in the darkness that swallowed her.

Chapter 23

It was getting lighter. She was floating up towards the surface of... what? Pain beyond anything she had ever been able to imagine racked every cell of her body. She couldn't breathe. She couldn't move. Was she alive or dead?

The light grew stronger. Warmth flowed across her face, warmth like breath. Someone was with her. Her eyes flickered open – and she stopped breathing, for a moment her pain forgotten in her terror. Less than an arm's length from her face, the muzzle of a lion – an enormous, golden male lion – stared down at her, his front paws straddling her shoulders. She screamed, only no sound emerged. Her organs, her lungs, had been crushed so badly by her fall that they were unable to draw in enough air to allow even a whimper to escape.

The lion lifted his head and roared, a roar that shook the ground she lay on. It was the sound that had woken her that morning. This time, in that roar, Calista heard the symphony of the galaxies, and in his eyes, as blue as the midday sky above her, she saw the cosmos – millions upon millions of stars, stretching into eternity. Sparkling silver clouds of stardust. Towering nebulas of every colour and design. She saw in them the birth and death of worlds and suns, rising and fading, from the beginning of time. And in his breath, she felt the breath of creation, warm and moist on her skin. She sucked it into her body as deeply as her ruined lungs would allow, drawing it into her shattered limbs and broken flesh.

'Welcome home, little One.' Words that were more a feeling than a thought. 'Welcome home.'

*   *   *   *   *

Many hours later he was still with her, lying close against her. Protecting and shielding her, keeping her warm with his body as night fell and with it, the temperature. Through her tunic, Calista felt the rise and fall of his flanks and the heat of his body. Her fear gone, she welcomed his nearness with an instinctive understanding that this was the one Muu-nan had promised would come. The one who had come to guide her. It was a knowing that had been born in her the moment she had gazed into those blue, blue eyes and seen the universe reflected back.

Chapter 24

Calista opened her eyes to a clear, sparkling sky. For the first time since beyond her remembering, her mind was equally clear. What though of her broken body? She took stock. The agonising pain that had seared through her entire body when she had first regained consciousness after the fall had gone. In its place, a dull ache throbbed remorselessly. It hurt, a lot, but it was bearable. Surely that had to be a good sign. Tentatively she focussed on each area. Her feet and legs; she could move them, if stiffly. Her back. Her belly. Nervously she took a deep breath and her lungs responded. Slowly she pushed herself up to a sitting position, closing her eyes to the wave of dizziness that swept over her. She was weak. She still hurt. But by some miracle, her shattered bones had set and her torn flesh healed. She was alive.

Where was the lion? Was this his doing? Had he somehow healed her while she lay oblivious? The mighty beast, who had guarded her and kept her warm throughout the cold, dark hours, was nowhere to be seen.

Muu-Nan! Where was the skull? How could she have forgotten about him? Her heart constricted and fingers of fear clutched at her skin. He was no longer tucked into the front of her tunic; he must have slipped out as she fell. She had landed on a wide ledge several feet above the lake's surface. Far off to her left, the ledge and the cliff behind it climbed steadily to meet with the gentler slopes, the ones she had planned to cut across. Frantically, she scanned the slab of rock. It was bare, thank Sirius. If the skull had landed there, he would surely have shattered into a hundred thousand splinters.

Above her, the cliff rose steeply from a jumble of fallen rocks. Her heart sank. If he had landed among those, she would never find him. That is, if he had survived at all and not been smashed to dust by the impact.

Or… She stared in dismay at the lake, lying calm and unruffled below the ledge, its waters plunging who knew how far to the bottom. Far beyond where her vision could reach, certainly. If the skull had escaped the rocks and had instead landed in the lake... Well, he would be equally lost to her. She had no way of retrieving him, even if she could find him.

'Muu-Nan?' Desperation filled her call to the ancient skull. 'Muu-Nan? Are you safe? Where are you?' Silence answered.

She buried her head in her hands and wept. She had failed. Failed Omar and the Temple. Failed the other twelve Priests and Priestesses of the Light who, like her, were risking everything to keep the sacred skulls safe. Most of all, she had failed Muu-Nan, who had chosen her explicitly, entrusting her to take him to safety. For a long time she wept, bitter tears of loss, despair and frustration streaming between her fingers.

'Do not worry, dearest One. You do not need to search for me. I am coming back to you.' Muu-Nan? It most definitely was but what did he mean? How could he be coming back to her?

She swung around at a low growl. The lion had returned and was padding across the ledge towards her, his huge paws silent on the stone. In his mouth, he carried a clear, spherical crystal. Muu-Nan. The great beast lowered his head and gently laid him on the bare, grey rock, where the skull sparkled rose and lavender and fire in the fierce sunlight. With one swift gesture, Calista scooped him up and clasped him to her breast, her heart beating a rapid rhythm against her ribs. He was safe. He hadn't been smashed to splinters or lost in the dark waters of the lake. He was safe.

'Thank you.' Her eyes locked onto those of the lion, bluer than the noon day sky. For a fleeting moment she saw once again the cosmos swimming in their depths, then it was gone.

Now she was next to him, she realised that the lion was even larger than she had estimated, his shoulder standing as high as hers and the tips of the ears on that massive mane-haloed head reaching way above the crown of her head. Still she was not afraid, for in those eyes she had seen something else, something greater even than the cosmos. She couldn't name it. She didn't understand it. She knew only that it was older than time and vaster than the universe that stretched into infinity above them. All at once, faced with such immense power that it eclipsed even that of the skull still clasped to her breast, Calista felt very humble and small. She sank to her knees, lowering her eyes in reverence, and held out Muu-Nan.

The beast growled again, low and soft, and in the sound, Calista fancied she heard amusement. Laughter even. A deep, slow voice, like the rumble of waves crashing on the shore, filled her mind. The voice of the lion.

'Peace be with you, Child of Earth. You have no cause to kneel before me. The courage and strength that you have shown prove that you are an equal to all you encounter. Rise, blessed One.' His soft muzzle nudged at her forehead, lifting her face to meet his. 'Peace be with you,' the rumbling voice repeated. 'Have no fear. I shall return.'

With that, he turned and padded away, vanishing into the scrub of the hillside, his tawny gold coat merging so perfectly into the sandy yellow of the soil that it appeared he had simply dissolved into the air.

Calista stared after him. Would he indeed return? She had to trust that he would. She tucked the once more quiescent Muu-Nan back into the front of her tunic and eased her aching limbs into a crevice formed by several fallen boulders where she could shelter from the fierce, burning rays of the sun. She was still desperately weak, physically empty of strength and in dire need of proper nourishment, even if her injuries were healing. She had only a couple of handfuls of berries left and would have to find food soon... but not now. Not today. She ate barely half of what was there before tiredness claimed her and her eyelids closed. She dozed fitfully, the rocks that dug into her back eliminating any possibility of deeper sleep, until a muffled dragging noise roused her. Night had fallen and in the darkness she could distinguish only a dim silhouette moving across the ledge. It was shapeless – or at least so strange a shape as to be unrecognisable – and Calista shrank as far back as she could into her tiny shelter. What in Sirius' name was it?

A familiar low rumble allayed her fears. The lion had returned. She crawled out of her hiding place and picked her way carefully across the ledge towards the shadowy outline. The ground was hidden by the night and suddenly she tripped and stumbled, only avoiding a painful tumble by thrusting her arms forward to save herself. Yeuwww! What was that? Her hands had landed on skin, warm and covered in short hair and damp stickiness. An animal of some kind, she guessed, once her heart had steadied its beat, and a large one by what she could tell, though she could make out nothing more. The last sliver of the waning moon, a silver crescent-shaped thread, shed no light on the sleeping land. She would have to wait until dawn.

Chapter 25

The pale light of a new day revealed the body of a large, horned animal that resembled the deer that ran in the forests around Yo'tlàn. The only difference was that this creature carried a single pair of corkscrewed horns the length of her arms in place of the familiar multi-branched antlers. The lion stood guard over his kill as he had since his return, his muzzle red with its blood. Now Calista had woken he bent his head, seized one of the animal's hind legs in his jaws and pulled, wrenching it free to a stomach-churning sound of tearing flesh and tendons. Taking it in his massive jaws, he moved closer and laid it at her feet. This was her share.

The lion tore hungrily at the mutilated corpse, ripping into its belly to reach the soft entrails inside. Although nauseated at the spectacle, Calista's revulsion was overridden by the prospect of a full stomach and hunger sated. She would make a fire and roast the haunch; there was plenty of dry wood in the dead shrubs that littered the base of the cliff. Ravenous as she was, the prospect of chewing on raw flesh made Calista sick to her stomach.

Leaving the skull safely at the inner edge of the rock shelf, she gathered a pile of flat stones and built a low, crude, circular wall the length of her forearm in diameter and as high as her knee. She filled the centre with twigs, dead leaves and small branches, keeping to one side the larger pieces of wood for when it was fully alight. The gaps between the stones would allow air in to fuel the fire and she would rest the haunch across the stones above the flames, turning it regularly. It was a huge chunk of flesh and would take a long time to cook but that couldn't be helped. She had no means of cutting it into smaller pieces.

Skinning the meat was an easier task than she had anticipated. Where the lion had torn it from the carcase, the skin was ragged and loose. She took a good grip and with a sharp tug, the skin separated from the underlying flesh, like the peel from an orange. Now, how to light the fire? In her excitement, Calista hadn't considered that problem. She had no flint, no fire-making equipment. Everything she had taken from Yo'tlàn was either lying at the bottom of an ocean or in the boat that perhaps still drifted aimlessly somewhere on its surface.

She picked up a couple of loose stones hopefully but when she knocked them together, hoping for a spark, they crumbled. Too soft. Light flickered briefly at the corner of her vision. Muu-Nan was glittering in the sunlight. Of course! Crystal, even if not completely clear, would focus the sun's rays into a single beam powerful enough to ignite any combustible material. She lifted the skull onto the edge of the fire pit. While it wasn't a proper sphere, and the carved jawline and facial features sent the rays in unexpected directions, she manoeuvred it until the concentrated sunlight shone directly on her pile of kindling.

Very quickly, the dry grass began to smoulder. One of the twigs smoked, glowed and burst into a tiny flame. A quiet cluck of triumph escaped Calista's lips. Quickly, she fed the flame with more twigs and dried leaves and soon a small fire burned merrily. She lifted the skull away and set him down by the cliff once more, whispering her thanks.

She tended the fire closely, building it up until it settled into a glowing mountain of white-hot embers before she placed the meat across the top of the stones. She had to wait an agonisingly long time before the mouth-watering smell of roasting meat drifted across the ledge, all the while her empty, ravenous belly growling and cramping in protest, made more acute by the teasing promise of the aroma. When she could stand it no longer, she wrapped the remains of her food sack around her hand, lifted the haunch from the heat and sank her teeth into the cooked surface layer until the juices poured down her chin, only stopping when she reached the still-raw flesh beneath. Her hand shook with the emotion of starvation avoided as she placed the haunch back over the firepit to continue cooking.

Chapter 26

Calista walked on, accompanied at every step by the great golden lion who only ever left her side to hunt for food. He was her protector and he was her guide. Whenever danger lurked near, his instincts would sense it long before it became visible and he would lead her safely around it, although there had been a few close calls when she had ignored his guidance, obstinately taking the path she wanted to take.

At first, when she had headed off confidently in a direction he didn't wish to go in, he had simply stopped, refusing to follow her. His recalcitrance had irritated her and she had set off stubbornly, believing that Muu-Nan was guiding her way, only to quickly come up against some insurmountable obstacle; the raging torrent of a flood-heavy river, a barricade of needle sharp thorns as long as her palm, the unscalable cliffs of a deep chasm. Deflated, she would turn around and return to where the lion waited for her patiently.

A dozen or more times, she had made such fruitless and draining diversions, firm in her belief that Muu-Nan was leading her forward. Until the day when, leaving the lion standing patiently on the side of a low gully, a giant puff adder had reared up only a couple of paces in front of her, hissing its anger as it readied to strike. Frozen in the face of certain death, a flash of amber-gold had flown past, seized the snake just behind its deadly head and hurled it into the scrub with one toss of his powerful jaws. After that, Calista followed her guardian without question, conceding that Muu-Nan had sent the lion to her and the skull was leading the way through him. She could no longer ignore it.

Nor could she ignore any longer the physical changes in her body. It wasn't only that she was now stronger, leaner and fitter than she had ever been throughout her comfortable life in the Pyramid Temple where, although she had nurtured and cared for herself, the physical demands had been moderate. The exertions of this endeavour – day after day walking and scrambling over rugged terrain, climbing and descending steep hills and gorges, wading through thigh deep currents – combined with the high protein diet provided by the lion's hunt, had toned her muscles and eliminated any excess flesh from her frame.

No, this was something more. Something – dare she think it? – not quite natural. When she studied her reflection in the still, clear pools they occasionally passed, she saw a face that had become softer and smoother. Her skin was firmer, despite the rigours of her existence, and appeared to have regained a youthful freshness in defiance of the perpetual aridity and heat. Her limbs were lithe and supple, her body no longer that of a woman nearing her seventh decade.

If initially she could put the changes down to her increased fitness and wishful imagination, that reasoning was completely extinguished the morning she woke with a dull ache in her belly and her thighs red with blood. Her moon cycles had returned, more than fifteen years after their last visit. Her womb, which had never known the fullness of a pregnancy, was by some miracle blossoming once more. Her first reaction was fear. Was she ill? Had her body succumbed to some disease she had been unaware of? Was some malignant growth taking over her flesh? In the Temple, there had been priests trained in the healing of such disorders. She was not one of them. She had had other duties and had never learned their skills.

'Peace, Child. Your body is well.' Muu-Nan's melodic words whispered through her fears. 'It is healing. It has been healing since you set foot on this continent. Your cells are rejuvenating, returning to their optimum functioning.'

'Why?' Calista could think of nothing else to say in her confusion. Why now? Why her? And, if Muu-Nan was the cause of the changes, if he had that power, why had it never been used before? Why had they not known of it in Yo'tlàn? And why, after so many months of silence, was the skull speaking to her today?

'Because it is necessary now. It wasn't necessary then,' the soft voice answered. 'You have much to accomplish, descendants to bear who will carry your work and your lineage forward. Do not let this concern you now. You will learn all when the time is right. Accept what is being given to you and continue on your way.

'You are blessed, Child, more than you know. The task that lies ahead of you is greater than you can as yet conceive. Do not fear this. I and many other allies will be with you, guiding you at every step. Fall into this fearlessly and let it carry you into the great joy that lies ahead. This is my promise to you.'

Chapter 27

She had been trudging through the range of jagged, rocky hills for several days. It was difficult terrain and she was making slow progress. These were the kind of days when Calista questioned everything: why she had taken on the mission of protecting Muu-Nan (although in her heart she knew she would make the same choice again); whether she had the strength to carry on much longer; indeed, whether she would ever reach her destination, wherever that was. There had to be one, otherwise why would the Great Lion have been sent to guide her. She couldn't begin to guess how much further she would have to travel and at times like these, when the path was so hard and fatigue had worn her down, she doubted that she would live to find out. She had lost track of how long it had been since she had left Yo'tlàn and the Pyramid Temple. It felt like another world and another lifetime. Surely it had to have been nearly two full sun cycles ago, close to seven hundred and thirty days, and still she could see no end to her journey.

On the fifth day, during the period of brief twilight before the black night enshrouded them, they passed through a cleft between two shoulders of grey rock and entered a narrow valley. The steep stone walls blocked out all but a slender strip of darkening sky and a sprinkling of emerging stars. Her lion companion padded silently and peacefully beside her, guiding the way.

Calista shrank back. Despite the powerful bulk of her companion at her shoulder, fear clutched at her belly, yet the fear was nothing compared to the wonder that swept through her. Blocking their path was a colossal snow-white lion, a mighty beast, larger by far than her golden guardian. Her head, she estimated, would barely reach to its shoulder. He stood calmly; she could feel the power emanating from him. A succession of thundering roars burst from his throat, their echo reverberating on and on around the stony slopes of the valley, until every cell in her body trembled with their force.

Questions flooded into her mind. What was this creature? An albino? No, even in the rapidly fading light she saw his eyes clearly. They were the same vivid blue as her companion's, the colour of the noon day sky, and they blazed like light pouring through the purest of sapphires.

She sensed the golden lion move beside her and laid a hand on his shoulder as he stepped forward, fearing a confrontation. Powerful as he was, he would be no match for this majestic creature. He paid no attention to her warning touch. A few paces away from the snow-white beast he stopped and, to Calista's astonishment, bent the knees of his front legs and lowered his brow to the ground in a gesture of respect and submission. The white lion bowed his head briefly in acknowledgement then lifted his gaze to settle on Calista.

'You know what to do.' Muu-Nan, his words whispering softly through her thoughts.

Suddenly, and out of nowhere, she did. Reaching into her now tattered bag she drew out the skull and held him aloft. He glowed with a soft, radiant light that illuminated the gloom of the gorge floor. In all her time with the skull, Calista had never seen this. The white lion walked towards her past her still-kneeling guide and she was no longer afraid; with crystal clarity, she realised that this lion and Muu-Nan were linked in ways she couldn't understand. She too fell to her knees, holding Muu-Nan out to the huge white lion who was so close that she felt his warm, moist breath on her face.

The lion bent his head and rested his brow on that of the skull she offered up to him, his touch so gentle she barely felt the weight of his massive head. The black of the new night settled around them, the only sound the soft breathing of the three of them and the thud of her heartbeat; the only light the slender river of starlit sky above them and Muu-Nan's otherworldly glow. They had been taken out of time and space.

She stayed there for a long time, floating in this other place. It was only when the skull's weight grew too much to hold any longer, bringing a dull cramping ache to her arms and shoulders, that she remembered where they were. As if in response to her discomfort, the white lion lifted his head, breaking contact with Muu-Nan. She lowered her arms, setting him down on the ground. Still she had no idea of what was going on or why the snow-white lion had come to them, and Muu-Nan did not enlighten her. He had fallen dormant and unresponsive once more, his luminosity extinguished. What she did carry within her was a profound understanding that this meeting had been of the utmost importance. It had been the reunion of old friends, the re-establishing of an ancient and much-missed connection during which the two had shared important information.

She became uncomfortably conscious that the lion was watching her, his alabaster muzzle barely an arm's length from her face. Blue, blue eyes looked deep into her soul, reading it as if it was an open book. There was nowhere she could hide, no part of her she could shield from that penetrating gaze. Still she wasn't afraid. Those eyes held only the most profound compassion, love, and wisdom, more than she had ever witnessed even in Omar and the Elders of the Pyramid Temple whose light and high vibrational frequency had always left her in awe. This creature was as far above them as they were above the Shadow Chasers. She stared at him. What *was* he? Where had he come from?

The great beast bowed his head; to her astonishment, Calista could have sworn a smile flickered around his muzzle. With a final bow of his head to the golden lion who waited unmoving in the shadows behind her, he turned and padded away into the darkness, a ghostly white shadow fading into the night.

Her guardian nudged her gently with his massive shoulder, breaking the spell. The valley was as black as pitch, the tiny glimmer of starlight making no difference to the darkness. They could go no further that night. Her hand on his warm flank, he guided her to a patch of soft, sandy soil where she spread out her cloak and lay down.

'His name is Rasalus. He is your ally. His home is amongst the stars and his ancestors were of those who brought Muu-Nan to your world. He will watch over you. He will help you to achieve what you are here to do.'

With her guardian lion's whispered reassurance calming her confusion, it wasn't long before Calista fell into a deep sleep.

Chapter 28

For days they had been heading north along the banks of the Great River. Whereas for so long she had had no real way of marking time and had early on given up the attempt as days turned into months, or maybe that was years, now she had a reliable means of keeping track of the days passing. Her moon cycles had continued regularly since their re-appearance and she had counted four full flows since they had first approached the tumbling waters of what had been, at first, a narrow ribbon of water carving through the landscape. They had skirted the blue expanse of the vast inland sea fed by that watercourse until they had come to a wide river that flowed northwards from the lake. This was the route they were to take. The river had grown wider and ever more mighty as it traced its path through the wilderness, sometimes as a single, deep, fast flowing current, at others breaking into meandering channels through low sandbanks where terrifying giant lizard-like creatures basked in the hot sun and from time to time slid without a sound beneath the waters until only their eyes were visible. They negotiated cataracts where the path fell away down near vertical cliffs, and treacherous marshlands where she kept a sharp look-out for the giant scaly lizards that lurked unseen amongst the reeds. Still the lion led her on.

*   *   *   *   *

They were walking across a small shingle beach on the inside bend of the river. A rugged, steep cliff rose high above her, climbing up the ragged incline in a series of ridges. Calista slowed and peered more closely at the vegetation-covered face. Was that...? What looked to be a crude path zig-zagged up from the slender crescent of sand they stood on. A few paces further she stopped, dumbfounded, staring wide-eyed at a short, timber pier that thrust out from the bank into the strong current. Though rudimentary, it appeared solid and sound. It also looked well-used.

Did this mean that she had at last reached her destination? Surely it had to be so. The pier had been built by someone, which meant there had to be people here. Since the morning, so long ago now, when Kal and the woman had helped her escape from their village and left her on that desolate hillside, she hadn't encountered a single person. All through her epic trek, Muu-Nan and her lion guide had had no human contact, whether by accident or design. Now it appeared that this isolation was about to end. Her legs crumpled and she sat down hard on the pebble-strewn beach. She had been waiting for this, had anticipated this moment for such a long time, so where was the joy, the excitement, she had been expecting? Sitting there on the slender shingle crescent, she felt only the emptiness of anti-climax and the numbing exhaustion of years of journeying that now swept through her, and with it came a spreading anxiety. What was she to do?

Walking the landscape in the lion's company, guided and protected by him every step of the way was all she had known for so long. However challenging it had been, it was familiar and reassuring. She had felt safe. Now, she was facing the loss of that life. The loss of another life, for Atlantis, Yo'tlàn – even the Pyramid Temple itself – had long been left far behind her, nothing now but a hazy memory. One challenge was over. The next, it seemed, was about to begin. What that would be, she could not guess. In her mind swirled Muu-Nan's words that the task that lay ahead of her was greater than she could conceive.

A low rumble broke into her thoughts. The lion was speaking, his words deep and kindly in her mind.

'This is where we say Farewell, my cherished Calista. My work is done. I have brought you here safely. I have brought you home. I have fulfilled the mission given to me by the thirteen Skulls of Light and now you must go on without me. There is much for you to do here.'

'Go on? Where?' In her heart she had known this, known that once she arrived at her destination, the lion would leave her. She had pushed the thought away stubbornly every time it returned, unwilling to contemplate a time when he would not walk at her side.

'There.' She followed his sky-blue gaze to the cliff base and the narrow path that led up steeply from it. 'That is your way.'

'But...' Her eyes filled with tears. He had been with her for so long, her protector, provider, guide. She could no longer imagine life without her golden-pelted companion.

'You will not have to do this alone,' he promised. 'For a little while, yes. Soon though, others will come to help you. One in particular. He has been tasked with a mission as important as your own. He will come and he will walk through life by your side. Beloved Child, it has been my honour to journey with you. You will always be in my heart.'

She turned and stared at the track, still unsure.

'Who lives here?' she asked, unwilling to let him go. Getting no answer, she whirled around. He wasn't there. As silently as only a cat can move, he had slipped away.

Fear gripped her, clutching at her chest. She couldn't breathe. He had gone. She was alone. Warmth touched her through her tunic, caressing her back where the bag holding Muu-Nan rested. She drew in a long, slow breath, her courage returning. Of course she wasn't alone. Muu-Nan was with her, as he had always been. With the lion's help, he had brought her safely this far. He would lead her safely forward too. She had nothing to fear as long as he was with her. She squared her shoulders, took a last glance over her shoulder back the way she had come, and started up the path.

Chapter 29

The settlement – bigger than a village, almost large enough to be called a town – spread out in front of Calista. She had clambered up the final dogleg of the steep path and emerged onto a flat, stony plateau in front of a settlement of square, flat-topped mud-brick buildings. After so long away from any form of civilisation, she hesitated, apprehensive. Would they welcome her and Muu-Nan? Or would they reject her, fearful of the skull, as Kal's people had done?

She looked around. There wasn't a soul in sight, the only sounds those of the goats and chickens that roamed between the buildings. Far below, the lush green fields that stretched out along the river's bank, irrigated by its waters and made fertile each year by its floods, were deserted. They were here though, the inhabitants of those homes, watching her from behind the shuttered windows or the low walls of the roof terraces. She felt their eyes following her as she passed by.

She gathered her courage and with as much confidence as she could muster, shoulders squared and head held high, walked through the dusty, empty streets where, here and there, the framework of a well indicated that fresh water flowed beneath this land. She went on until she came out of the buildings onto open land, an arid, barren plateau from which a large, irregular outcrop of rock rose, two thousand and more paces ahead. She had reached the edge of the town.

Retracing her steps, she took a wide alleyway off to her left and soon came out into a large, clear space between the buildings. The town square? A market place? Certainly an area for gatherings. Again, the place was empty of people. She turned, slowly, looking for some indication of what she should do and where she should go.

'Honoured One, welcome.' She spun around, startled at the greeting that had come from nowhere.

The man was small and wiry with skin the colour of walnut, eyes of the blackest ebony and hair that still showed strands of the same colour, though it was now heavily cast with white. He was, perhaps, in his eighth decade? He wore a short sarong around his waist and on his naked chest rested a heavy breastplate of what appeared to be pure gold, thickly inlaid with gemstones. Lozenges of vibrant lapis lazuli, blood-red garnet, fiery carnelian and flowing green malachite surrounded a central crystal as big as Calista's fist that sparkled fire in the sun's rays. He had to be the leader of these people; the aura of his authority filled the square. To her surprise, he bowed low.

'I am Da-Lim and this is my land, a land blessed by the gods.' His words overflowed with warmth and welcome. 'Welcome. We give thanks to the gods for bringing you safely to us. We have waited long for you.'

Calista's brow wrinkled. She didn't understand. How could this man have known she was coming here when she herself hadn't known?

If Da-Lim saw her bewilderment, he ignored it. 'We will talk later when you have rested and eaten,' he continued. 'Come. We have prepared lodgings for you.' He led the way to a small, single-storied building just off the square, pulled aside the heavy curtain that served as the door, and ushered her in.

'This is your home. Do what you wish with it to make it your own. There is food here and a soft bed. We will speak tomorrow.' He started to leave then turned back, remembering. 'When will the other arrive?'

'What other?'

Da-Lim frowned, taken aback by her question. 'You do not know?' Calista shook her head. 'There is another who comes.' He spoke with certainty. 'The prophecy says so.' He held up his hand, forestalling her questions. 'We will speak tomorrow,' he repeated, then turned and slipped through the curtain leaving Calista in a fog of restless confusion.

* * * * *

The following morning, the town was bustling. Everyone she encountered was of the same build and colouring as Da-Lim, small in stature and dark-skinned. They watched her with undisguised curiosity as she wandered through the streets, not wishing to be discourteous by staring too openly yet fascinated by this tall, fair-skinned woman with a river of silver-gold hair who walked like a queen. Only the giggling, doe-eyed children paid no heed to politeness, crowding around her chattering and giggling, reaching out to touch her.

'Calista.' Da-Lim was in the square and had clearly been waiting for her. 'Come.' He led her to a canopy, the rough ground beneath which had been carpeted in soft goatskins, and gestured to her to sit.

'How do you know my name and that I would come here?' She couldn't hold back any longer.

'The prophecy. The gods.'

'I don't understand. What prophecy? What gods?'

He smiled, revealing even, white teeth. 'The ancient prophecy, given by the gods who came from the stars in the time before time, repeated by those who came to visit my father when I was still a child.' He frowned. 'You do not know of it?'

She shook her head. 'No. What does this prophecy say?' Would it give her some clue to what she was to do next, now that she had completed her journey?

'That two strangers will come here from a distant land, although not together. They will be one woman and one man, and they will bring with them treasure beyond price and power beyond measure.

'It speaks of a tall woman with hair the colour of sunlight woven with moonlight and eyes the colour of springtime leaves. The sacred treasure she carries will bring lasting peace and abundance to our land.' He indicated the obviously heavy bag hanging from her waist. 'This treasure that you carry always.'

Instinctively, Calista hugged the bag more tightly. If Da-Lim noticed, he ignored it. 'The prophecy tells they will come when the Great Lion hangs high in the Eastern heavens and the call of his earthly sisters is heard on the winds. She comes here first. He joins her with the passage of time.' Da-Lim fixed her with a steady gaze. 'When will he come?'

Calista's head swam. Could it really be that another from the Temple would be guided to this place by the skull he carried? It had to be so, but who?

'I-I don't know,' she faltered.

Da-Lim relented in the face of her obviously genuine incomprehension. 'It is no matter,' he said gently, 'for it will be so. The prophecy speaks truly; he will come. In time, all will become clear. Tell me then, how did you come here?'

'I was brought here by a great he-lion, although I cannot say for what purpose. I have been told only that I would discover this after I arrived.'

Da-Lim nodded. 'It is the time, indeed. Your story confirms it. Lions are not usually seen in these lands yet for the past six moons my people have glimpsed a mighty she-lion roaming the far side of the plateau. I myself have heard her roar as the moon sails overhead. We have let her be, taking it as a sign that you would soon be here, for she has kept her distance, and our people and our livestock have remained unharmed.' He rose, the audience at an end. 'This is your home now. Treat it as such. All you need will be provided for you; you need only ask. When the moment comes that you learn of your purpose here, we will help you.'

Chapter 30

She was weary with an overwhelming exhaustion that had come upon her two days earlier and brought her to her knees. Now that she had stopped, had reached her destination with no clue what she was to do next, and therefore with nothing she could do, she had begun to relax. It was this unaccustomed inaction, this letting go, that had opened the door to the bone-crushing fatigue she had been holding at bay for so long.

For two full moon cycles, she rested, settling gradually into her new life, feeling the fatigue drain from her limbs. It was difficult to adjust after so long on her own with only the lion for a companion. Then there had been no conversation, the only sounds those of the natural world around her, and the continual moving forward. Here, the world she found herself in was bustling and lively, filled with chatter, laughter, and the occasional argument. Here, she stayed in one place, the scenery unchanging. Often she felt trapped, suffocated by the walls and narrow alleyways, and to ease the discomfort she took on the daily habit of long walks with Muu-Nan, crossing the plateau to its furthermost edge.

Each time, she found herself at the foot of the strange stone outcrop that pushed up out of the bedrock, as if she had been drawn there by a magnet. She would shelter from the fiercest heat of the day in the shade that it cast, take the skull from his wrappings and gaze into his pale depths asking for guidance. Each time she was met with silence. At first, she accepted that it was not yet time for her to know. When day after day after day passed, however, with no communication, the doubts began to grow. Now that she had done as she had been tasked, now that she had brought Muu-Nan to this place, would the Heart of Regulus ever speak to her again?

* * * * *

Calista woke suddenly, her heart racing. In the darkness of her room nothing stirred and yet… Not daring to move, she strained to listen. It was faint but it was there, a slow, rhythmic breathing. Not human. An animal, and a large one at that. Had the huge she-lion that roamed the plateau chosen to come into the town to fill her belly tonight? Slowly Calista opened her eyes, fearful of what she might face.

Instead of a she-lion's sleek head and tawny-brown coat, the doorway was filled by a giant male lion whose coat glistened like virgin snow in sunlight. But this was not day and the night was black as pitch. The light came from within him, spreading out around his body, spilling into the darkness. She recognised this magnificent creature at once; she had met him before, on the boulder-cluttered floor of a narrow canyon.

'Rasalus,' she whispered, sitting up. He bowed his massive head in greeting, shimmering and noble.

'It is time.' His deep, rumbling growl reverberated through her body in words she could understand.

'Time for what?' she asked, silently, meeting his thoughts with hers. 'What is it I am to do?'

'Come, I will show you.' She rose to follow, unafraid, even though the great lion's shoulder stood level with her head and his massive jaws could crush her as easily as she could crush a beetle.

There was no moon. It was the time of its cycle when the old moon had died and the new had not yet been born. Free of moonlight, the sky dazzled, thick with stars. Sparkling diamond dust on an indigo velvet backdrop. Three stars, those of the Hunter's Belt, outshone all others. It was magical, enchanting, yet little light touched the world below.

It didn't need to. Rasalus was radiant, his white-gold aura reaching out for an arm-span all around his body, illuminating the ground within its sphere. As long as Calista stayed close to him, she could easily see to pick her way through the rocks and scrub.

A short distance from the outcrop, he stopped. 'You see the three stars of the Hunter's Belt?' he asked. She nodded. They were alive with light tonight. 'Where their light falls on this plateau, three monuments will arise in the likeness of the Pyramid Temple in Yo'tlàn. In time. That task belongs to another.' He turned to face the outcrop. 'Your work is here.'

'What work? What is it that I am to do?'

'You will build a home for the Heart of Regulus, fashioning it from the flesh of Tera that rises up before you from the bedrock.'

'The outcrop?' Had she misunderstood? She had not. Rasalus bowed his head. Yes, the outcrop. But how?

'We shall guide you. Muu-Nan will guide you.'

'What is this home to be?'

'In time.'

'So I am not to know what I am building until I build it.'

Rasalus' eyes flashed. 'Each step will be revealed when you need to know.'

'But...'

His eyes flashed again, fire and starlight. She would learn no more tonight. Again, a bow of acknowledgement.

'The first task is to excavate the ground around the rock to the height of three men and level the floor to create a courtyard.'

'So be it.' Irritated and frustrated, Calista turned away.

'Calista.' The growl was conciliatory. 'Let that be enough for now. In time, you will know all. Start today with what you have been shown. I will return, often, to guide you in this.' He lifted his head to look at the eastern horizon, already paling with the dawn. 'I will return,' he repeated.

The immense beast shimmered, flared, and was gone, leaving Calista alone with her thoughts. The sun was high overhead when at last she returned to the town to speak with Da-Lim.

Chapter 31

The whole town was making its way towards the square. Tonight, they would feast. A band of travellers had arrived and word had quickly spread that they carried with them the second treasure of the prophecy, a rumour Calista had not heard until she returned home late in the day having been occupied at the outcrop site since dawn. She hadn't yet seen the newcomers; they had been resting in their accommodation when she had returned, and she was fiercely impatient to meet them. If this was indeed the fulfilment of the prophecy Da-Lim had spoken of, they would be from Atlantis – and amongst them would be a Priest from the Temple. A familiar face. A flash of intense homesickness swept through her when she heard the news, and she bathed and dressed quickly. Filled with anticipation, she pushed aside the curtain door and stepped out into the street.

Her heart missed a beat, then another. She couldn't breathe. The world stopped around her. What in the name of Sirius...? It couldn't be – and yet it was. Kua'tzal, the man she had once loved more than life itself. Still loved, if the roar of the blood racing through her veins spoke truly. The unexpected feeling was so raw and so intense that her legs almost gave way beneath her. This was the man she had believed lost to her – and to the Light – forever. The man who had become a traitor, a friend of the Shadow Chasers and the misery they spread. How could he be here?

Yet he *was* here, not a dozen paces from where she stood rooted to the ground. The words of the prophecy echoed in her mind: *'They will be one woman and one man, and they will bring with them treasure beyond price and power beyond measure.'* Could it be that Kua'tzal was that male, chosen Guardian of one of the Skulls of Light? It was impossible and yet… If he was here and if he carried with him another of the Skulls, it had to be so. What other explanation could there be?

He was turned half away from her, hadn't seen her. She watched him, not moving, not speaking, dragging her emotions back under control, waiting for her pulse to slow and her breath to calm. The man standing before her was no longer the pinched, cold, old-before-his-time Priest she had last seen pacing the corridors of the Pyramid Temple. This Kua'tzal seemed younger – much younger – filled with vigour and life. Strong and… Well, happy and relaxed. This was the Kua'tzal she had known all those years ago when they had laughed and loved together. He had changed since he had left Atlantis, just as she had.

'Kua'tzal? Is it really you?'

He turned slowly, his face a mask of disbelief, and stared at her, unable to speak for a very long time.

'Cleantha,' he sputtered eventually. She put a finger to her lips to forestall any further comments, lightly took his arm and steered him to a quiet corner. 'Cleantha?' he repeated.

'Here I am known as Calista. Muu-Nan requested it,' she told him. Her hand, still resting lightly on his arm, was trembling. A maelstrom of emotions, long locked away – confusion, hurt, love – churned and ached within her. Somehow, she kept it in check, if barely, and held her voice steady.

By unspoken mutual consent, they spoke of other things; of the skulls, of the perils and challenges they had faced to reach this place, and of the immense responsibility that they had learned lay ahead of them. Inside, however, Calista was fighting a losing battle with her feelings.

'Let's go back to the celebrations,' she said. She needed crowds, noise, laughter. Anything to keep her attention away from the chaos of her emotions. 'After all, they're in your honour.'

* * * * *

By keeping a distance whenever possible between herself and Kua'tzal, she held on to her composure for the rest of the evening, functioning as if life was normal. It wasn't though. Kua'tzal was here. How could it ever be normal again?

The instant she reached the sanctuary of her home, all of the long-repressed emotions, the pain and anger – so much anger – the despair and the love overwhelmed her. She curled up on her bed like a wounded animal, knees clutched to her chest, shaking so much her teeth rattled. No tears. Not now. They would come later.

And somewhere, as fragile as a candle flame in a storm, a spark of hope flickered. In his shock at seeing her, he hadn't hidden it. In those first moments when he had turned, recognising her voice, she had seen it. Love, laid bare and vulnerable. Love that reached back through the decades, undimmed and untainted. Love for the only woman he had ever wanted.

So much had passed between them since. So many harsh words, so much bitter rejection. Was it too late?

'It is never too late,' Muu-Nan whispered softly to her heart. 'Trust, blessed One, and let the life that lies before you unfold.'

Chapter 32

Calista watched the river swirl lazily past, serene and eternal, the deep green waters echoing the depths of her feelings. She closed her eyes, soothed by the rays of the early morning sun that flowed like warm honey over her skin, and the delicate fragrance of the pale blossoms that surrounded her, tickling her nose. She desperately needed these few moments of peace before the ritual she would lead later, the culmination of the task that had occupied her since her arrival here on the plateau so many years earlier.

She stretched out on the soft herbs that covered the sandy ground, Muu-Nan cradled in her lap, and drifted back through time, remembering...

Under her supervision, and with the guidance of Rasalus, the Great Stone Lion had emerged from the bedrock as if awakening from an aeons-long slumber, to rise proud and mighty from the dusty, drab ground. It had been hard, challenging, even with the Star Lion's help. She had had to learn new skills and make sense of concepts and theories that verged on the inconceivable even to her Temple-trained mind. Muu-Nan had been with her throughout, giving her strength, clarifying her understanding, and opening her mind to accept the truth of these impossibilities. Despite – or may be because of – all of this, Calista had found her work immensely satisfying and enjoyable.

A soft smile played on her lips and her closed eyes wrinkled a little at the corners. The Great Stone Lion was not the only reason for her happiness. There was also Kua'tzal and the love that they shared. Once buried so deeply in an abandoned corner of her heart, believing both him and that love lost to her forever, they had been returned to her. One more impossibility that had come to pass. Muu-Nan had once promised that great joy would be hers. With Kua'tzal, she had found it.

Their work had kept them busy and at first there had been few chances to speak at length. Those times they had, neither had been able to hide their pleasure. Calista's smile deepened. Regardless of the demands of the tasks they were undertaking, they had contrived to meet, to talk, more and more often. Their once shattered bonds healed and grew ever stronger until they became unbreakable.

Tears now dampened her lashes. Not for herself, even though her heartbreak had been unbearable. No, this morning on the tranquil riverside, she wept for the man she loved. For the sacrifice he had made for Atlantis, for the Temple, and for the Skulls of Light. And for what that sacrifice had cost him. No matter that it was in the past, the scars it had left on him would never fully heal. She saw it in the shadows that even now sometimes darkened his eyes in his quiet moments. Those were the times she would take him in her arms and simply hold him until the shadows dissolved.

Their love, reawakened, was stronger than it had ever been. She flushed. It had been here on the river's edge in the nearby bathing pool that he had come to her, and she had welcomed him with her body. And her body had welcomed him without condition; that morning, new life had been sown in her belly. The following night, they had wed.

Yet... and this morning, for the first time, she could admit it; in all the time they had been together, with all the love she felt for Kua'tzal, she had kept a piece of herself back. She'd been aware of it for a long time, had never been able to discover why. It had always floated a fraction too far below the surface for her to grab hold of and explore. Why then had it now stolen up to pinch at her heart and remind her? Was she at last ready to let that piece go and to give him everything that she was?

A breeze plucked at her hair, pulling her away from her thoughts. Muu-Nan was still cradled heavy on her belly, her hands resting lightly on his cool, glassy surface. Out of nowhere, her heart filled with sadness.

'What now, Muu-Nan?' she murmured. 'What do I do? I always knew you were never mine to keep and yet we have been together for so long and been through so much. My heart breaks to let you go, though I must. That is why you brought me to this place, so that this day would come.'

The skull pulsed beneath her fingertips, blazing with his unusual lavender-pink light. 'Blessed Child, always I will be but a thought away. When you call on me, I will answer. The road you walk now takes you to another calling. You, together with Kua'tzal and those who came with him from Atlantis, will build the foundations of a new civilisation. It has already begun.

'Do not feel sorrow for what is past, blessed One. Rejoice in what is to come and in he who walks this road with you.' The light faded and the skull fell silent.

'Calista?' Her name rang out through the still air. Kua'tzal was looking for her. Gathering the skull, she scrambled to her feet and waved in greeting.

'Come, wife,' he called. 'It is time.'

Chapter 33

Calista took a few moments to absorb the spectacle that greeted her. Below was the immense sunken courtyard surrounding the Great Stone Lion who stared unseeing out over the plateau, eastwards towards the rising sun. Towering behind him were the part-built structures of the three pyramids that marked the point where the light of the three stars of the Hunter's Belt fell onto the land. Just as Rasalus had told her so long ago.

The contrast could not have been greater. The lower sections of the three huge pyramids, still far from completion, were already sheathed in inky black obsidian quarried in distant lands and brought here along the Great River. Against them, rising up from the basin of polished coal-dark basalt that formed the courtyard, was the glistening, pure white, marble clad Great Lion, sparkling in the sunlight like freshly fallen snow. Black and white. Night and day. Kek and Kauket. Balance and harmony.

It was time for her to relinquish her guardianship of the skull. Sharply aware that she was the sole focus of the entire town, who had gathered there for this ceremony, she descended into the courtyard, Muu-Nan held to her breast, and moved forward until she stood between the huge stone paws. She closed her eyes, waiting for the words that would flow through her from another time and place. She lifted the skull high above her head, the sun's rays flashing and blazing on its surface, and spoke in clear, vibrant tones.

'Muu-Nan, Skull of Arcturus, Heart of Regulus, guide us well. Bestow on us your wisdom, your knowledge, and your love as today we bring you home. Watch over and protect us, that we may always live with loving hearts, open minds and generosity.'

The air hummed, electricity prickling skin and a shiver of low voices stirred the crowd, wonder mingling with fear. In front of Calista, a ball of blue light had appeared, spinning and rippling, growing larger with every moment that passed. The shiver turned to a sharp intake of the collective breath. The ball of light had vanished and in its place stood two lions, as pure white in colour as the marble that clad the great monument. They were colossal, their shoulders standing level with Calista's head, and yet the woman didn't move, undaunted by their closeness.

She was used to the mighty Rasalus appearing from empty air. Those around the perimeter of the courtyard, however, had never witnessed it; they drew back, hesitant and afraid, some whispering of sorcery and ill-magic. Calista turned to them.

'Friends, I ask you to welcome our guests from Regulus who honour us today by sharing in our ceremony.' The muttering faded. They trusted Calista. They would believe her despite their fear.

The two lions held Calista's gaze and, once again, she watched all the wonders of the cosmos unfold in the infinity of their eyes. At last, with a toss of their mighty shoulders, they planted their forepaws firmly on the ground, raised their heads and roared, loud enough to shake the ground beneath her feet. On and on they roared, louder each time, the sound echoing in crashing thunderclaps across the plateau. Day turned to night and then back again in the space of a hundred heartbeats and the lions fell silent. No-one moved, no-one spoke, wondering what would happen next.

'Come.' Calista turned to address the crowd. 'It is time to enter the Hall of Mirrors. Let the ceremony begin.'

Led by the two great beasts, she turned towards a doorway in the tip of the left-hand stone paw. Da-Lim and Kua'tzal followed. Hesitantly at first, a hesitancy soon overtaken by curiosity and a burning desire not to miss out on the coming events, the crowd descended into the courtyard in their wake.

The opening led onto a narrow, low passageway that sloped steeply down for some considerable distance before climbing again. It was dark and cramped, lit only by the widely spaced lamps set into the wall, and no-one dawdled in its claustrophobic gloom.

The Hall of Mirrors was vast, hollowed out from the living rock, the perimeter set with highly polished mirrors fixed onto wooden frames, the reflected light of the lamps and torches creating an eerie, flickering atmosphere. Those present were standing, literally, within the belly of the beast.

Calista didn't move. Her consciousness had left her and was travelling far out into the farthest reaches of the galaxy and beyond. Constellations, nebulae, and galaxies swirled around her as she soared through the infinity of space to a small room on a distant world. The room was lit by the glorious radiance of a colossal quartz bed that filled its centre, glowing like the sun. Ice-clear points the length of her arm thrust up into the darkness illuminating those who stood around it.

The Arcturans she recognised from the Temple records of their once frequent visits to Yo'tlàn. With them was a powerful golden she-lion, a tall well-built man with a halo of tawny gold hair and a tall, slender being – she was unable to discern whether it was male or female – with white skin and the palest of pale blue eyes. All were focussed on the crystal cluster, a couple of handspans above which a skull was materialising in the air. Its colour was an unusual pale lavender-pink and it was as clear as water, shot through with rainbows and delicately folded veils. This was Muu-Nan's birth, she realised with a jolt. She had been brought here to witness it.

Those surrounding the crystal cluster had closed their eyes and were chanting in low, slow tones. Electricity crackled through the air, coalescing into the finest of gold filaments that, rooted in their hearts and brows, reached across to the newly created skull, penetrating and merging with it. The light strengthened. A column of light burst upwards from the crystal bed into the skull, exploding it into life. In its depths, light sparked, intensifying rapidly, spreading to spill out past its physical boundary.

Calista's eyes flew open. She was back in the Hall of Mirrors; in her hands Muu-Nan now blazed as brightly as in her vision. He was ready. Tingling raced up and down her spine, her arms, her legs. She couldn't move, rooted firmly to the bedrock beneath her feet. The skull's aura expanded further, enfolding Calista completely until she shone as brightly as he did. In the background, the lions continued to sing. It was softer now, more harmonious. Hypnotic and compelling, it carried those who watched, wide-eyed and open-mouthed, out of time and space.

They forgot where they were. They forgot who they were. All that mattered was the Heart of Regulus and his Guardian, Calista.

Moving slowly, deep in trance, Calista raised the skull high above her head and began to chant. *'Ot thekat sti partash.'* Over and over again, her voice joining with the lions' call. *'Ot thekat sti partash. Ot thekat sti partash.'*

The Heart of Regulus sparked and flared, trembled briefly, and lifted out of her hands, disappearing into a tiny shaft directly above her that led to the exact centre of the stone head. The growls changed pitch again. This time they carried a slower, deeper tone that vibrated through flesh and bone. The air in the shaft thickened, grew opaque and solidified into stone until no trace of the opening remained.

Calista fell to her knees, drained, her arms limp, her head hanging to her chest. She no longer had the strength to stand. In a heartbeat, Kua'tzal was at her side, lifting her into his arms and cradling her like a child. Behind him, the lions blazed silver and starlight. Their thanks rippled through every mind.

'It is done. Our blessings upon you. Honour Muu-Nan, Skull of Arcturus, Heart of Regulus. Let him guide and protect you. You are blessed to hold two of the sacred Skulls of Light in your safekeeping. It is not by chance. This is a great land, a land of power where Tera's energy flows strongly and freely. Here, your potential is unlimited; let the skulls guide you to it. Use that power but use it wisely, Children of Tera. Do not let fear and greed contaminate the gifts you have been given.

'Remember us when you look upon this great monument. We will return from time to time to walk beside our Earth family. We take our leave of you, offering you the love and light of the cosmos to hold in your hearts.' They bowed their heads to the floor. 'Farewell, friends.'

Radiance flared and condensed into a ball of vibrant white light that hovered for a moment – and was gone. In the stunned silence that followed, Da-Lim stepped forward.

'Come, friends. Today is a day that will be told of in legends for generations to come. It is time to celebrate, to feast and drink and dance. We have been blessed indeed by the gods. Let us show them our appreciation and gratitude through our celebrations and joyful hearts.'

Followed by Kua'tzal, carrying Calista in his arms, Da-Lim led them back through the passageway and into the evening sunlight. True to his command, tables shaded with wide, woven canopies were set up in the courtyard and laden with food and wine. The sun's burning heat had mellowed to the blissful warmth of evening and the people feasted and drank, sang and danced until the first streaks of crimson heralded a new dawn.

* * * * *

Everyone but Calista and Kua'tzal. She was simply too exhausted. He carried her home to the sounds of revelling drifting across the plateau, taking pleasure in the feel of her soft, warm body against his. As he lowered her to the bed, her arms encircled his neck and her lips pressed to his.

'I love you, husband,' she whispered.

'I love you too.'

Their lovemaking was slow and unhurried, of soft kisses and tender caresses. When he pushed against her, she opened to him, moist and eager, and he moved within her slowly and selflessly. She moaned softly, the sensations carrying her up and up towards her climax. Her heart opened to him so completely that tears of joy spilled onto her flushed cheeks. Nothing held her prisoner any longer, not fear, or hurt, or her Guardianship of the skull. Her legs wrapped more tightly around him, her arms pulled him closer and she drew him into her more deeply than she had ever done before. He felt the shift and he responded, his thrusts more urgent, his kisses hungrier.

Her release came quickly, shattering the last of the walls she had built over the years, hurling her into wave after wave of shuddering ecstasy that swept her far from the mud-brick house, the barren plateau and the Lion Temple, sending her soaring through a kaleidoscope of shooting stars. When, finally, she came back down, Kua'tzal was gazing down at her, looking bemused – and not a little pleased with himself. She smiled and caressed his cheek with her fingertips. Muu-Nan may no longer be part of her life, but she wasn't alone. She had Kua'tzal: her husband, her lover, and father of her child. What would unfold in the future was still untold. Whatever it was, they would meet it together.

GEMMA, 3

Chapter 34

I shivered, the hairs on the back of my neck prickling. Someone was walking over my grave. It certainly wasn't from cold. It was an unusually hot April lunchtime with not one cloud to be seen in a sky the colour of speedwell. Even in a vest top and cotton skirt I was sweltering. The shiver came again, raising goose-bumps on the bare flesh of my arms. This time, though, there was something else – the sensation that eyes were boring into my back. Someone was watching me. Studying me? I whirled around, my gaze flashing left to right and back again, searching the crowds.

In the busy, tourist-packed Bath street, I had no chance of finding him… Or her. People of more than a dozen nationalities bustled and chattered and snapped souvenir photos, and after I was nearly knocked off my feet for the third time by this unyielding human tide I gave up. I was looking for a needle in a colourful, endlessly moving, multi-cultural haystack.

Lost in my thoughts, not really paying attention to where I was going – my mental autopilot moved my feet in the right direction and stopped me crashing into any lamp-posts – I made my way to the café where I was meeting Cathy for lunch.

'What's wrong?' Cathy, I would remind you, is extremely psychic. I'd never been able to hide anything from her and she had immediately sensed I had something on my mind.

'I think I'm being watched. Or followed. Or something.' At least, I had thought so. Now, sitting at our table on the sun-drenched pavement in the shade of a huge parasol, doubts were creeping in. 'Of course, I could have imagined it.'

Her eyes narrowed, studying me. 'No, I don't think so,' she pronounced after a lengthy pause. 'You did pick up on something. Genuinely. Trust what you felt. Is it still there?'

I closed my eyes and concentrated. 'No. There's nothing.'

The pressure, like thumbs pressing hard into the flesh between my shoulder blades, had gone. My shoulders dropped, my jaw unclenched, and I relaxed back in my chair. I was becoming paranoid.

'It was probably just a fan of my books who recognised me and was wondering whether to speak to me,' my voice of reason argued, 'then they lost me in the crowd.'

'Don't kid yourself,' retorted the other voice – the one that kept me on alert. 'Remember Callum? Remember how you and Joe were almost killed by that goon in the Range Rover only a couple of weeks later? That wasn't paranoia. That was serious Danger with a capital 'D'.'

'Gemma?'

'Sorry. My mind was taking me places I didn't want to go.' I held her gaze. 'I'm scared, Cathy. I'd managed to shut it all away and pretend it didn't happen. Most of the time, anyway. But just now… That feeling. It brought it all back, too vividly for comfort.'

'It's hardly surprising.' She took hold of my hand and squeezed it gently. 'Why don't you talk to the Skulls and ask them to protect you? Surely they can do that?'

I laughed, rather drily. 'You'd think so, wouldn't you, seeing as how they are supposed to be these mystical power-houses. Given the fate of too many of their Guardians though, I'm not sure I can rely on it.'

'There are those, close, who will help. Those who have sworn to protect the Skulls and their Guardians as they prepare to return to the world. With their lives if necessary.' Cathy had that distant expression that came over her whenever she was tuned in to her guides.

'Who?'

She shook herself, refocussing on the café and the sunshine. 'I don't know.' She closed her eyes, turning her awareness inwards once more. 'You need to be careful though. Not take any silly risks. Those who are here to help you are gifted. Skilled. Courageous. They will do everything in their power to protect you. But they are not invincible. They are men and women. Human. Mortal. Just like you and I. Oooh, that looks delicious.' The waitress had placed a plate of spiced, seared duck breast, salad and buttered new potatoes in front of her, breaking her concentration. She shook herself and changed the subject. 'Now, tell me what you've been up to these last few months, Gemma. We haven't seen each other for ages.'

A tantalising aroma of grilled seabass and samphire was pulling my attention to my own plate and I was more than happy to shift the conversation back to a less stressful topic, chattering on, catching up as we ate. By the time our plates were cleared, our desserts demolished and our coffees drunk, I'd let go of my earlier fears.

Which lasted until I met up with Joe that evening…

*   *   *   *   *

'I'm not sure whether I should tell you this or not.' Joe was sprawled on the sofa, doodling in the margins of a magazine.

'Tell me what? What's up, Joe?'

'Nothing specific, not really.' He hesitated. 'It's just that for the last week or so, I've had the uncomfortable feeling that I'm being followed. I can't prove it. I've not *seen* anyone. But the creepy sensation won't go away. Maybe it's simply my imagination racing into overdrive after all that's gone on. Though if so, why now, after so many months?' He looked across at me. 'Forget it, Gemma. It's probably nothing. I don't want to give you the jitters. It's just that… Well, I thought it best to let you know. Better safe than sorry.'

'I'm glad you did because I had that same feeling today on my way to meet Cathy. She went into her weirdness for a bit and apparently we have people around us – though God only knows who they are – who are watching out for the Skulls and their new Guardians.'

'I hope she's right.' He held up his hand, forestalling my objections. 'I have no doubt about her abilities Gemma, not after she nailed finding Callum. That's not what I meant. But I don't think we should put all our trust in this group of, what was it she called them? Protectors? You said she talked about the Skulls and their Guardians? Well, you aren't a Guardian, and neither am I. We can't guarantee we're on their radar.'

'What do we do?'

'We stay alert, trust no-one other than Cathy and Duncan, and lie low. We don't do anything to draw attention to ourselves. And hope it's enough to make them – whoever they are – believe we don't have anything they want.'

'Which we don't.' I dropped down next to him on the sofa.

'Except for knowing where Gal-Athiel is hidden. And the gold key in your safety deposit box.

I groaned. 'How did I forget? When is it going to end, Joe?' His arm went around my shoulders and he hugged me, unable to answer. There was no answer to give.

Chapter 35

Someone was in my room. I didn't move a muscle as I peered through my lashes trying to pierce the gloom. The blurred outline of a dark, bulky shadow was moving towards the bed and, for a split second, polished metal glinted in the moonlight that filtered through a crack in the curtains.

'JOE!' I screamed, throwing myself sideways away from the intruder in a frantic bid to escape the knife he held. 'JOE! Help!'

I was going to die!

It felt like a lifetime but it could only have been a second or two before the bedroom door burst open and a second shadow flew into the room and crashed into the first. They landed heavily in a jumble of arms and legs and bodies and a loud grunt of pain across the bed where I floundered half in and half out of the covers.

For a few long seconds, no-one moved. I couldn't; the weight of two large bodies on my legs and hips had me pinned, helpless. A disgusting warm wetness was seeping through my pyjama bottoms onto my skin.

'Joe?' I breathed anxiously. The weight on top of me eased a little.

'Gemma? Are you alright?' he wheezed. He flicked the light switch and the bedroom flooded with welcome bright light. 'I must have knocked him cold.'

'You're hurt.' I gasped, horrified. Joe's t-shirt was crimson, sticking to his body.

'No, I'm OK. Knocked the wind out of me, that's all.' He shuddered at the sticky blood growing cold against his flesh. 'It's not mine.'

Simultaneously we stared at the well-built, black clad figure lying motionless across my bed, his head and most of his face hidden by a black balaclava. He was dead, there was no doubt about it. A knife – the knife that had been meant for me – stuck out grotesquely from his neck. He must have fallen on his own weapon when Joe hurtled into him. Joe had been lucky; if it had come to a real fight, he wouldn't have stood a chance.

'Get him off me.' It came out as a panicky wail. Bile burned my throat. I felt sick. 'Get me out of here.'

How could this be happening? It was the stuff of spy novels, not real life. But happening it was, the body and the blood soaking my bed proof that I was in deeper than I knew how to handle. A killer had broken into my house, my bedroom, with one aim – to end my life!

Grimacing with revulsion, Joe seized the dead man's muscular shoulders and hauled him onto his back. I scrambled out from under the duvet, nauseated by the clammy touch of my pyjama bottoms sticking to my thighs.

'You go first,' he said quietly.

Doing my best not to look down at my blood covered legs, I raced for the bathroom. I couldn't get out of those pyjamas quickly enough. I stripped them off, shoved them into a refuse bag and stepped into the shower, turning the flow to maximum. Long after all trace of blood had washed away, I stood there letting the hot, steaming water pour over me. Until I remembered Joe and his gore-soaked t-shirt. I wrapped myself in the towel and opened the door.

Joe handed me a pile of clean clothes as he passed me on his way into the bathroom. 'I grabbed some things for you. I didn't think you'd want to go back into your room just yet.'

Still in severe shock, I could only nod my thanks, thanks that there could never be enough words to express. Not for the first time, I wondered what I'd done to deserve his friendship and support.

Thirty minutes and a large slug of whisky later we were sitting at the kitchen table, each of us nursing a large mug of strong tea. It wasn't helping; neither of us was yet able to speak.

* * * * *

The wall clock said 3.15am. We'd been sitting there in silence for an hour, unwilling to emerge from the numbness that had seized us and somehow made what had just happened seem less real and more like a bad dream. It couldn't last. We had to wake up and face reality sometime.

'What do we do?' Joe muttered eventually. He was white as a sheet, the mug he still held rattling on the table. Trying to come to terms with the fact that, however inadvertently, he had been instrumental in a man's death only an hour or so before.

Chamberlain's face flashed into my mind. 'We could call the police,' I ventured. 'Or rather, we could call D.I. Chamberlain.' Where had that idea come from?

'What? I grant you he acted a bit strange when he interviewed us but that doesn't mean anything. How do we know we can trust him? We can't trust anyone, remember?'

'There is a dead man sprawled on my bed with a knife in his neck, Joe. What do you suggest we do? Wrap him in a tarpaulin and bury him in the woods?' We were both a bundle of nerves, terrified out of our wits, and as a result, overwrought and short-tempered.

'Oh, I don't know.' Joe dropped his head into his hands. 'All I know is that because of me that man is dead and I'm the one who'll have to answer to it.' My heart went out to him.

'You saved my life, Joe,' I said softly. 'You didn't intend to kill him. It was an accident and it was self-defence. There's no doubt he was going to kill me and most likely you as well. I mean, look at him. No-one will believe he was here to ask me to sign a book.'

'Doesn't alter the fact that I'm responsible for his death.'

'It wasn't your fault, Joe.' I got up, walked around the table, and wrapped my arms around his chest. 'But it happened, and we can't just sit here and do nothing. Look, I don't know where the idea came from, but it does feel the right thing to do. No, I don't know if we can trust Chamberlain. Honestly though, what other choices do we have? I'm not inclined to call the local police. Cathy? No way. I'm not getting her involved in this. Or Duncan either. He's put himself out there for us too much already.'

'Chamberlain it is, then,' Joe agreed reluctantly. 'Let's hope he's on our side.'

It was still only half past three in the morning; nevertheless, I pulled out the inspector's card and punched his number into my phone.

Chapter 36

He came alone. That should have given us a clue, but we were still too traumatised, too scared, and too bloody well emotionally mangled for the implications to register. He walked, grim-faced, into the kitchen and sat down uninvited on the nearest chair. Joe and I hovered by the worktop. Now that the first shock was easing, we were restless and unable to settle.

'Tell me,' he demanded, so I did. It didn't take long; the nightmare had been over so quickly. When I finished, his expression was darker than ever.

'Stay here,' he ordered as he left the room and headed upstairs to my bedroom where the still-warm corpse lay spread-eagled on my bed. Neither Joe nor I needed to be told twice. Nothing would have got us back in that room until the body had been taken away.

A couple of minutes later he was back. 'Clear case of self-defence,' he stated. 'I've got people coming to remove the body. Should only be half an hour or so.' Joe and I looked at each other in bewilderment. Where were the questions? The forensic team? The swarm of police officers that usually took over a crime scene.

'Not necessary in this case.' He had answered our unspoken questions.

My mind was a fog of incomprehension, misgivings and what? Suspicion? Had I made a mistake in insisting we call him? Something was definitely not right here. We'd braced ourselves for – oh, I don't know – more people? More activity? More investigation certainly.

Statements taken. Evidence logged. And photographs. Lots of photographs. Not just one man.

I jumped, startled by a loud knock at the door. It's safe to say my nerves were shot to pieces.

Detective Inspector Chamberlain, on the other hand, had evidently been expecting it and went to open the front door. 'Good, you're here. Upstairs.'

I still expected to see a swarm of uniformed officers walking into my house. I was wrong. Through the open kitchen door, we saw two tall, burly men in overalls enter and head straight upstairs without giving us a glance, the first carrying what appeared to be a large rectangle of folded thick polythene. Chamberlain followed on their heels, the murmur of their conversation too low for either of us to make out. A few minutes later footsteps descended the stairs while a series of bumps and thumps echoed through the ceiling. Chamberlain came back into the kitchen, closing the door behind him.

'They're taking away the body now. They'll take the mattress and bedclothes as well.' He saw our frowns. 'For forensic purposes.'

I didn't believe him. Glancing across at Joe, it was clear that he didn't either. What was going on? We'd both suspected there was more to D.I. Chamberlain than he'd let on after he had interviewed us following Callum's murder. That suspicion now settled into certainty. The doubts I'd pushed aside returned with all the force of a hurricane. Who was he? What was he up to? What did he want from us? And crucially for us, whose side was he on and could we trust him?

'Just a minute, Detective Inspector.' Joe wanted answers. 'This isn't how the police work. What the fuck is going on?'

More bumps and thuds outside the closed kitchen door. Judging by the sounds and the accompanied grunts and stifled curses, the two men were attempting to manoeuvre a large object down the cottage's narrow dog-leg staircase. I flicked a glance towards the closed door.

'No, Mr Cunningham, it isn't. It is, however, how we work.' He held up his hand, stopping any further questions. 'Ask no more. Know though that there are those who wish you to succeed. Listen to the words the Skulls have spoken and trust them, even if you do not trust me. At the right time, you will have the answers you are looking for.' There was a low tap on the door. 'Ah, good. We're done here.' He reached for the door handle, then turned back. 'Tonight never happened. There will be no police investigation, no questions, no inquest. It has been a frightening experience. Do whatever you have to do to recover from it but do not speak of it. It didn't happen.' he repeated.

'Why should we trust you?'

'Ask the Skulls.' His hand rested briefly on the worktop then he was gone, leaving Joe and I staring after him, speechless.

'What the… Did that really just happen?' Incredulity dripped from Joe's lips.

I shut my eyes and leaned back against the worktop, trying to make some sense of the whole episode, and failing spectacularly. Outside an engine roared, then another. Wheels crunched on the gravel on the driveway, the engines faded into the distance, and were gone. At the edge of my mind, an elusive thought prodded at me, trying to get my attention. I turned to look at it and suddenly I knew what it was.

'How does he know about them?'

'Know about what?'

'The Skulls. It's just clicked. Twice in two minutes he mentioned the Skulls. How did he know about them and that they communicate with me?'

'Uh… I think our friendly detective knows one hell of a lot more than he's letting on.' Joe held out his hand. In his fingers was a gold ring, narrow-banded, the face inset with a flat, deep black stone. Onyx maybe, or tourmaline? 'It was on the worktop where he put his hand. Look at it, Gemma. Look at the stone.'

He dropped it into my open palm where it lay, heavy and gleaming. It was a type of signet ring, just like so many others. Except… My eyes widened. It couldn't be. Yet there it was. Unmistakeable. Etched into the black stone was a symbol I knew only too well. It resembled an 'f' and a 'j', joined at one hundred and eighty degrees to each other by a small circle…

* * * * *

We were crashed out in the living room, too wound up to even try and sleep. Moreover, I didn't have a bed to go back to.

'I'll take the couch until you get a new mattress,' Joe stated, 'and we need to increase the security on the house. Do everything we can to protect ourselves from another unexpected visit like *that*.' He pointed to the ceiling, above which was my bedroom.'

'Like what?'

He leaned forward. 'Your burglar alarm is live now, yes?' I nodded. 'Right, we can tick that one off. From now on we set it when we go to bed, not just when we go out. We double check all outside doors and windows are locked at night and we keep them locked at all times. And we sleep with the windows closed. Tomorrow, I'll head into town and buy a couple of hefty bolts each for the front and back doors.'

Normally, I'd have teased Joe mercilessly for his worrying. After tonight's events, however, I wasn't going to argue. While we might cook in the summer heat, it was better that than ending up face down in a canal like Callum.

'Joe, who do you think Chamberlain really is?' I asked as I snuggled down next to him on the sofa.

'I have no idea,' he muttered, pulling the blanket up over the both of us. 'But I'm pretty sure it won't be too long before we find out.'

Chapter 37

Oh, this was ridiculous. I couldn't stand it any longer. The temperature outside was in the mid-twenties Celsius and here I was shut away indoors with all the doors and windows locked and bolted. I felt trapped and suffocated. I was going stir-crazy! I'd made myself a prisoner in my own home, victim to my fears. Yes, that brute had broken in intending to kill me, I couldn't deny that. Nor that it had been beyond terrifying. The question I now had to face was: was I going to live the rest of my life – no, *exist* the rest of my life, because I certainly wasn't living it now – hiding away, too frightened to set foot outside the door in case they (whoever the unidentified 'they' were) were waiting for me?

Or was I going to grab my courage in both hands, stick two fingers up to all of it and do what I had to do? Of course the danger was real. Callum's murder and the two (to date) attempts on my and Joe's lives had made that horribly obvious; and yes, I was bloody well scared. But we had survived both attacks. Maybe it was time to trust in the Skulls, to trust that they would protect me. They had asked me to do this, so surely they would ensure I stayed alive to fulfil the task? Then there was the message that had come through Cathy, telling me that there were those close who would be watching out for me. OK, yes, Joe was right when he'd said we weren't Guardians but wasn't my – our – role just as crucial?

It had been three weeks since that night. Three weeks during which we'd put ourselves under virtual house-arrest, shut away from the outside world and only venturing out when absolutely necessary. Three weeks of glorious weather that I'd experienced through the glass windowpanes. Enough! That time was over. We could no longer be ruled by our fears. There was a certainty within me that the challenges had really only just begun and that more, so many more, frightening, challenging, impossible, perilous situations still lay ahead of us. If I – we – gave into our fears now, we might as well give up. With that mindset, there would be no way we could overcome those situations, and overcome them we had to. We had agreed to take this path and we had to travel it to the end, wherever that may be.

It was time we took the decision once and for all that we wouldn't let 'them' stop us and that we stepped up to continue with the mission we'd been given. I say 'we' because I no longer questioned that Joe and I were in this together and that we had been since the beginning.

Certainty wrapped itself around me in a soft blanket. Yes, it was time to trust. I went to the windows, unlocked them, and flung them wide open. A shiver of fear caught me unawares and I almost slammed them shut again, stopped only by the fresh air, warm and laden with the scent of honeysuckle and Virginia stocks, that flooded into the room. I breathed it in with slow, deep breaths, filling my lungs. Letting it soak, soothing and reviving, through my body lifting my spirits and my resolve.

Next were the French doors. For those few moments, the Skulls were with me, reminding me of the truth of me. For those few moments, I believed totally that nothing and no-one could harm me or push me off course. I walked through them like a goddess, feeling powerful and untouchable, delighting in the heat of the sun on my skin and the soft tickle of grass beneath my bare feet.

I picked up my notepad, pens and a blanket and sat down in the shade of the ancient, gnarled apple tree, intending a couple of hours productive writing in the peace of the garden. It didn't happen. The sun was too deliciously warm, the air too fragrantly scented, the hum of the bees too hypnotic. I couldn't resist. Setting down my pen and paper, I lay back on the blanket and marvelled at the filigree of twisted, lichen-covered branches etched against the cloudless, periwinkle blue sky. My breathing slowed, my eyelids grew heavy, and I drifted.

* * * * *

'There is more to this than you yet see.' Rich, mellow tones broke into my sleepy mind. Who was this? These were not the familiar gentle, melodic tones of Gal-Athiel.

'No, I am not Gal-Athiel.' A black skull, shining like glass, hovered in front of me. Real, if not quite solid. I knew this skull; this was Gileada. I sensed his acknowledgement.

'I come to you today to reassure you so that you do not falter. Earth cannot afford for you to doubt in these times when the threat to humankind rises up in starkly illuminated detail. Your world is descending once more into division and hatred, a situation that it has experienced to its cost many times before. It is a descent driven by leaders who act from fear. Sometimes this fear is for the welfare of the people they govern, driven by concern. Although their intentions are worthy, their reactions are misguided. More often, more insidiously, however, it is fear for the weakness of their position that drives them to entrench their power. They seek to strengthen their control by standing race against race, skin colour against skin colour, religion against religion, for divided societies always look to leaders they believe to be strong even though that illusion of strength is itself born of fear.

'It is too easy to throw up your hands, to say 'I cannot do this.', 'I am not strong enough.', 'I am too scared.' It is too easy to back away and hide, believing you are not enough, believing that your contribution is not needed. We say to you that you can do this, that you are strong enough and that your contribution is of the greatest importance in creating the change your world hungers for. We will help you.

'Many hear our call. Too many ignore it, keeping silent even as they watch in despair, afraid to speak up And yet it takes only one to stand up, one alone in a crowd, for the man or woman next to that one to find the courage to do the same. And so it ripples out, one and one, and one, and one. Until, instead of one standing alone, a thousand, a hundred thousand, a million human voices rise up together. And because one had the strength to stand up and take action, despite believing in the hopelessness of that action, now a million and more stand up alongside her. A million and more join their voices with his. And your world is changed. Division melts into unity, competition into co-operation, hatred into love, and conflict into peace. And all because one man or woman dared to stand up and speak their truth.'

'This is what we ask of you, dearest Child. That you continue to stand up and speak through your writing. To share the knowledge of us and our desire to return amongst the people of Earth once more. To guide the new

Guardians to Us. To do what you must do, no matter where it leads you, breaking through the fears that would hold you back. To accept this with all the difficulties and dangers that are to come. For if not you, then who?

'You will meet others chosen to guide this revolution, and do not doubt that it is a revolution; a revolution in consciousness, a revolution in humankind's understanding of itself, of its origins and of its place in the Universe. If you are to survive the ills you inflict on this planet and on one another, if your world is to recover so that She may sustain your ongoing existence, it must be so.

'That is why we are preparing to return sooner than we would have wished. We see clearly that there is much to be hopeful about, much to cherish, and we return to show you this and to open your eyes to another way. A way based on love instead of fear and hatred. A way based on one-ness instead of separation. A way based on creation instead of destruction.'

'Gemma?' The spell was broken. The black skull had vanished. I opened in my eyes, blinking in the sunlight to see Joe peering down at me. 'Is everything OK?'

I shook away the lingering remnants of another world. 'I think so, yes.'

'What are you doing out here? You should be in the house.'

I stood up, linked my arm in his and led him towards the house. 'Do you want a cold cider, Joe? We need to talk.'

MUU-NAN

PART 4

THE FIVE RUNAWAYS

Chapter 38

It had been a good day, Dar-Ra mused, leaning back contentedly against the smooth boulder, still warm from the torrid heat of the afternoon. They had swum in the cool waters of the river and dozed through the hottest hours under the shade of a palm grove. Later, they had caught fish and cooked them over a fire on the riverbank.

In two days, the sacred Star would be directly overhead and the entrance to the Lion Temple would open, as it did every year at this time, the day signalled by the position of that star. No-one who had not seen sixteen full sun-cycles was permitted to enter the Lion's belly; this year, he and his friends had reached the age and would enter the sanctuary of the temple for the first time. All except Amisi, the youngest of the group. She would have to wait another two cycles. To enter the belly of the Great Stone Lion and hear the priests speak directly with the gods was something Dar-Ra had dreamed of since he was a small boy and now it was here. He was so excited he believed he might burst.

Life was good. Pharaoh was a compassionate ruler, driven by a powerful desire to see his people thrive, and through the Holders of the Lion Wisdom he was guided in this by the sacred and never seen Heart of Regulus, a priceless treasure hidden away within the fabric of the Great Stone Lion. So it had been for generations, and so it would be for generations to come.

The fire flared. Showers of golden orange sparks burst up into the indigo evening.

'That's the last of the firewood.' Kulak settled himself back down onto the soft, warm earth.

'I have to go anyway.' Kyky scrambled to her feet. 'It's late. Mother and father will be looking for me. Amisi, are you coming? Amisi?'

In reply, the young girl raised her hand and pointed. 'Look,' she breathed. They followed her gaze to where the fire crackled and sparked.

'What in the name of all that's sacred…?' Kulak sputtered. Though not yet a grown man, he was already a giant. 'Tell me you can see it too. That I'm not the only one going mad.'

Above the dancing flames spiralled a sphere of white light, a little larger than a human head.

'I… I see it,' Dar-Ra stuttered.

'I wish I didn't, but I do.' This was Djal, the fifth member of the group. 'Look, there's something in it… A face.'

Sure enough, within the sphere an image was taking shape; at first indistinct and dim, it quickly settled into that of a skull of a clear, pale lavender crystal. What sorcery was this?

'I'm scared.' Tears trickled down Amisi's face.

'Do not be afraid.' Words, deep and melodic, resonated through the still dark air. 'I will not harm you.'

'Wh-who are you?' Dar-Ra found his voice at last.

'I am Muu-Nan, Skull of Arcturus, Heart of Regulus. I rest within the Great Stone Lion. I come to you tonight to ask for your help.'

'Our help?' Kulak snorted, despite his fear. 'How? We're children. What can we do?'

'You are far more than just children. Within each of you beats the heart of a warrior. I would not have come to you if you could not do what I ask.'

'What is that?' Dar-Ra took a step towards the fire, speaking far more boldly than he felt. 'Exactly what is it that you want from us?'

'Although you do not yet see it, the winds of change blow across this land. They are coming quickly, and they cannot be stopped. Within a very short time, nothing will be as it has been. On that day, I must not be here. Those who come on those winds seek me out. Should they find me, they will use my power in ways that will destroy this land, far beyond the borders of this kingdom. That must not happen. I come to you tonight to ask that you take me from the Great Lion and carry me far from here.'

'We can't do that,' Djal burst out. 'We're *children*. None of us has ever even been out of sight of the City. How do you expect us to do as you ask?'

'Because you can. Because you are courageous, intelligent and resourceful.' The skull began to spin slowly. 'I ask this not for me, for I will not suffer in this. I ask it for your people, for your friends and for your families. Their lives are about to change greatly, to become much harder. If those who come gain possession of me, that hardship will be multiplied many times over.

'I ask much of you, this I understand, but you will not be alone. I will be with you. I will help and guide you and give you the strength you need.'

'If you are as all-powerful as the Holders say, can you not act to prevent this?'

'I am powerful, yes, more powerful that you could imagine, yet there are some things I cannot do. My power cannot change human hearts and minds. You have free will. You make your own choices from that free will, for good or for evil, and you live with the consequences of those choices.

'If you ask for my help, I can help you. If you do not, I cannot. If you choose to help me, I can help you. If you choose otherwise, I cannot.'

'You ask much of us, blessed Heart of Regulus.' Kyky stared into the flames, her mind in turmoil. Her heart cried out for her to say yes, her head was filled with all the reasons to say no. 'How do we decide what to do?'

'Go home. Sleep. When daylight comes, with it will come the answers. You will know what to do. When you have made your decision, I will know.

'The love and blessings of the Skulls of Light surround you all.'

Chapter 39

The massive figure of a he-lion in all his power stood guard in front of the pyramid complex on the plateau, watching over the thoroughfare that led to it. The monolith measured over ninety paces from the toes of its strangely elongated front paws to its tail and had been carved directly from the bedrock from which it rose. Sheathed in the finest layer of snow-white marble it dazzled the eyes in the intense rays of the early afternoon sun. The moat that surrounded it, excavated from the bedrock and lined with polished black basalt, was filled with water that captured the celestial bodies of the night sky and transported them down onto the Earth.

Surrounded by the crowd that stood waiting silently, their expectation tangible, the five young friends stood on the lip of this moat, every one of them fixed on Zek-Har, most sacred Holder of the Lion knowledge, who stood at its far end. His tall, golden-robed figure shone like fire in the fierce sunlight. In his upraised hand, held high above his head, gleamed the heavy lion-headed staff, forged from the purest gold. His arm dropped, the signal for the ceremony to begin, and the crowd strained to get the best view. Imperceptibly at first, becoming more noticeable with every heartbeat that passed, the level of the water in the moat fell. It would soon be time.

If the rest of those present were taut with eager expectation, it was nothing compared to the tension and apprehension building in the five friends. Very soon, the basin would be empty and Zek-Har would step forward to begin the ritual that would open the entrance. None of the five spoke; they were all too pre-occupied with thoughts of what lay ahead and what they were about to do, an action that would change their lives forever.

This was the much anticipated once a year opportunity for the people of the kingdom to hear for themselves the words of the Lion gods who had inspired this monument. During its construction, the sacred skull Muu-Nan – known to all as the Heart of Regulus – had been placed in its head at the location of the pineal gland, the point where Heaven meets Earth and Spirit meets Matter, from where he had watched over, protected and guided the people of this land. Every year, when the star Regulus positioned itself directly overhead and its light pierced the tiny channel at the crown of the stone lion's head, the Lion gods themselves spoke directly with the people. It was a time of celebration and thanksgiving, for Muu-Nan had indeed blessed them with his presence.

For the five young people waiting nervously in the midst, this was much, much more. They had been asked – summoned would perhaps be a better choice of word, Dar-Ra mused – to undertake a task that was the worst of heresies and would lead to certain death if they failed.

Dar-Ra was the unspoken leader of the group, the eldest by barely two moon cycles and, the others agreed, by far the smartest and quickest thinking. Somehow, he always managed to find a way to get himself and his friends out of the scrapes he led them into. Excitement bubbled within him, overpowering his fears, at least for now. Whatever else it turned out to be, this would without question be the adventure of a lifetime.

He took a deep breath. If they couldn't carry out their plan today, it would be a full sun cycle before the opportunity came again. Once the moat was reflooded, it would not be emptied again until Regulus was once more overhead. Even if it was, the boy reflected, there was no way to access the Hall of Mirrors, the inner sanctum of the monument, which was only accessible on this one day of every cycle.

Only the Holders knew the secret of opening the stones. From the little he had learned when listening to those who had experienced the ritual before, the Holders opened the portal with a special series of sound frequencies which agitated the molecules of the stone. Solid rock turned to thick mist, like that which sometimes rose from the Great River in the early morning. The sensation was like moving through water, they had told him, preparing him for his first visit. It required some effort to push through the mist, but not enough to prevent them entering. When they left, another series of notes reversed the spell, returning the mist to solid stone once more. Except that – Dar-Ra's stomach lurched – he wouldn't be leaving.

A stirring whispered through the crowd, alerting him. The moat was empty and a procession of twelve Holders, each wearing the same golden cloaks as Zek-Har and headdresses that resembled a luxuriant lion's mane, was making its way across the base to halt between the great stone paws.

'Only two of the most senior Holders know the sound sequence,' Kyky whispered in his ear. He glanced at his friend and she nodded. 'Mother told me.'

Sure enough, two Holders now stepped forward, each holding a flute-type instrument to their lips. Moments later, the air filled with an unexpectedly inharmonious symphony of jarring notes – random, and yet not random

– that rose and fell with a stridency that was painful to hear and which increased steadily in volume so that everyone on the waiting crowd clapped their hands over their ears to ease their discomfort. Abruptly the noise stopped, the notes falling away in the still air. A low murmur rippled through the gathering. In the stonework at the front edge of the massive left-hand paw, a dark rectangle had appeared. Shimmering silver drifted across night black. The portal was open.

Immediately, the crowd gathered on the rim scrambled down into the moat and made its way across its still damp base, following the gold-clad Holders through the newly opened doorway without hesitation. With a 'Let's do this before we come to our senses' glance at his companions, Dar-Ra joined them. Would anyone notice their fear and question it? No. Several of those around them looked as nervous and uncertain as Dar-Ra and his friends did; those who, like them, were just on the boundary of adulthood and had never experienced the ceremony before.

He looked across at Amisi. She still had two sun cycles until she reached the permitted age. Fortunately, she was tall and her height helped to disguise her lack of years. She walked with her head down, her eyes lowered to the floor and she had pulled her shawl forward over her forehead to hide her features, for many of those here knew her. She would have to keep her distance as far as possible and pray she remained unnoticed. In her favour – no-one would expect to see her here.

Entering the black passageway, pushing blindly through the thick silvery air, was unpleasantly disorientating. The floor sloped down steeply before rising again and it was with a deep sense of relief that he emerged at last into the vast, dimly lit chamber in the lion's belly, only to be assailed once more by the discordant notes of the flutes echoing around him, amplified by the curve of the ceiling. The noise was reaching an unbearable level when again, suddenly, it stopped. A narrow shaft of brilliant violet-white light the diameter of a man's thumb had pierced the gloom, casting directly down from the lion's head to hit the floor of the chamber below. This was the light of Regulus. It had penetrated the tiny shaft at the crown of the mighty stone head and travelled down through the skull, which had amplified it ten thousand-fold and more on its path into the chamber below.

A hundred tripods, each taller than a man, lined the perimeter of the space, and each tripod held three polished silver discs that reflected the light of the myriad of lamps that had been set around the floor and were now being lit. Soon the room appeared filled with fireflies flickering in the blackness of this place where daylight never reached. At a sign from Zek-Har, a thickset Holder stepped forward pushing another tripod, this one bearing a single disc the diameter of a man's arm-span, and carefully positioned it under the narrow beam of light. The ray flashed from the perfectly angled disc to the next, reflecting onto the next, and the next, until the entire perimeter was cross-crossed with a dazzling web that transformed twilight into midday and held within its boundary all who were gathered there.

A hazy curtain of shimmering gold danced on the front wall at the exact point where the great stone beast's heart would be. They watched, silently, filled with anticipation; anticipation that turned rapidly to astonishment, for within the gleaming mist, the head of an immense he-lion was now visible. Gasps, quickly stifled, broke from the watching men and women. Even the Holders appeared startled. This was not the way it usually went.

'What's going on?' Kyky breathed. 'This isn't what usually happens, is it?'

'I think we're about to find out,' Kulak murmured in her ear.

'Greetings, Earth brothers and sisters.' They stared, startled, at the lion's image. Although only a low, deep-throated rumble had come from his throat, they had understood perfectly.

'Greeting, Star Brother.' Zek-Har had quickly regained his composure and stepped forward to address the image, bowing low. 'You grace us with your presence. May I ask to what we owe this honour?'

'I have come with a warning. There are those who have learned of the treasure you hold, of the sacred skull Muu-Nan, he who you have sworn to protect. They have determined to possess him, no matter what the cost. You must take action, for they will come, very soon, and they will not allow anyone or anything to stand in their way.'

'Muu-Nan is inaccessible, Star Brother. You know this as well as I. Once the chamber is sealed, no-one can reach him.'

'They know of the Heart of Regulus and where he lies, and they will destroy everything that stands in their way in order to possess him. Do not make the error of believing him unassailable, my Friend. There are some in your midst who have betrayed your trust, who have aided and advised those who move against you.' He paused, amber-gold eyes flashing fire. 'You doubt my words, Brother.'

'Great Lion of Regulus, I would not disrespect you in such a way. However, it is difficult to accept. Our order is handpicked from the most honourable men and women. Our people cherish the skull as they do their own children. I do not – I cannot – believe that anyone here would endanger him.'

'Nevertheless, it is so. This is our warning to you, Zek-Har. Hear me and act now, even though I weep for you as I speak these words, my Earth Brother. Seek out those traitors and put an end to their treachery. Prepare for war. Prepare for death. Much death. We cannot stop it. By the laws of the Galactic Alliance we are forbidden to intervene. I can, however, send you this warning so that you may prepare. Prepare well, Zek-Har. This day *will* come and sooner than you wish.'

The image rippled and dissolved. The web of light criss-crossing the Hall of Mirrors dimmed and vanished as Regulus moved on its journey through the heavens taking its light with it. All that remained was the pale firefly glimmer of the lamps and the anxious mutterings of two hundred deeply disturbed citizens.

'So that's why we're taking the Heart of Regulus today,' Kyky breathed. 'The gods had better be with us.'

'Muu-Nan is.' Amisi squeezed her friend's hand. 'He won't leave us on our own.'

'What does he mean, Zek-Har?' The voice came from the centre of the crowd. 'Who are these traitors he speaks of? Who is coming for our beloved Muu-Nan?'

The elder faced the crowd, his expression for once lacking its habitual serenity.

'I do not know,' he admitted. 'Our brother's warning was as unexpected to me as it was to you. However, we have now been forewarned and it is my promise to you that we will find out who acts against us and that we will do what we must to prevent this.' He spoke with all the authority of his position, his voice strong and his words reassuring. 'We will succeed. We will ensure that the events spoken of do not come to pass. We give thanks to the Star god for his warning; however, Muu-Nan is safe, of that I am certain. For the rest, we will prepare. We have time. Leave now, my friends. The Holders of the Lion Knowledge must meet with our gracious Pharaoh. We have much to discuss and plan.'

Rather than the uplifted mood which usually prevailed on this occasion, the atmosphere among the crowd was subdued and troubled as they drifted towards the passageway and out through the doorway to the sunlit outer world. All but the five young friends who crouched in the shadows behind the furthermost tripods until the last of them, the Holders, had disappeared from view.

Not one looked back. Why would they? Very soon the chamber would be resealed and would stay that way until Regulus once more shone overhead, a full sun cycle away. No-one would choose to stay behind to be entombed alive, facing a certain and monstrous death from starvation or asphyxiation, whichever came first. There was no way to escape once the stone re-solidified.

Chapter 40

'Quickly, Kyky. Go. You haven't much time. As soon as they're all outside, they'll close it up.'

The girl nodded, nervously. This was it. She was the only one who could do this and do it, she would. They'd made their choice and would now live – or die – by it. Nonetheless, her legs were wobbly, and her heart raced.

With an urgency born of fear, Dar-Ra pushed her towards the small, dark opening of the shaft that led to the lion's head, and Muu-Nan. 'You have to be down out of there before that happens.'

Kyky didn't need telling twice. A fraction too slow and she would be trapped in the stone as it set around her. She shook off the thought. Worrying about it would only serve to slow her down. Agile as the creature she was named after, she sprang up onto the shoulders of the human mountain that was Kulak and a moment later all they saw were her disappearing feet.

'Hurry,' Kulak called anxiously, echoing the unspoken tension that had the whole group in its clutches. Kyky had only a scant few minutes before the shaft turned back to solid stone. Dar-Ra glanced at his friend. As well as he thought he hid it, Kulak's feelings for her were written all over his face.

Every second felt like an hour to the four who waited below, all of whom were aware that the Holders would even now be working the ritual to reseal the rock. The lamps set around the floor were dimming, almost at their end. Amisi fumbled in her tunic and drew out her own small lamp which she lit with a flint. Although the weak flame gave only an unsteady light, it was a reassuring beacon in the deepening gloom.

'Kyky!' They called more urgently now. A series of notes, faint but unmistakeable – the harsh tones of the flutes – was filtering through into the chamber. In the entrance way, the silver mist was thickening. The stone was solidifying. 'KYKY!'

'Here. Catch.' Kyky's face peered out of the shaft. 'It's getting a bit thick up here.' She dropped the skull into Kulak's huge hands and twisted to bring her feet under her body.

'Oh no. The gods save me!' she gasped and dropped with a stomach-churning scream to the floor, crumpling as she landed to lie groaning and rocking, clutching at her left hand.

'Kyky? KYKY? What happened. Oh gods!' Dar-Ra fell back on his heels, his face ashen in the dim light.

'What is it? What's wrong?' Kulak pushed forward, anxiety clouding his eyes. 'Kyky?' He leaned over the whimpering girl, gently taking hold of the hand she was cradling. It was slippery with blood and...

'What ...? Where are they?' He stared, horrified, at Dar-Ra, his words a hoarse whisper. Where the third and fourth fingers of Kyky's hand should have been was a ragged, gaping wound and the outer half of her hand was missing. Handing Muu-Nan to Amisi, he quickly shrugged off his shirt and tore the soft cotton fabric into strips which he used to bind the injury and stem the blood flow. It wasn't until he had finished and was cradling the softly moaning Kyky in his arms that he spoke again.

'What happened?'

'I don't know.' Dar-Ra was shaking, feeling sick and weak. He had known Kyky his whole life, she was like a sister to him, and now this... The exciting adventure he had been anticipating had, in just a few heartbeats, turned into a nightmare. They had always known the danger, or they believed they had. Except that they hadn't, had they? Not really. It had still been an adventure, a game, like their other escapades. Not really real – not until this moment. It was only now that he grasped the gravity of the task they had committed to, the danger it posed. Kyky could have been killed. As it was, she had been badly injured. Their situation was deadly serious, and they all had to start treating it as such.

'She ran out of time. Look.' Amisi's voice trembled, barely above a whisper. She was staring upwards at the spot where the shaft entrance had been. Three pairs of eyes followed her gaze. The opening had disappeared, empty space now replaced by solid rock.

'What's that?' Djal was squinting through the half-light, pointing to a dark blob in the stone.

'My fingers!' Kyky had pushed herself to a sitting position, her voice wracked with pain, cradling her mutilated hand. 'The stone was closing in around me. I could feel it getting thicker and thicker so I had to jump and hope.' Her voice shook. 'I knew as soon as I did that I was a bit too late. I felt the stone trap them as I dropped.' She forced a weak smile. 'Nothing like leaving it to the last minute!'

The dark patch came gruesomely into focus as a ragged lump of bleeding flesh protruding from the roof, dripping crimson onto the floor below.

Kulak hugged her gently. 'You did it, Kyky. You rescued Muu-Nan, just as he asked. None of us could have done what you did.' He took the skull from Djal and laid it in her lap then looked up at his friends. 'Now what?'

'We find the way out of here.' A deep frown betrayed Dar-Ra's worry. They had had no way to investigate the chamber in advance and were acting out of a total faith in Muu-Nan's word. If that faith was misplaced, they would all die a long drawn-out and very unpleasant death, trapped in the bowels of this monument. He shivered violently; they would be eaten alive by the Great Stone Lion. No, he rebuked himself, he couldn't think like that. He wouldn't think like that. That would not be their fate. There was a way out and with Muu-Nan's help, they would find it. 'Where are the other lamps?' he called.

Four more small stone dishes appeared from beneath robes, were filled with oil from pouches similarly concealed and, with the flash of a flint, were lit.

'Alright. If we've understood correctly, the hidden doorway is somewhere around here at the front of the chamber, beneath the floor. To open it, we have to find the trigger. Which could be anything and anywhere,' he finished despondently. 'How do we know where to even start looking?'

'Like this.' Amisi had stepped forward, holding the skull level with her head and gazing into its eye sockets, her unusual violet irises darkened further by the reflection of the crystal. She stared blankly, focussing on somewhere far away from the gloom of this dark and increasingly oppressive place; when she spoke next, her words echoed with a resonance and authority that the young girl's voice could never carry.

'There.' Again that rich, sing-song tone, only this time the others forgot to wonder at it. They were no longer paying attention to Amisi. An incandescent kernel, no bigger than a date stone, had burst into life in the centre of the skull and from it a thread of brilliance sped through the darkness, striking the mirrored disc and reflecting off to land on the wall behind at the exact point where the lion's heart would sit.

Djal was first to reach the spot. He turned, confused. 'There's nothing here.'

'There has to be.' Dar-Ra joined him, studying the surface closely. But Djal was right. There was no doorway, no trace of one, only a blank wall of stone whose blocks were so tightly fitted together that he couldn't have pushed a blade of grass between them. 'I don't understand.'

'The door is there,' Amisi repeated.

'The bloodstone.' Kyky's voice was barely a whisper. 'The bloodstone.'

'What do you mean, Kyky? What bloodstone?' Kulak peered at her anxiously. Her face was an ash-white blotch in the dim light, her eyes closed. 'She's hallucinating.'

She struggled to sit up, her eyelids flickering as she fought to open her eyes and look at them. 'No. No, I'm not...' Her voice was faint, wavering, and yet it held a certainty that they couldn't ignore. 'You have to find the bloodstone. That's the key.' She slumped down, spent and only half conscious.

'Do we believe her?' Djal looked doubtful.

'It's all we have, unless anyone has a better idea?' Dar-Ra's gaze swept across his companions. They all shook their heads.

'Nothing.' Kulak admitted. 'But we still have no idea what Kyky was talking about. I haven't seen any bloodstone.'

'Nor me. If she's right, though, it's here somewhere and we have to find it. Quickly.' The first of the lamps had just sputtered and died. That left four. Four lamps and the dazzling thread of light still emanating from Muu-Nan and bouncing off the mirror. The tiny lamps wouldn't burn for much longer. 'Can Kyky tell us?'

'Kyky. Kyky.' Kulak gently stroked her cheek. The girl stirred and looked up at him through eyes clouded with pain. 'Where is this bloodstone, Kyky? What does it look like? Do you know?'

'Can't you see it?' She blinked, rubbed her eyes unsteadily with her uninjured hand and stared past his shoulder to a point on the wall several paces to the right of the spot where the light beam touched it. 'It's there.'

'Where?' Djal moved slowly, following her gaze.

'More. Across a bit more.' Her voice wavered.

'There's nothing here, only blank wall.' He turned, again confused. 'Are you sure?' Kyky nodded.

'This one?' He pushed on it hard. Nothing. He tried to turn it. Nothing. It wouldn't move even a fraction. 'Are we going to die in here?' There was no fear, no panic in Djal's question, simply an acceptance touched with curiosity.

'No. Muu-Nan told us that there's a way out and we're going to find it.' Dar-Ra turned back to the wall. He was the one who always found a way out of their scrapes and he would find a way out of this one too.

'Kulak, help me.' Kyky struggled – and failed – to get to her feet. 'Help me to the wall.' The boys looked at each other, the question unspoken but clear.

'No, Kyky. You're badly injured. Rest.'

She wouldn't listen, again pushing herself up until, with an immense act of will, she stood, swaying with the effort. She took an uncertain step and crashed to the ground, landing on her mutilated hand with a scream of agony. Immediately, Kulak was at her side.

'Stop, Kyky. I'll take you.' He picked her up and carried her across the chamber.

'Closer,' she panted, 'so I can touch it.'

Gasping in pain, her skin whiter than the limestone that newly clad the Great Pyramids, she reached out her injured hand and laid it on the smooth, cool surface. Dark wetness glistened. Though she whimpered at the slash of invisible knives that pierced her mangled flesh and bones, she didn't draw it away. Instead, she began to chant, a low murmur of words in a language unknown to the three boys standing around her. All the while, Kulak held her in his arms, cradling her as tenderly as if she was a baby, wanting only to protect her and keep her safe.

Three times she spoke, then her eyes rolled and her hand dropped from the wall, leaving a grotesque smear on the pale surface. She had fallen unconsciousness. They waited, tense. Nothing. It hadn't worked. Kyky's action has been nothing but the hallucination of a grievously injured girl in pain.

Chapter 41

At the far end of the chamber, Amisi stood like a statue, her expression blank, as if she had vacated her body and mind. Kulak carefully lowered Kyky to the floor and sank down beside her.

'It's over. The Heart of Regulus betrayed us. He promised to help and instead he got us trapped here. We were caught up in our imagination and now we'll pay the price.' There was nothing they could do. By the time the entrance was re-opened, the five of them would have been long dead.

A soft click echoed at their backs. They whirled around; three mouths fell open. The blood-stained block had moved – or rather, the front face of it had. A panel, a thumb's width thick, had slid downwards to expose a shallow compartment cut into the stone. From within the compartment, deep crimson glowed softly.

Dar-Ra was first on his feet, stretching up to peer into the cubbyhole. Inside lay an oblong jewel of the richest ruby red, its facets reflecting the pale, flickering flames of the lamps in a hundred pinpricks of light. It was huge, longer than his middle finger, its width easily that to his second knuckle.

Kulak and Djal jostled to get a view. 'Is it real?' Even their whispers sounded too loud.

'What else can it be?'

They fell silent. The gemstone was breath-taking. Surely there could be none other as beautiful and captivating on the Earth. They looked at each other, unable to form the question that filled all their minds. They had the bloodstone, what did they do now?

'Kyky?' But the girl was lost in the humane darkness of the unconsciousness that was shielding her from her pain.

Dar-Ra shrugged. What did he have to lose? If they didn't find the way out, they were doomed anyway. He reached in and lifted the jewel from its rest, shivering at its touch. It lay chill in his hand, like frozen blood. He turned back to his friends, uncertain. What was he meant to do with it? How did it open the door? Come to that, where was the door?

He spun back to the wall. Kulak was staring past him, grinning, and no wonder. A dark rectangle had appeared in the golden-white stone. He looked down at the jewel in his hand. Could it have been that straightforward? Had simply removing it from its compartment been the key? It seemed too easy, and yet… There was their way out.

'Amisi, come on. Let's go.' The girl didn't move. 'Amisi!'

Gently, Djal took the skull from her and pushed it into the front of his tunic. 'Amisi,' he repeated.

The girl shook her head, dazed and disoriented as if waking from a deep sleep.

'Come on, Amisi. We've found the way out. Hurry.' He pulled her to the small opening and thrust a lamp into her hands, taking one for himself too. 'I'll go first, you follow.'

As small and slight as Djal was, he had to stoop to negotiate the low ceiling. The taller Amisi was not so lucky; she was forced to stumble along bent almost double. Stifling blackness surrounded them in a heavy, musty shroud. Despite the discomfort, they kept going.

This was their only escape route. The alternative was to wait to die, prisoners of the Great Lion.

Dar-Ra eyed the tiny opening doubtfully. Transporting the unconscious Kyky seemed an almost impossible task.

'We'll do it,' Kulak stated firmly. 'We'll get her out. Somehow. I'll go backwards and pull her along. You follow with the lamp and watch out for her hand. Make sure it doesn't get caught in anything.'

Dar-Ra slipped off his tunic and spread it on the floor, and Kulak gently laid Kyky on top, hoping the fabric would give some protection to her skin as he dragged her along. Kulak reversed into the passageway on all fours and took hold of her inert body under her arms, encircling her slender frame with his powerful grip. It was awkward, and within only a few steps his back and stomach muscles were protesting angrily. He gritted his teeth and hauled her backwards, step by laborious step.

Now it was Dar-Ra's turn. He stuffed the ruby gemstone into his cloth belt, picked up the final lamp and bent to help Kulak. In truth he could do little of use other than encourage his friend and watch that Kyky's maimed hand didn't suffer further injury. Progress was difficult and exhausting. The tunnel sloped steeply downwards for a long way, much deeper and further than the route by which they had entered. The only sound was the puffing and grunting of Kulak's exertions and the soft drag of fabric on stone. Kyky was still lost in oblivion.

Eventually, the floor levelled out. They had come out into a small natural cave, the roof high enough that they could stand, where Djal and Amisi waited for them. Only one flicker of light greeted the two boys – Djal's lamp.

Amisi's had died long before. Kulak straightened up stiffly, stretching his cramped, aching back with a groan.

They could see little of what surrounded them; the feeble light reached only a pace or two through the blackness. Exploring by touch more than vision, they discovered that the passageway continued at the far side of the space in an uninviting black maw that led to who knew where. Well, they had no other option. That was the way they had to go. No sooner had Djal taken the first step towards it than Dar-Ra's lamp sputtered and went out. That left one.

Djal ducked his head and slipped into the darkness, the others hurrying after him. Every one of them understood only too clearly the gravity of their situation. If the remaining light died before they reached the surface, they would be lost in this underground maze forever. Amisi was swallowed up next then Kulak, who had swept the limp Kyky into his arms, cradling her gently and carefully. Once more, Dar-Ra brought up the rear. This time he shuffled forward in near total darkness, the black bulk of Kulak barely visible no more than a pace in front of him.

They had been walking for what felt like hours, although time had long since lost all meaning for the four young friends as they stumbled through the pitch-dark passageways and caverns of this underground kingdom. Throughout, Kyky remained lost in a different darkness, hers warm, healing, and protective. If she grew heavy in Kulak's arms, he never gave a sign.

Dar-Ra was puzzled. If they had been trudging on for even a fraction of the time he believed, Djal's lamp should have died long before, yet the tiny flame still flickered as strongly as it always had. Could it be...? No, that was nonsense. Yet the thought came back and back again, refusing to be swept aside. Was this the skull's doing? Was the Heart of Regulus somehow keeping the flame alive until they reached safety? How was beyond the boy's understanding, but the more he thought about it, the more it made sense. Muu-Nan had reached out to all of them with his cry for help, so he would ensure that they stayed safe. Wouldn't he? His escape depended on it. And then there was Amisi's odd behaviour, and Kyky somehow knowing exactly where the bloodstone was concealed. It was all very, very weird.

The bloodstone! He felt into his belt. Yes, there it was, hard against his fingers. Dismay and terror crushed down on him, knocking him off balance so that he lost his footing and smashed his shoulder against the hard rock. He stifled a curse. He had in his possession a gemstone that every ruler on Earth would trade his kingdom for, a gemstone he had taken from the Great Stone Lion. What was he going to do? If he was caught, he would be branded a thief and his punishment would be the ultimate. Panic caught in his chest, tightening. He had to go back, return it. Only he couldn't. He had no light and even if he had, he'd never find the way...

'Peace, child. The bloodstone is yours to keep, a gift from the Lion gods to you and your friends.' The low, vibrant voice filled his mind until he was aware of nothing else. His fear evaporated, replaced by the feeling that he was safe and protected, just as when, as a baby, his mother had wrapped him snugly in a warm, soft blanket. 'You have shown great courage and one of you has already paid a heavy price. Do not doubt that much more will be demanded of you in the times to come. Take this bloodstone and use it as you must.'

'Muu-Nan?' Dar-Ra shook himself. The unremitting dark, hunger, thirst, exhaustion; they were playing tricks with his imagination. Weren't they? But what if...? After all, hadn't he come to them the previous night?

A low chuckle echoed softly through his mind. 'Believe what you will, child. I have no issue with that. Know though that I will guide you and protect you. Even when the way ahead is unclear, when you cannot see the next steps to take, trust in me. All will be shown to you when it is needed.'

'Noooo!' Djal's anguished cry hurled Dar-Ra back into the reality of their plight. 'My lamp. It's gone out.' The words were unnecessary. The blackness that enveloped them was as thick as tar.

If there was ever a time to test the truth of Muu-Nan, it was now. *If* he hadn't been hallucinating, the Heart of Regulus had only moments before promised to protect and guide them. Right now, blind and lost in this underground world, they desperately needed that protection and guidance.

'Seek well what you need. Look and you will find.' The thought came unbidden. What in the name of the Lion gods did it mean?

'Seek well what you need?' Amisi's disembodied question startled him.

'You heard it too?' Kulak's question prickled with astonishment.

'We all did, I think. Does anyone have any idea what it means? Because I absolutely don't!' Djal added.

'It's a riddle. I hate riddles.' Kulak's irritation was tangible, echoing around the walls of the unseen tunnel.

'No, it's not a riddle.' Djal burst out excitedly. 'Look. Up ahead.' Four pairs of eyes peered through the darkness.

'Djal's right. It's lighter over there. Only a tiny bit but...' Moving blindly, testing every step with hand and foot for danger of any kind, Dar-Ra inched past his companions towards the point where the blackness appeared marginally less solid.

'I see light,' he called back, excitement raising his voice to a high-pitched squeak. 'There's a sharp bend in the passageway here. Now I've got around it, I can see a tiny spot of light. It has to be daylight. Come on.'

Strength and spirit revived by the prospect of fresh air and sunshine after so many hours underground, Djal, Amisi and Kulak, still carrying the senseless Kyky, hurried as fast as caution would allow to where Dar-Ra waited for them. He was right. The pinprick of light was still a long way off, and who knew what obstacles still lay between them and it. It didn't matter. The end of this subterranean ordeal was now in sight.

* * * * *

The young friends edged their way closer to sunlight and fresh air, the same thought occupying each of their minds. What now? They could not return home. They had vowed to take Muu-Nan as far from here as they were able, to keep him from the clutches of those who would soon come, and they would not abandon that vow even if where that would be remained a mystery to them all. It seemed an impossible task. They carried nothing but their trust in Muu-Nan and his promise that he would guide and protect them. With such a vast unknown lying ahead, none of them had ever felt so young, so vulnerable and so completely unprepared for what might lie ahead.

They also had Kyky, who had still not regained consciousness. They would not, could not, leave her. Kulak – and when he faltered, Dar-Ra and Djal – would carry her for as long as necessary, until she regained the strength to walk on her own, or... No, they would not even consider that outcome. Taking her back to her family, who would care for and nurse her, was out of the question. Her wounds would be tended, yes, but how could she answer the endless questions as to how she had sustained the injury? Questions that would become ever more probing and difficult when the disappearance of her four friends came to light.

Dar-Ra's heart contracted painfully. He would never see his home or family again. None of them would. They would vanish like ghosts in the night. Grief slashed at him like an obsidian blade and guilt rose up and battered him so brutally that he almost fell. Their families' pain would be worse. Not knowing what had happened to them, always wondering whether they were dead or alive. Unable to say goodbye or to mourn properly. Their loss, their distress, their never-ending torment at the disappearance of the five young friends…

'Peace, child.' Amisi was speaking, though it was the voice he had come to know as Muu-Nan's that flowed from her lips and broke through his anguish. 'Let heaviness and sorrow have no place in your heart. They will understand for I will help them, as I will help all those you leave behind, to find peace and consolation. That is my gift to them for your courage.'

Chapter 42

Their road was long and arduous, even harder to endure because they had no knowledge of where they were going other than that they had to head east. Always east, Muu-Nan had told them, into the rising sun. The skull guided their feet, speaking to them through Amisi, and they quickly learned to trust him implicitly. He led them across barren, arid lands where little but stunted dry shrubs survived, and across high, craggy, ice-bound ridges. Often their stomachs were empty and thirst caught in their throats. Always though, the skull would lead them to food and water, sometimes in abundance, more often meagre and unappetising. Always enough to satisfy for a while their complaining bellies and parched tongues. A tiny spring would bubble out of a crack in a rock to vanish almost immediately, swallowed up by the dry, sandy soil. They would stumble across the fresh carcase of some small mammal as yet untainted by the heat of the day. A scraggy plant would provide a handful of tart berries, or an unlikely clump of leathery leaves would yield sweet, juicy flesh.

Kyky's hand healed rapidly. Before many days had passed, she had regained her strength and kept up easily with her friends, testament to the power of the skull. Although she carried only a faint memory of what had happened, her maimed half-hand served as a permanent symbol of her courage and sacrifice.

One morning, well over four moon cycles into their trek, they came across the remains of a camel, its load scattered around. Not far away lay the sun-bleached bones of its owner, picked clean by carrion hunters beneath the tattered rags of what remained of his clothing. The camel was undergoing the same fate. It's shrunken, desiccated hide was shredded and torn by the scavengers that had fought to tear apart the tough, dried skin.

Amongst the goods they found cloth and clothing, rope, blades and gourds. This had been a merchant on his way to trade in some big town. They seized eagerly on the treasure trove, fashioning a secure sack for Muu-Nan and collecting as many gourds as they could carry for storing their precious water. They found no food; any the merchant may have carried had long since disappeared. They saw no-one else. It was as if the desert had swallowed up every sign of human life.

They walked and they walked. Their bodies grew lean, fit and strong and, as they travelled through season after season and celestial cycle after celestial cycle, they left childhood behind.

* * * * *

It was late in the afternoon when they crested a low, boulder-strewn rise and came to an abrupt halt, unable to believe the sight that lay before them. The land was vibrant with colour and a wall of noise rose up to greet them from a tented City that had blossomed in the desert, stretching to the rise of the hills on the far side of the plain. As one, they dropped to the ground in the cover of one of the large boulders that stood sentinel on the ridge.

'Who are they?' Dar-Ra whispered, more to himself than with the expectation of an answer. 'Will they help us or kill us?'

In these wild regions, bandits and warlords who would slit your throat for the shirt on your back were a very real threat. If they entered the camp, they could as easily be walking to their death as to their salvation.

'Muu-Nan?' Amisi had pulled the skull from his wrappings and now held it level with her face, gazing into his empty eye sockets in search of some guidance. The skull was silent.

'It seems we have to make our own decision in this,' the young girl announced glumly.

'Surely if we were heading into danger, Muu-Nan would warn us, wouldn't he? He wouldn't risk being caught by those he asked us to save him from.' Dar-Ra stared at the skull, willing it to give some sign. It didn't. He peered over the boulder's rough top. 'This is no bandit camp. It's huge. It has to belong to a king.'

'Doesn't mean we wouldn't die though. Or be captured as slaves.' Kulak muttered gloomily. 'There are precious few good kings around.' He slumped back onto the stony ground.

'Please Muu-Nan, help us. What do we do?' Amisi pleaded. Still the skull did not answer. She rested her head against the rough, sun-warmed stone and closed her eyes in frustration. They were so close to good food and water, and maybe even a proper bed, yet they dared not risk revealing themselves to those who camped so close by.

'Kulak's right, we can't take the chance. We risked everything to take Muu-Nan out from the Great Lion and it cost us dearly. We can't throw all that away now. I say we wait until dark then make our way around this edge of the camp and up into the hills beyond.'

His companions nodded. Too much was at stake to do anything else.

They dozed fitfully in the shade of the rocks for the rest of the day, waiting for nightfall. It seemed it would never come, but at last the sky to the east began to darken. Brilliant, sparkling blue skies deepened to indigo, swept over with a constantly moving collage of gold, violet and red. Above, the first stars glittered and the dazzling globe of the full moon climbed above the horizon. It was time.

Cautiously, for the slope was steep and the ground underfoot littered with loose stones that would easily turn an ankle, the five friends began their descent. They had gone no more than a quarter of the way when Amisi cried out in dismay.

'Muu-Nan...' With no further thought either of stealth or her safety, she sprinted slipping and sliding after the skull which was tumbling rapidly down the incline, starlight glinting on its polished surface.

'What is it?' The agile, sure-footed Kyky was on her heels.

'The Heart of Regulus,' Amisi panted. 'He dropped out of the bag.' She pointed to where the skull rolled and bounced, momentum carrying it ever faster away from her.

The five stumbled and lurched down the hillside after the skull, onwards, downwards; nothing, it seemed, would stop its descent. It was only when it reached the floor of the sandy valley that it slowed, coming to rest in a small, sand-filled depression where it lay still, sparkling in the moon's cold, white light.

'Muu-Nan!' Amisi seized him and lifted him to the light, examining him carefully. 'He's alright.' In spite of the violent descent, the skull was miraculously undamaged.

'What happened?' Sand showered from Djal's hair.

The girl shook her head in bewilderment. 'I don't know. I'd wrapped him away carefully, just like I always do. I know he was safe. And then he wasn't. He dropped onto the ground and rolled down the hill away from me.' She swallowed. '*He* did it. I know it sounds mad and I don't know why he did it, but he did. He escaped from the bag.'

'Well, what do we have here?'

Slowly, fearfully, they turned. They had been so caught up in checking Muu-Nan had come through unscathed that they had forgotten about the encampment and the danger it might hold for them. And now, they had been caught.

'Your Highness.' They dropped to their knees and bowed their foreheads to the ground. He had to be a king yet for all his authority, and the strength and power that he emanated, there was a kindness in his curious gaze. He was young, in his mid-twenties, with skin of a rich, deep brown and ebony dark eyes that glowed with life. Beneath his head-cloth, held in place by a plain gold band, a tightly braided narrow leather thong held back chestnut hair of the same colour as the closely trimmed beard encircling his mouth.

'What is that? Show me!'

Not daring to disobey, Amisi rose and, her eyes lowered, handed him the skull. His eyes lingered on the young woman who despite her tender years, ragged appearance, and the marks of the hardships she had endured, held the promise of a passionate sensuality and fire.

Under his scrutiny, she blushed fiercely. Recognising her discomfort, the King shifted his attention to Muu-Nan, lifting the skull so that the moonlight fell directly onto it, the unusual lavender-pink quartz sparkling with an unearthly light in the silver rays. His focus softened; he had been taken far from this desert valley and it was a long time before he returned.

'Your Highness...?' The General at his right shoulder had become anxious and had ridden forward, concerned that the skull and the five young people were casting some harmful spell. The King raised his hand, commanding silence; reluctantly the man dropped back to his place. It was some moments more before the King spoke.

'It has much to tell me,' he declared, 'but for now it has asked me to return it to the care of those who have been its Guardians for so many difficult days.' To everyone's astonishment, not least that of his men, the King held it out to Amisi.

'Take it and come with me. You are in need of food, rest, and new clothing to replace those rags. You are my guests, and my hospitality is yours to enjoy. I will speak with your skull again in due course.'

The five friends didn't move, unsure whether to obey or attempt to flee.

'I am Karga, King of this realm, and this is my army.' He gestured to the massive encampment behind him. 'I had a dream to set out in search of a treasure that would ensure the safety of my people. It was a dream like no other and one I could not ignore. I didn't know what that treasure would be, only that I would know it when I found it.' He smiled. 'There were many, I know, who whispered behind my back that I had gone mad, that I was chasing phantoms.' He glanced at Muu-Nan, glittering in Amisi's hands. 'Maybe I was but if so, I have found them. *This* is the treasure I was seeking.' Kyky wasn't sure whether he meant the skull or Amisi. '

Come,' he repeated, turning his horse back towards the tents. Gently given, it was a command nonetheless, not a request. Uncertain of what awaited them, the young guardians followed.

Chapter 43

Five times the Earth circled the sun and they remained in Karga's court, content to be there. It was a joyful place, for Karga was indeed a good and just king and his people were happy, content and prosperous. Muu-Nan's arrival had only increased that wellbeing and the abundance of their lives, and the people of the kingdom gave thanks every day for the skull's gifts. Muu-Nan – who the people here had renamed Bringer of Peace – had not given any sign that he wished to move on so the five friends stayed and found a purpose and a new life.

Dar-Ra and Kulak enlisted in Karga's army, learning to wield weapons as skilfully as any other soldier in the ranks. The training increased even further their strength and fitness, and as Kulak's body reached its full maturity, the towering youth grew into a virtually invincible colossus, a man-mountain that few could best.

Kyky wanted to become a warrior too, to fight and stand alongside her friends, and it was to her constant frustration that she could not. Even if she had had two good hands, in Karga's kingdom it was strictly forbidden for a woman to become a warrior. It wasn't all disappointment, however, for she discovered a new passion, that of herbs and healing plants. She learned quickly and eagerly, filling her days gathering leaves, roots and flowers from the land outside of the City walls, distilling essential oils and potions and brewing elixirs under the guidance of the court's healers. Nor was she totally thwarted in her desire to learn to fight, persuading

Dar-Ra and Kulak to train her in their free hours. Under their tutelage, she learned to wield a blade well enough with her good hand.

The hardships of the trek from the Great Stone Lion had taken a toll on Djal's health and he had fallen seriously ill after their arrival in Karga's City. Although he had recovered, he was no longer the strong, vital Djal of before. He could not fight, not that he wanted to. He had never been a warrior. His gifts were his mind, which was sharp and insightful, even psychic at times, with an uncanny ability to pierce through any fog of confusion and deception, and his heart and soul which sought justice and truth always.

As for Amisi, she had indeed grown into the woman who fulfilled the promise Karga had glimpsed on their first meeting. She was beautiful, intelligent, passionate, and kind, and it hadn't taken long for the king to fall head over heels in love with her. She returned his love as deeply and the two had become inseparable. Since their arrival in this land, Muu-Nan had communicated only through Amisi; she was his main Guardian and his mouthpiece. She cherished the Heart of Regulus and kept him with her constantly, sharing his guidance with her beloved Karga and his Council.

That is not to say that the kingdom was without its problems. Its wealth, strategic location and rich, fertile lands were a prize coveted by many, most of whom were willing to take it by any means necessary. Muu-Nan was not just the bearer of joyful days and full storehouses, however. Since the Heart of Regulus had come to his palace, Karga's armies had been indomitable. Whenever he rode into battle, Amisi – and Muu-Nan – rode out beside him. With the skull's power on his side, every battle had been won and every enemy set to flight, cruelly weakened. Each time, Karga rode out to meet his enemies far beyond the borders of his realm, cutting them down long before they drew near enough to threaten its borders. And no matter how huge the opponent's army, no matter how grave the danger, Amisi rode always at his side, carrying Muu-Nan in a casket of gold filigree that was set firmly onto the saddle of her camel.

Until the battle they lost...

*   *   *   *   *

'Karga!' Amisi's scream pierced the pandemonium of the battlefield. 'KARGA!'

She wheeled her camel around, reaching for the king who was swaying dangerously in his saddle. He stared at her for a brief heartbeat, disbelief mingling with pain, then toppled and crashed to the ground, the shaft of a lance protruding grotesquely from high up on his side under his arm. She leaped down and dropped to her knees at his side. The skull! The Heart of Regulus could help him.

With her fingers fumbling to open the casket, however, the agonising realisation exploded in her that even Muu-Nan's formidable healing power could not help him. Karga had been dead before he hit the ground. The well-aimed lance had found the vulnerable spot in his armour, at the point just below where his arm joined his body, the one spot unprotected by its tough leather and wadding to allow him to wield his blade and bow without hindrance. The razor tip had pierced the exposed skin effortlessly and found his heart. Already the armour was stained crimson, soaked through with the blood that gushed from the wound and pooled on the rough ground.

'NO!' Amisi screamed, her shaking hands gently lifting his helmet to caress his precious face. Silent, wracking sobs shook her; grief cut brutally short, the anguish on her face replaced by incomprehension. She stared down. A blade, dripping red with blood – her blood – protruded from her chest. And yet she felt nothing. The world slowed. The chaos of the battlefield receded. She was aware only of the blade and her blood – and that someone was watching her through cold, mocking eyes. A gauntleted hand reached for the casket holding the skull.

'No...' It came out as an unintelligible gurgle. Agony exploded in her chest and the metallic saltiness of her blood filled her mouth. Darkness closed in rapidly from the edges of her vision, the final image burned into her consciousness that of a twisted, mocking grin in a hard, pitiless face. She slumped, lifeless, over Karga's body, her life-blood mingling with his in their final death embrace on the gore-soaked ground.

* * * * *

Their king may have fallen, but Karga's army was well-disciplined and committed, led by strong, intelligent generals who fought not just for him but also for their homes and for the lives of their wives and children. They would battle on until they dropped. This time, they didn't have to. The enemy troops were falling back, retreating, just at the moment victory was within their grasp. Karga's men didn't hide their jubilation. Jubilation that swiftly withered and died as word spread that their king had been killed.

The news took some time to reach Dar-Ra and Kulak who were on the outermost flank of the battlefield and who had fought side by side throughout. When it did, ice-cold dread clawed at their bellies. If Karga was dead, what had become of Amisi, who never left his side in battle? There was no news of the King's consort. Was she still alive? And what of Muu-Nan?

Clutching his left arm, which had been slashed almost to the bone and hung useless at his side, bound with a bloodied strip torn from his undershirt, Dar-Ra stumbled through the exhausted soldiers, slipping on the blood-soaked earth, tripping over the bodies of the dead and injured that littered the ground. Kulak kept pace, himself dazed and unbalanced from a crack to his skull which still oozed blood that trickled down his neck and darkened his sweat-blackened armour even further. The stench of death and the agonised screams of the wounded filled the air and rattled their senses.

A grim-faced group had gathered around Karga's body and were speaking in low voices. Among them, Dar-Ra recognised Portek, General-in Command of the King's troops. The general turned as they approached, grief and fury mingling on his time-worn face. His shoulder looked to be dislocated; he paid it no attention.

'The King is dead?' Normally such a question from a rank and file soldier would have earned at the very least a sharp reprimand and a curt order to go and help with the wounded. Instead, recognition flared in the old General's eyes and a flash of sympathy shadowed his features.

'Yes.' His voice cracked with the pain of losing his beloved King. 'But not just him...' He stepped aside.

Dar-Ra staggered and would have fallen had Kulak not seized his arm in his powerful fist and held him upright, even as he heard the big man beside him draw in a shuddering breath. Amisi? No, this couldn't be, not after all they had gone through, all they had overcome, together. How had Muu-Nan let this happen? Why hadn't the skull protected their beloved friend?

The girl lay across the king's body where she had fallen in a final, grotesque embrace with her lover. Beneath her cooling, inert body, Karga stared up at the darkening sky of twilight, his eyes wide and unseeing, the thick shaft of a spear still protruding obscenely from his side.

'I saw it happen and I couldn't reach them. The fighting around me was too fierce. I failed my King.' The dark gleam of shame in Portek's eyes was echoed by the sorrow in his words. 'He came for them with a purpose. He went straight for my Lady Amisi and the Bringer of Peace. My King was killed as he tried to protect them. He was after the skull. That was all he wanted. He raced off as soon as he had it.' He stared at the retreating enemy soldiers, tiny specks now disappearing into the distant river gulley. 'They have what they came for.'

He turned to his men. 'Take our King and his Amisi to the palace for burial.'

Gentle hands lifted the bodies onto a rough bier constructed of lashed-together spear shafts and anything else the men were able to find. The two lay as inseparable in death as they had been in life, even for such a brief time. The enemy may have fled, the King's army remained unvanquished, but none felt the thrill of victory. It was an army with a heavy, grieving heart that returned home that day.

Chapter 44

'We can't let them take Muu-Nan. We have to get him back.' Kulak spoke in hushed tones in the corner of the barracks. 'We've risked so much, endured too much, to simply give up and not even try.' His voice dropped further. 'We owe it to Amisi.'

'I agree.' Dar-Ra glanced around to check no-one was listening. 'When do we leave?'

'First light. It'll be almost impossible to track them in the dark. They've got a good few hours start, it's true, but that shouldn't matter. Most of their men are on foot and we'll be riding. We'll cover the ground a lot faster than they can. We'll gain on them with every hour that passes.'

* * * * *

Kulak found Kyky standing vigil over Amisi's body.

'Kyky?' He spoke softly, unwilling to break into her grief. Over the years, his adolescent feelings had developed into a deep, if unspoken, love for the young woman.

She looked up at him, her face white with strain and anger though as yet untouched by tears. They would come later. His heart, already aching deeply from Amisi's death, cracked further open at the sight of her bitter pain.

'Why?' she whispered. 'Why didn't Muu-Nan protect her? She kept him safe for so long. Why wouldn't he do the same for her?'

'I don't know.' He had been asking himself the same question and he had no answer. He enveloped her hands in his. They were icy cold despite the warmth of the night.

'It's not fair!' Kyky's wail was too much for him to bear. His arms went around her and he pulled her close, rocking her gently as heaving, dry sobs shook her body.

'No, it's not,' he murmured softly.

He held her for a long time after the sobs had subsided, her closeness giving him strength as he gave her courage. 'We're going to get the Heart of Regulus back,' he told her. 'Dar-Ra and me. We're leaving first thing in the morning.'

'I'm coming too.' She cut him off before he could protest, lifting her maimed hand. 'I paid a price once to keep the skull safe. I will not be kept out of it this time.'

'But Dar-Ra...'

'Dar-Ra will just have to deal with it.' She raised up on tiptoes and kissed his cheek. 'There's no point in arguing, Kulak. I'm coming with you.'

No, there was no point. Kyky had made up her mind and nothing either he or Dar-Ra said or did would be able to stop her. If he was honest, he didn't want to.

*   *   *   *   *

They slipped through the City gates at daybreak the following morning and pulled up sharply. This was not the covert departure they had planned. Around fifty men were waiting for them, mounted and ready to leave. And Kyky. She rode out of the pack to greet them. Dar-Ra threw a glance at Kulak who had the grace to look sheepish.

'Ahhh, yes. Kyky's coming along too. I forgot to tell you.'

'Forgot?'

'Well you try to stop her. I couldn't. And we shouldn't either. She's as much a part of this as we are.'

'Amisi was my friend too,' the young woman declared fiercely.

One glance at Kyky's stubborn expression and squared, set shoulders and Dar-Ra saw that he would have no more success than Kulak. He conceded defeat.

'That's true enough. Alright Kyky, you're in. What about Djal?'

'I'm staying here.' He had followed them through the gates and stood behind them. 'I'm no warrior but I am a good friend and advisor to young prince Kalto and his mother. I have her trust and respect and that of the council and the court. Prince Kalto may now have to assume the role of King but he is only eight years old and he is young and vulnerable. He needs my support and guidance until he learns to be as good and wise a ruler as his father.'

He pulled a tattered piece of hide from his robe and handed it to Dar-Ra. 'Here. It's a map. One of the prisoners um... volunteered... the information after a little gentle prompting. It's the route they took to reach the plain where you encountered them. It's their most direct route home and there is no reason to believe that they'll return a different way. He confessed their target was Muu-Nan, so they've got what they came for. They'll be in a hurry to get the skull back to the safety of their own land.

'As for these men,' he gestured to the waiting troops, 'they are Karga's most loyal and trusted – strong, brave and skilled. Each one of them is willing to give his life to avenge his King's death. Do not deny them this opportunity, Dar-Ra. You may need them.'

Chapter 45

Crouched behind the boulders that littered the parched earth, they peered up at the massive fortress perched on top of the stone outcrop that thrust up incongruously for hundreds of feet from the flat lands that surrounded it. It was the perfect defensive position, the sheer rock faces unassailable and the gate unreachable. The group were over a thousand paces distant and even from there they had to crane their necks painfully to view the stark buildings at the summit.

'I can't see much.' Kyky squinted through the sunlight. 'It's too far away.'

'Here.' Jalk, a short, wiry man who in his three decades had seen more battles than most twice his age handed Kyky a clear disc the length of his forefinger in diameter and polished to a smooth mirror finish. Each face curved gently outwards. 'Look through this.'

She put it to her eye, blinking in disbelief. The whole cliff face had moved towards her, so close that she felt she could reach out and touch it. Amazed, she lowered the disc and lifted a questioning eyebrow at the man who had given it to her.

'I came across it after a battle. One of the enemy warriors had it tucked into his tunic. King Karga said I could keep it as a prize.'

One by one, the others peered through the disc, their mission temporarily forgotten at the marvel. Each one handed it on with wonderment written all over his face.

'Kyky,' Dar-Ra gave it back to her, 'you have the sharpest eyes. What do you see?'

She lifted it to her face once more. 'Two platforms. One huge, one smaller. At the top of the rock face at the base of the outer walls. Behind them is what looks to be an entrance gate and I think there are ropes and pulleys and some odd-looking wheels stuck together. More ropes holding the platforms up onto a framework of massive timbers.' She looked puzzled. 'Where did they get all those huge pieces of wood? There's nothing like that anywhere near here.'

She rubbed her eyes and studied the fortress again. 'The walls seem to be rough blocks of stone, and not that well-built either. It all looks really old and a bit tumbledown. Why would they choose to come here?'

'Because no-one can touch them up there. Even the full might of the King's army couldn't breach those walls. How would they get up to them?' Jalk scratched his head. 'How does *anyone* get up there?'

'The platforms. They must be for lowering people up and down.' Portek took the disc from Kyky and squinted through it. 'That large one could easily carry four camels. Once they are raised, the place is impenetrable.'

'Including to us!' Dar-Ra slumped to the ground. 'Even if we could get in, there are – how many of us? Fifty-three? Against an entire army. We'd be trapped and outnumbered. We wouldn't stand a chance.'

'I wouldn't be so sure.' A sea of heads turned towards Kyky. 'Muu-Nan is here; I can feel him. But I don't think there are very many soldiers here. Why would there be? I mean, who could storm this place and steal him? My feeling is that they're keeping a small group here to guard the Heart of Regulus while they try to discover his secrets and that the rest of the troops have been sent away. If nothing else, it would take forever to carry an army with all their camels, horses and equipment up to the fortress on those platforms.'

'If Kyky's right, and what she says makes sense, it would answer one problem. It doesn't solve our biggest obstacle though. How are we going to get from down here,' he pointed at the ground beneath his feet, 'to up *there*? We could reach the cliff base unseen at nightfall. Then what?'

'There's another way in. There has to be.' A tall, muscular man who bore a scar that puckered his neck from jaw to collar bone spoke up. 'Look, this place is impregnable, yes? No-one could take it by force. But what about another form of attack, one that would leave it wide open to defeat?'

'Siege!' Kulak clapped his hand to his forehead.

'Exactly. All an enemy would have to do is set up camp down here and starve them out. Anyone who had the ability – and power – to build a fortress up on that rock would also have had the foresight and ability to create a second entrance. What's more, unless the fort is manned permanently, someone would have to get up there initially to work the platform system. There has to be another, hidden, way in.'

'Where?'

He looked around and shrugged. 'I have no idea. A good distance away. Anyone making their escape would want it to be as far away as possible so they wouldn't be spotted, and very well hidden so that no-one would stumble on it accidentally.'

The outcrop rose up perpendicular to the scrubby land, thrust up out of the belly of the Earth by some long-forgotten seismic shift, a hard, black rock very different to the softer grey-cream stone that scattered the landscape and had suffered from eons of battering by the elements in this god-forsaken place. It alone had had the durability to withstand all that had been thrown at it and it towered over the surrounding scrubland, its sheer dark sides repelling all who would attempt to scale its heights. The men who had been out scouting came back reporting that this was the case on every aspect. Other than by the lifting platforms, the outer face was impossible to ascend.

'Which reinforces the likelihood of another route to the summit,' Kyky pondered. 'Someone found the way in, and they didn't go up the side.'

'If they found it, we can too. We need to act quickly. We have no idea of what supplies they have or how long they can – or plan to – stay holed up in that eyrie. We, on the other hand, have supplies to last only a few more days. It's a pretty safe bet that we'll run out before they will, and there's precious little chance of finding more in this place.' Kulak surveyed the arid, stony land. 'We have to find that entrance and we have to do it quickly. Once our supplies run out, our strength will too. If that happens, there's no way we'd be able to take them on and win.'

Only… Where to look?

*　*　*　*　*

Dar-Ra opened his eyes to a star-strewn sky and listened. Voices, speaking in an unknown language, had woken him. Whoever it was couldn't know that anyone else was around for they were making no attempt to hide their presence. He sat up cautiously and squinted through the darkness. He could see nothing. The moon was well past its last quarter, its slender silver sickle casting little light on the land below.

'Where are they?' Kyky had materialised at his side. 'I can't see a thing.'

'Nor me. Let's go and find them.'

Waking Kulak with a warning that enemy soldiers were roaming the night and could discover their camp, Dar-Ra and Kyky slipped through the darkness on the trail of the voices. They moved as silently as ghosts, stopping every few paces to take their bearings, for it would be too easy to lose all sense of direction in this blackness. Progress was slow; while the two friends were invisible under the cloak of night, so also were the hazards that awaited them underfoot. They passed the foot of the rock tower, which loomed even blacker against the sky, blotting out the stars with its bulk. Still they crept on.

The world had fallen quiet around them, the voices no longer detectable. Where had they gone? No sooner had the question formed in Dar-Ra's mind than a raucous burst of laughter cut through the night directly ahead of them. His hand sought the hilt of the blade that hung at his waist.

'I hear them. They have to be near but I can't see a thing,' Kyky whispered into his ear, taking a pace forward only to be yanked back by his sudden iron grip on her wrist. She had been about to walk over the edge of a steep drop; how far down it plunged, she couldn't tell in the darkness.

'Thank you,' she breathed then straightened, pointing. 'Look. Over there.' Below them and a good few hundred paces to their left, the faintest glimmer of light flickered yellow against the darkness. Snatches of conversation drifted on the air. She nudged Dar-Ra. 'We've found them! Come on.'

They edged their way carefully down to the base of the steep slope, holding their breath at every step in fear of the slightest sound which would give them away. Fortune was smiling on them; not one dislodged pebble or breaking twig from a misjudged step betrayed them. At the bottom, they found themselves in a narrow gash in the land, perhaps forty paces at most in width. They had descended perhaps the same distance. The ground beneath their feet was sandy and smooth, an ancient riverbed that had eroded the sliver of softer rock which had once wound its way between the more durable stone of its banks. They crept nearer to the weak light.

Now it was Kyky's turn to grab Dar-Ra and drag him urgently behind the skeleton of a stunted tree that had at some point in the past blown into the ravine. He cursed silently as his knees skinned on the rough ground. They were only just in time. Kyky's sharp ears had picked up the sound long before his had and only now did he hear the thud of rapidly approaching hooves. Seconds later, a battalion of camels and their riders, followed by the same of horses, thundered past almost within touching distance. After them, half blinded by the dust cloud kicked up by the beasts, rank after rank of foot soldiers followed at a fast trot.

The army was leaving, but what about the skull? What about Muu-Nan? Were they taking him?

'No.' Kyky shook her head. 'He's still up there.' She tilted her head in the direction of the fortress. 'I don't know how I know but I do.'

'And that is our way in.' Dar-Ra pointed to the dimly flickering beacon. 'Come on, let's get back up top. We'll get a better view from there and it'll be safer.'

* * * * *

They studied the jagged entrance in the far wall of the cleft, barely lighter than the darkness around it. The opening was around three times his height, Dar-Ra estimated, and around only ten paces wide.

'Big enough for the camels and riders,' he mused.

Sounds of movement and the occasional harsh cough came from within. Apparently not everyone had left.

Satisfied that they had gathered all the information they could, they committed the few features of the area to memory and took a rough bearing from the massive black bulk of the fortress rock. It could only be approximate; the darkness concealed virtually everything they could use as markers. Kyky pulled off the ribbon that tied back her hair and fastened it around the stem of a small, shrubby bush, close to the ground. When they found the ribbon, they would have found the location of the entrance.

A soft glimmer was lightening the eastern horizon. Dawn was on its way. They had to get back to their companions before daylight stole any chance of concealment.

Chapter 46

The next evening, with the encroaching night concealing their movements, all but five of Dar-Ra's small band left their camp to retrace the steps he and Kyky had taken, keeping low and using what cover they could find. Although the fortress appeared deserted, as it had since their arrival, there could still be sentries on guard. The five who remained would keep watch for any activity at the lift platforms.

It was easy enough to find the cleft in the land; they simply headed past the fortress pinnacle until they reached it. Finding the entrance in the wall proved to be a lot harder. It simply wasn't there. The rock face below where Kyky had tied her ribbon was sound and unbroken. They slid down the bank and searched in the fading light. Nothing, not a crack, not a rodent hole, broke its uniformity.

'I don't understand. This is the right place. The ribbon proves it. So where is the entrance?' Kyky leaned back against the rock face that was still warm from the blazing sun that had beat down on them all that long day, and wearily rubbed her forehead. A heartbeat later she jerked forward again as if scalded.

'The rock. It moved. I swear it did.' She turned to stare at the vast slab of solid, unbroken stone, running her half hand across its gritty surface. Nothing.

'You imagined it Kyky,' Dar-Ra muttered dully. 'You're exhausted, like the rest of us.'

'No, she didn't. Look. That wasn't there before.' Portek pushed Dar-Ra aside, pointing at the slenderest of cracks, barely a hair's width across, that traced a faint yet distinct line from the ground to well above their heads. 'Lean back again, Kyky, in exactly the same place as before.'

She did as he asked and this time there was no doubt. The hairline crack doubled then trebled in width. She leaned harder; with a soft scraping sound, a large section of the rock face swung inwards. Dar-Ra grabbed her and pulled her back before she too tumbled in. On the far side, the others had flattened themselves against the wall. None of them had any idea of what might be waiting for them inside, or who might charge out with blades and spears flying.

The expected charge didn't come. Instead, a short, bearded man stepped out into the light blinking and scratching his head, wondering why the gate had opened. The mechanism was precise. It had to be triggered in exactly the right place, which would be impossible for anyone who had come across it by chance. In any case, who would be wandering around out in these god-forsaken lands? The last thing he expected was an attack.

Too late he spun around as a careless foot rattled against a pebble. The blade opened his throat before he could reach for his weapon and he dropped lifeless into Kulak's waiting arms. The giant hoisted up the corpse and dumped it behind a clump of woody shrubs. Although the eagerly searching vultures would reveal its whereabouts as soon as daylight came, his assailants planned to have retrieved the Heart of Regulus and be far away long before then.

They were in a large rectangular vault that had been hewn from the bedrock and was thick with an acrid stench that emanated from the rows of stalls it held, twenty or more on each side. To the left, a handful of camels snorted and stomped, glaring malevolently at the intruders as they passed. To the right, at least thirty small, sturdy horses shuffled restlessly. The whole area was dimly lit by sputtering torches held in crudely forged wall sconces.

'Thirty horses – that means at least thirty men,' Portek murmured. 'Well, we have the element of surprise. With luck, we can be in and gone before they realise what's hit them. From the way that one reacted,' he nodded towards the doorway, 'the last thing they're expecting is visitors. We'll take all the horses and camels with us when we go. They won't keep up with us if they're on foot.'

'That way.' Kyky pointed to the far end of the chamber where a rectangular shadow stood out against the paler walls. Beyond, a roughly hewn tunnel disappeared into the darkness, its roof roughly the height of a man; no horse or camel would ever go past this point.

'From now on, not a sound,' Portek commanded. 'If they hear even a whisper, we've lost.' Leading the way with cautious speed, he ducked through the low opening and into the passageway followed by Dar-Ra, Kyky and the remainder of the men, with Kulak bringing up the rear.

The tunnel had been hacked out without finesse, created as a means of escape not a pleasure stroll. After only a short distance, it plunged steeply down, not levelling out until it was far beneath the valley floor. They walked blindly, feeling their way with hands and feet, heads and shoulders frequently – and painfully –

cracking against protruding lumps of rock. There was no room for torches in this cramped, airless burrow.

An eternity passed, shuffling painfully and slowly forwards. At last however Portek's foot kicked against stone. Above it and a little way ahead it stubbed against another. They had reached a second staircase, this one leading upwards. This had to be the route up to the fortress. The steps were narrow, uneven, jagged – and treacherously steep. One false footfall in the all-enshrouding blackness would be fatal, both for the one who slipped and for all those below who he would inevitably carry down with him to their deaths. On and on they climbed, up and up, until the legs of even these strong, battle-tough warriors burned like fire and their lungs gasped for air in the cramped, unventilated space.

A splinter of light signalled the end of their misery. Daylight, creeping in around the door to the fortress – or so they hoped. Dar-Ra pushed past Portek, grasped the catch and lifted. It opened smoothly, without a sound. They strained their ears, listening. Hearing nothing. They could only hope that meant the courtyard was empty. They had no way of knowing for sure until they left the relative safety of the stairwell. Taking a deep breath, Dar-Ra grasped the hilt of his blade, ready for a fight, and pushed the door wide open.

The stairs had taken them to a quiet corner of the inner courtyard, which was encircled by surprisingly low, crudely built walls, more evidence of the fortress's impregnable location. Across the yard loomed the bulk of the main building, accessed through thick double doors set into the centre of its facade. One sat lazily ajar; those living here felt safe from any intrusion. Behind where they huddled, in the opposite wall, barred gates led to the outer yard. Through them he spied the hulk of the hoists and the lifting platforms they raised and lowered. It was deserted. There were no soldiers here, no-one to challenge them. There had been though, and not so long ago judging by the refuse heap piled up against the far wall that was shrouded in a living, crawling cloak of buzzing, fat-bodied black flies.

Moving as silently as wild cats, the group skirted the walls until they reached the open entrance of the main building; inside a long, wide corridor lined on each side by doorways stretched away leading to square, featureless rooms: barracks for soldiers garrisoned here.

They searched each one. Only the four nearest the entrance looked to have been recently inhabited. The others were empty and had been for a very long time, to judge by the thick layer of dust that covered every surface. There was nothing that gave any clue as to who had been there in distant – or more recent – days. They counted twenty rooms in total, ten to each side, with fifty cots crammed into each. The barracks had been built to house two thousand men; only a tenth of that number had been here recently. How many remained, and were they really so confident of their unassailability that they had left the gates unguarded? Or were Dar-Ra and his friends walking into a trap?

Another set of double doors at the far end of the building gave onto an open inner yard surrounded on the other three sides by low, single-storey buildings. From the one on the right, the spicy aroma of a cooking pot hung in the breeze and the sound of men's laughter mingled with the soft notes of a pipe. The left-hand building appeared abandoned, a single broken door hanging crookedly on its hinge. Quietly, the group drew back into the barracks hall, closing the door.

Portek chuckled softly. 'We're going to give those rats a surprise they'll never forget.'

Keeping low and to the cover of the perimeter, they crept towards the occupied building, each unsheathing his blade as he moved. Kyky slipped a short, razor-sharp dagger from her boot and weighed it, her heart heavy. Today, she would exact revenge for Amisi.

Chatter and laughter and the clatter of knives on tabletops spilled out into the heat of the morning. The soldiers who remained in the fortress were relaxed and off guard; after all, their hideaway was impregnable.

They soon learned their folly. With a blood-curdling yell, Kulak charged into the mess hall, slashing and slicing, Kyky and Dar-Ra close on his heels. Behind them surged Portek with over forty well-seasoned warriors, all of whom kept an ice-cold control despite their rage and desire to avenge their king.

Within moments, chaos filled the dining hall. The men eating inside were as well-trained and disciplined as Portek's and it took only a split-second of hesitation for them to grasp the situation and switch into fighting mode. Knives that seconds before had speared meat from platters now stabbed and hacked. Other weapons, left resting against the wall as the soldiers ate, were swept up and wielded within a heartbeat.

They were skilful and experienced. So too though were Dar-Ra and his band, and they had had surprise in their favour; two of their opponents fell dead before they had had time to react. The fight was fierce, brutal, and ugly. In the confined space, both sides tripped over tables and benches and slipped on spilled wine and food. Kyky could not match the strength nor the size of the men but she was wiry and agile, leaping easily over upturned tables and slipping between and under those that still stood. And although her dagger was no match for their long blades, while they were occupied with her friends, she would appear behind them as silently as a wraith, stabbing and hacking. Opening an unsuspecting throat from ear to ear or plunging her blade into a sword arm raised to deliver a fatal blow.

'KYKY!' Kulak's shout registered as she tore her blade from a blood-sodden shoulder whose tendons it had just severed. She spun around. The knife whistled through the air, about to strike her between the eyes.

It vanished. A huge bulk had hurled itself between her and an inevitable death, gasped, and collapsed to the floor with a heavy, dull thud. Dull eyes stared up at her; blood gushed over the already gore-soaked rushes. She bent and retched. While she had learned the skills of combat well, until today she had had no experience of its ugly reality. The next instant, she was fighting for breath, the world spinning out of con troll around her. It was Kulak lying at her feet, his skin white and clammy, a mother-of-pearl hilt protruding from his chest, its pale opalescence stained crimson. No! It couldn't be. And yet it was. A keening wail filled her ears and she realised with a shock that it was coming from her lips.

She fell to her knees at his side, oblivious to the slaughter continuing around her. This was Kulak. He couldn't die. He mustn't. He was invincible. They had been through so much together. Hadn't he carried her for days after they had escaped from the Great Stone Lion?

'Kulak?' she whispered, stroking his cold cheek. His eyelids flickered and opened, focussing on her with difficulty, his eyes filled as much with love as with pain.

'Kyky.' He tried to smile and a trickle of crimson seeped from the corner of his mouth. 'I told you once that I would joyfully give my life to save yours. Today I am filled with joy that I have done so.' His voice was weak and faltering, his breath rapid and shallow. With the last of his strength he lifted a trembling hand and touched the tears flowing down her cheek. 'You know I have always loved you, and I have always known that I could never have you. You didn't love me, even though you tried. But I could keep you safe, and that I have done. Do not cry for me, my beloved Kyky. I go through this doorway at peace and content.'

'Kulak!' But he was gone, what light that remained in his eyes fluttering into darkness like a candle flame extinguished. She bent her head and kissed his forehead, then gently drew his eyelids closed. She may not have loved him as he had longed for, as a lover, but as a friend he had held her heart more dearly than anyone she had ever known, and she wept for him bitterly. He had sacrificed his life to save her and now her heart was breaking.

'Kyky?' Dar-Ra was standing there, tears in his eyes, staring down at the lifeless body of his friend at whose side he had fought so many battles. He knelt beside Kyky and he too bent to kiss Kulak's forehead in a last goodbye. With a monumental effort, he forced down his grief and stood. There would be time to mourn him later. For now, they had come here for a purpose and that purpose must be fulfilled. Kulak would not have held back his anger if they had given up at his loss. Kyky looked up at him, finally becoming aware that the clamour of battle had silenced.

'We must find Muu-Nan, Kyky, or he will have died for nothing.' He held his hand out to her.

She nodded mutely and let him pull her to her feet, seeing properly for the first time the slaughterhouse that surrounded her and sickened by it. The floors ran crimson, corpses and disconnected limbs scattered across its sticky surface. How many had died here?

'They're all dead,' Dar-Ra informed her flatly. 'Around forty of them. We have ten dead and fifteen wounded, ten seriously, most of whom are unlikely to survive until tomorrow.' The hall echoed with their groans and cries.

'We've searched this building. There's nothing here. That is the only other possible place where Gileada can be.' He pointed to the far building, a squat, windowless structure of dark grey stone with a single, closed door set a little way right of centre.

Chapter 47

Accompanied by thirteen of their unwounded companions, Kyky and Dar-Ra marched brazenly up to the silent stone building. There was little point in sneaking around any longer. Anyone inside had to know of their presence by now, all element of surprise having vanished at their first assault and the uproar of the battle that had ensued.

As expected, the door wouldn't budge. It wasn't a problem for long. Jalk, bruised and battered and still fuelled with adrenalin from the fight, seized a battle-axe from the dead troops' weapons haul and with a din to wake the dead made short work of the thick wooden planks which quickly splintered and cracked under the onslaught. The interior was gloomy and dark, lit only by the small amount of sunlight that filtered through the wrecked door. Torches sat unlit in wall sconces. There was nothing else there. Where was the skull?

'He's here, close by. I sense him,' Kyky muttered. 'Only where? Where ARE you, Muu-Nan?'

'Here. Look.'

Now that their eyes had accustomed to the low light, they could clearly make out footprints marking the dust on the floor, all leading to... Nowhere. They just stopped.

'Not another secret door,' Jalk groaned.

'It all looks solid.' Portek was pushing hard at the stone walls. 'There has to be some mechanism to open it, though only the gods know where.'

'Follow the birds.'

'What?'

'I don't know. The words just popped into my head.' Kyky retorted. "*Follow the birds.*" Maybe Muu-Nan is helping... Only there aren't any birds here.'

'Yes, there are.' Dar-Ra pointed excitedly at the wall they were facing. 'I can just about make them out. Carved into the stone.'

He snatched one of the torches from its sconce and struck a flint. The dusty head sparked and then flared, revealing faint lines etched onto the wall. They were worn and ancient, the all but vanished marks of an ancient engraving: battles, a queen leading her army, a king on his knees, and hovering above them all were several strange dish-shaped structures from the underside of which sinuous lines traced downwards. Next to those unfamiliar objects, a line of seven eagles flew right to left, beak to tail feather.

Birds. Eagles were birds. The images were beyond the reach of most of them except Loras, the tallest by far, who stood a good head above the others. Kulak would have been able to see too if he was here, Kyky brooded, but Kulak was... No, she wouldn't go there. Not now. Grieving – proper gut-wrenching, heart-crushing grieving – would come later when the Heart of Regulus was safely back in their hands.

Loras touched his finger to the wall, tracing the outline of the eagles to the tip of the front-most beak and then on to the far corner of the wall, pressing as he went. Nothing. He turned, discouraged.

'Follow the birds. FOLLOW! Go the other way.' Kyky was hopping with impatience.

Loras moved to the tail of the last bird and began to track his fingers back in a level line to the opposite corner. He had gone around a third of the way when he stopped and peered at the wall. 'There's a tiny depression in the stone here. I can't see it very well, but I can feel it.' He squinted. 'It could be a star, or a sun?' He pressed and waited. Nothing happened. Nothing moved. The wall in front of them remained as solid and unbroken as before.

Only... The hidden entrance wasn't in the wall.

'Look out! The floor.' Portek leaped back in alarm as a large square of paving beneath his feet dropped and slid sideways. Flickering candlelight spilled up and out over the flagstones, illuminating a flight of steps that led downwards.

'They're coming.'

Running feet sounded below; a split second later, five heavily armed men charged up the stairs and into the room, forming a protective ring around the trap door, their faces set and their weapons raised. Five. Against Dar-Ra and his fourteen resolute, if exhausted, companions, there could be only one outcome. The battle was bloody but brief.

Dagger in hand, unsure of what awaited them in the underground room, Kyky led the way down the staircase, slick scarlet with blood from the battle. It spiralled for twenty steps or so down into a small circular vault no more than thirty paces in diameter, whose ceiling shimmered iridescence and whose walls glowed golden with symbols traced in what appeared to be flowing, liquid light. Kyky shivered. The whole space had an unearthly feel, as if it had landed here from a strange and unfamiliar world.

Thirteen large candles set on slender metal stands encircled the perimeter of the chamber, casting an unsteady light. Opposite the staircase, hard against the wall, was an octagonal column of glittering black stone, crowned with a polished gold disc as thick as a man's thumb. On top of the disc, gazing at her through his blank eye sockets, was Muu-Nan.

In front of him stood a giant of a man, taller even than Kulak had been, strong and muscular with a shock of thick, black hair and dark, almost bronze skin. He wore a long purple cloak and oiled leather vest over a silken tunic that reached half-way down his thighs, and a sword belt of dark leather embossed with golden skulls circled his waist. The scabbard was empty, the weapon in his hand, a massive blade that glittered blood crimson in the candlelight. Portek recognised him immediately, the face seared onto his memory the moment when, across the battlefield, he had seen him plunge that same sword into first his king, Karga, then Amisi.

'You,' he hissed, fury flaming in each word. 'You murdered my king.'

'A necessary sacrifice,' the giant snarled, unfazed by the numbers facing him. 'Now leave, before I slaughter every one of you,' Looking at him, dwarfing over the tallest of their men, Kyky believed he could do just that.

'One against fifteen? I don't fancy the odds.' Dar-Ra had stepped forward and was bluffing it out, challenging him. 'We've come for justice, to avenge King Karga, his beloved – our beloved – Amisi and to take back the Heart of Regulus.'

The giant laughed, genuinely amused, Kyky thought. 'You can try, little man. You will fail, as all those who challenge me fail.' Arrogance dripped from his tongue. 'I am Kri-Angar, son of Har-ka, son of Piontas. The Skull of Arcturus was stolen from my ancestor, Horin Shadowchaser at the fall of Yo'tlàn and my fathers have been seeking to regain it ever since. I, Kri-Angar, have succeeded when all before me failed. I have earned my title to it and I will not relinquish it again. With the Skull of Arcturus in my possession, I will never be defeated. Every land I conquer will be the evidence of my power and might. Now tell me, little man, who are you to think you can take it from me?'

'You are nothing but a murderer and a thief,' Kyky hissed. 'Muu-Nan is not yours to take.'

'You think you can take it from me?' The sneer that crossed his face made the girl even angrier. 'Me, Kri-Angar, descendant of Horin Shadowchaser, first among the Dark Ones and conqueror of Atlantis? No, you are wrong. It is not *yours* to take, girl.'

'The Heart of Regulus chose us as his Guardians. We shall have him – and your life.' Fearlessly, Kyky stood strong before Kri-Angar. 'You killed Karga, a good and just man in whose possession Muu-Nan had chosen to stay and you slaughtered our dear Amisi. Today, your men killed my friend Kulak. For those crimes, if no other, you will pay with your blood.'

Even before she had finished speaking, Kyky fell to her knees. Some malevolent force was sucking the energy from her muscles, her nerves and her will, and Kri-Angar was controlling it. She had no strength to fight. She stared up at him. This was no mere man. He was a sorcerer, able to draw on the powers of the darker dimensions to help him. Turning her head, she saw with dismay that the others had fallen prey to the same force.

But his wasn't the only unseen power in the room. Soft, tinkling chimes fluttered in, filling her mind and prickling through the cells of her body. The heavy blanket of inertia that enveloped her began to lift. She turned her head to look at the skull; he blazed with light. Muu-Nan was freeing them from Kri-Angar's control. Rapidly her strength returned and with it came the absolute certainty that the sorcerer could not win. He was one, however strong; they were fifteen. And they had Muu-Nan.

The Dark One sensed the change and for a fleeting moment, doubt flashed in his eyes. It was enough. Dar-Ra and his men noticed it and it spurred them into action.

'On him!' someone yelled, and fifteen blades flashed in the candlelight.

The fight was short and brutal, punctuated by the cries of those cut down in the attack. Kri-Angar fought fiercely and skilfully, his reach long, his reactions swift, but he was no match for fifteen determined warriors. Nonetheless, by the time that it was over, five more of Dar-Ra's group lay dead or dying and another half a dozen nursed wounds of varying severity. Kri-Angar lay face up on the blood-slippery floor, his robes staining scarlet from its touch. Still very much alive. Blood trickled into his left eyebrow from a cut on his scalp and there was a deep slice to his right arm, which had effectively disabled him and led to his defeat. Neither was a mortal blow.

Dar-Ra straddled the stricken, prone man whose chin was tilted awkwardly back trying to escape the tip of the blade pressed into the skin of his throat. There was no fear in the Dark One's eyes, only blazing fury and hatred.

'You have won this battle, it seems,' he hissed, 'but do not think that this is the end. Even though you will be rid of me, I swear to you now that others just like me will come after. They will come down through the years, through the generations, for as long as it takes to reclaim what is rightfully ours. The day will come when all the thirteen Skulls of Light are in our possession. You will not be victorious forever.'

'Put an end to him. It'll be one less jackal to worry about.' Portek glowered hatred for this man who had murdered his King.

Dar-Ra nodded and gripped on the hilt of his blade even more firmly. Kyky's hand on his arm halted the thrust.

'No.' He glanced across at her, confused. 'Not that way. Bring him to the courtyard.'

A short while later, a corpse wearing a long purple cloak and oiled leather vest over a silken tunic that reached half-way down its thighs swung in the air currents that swept around the summit of the black pinnacle, lifeless fingers still clawing at the thick rope that encircled its neck. Five hundred feet below, the remainder of Karga's men clapped and cheered.

Dar-Ra sank to the ground, spent, and Kyky dropped beside him.

'What now?' he asked wearily.

She smiled. 'We take the Heart of Regulus home. We return him to the Great Stone Lion.'

Chapter 48

'Wait.' As they crested the low rise to the north of the sleeping City, Kyky came to a halt. 'It's not safe.'

Since their rescue of Muu-Nan, and with Amisi dead, she had been the channel chosen by the skull to receive his guidance. Twenty-three warriors waited for her next words, those who remained from the fifty who had started out from Karga's City. The others lay in stone-covered graves at the base of the rock tower. Kyky spoke slowly, piecing together the thoughts and sensations Muu-Nan was passing to her.

'Our City has changed, as we were forewarned. The old Pharaoh is dead, murdered. His successor is weak. He lives in fear that he will lose his throne and to protect himself, he has surrounded himself with a small group of men who claim to be powerful sorcerers and allies. He has given them virtually unlimited power and freedom.'

She paused, concentrating. 'They control him with tricks and guile. He is being deceived and he refuses to see it.' She looked up, concern darkening her expression. 'Muu-Nan must not fall into his hands, nor those of his puppet-masters.'

'What then? The plan was to return Muu-Nan into the trusted hands of Pharaoh and through him to its rightful place in the Great Stone Lion.' Jalk looked at the others in dismay. 'What do we do now? Turn around and leave again?'

'No, we stay.' Dar-Ra spoke firmly. 'Muu-Nan guided us back here, which means that this is where he –

and we – need to be. Though why, and now where, I have no idea!' He shrugged helplessly. 'The one certainty is that, the way it stands, Muu-Nan must stay hidden. If those so-called sorcerers learn he is here, they'll stop at nothing to get their hands on him. And you can bet they won't use him for the good and wellbeing of all.'

Lorin spoke up. 'Someone has to go into the City and find out exactly what the situation is. Neither you nor Kyky can go. There's a risk you'll be recognised.' He held up his hand, stalling Dar-Ra's objections. 'I know that it's been a long time and that the chances of that are low. Still, it's possible and the consequences of that would be savage, for all of us.

'I suggest that a few of us, no more than three or four, enter the City when the gates open at daybreak. We'll simply be travellers heading west, looking for food and rest in the heat of the day. We'll find out what we can without raising suspicion and leave before nightfall, supposedly to put in some distance in the cool of the evening.'

'Alright,' Dar-Ra reluctantly agreed, 'but not you.' The big man was about to object when Dar-Ra continued. 'You look too much like a soldier and you'd undoubtedly attract some unwelcome attention.' He looked at Portek who nodded and called out names.

'Kisto, Hartos, Mikaste, are you up for the task?' The three men he'd named were ideal, their slight build and open faces masking completely their deadly combat skills. They nodded, grinning. The tedium of their long trek was about to break.

'The rest of us can't stay here. We'll be too exposed when the sun comes up. We have to move to somewhere less open.' Portek scanned the landscape as he spoke.

'Over there. That jagged ridge overlooking the plateau.' He gestured to the dark silhouette that reared up into the barely lighter sky to the south of where they rested.

Dar-Ra nodded. 'I remember it. It's rough, difficult ground, covered in rocks and hidden dips. We can hide amongst the boulders at its foot until Kisto, Hartos and Mikaste return with the information we need, then we'll decide on our next move.'

* * * * *

The three soldiers returned just after sunset, tired and sombre.

'It's not a good place to be.' Mikaste dropped to the ground. 'It's quiet. Too quiet. The City is under strict martial law with soldiers everywhere patrolling the streets and alleyways, handing out beatings and arrests for any perceived offence. Every stranger who enters the gates is searched and questioned. At length.'

'We didn't learn much,' Kisto added. 'The people are reluctant to talk. They're afraid, really afraid, and understandably so. It would only take a wrong glance for them to be marched off and executed as traitors.'

'What we did find out is that Pharaoh arrested all the Holders from the temple of the Great Stone Lion on the urging of his 'Council' – that's what these 'sorcerers' are calling themselves. It seems the Holders wielded too much power for their liking. The people were following them, listening to them and obeying them instead of following the new Pharaoh's edicts. Most of them have already been put to death. Those that haven't will be wishing they had. They're being questioned as to the whereabouts of Muu-Nan, and of course, they don't know.'

'But Pharaoh always respected them,' Kyky interrupted, shocked. 'He said that as Holders of the Lion Knowledge and Guardians of its temple and its treasure – the Heart of Regulus – he, who held himself above all others, had to acknowledge their gifts.'

'Not any more. It's all changed now that the new Pharaoh is on the throne. At his Council's command, they've even torn down the head of the Great Stone Lion and replaced it with one bearing Pharaoh's likeness.'

'So that is why we had to take Muu-Nan away. If we hadn't…' Dar-Ra's sentence tailed off as the implications settled over him.

Kyky shivered. The chill of the desert night was creeping across the plateau, but it wasn't just that giving her goose-bumps. It was an uncomfortable sensation that they were being watched. She stared out into the dusk, seeing nothing unusual in the fading light. She shook herself. She had to be imagining it, the questions, doubts and uncertainty that assailed her creating phantoms in her mind. Had their long trek home been for nothing? The skull had brought them to this place; he was meant to be here. Therefore they too were meant to be here. Only how, and where, now that the City and the Great Stone Lion were no longer safe?

'Let's sleep on it,' she yawned. 'Maybe we aren't meant to know yet. Muu-Nan brought us here for a reason and all we can do now is wait for that reason to be revealed.' Right at that moment, none of her companions had a better idea so, settling down amongst the sharp rocks and hard ground, they slept.

'Kyky, wake up.' Dar-Ra was at her side. 'There's a light up on the ridge.'

Sure enough, high above their heads amongst the jagged teeth of rock that thrust up into the sky from the top of the rise like the teeth of some terrifying beast, a sharp point of light swayed in the darkness.

'Soldiers?' She closed her eyes. 'No,' she murmured at last, 'not soldiers. Come on, we have to check it out.'

They woke the others and set off up the hillside, heading for the pinprick of light that darted around like a firefly. The full moon that had been rising when they had settled for the night was now completely hidden by storm clouds that had gathered as they slept, extinguishing its light as well as that from the carpet of stars beneath a thick heavy shroud. They stumbled and tripped at every step, blind in the oppressive darkness, the tiny beacon beckoning them on towards the top of the ridge.

'Where's it gone?' They stared across the craggy spine. The light had vanished.

No, there it was, some way ahead, flickering for a few moments and then vanishing again, teasing and tantalising. Drawing them onwards, inviting them to follow before disappearing again. They were closer now though. Just a little further and they would…

It had gone again, and this time it didn't come back. Was this some demon toying with them before it lured them, unsuspecting, to their deaths?

'What's that?' Some twenty or thirty paces ahead, as far as they could tell in the night's thick blackness, a faint glow nestled in the rocks. This wasn't the flickering orange-yellow dance of a candle flame or lamp. It was unlike anything they had ever seen, a soft, lavender hued light that shone steadily and evenly and cast no shadows. Luk, the nearest, picked his way cautiously towards it; as soon as he approached, it faded and vanished.

'There's nothing here,' he called, puzzled. Unable to see anything, he reached out his hand and touched the rock, still warm from the blazing heat of the day. His fingers met only a blank, unbroken wall of stone. There had to be something here. Slowly, so he didn't miss any possible clue, he edged across the slab. Nothing... nothing... nothing. Wait, what was that?

'Here,' he shouted excitedly. 'There's a lip in the rock and behind it there's a gap. It's not very wide. That has to be where the light went.' He tailed off for a moment and then came a muffled yelp of pain. 'By the gods, it's a squeeze.'

'Luk? LUK?'

A muffled reply. 'There's some kind of passageway inside. It's as black as a tomb.' Luk's indistinct silhouette loomed out of the night. 'By Atum's eyes...'

He rubbed his elbow. It was sending shooting pains up to his shoulder where bone had collided hard with solid rock and scoured off a thick layer of skin.

'Are you sure?' Dar-Ra was at his side, the others making their way over to join him.

'As sure as I can be without light to see by. The entrance is tight then it appears to open out a little. It slopes pretty steeply downwards.'

'Do we go in?' Horin peered over his shoulder into the narrow fissure.

Jalk stepped forward. 'The way I see it, whoever was waving that light wanted us up here. That's why they made such a big deal of it. Well, we're here and the only way forward is into that opening, so that's where we go.' He groaned. 'I hate being underground.'

One by one, and with a considerable amount of cursing from the more well-built men, they pushed through the opening and stood crammed into the narrow passageway beyond. None dared to move too far, knowing that countless unseen dangers might lie in wait.

'Down there. The light.' Kisto called excitedly. Sure enough, breaking through the relentless blackness some way ahead and below where they stood, a brilliant lavender sphere bobbed along. 'Someone's carrying it.'

'Let's go then.' Jalk was at his shoulder.

'No, wait.' Kyky grabbed his arm. 'We have no idea what's ahead. Even if whoever that is down there knows a safe path, we don't. It's too dangerous to follow if we can't see where we're putting our feet.'

'Ironwood. That'll burn slowly and well. I saw some when we came across the foot of the ridge.' Jalk turned and squeezed back out of the entrance. Before long, a pile of iron hard branches from which the tree got its name were lying outside the entrance to the passageway, wrapped in cloth from the men's tunics.

'It hasn't moved.' Luk appeared from inside. 'It's waiting for us.'

'Then let's get going.'

After several attempts, the stone striking on stone sparked and caught the dry fabric, flaring up before settling back into a weak flame that was just enough for them to see half a dozen paces ahead and no more. Far below them the peculiar, unwavering beacon hung motionless in the darkness. It was waiting for them, just as Luk had said.

It led them through a maze of tunnels, always staying in sight now though never letting them get too near or catch a glimpse of whoever was carrying it; allowing them draw a little closer when the route grew more tortuous or uncertain – when the tunnel forked, or they had to turn into a hidden side tunnel – so that they knew which way to go. The makeshift torches flickered and flared, casting eerie shadows on the walls that appeared to move and breathe as they passed by. When the cloth had been consumed by the flames, the iron-hard wood caught. It was poor illumination, but it was enough. Just.

Chapter 49

It was the faintest of glimmers against the blackest of blacks in this underground world, but it was there.

Portek rubbed his aching eyes. 'Is that sunlight? How long have we been wandering around down here?'

'Come on.' Dar-Ra gripped his torch, now barely flickering, and strode forward, looking a lot more confident than he was feeling. 'Let's find out.'

A hundred or so paces more, one more bend in the tunnel. What in Muu-Nan's name was this? In front of them, the underground world was flooded with light. Not the steady white rays of the sun. This radiance was golden, dancing over the walls and roof, constantly moving. Warily, yet consumed with curiosity to discover what other surprises this subterranean labyrinth had in store for them, they pressed on.

It was incredible. They had come out into a vast chamber, illuminated by a thousand or more lamps set around the floor. Once a natural cavern of immense proportions, it had at some time been enhanced by the hand of – who? man? – to create the extraordinary amphitheatre that lay before them. A hundred pillars, hewn from the living stone and carved with symbols that none of them recognised but sensed to be magical and mystical, rose up and were swallowed up in the dark heights. Below where they stood, open-mouthed and lost for words, three stone tiers encircled the perimeter, leading down to the lower floor, which had been levelled from the bedrock and shone like polished marble. Facing them, on the opposite side of the chamber, a long flight of steps of the same material led upwards and in the centre of the floor, a wide marble dais held the massive bulk of a sarcophagus. They stared speechless at the immensity and grandeur of the space. This was larger by far than the Hall of Mirrors in the belly of the Great Stone Lion, larger even than the greatest hall in King Karga's palace. They were like ants, wandering dazed and disoriented in an alien world.

Someone else was here! They were being observed. As one, they spun around to stare at the staircase on the far side of the cavern.

A woman sat there. They would all have sworn that she hadn't been there moments before and yet there she was, watching them with gentle amusement and a welcome in her eyes – as if, somehow, she had been expecting them. She rose and gestured for them to approach.

They walked towards her, spellbound. She stood taller than the tallest of the group, with silver hair that fell to her waist and glinted soft blue and lavender in the candlelight, and sapphire blue eyes that carried within them the light of the galaxies. Around her head, a delicate silver circlet dipped into a 'V' in the centre of her forehead, and the point of the 'V' was set with a lozenge the size of a plum, fashioned from the finest lapis lazuli.

She was strong of body, full-breasted and full-hipped, her form emphasised by her sheer, virtually transparent silver robe that did little to hide the nakedness beneath. But it was her skin that stopped the breath on their lips. It was the vivid blue of a midday sky.

She could not be described as beautiful by the standards of those who looked on her. Her jaw was too square, her features too pronounced and her brows angled sharply upwards to her hairline at the outer edge. She emanated a power, a magnetism, that was irresistible and she bore herself as regally as a queen, yet there was no arrogance in her manner. On the contrary, she carried around her an aura of warmth and approachability.

'Welcome.' Her voice, deep and resonant with the echo of another world, drew the newcomers from her spell. 'I have been waiting for you.'

The group could only stare at her. 'W-Who are you?' Mikaste managed to splutter.

'I am Nemerya. My people were amongst those who, in the far distant past, brought Muu-Nan and the twelve other Skulls of Light to this world. When they left, I remained. Why is not important. When I learned that you were bringing him back to this land, I knew he – and you – would need a sanctuary, a safe place to live, so I waited for you and brought you here. This has been my home for… Well, for as long as I have been here.'

'But...'

She silenced Portek with a flash of her sapphire eyes. 'No questions. It is not necessary. It is not for you to know more about me nor my reason for being here. All you need to know is that this is a safe place for you. If you are cautious and discreet.' She smiled at them and starlight sparkled in her eyes. 'You have been chosen as Muu-Nan's Guardians. He could not have better.

'Know though that some of you must leave this underground world and live in the City as obedient servants of Pharaoh and his Council. You who choose to do this will be the eyes and ears of those who remain in this place. You will be their lifeline, bringing food and information. Yours also is the task of choosing those who will take the place of the Guardians who remain in this underworld when they are taken by age. You will not have to search for them. They will be led to you as you were once led to Muu-Nan, and you will know them when they come.

'You who live above must watch and learn without giving the slightest cause for suspicion and gossip. Work, marry, raise families. Your sons and daughters will take your place when the years take you beyond the veil. Speak of this place to no-one other than those who walk with you and those who come to follow in your footsteps. Choose wisely, dearest ones, for those you draw close to you will be either your salvation or your downfall.'

She smiled again and the air shimmered. 'You have the gratitude and blessings of those who wish to see this world thrive. Your courage, hardships and sacrifices have not been in vain. The golden age that your actions have helped to initiate is still a thousand generations in the future. You will not live to see it, as I will not, yet it will come. One day, when all of humankind awakens from its sleep as you have, it will come. When the people of this world are ready to welcome and embrace the Skulls of Light without fear, greed, or lust for power so that they may once more come together to serve this world as they did before, it will come.'

Her sparkling eyes settled in turn on each of the dazed faces that stared at her. 'Now that you are here, I may leave. May the love and blessings of the Skulls of Light be ever with you.'

'You're going? Where?'

'To rest. To sleep the peace-filled sleep of those whose work is complete. The sleep that will carry me through the veil to a new beginning.' She gestured at the great sarcophagus. 'This will be my bed. Treat me well, dearest ones, that is all I ask. Anoint my flesh with sacred oils. Clothe me in the finest fabrics. Wrap me in soft linens infused with resins and those same sacred oils. Lay me on a bed of soft pillows.

'You will find all you need here. Muu-Nan will teach you how. And when you have laid me to my rest, place the great Skull of Arcturus at my head to watch over me as I journey onwards.

'From there, let him guide you as he has always done. Let him share his infinite wisdom with you. Let him teach you knowledge beyond all you can imagine and show you realities that will dazzle and stretch your minds past every limitation.'

Her smile now was one of deep serenity brushed with the slightest hint of sadness. 'My time is now, and I must leave. My only regret is that I shall not come to know you all. Farewell, blessed Guardians. The Skulls of Light are with you.' No sooner had her words faded in the air than she sank gently to the polished stone of the dais. Fifteen bewildered warriors raced to her side.

'She's dead!' Luk whispered, staring up at his friends in wonder, and not a little fear. 'Just like that. Like she CHOSE to go, and she went.'

'Maybe that's exactly what happened.' Kyky spoke softly. 'There is so much we don't understand about all of this.' With a wave of her half-hand she gestured to the vast amphitheatre and the sarcophagus, the skull she held and the men who stood around her. 'But if she spoke the truth, and there is no reason to doubt it, we are going to learn.'

GEMMA, 4

Chapter 50

I was nervous. Mostly though I was dancing inside with excitement. People loved my books. The stories of the skulls and their brave guardians had, it seemed, touched a nerve – or maybe awakened some ancient, dormant memories? Sales of the first novel in my series, '*The Skull Inheritance*' were sky-rocketing and first indications were that its sequel, '*Cosmic Legacy*', were doing the same. Both were doing far better than I had ever imagined possible. Which was why I was sitting on the London train at half past six in the morning on midsummer's day, speeding through the beautiful English countryside on my way to a book-signing event at a slightly off-beat bookshop in Covent Garden. I relaxed back into my seat, watching the trees that edged the track fly past in a kaleidoscope of greens.

Life had settled down. I no longer jumped at the random, unexpected bumps and thumps that were an inherent part of living in a four hundred year old house. The day that Gileada had spoken to me, I had made the conscious decision to set my fears aside as much as I humanly could and to trust that someone, somewhere, was keeping a close protective watch over us, just as Cathy had said.

The train pulled into Paddington Station dead on time. I had plenty of time before I had to be at the bookshop and the sun was shining, promising a pleasantly warm day to come, so I decided to walk rather than catch the Tube and take a detour through Hyde Park, delighting in the fragrant and colourful summer flowers that filled the beds and borders.

I was due to meet my agent and the publisher's representative at eleven o'clock, with the signing starting at half past. It wasn't even ten yet so, with the scent of fresh coffee tickling my nose, I found a pavement table and sat down with a cappuccino to watch the world go by.

* * * * *

Oh hell! I'd lost track of time. It was quarter to eleven already. I threw my chair back and stood up.

'Ouch!'

Hell, number two! I'd shoved my chair back onto the foot of a woman coming out of the shop just behind me. I turned to apologise, and the words died on my lips. The eyes grimacing in pain were of the deepest amethyst, framed with golden hair cut into a short, fashionable – and very expensive – bob. It wasn't the eyes in themselves, nor the bob, that shocked me, however. It was recognition. I knew her. I knew this tall, regal, golden-haired woman with the violet eyes. I had seen her before, but where? Suddenly, it hit me; I; had seen her in my skull dreams.

'Saphira,' I murmured.

The woman blinked as if, for an instant, she had recognised the name, nudging at some ancient, buried memory. Then it was gone.

'I am so sorry.' I found my voice again. 'I'm running late and I didn't look. Are you badly hurt?'

She rubbed her foot gingerly. 'No, it's OK. It was also my fault. I wasn't looking either.' Her voice was deep and rich, carrying the faint trace of a French accent. She looked at me closely. 'You are Gemma Mason, no?'

'Yes, but…'

'I recognise you from your books. I am a big fan.'

'Thank you,' I stammered. Wow! It was the first time anyone had said that, and it felt a bit weird. Good, but weird. It still didn't explain the feeling that I knew her.

'Have we met before? You look so familiar,' I asked.

She shook her head. 'No, we've never met.' She held out her hand and I shook it. 'Sophie. Sophie Montsegur.'

'Pleased to meet you, Sophie.' I glanced at my watch. 'Oh Lord. I don't mean to be rude but I have to run. I am so late. If you're sure you're okay.'

'Yes, of course. Don't worry, I'm fine.'

'Thanks.'

I hurried off. I had dawdled too long over my coffee, relishing people watching, and now there was a real risk that I might not get to the bookshop on time. Even as I rushed along, however, swirling into my growing anxiety at my lateness was the Sophie Montsegur puzzle. Could she really be Saphira, the queen and sorceress once shown to me in my dreams of Gor-Kual, the red skull? Surely it couldn't be. Yet, in this strange world I had been thrown into, I was learning that anything was possible. After all, weren't there times when I found myself living as Haa'nu, High Priestess of the Pyramid Temple? It was with some difficulty that I pushed down that train of thought. I had other priorities to focus on, like apologising for my lateness and my two-hour book signing event.

Yes, I was nervous about it. Would anyone show up or would I be left sitting there like a lemon, twiddling my thumbs and watching the hands of the clock drag around, trying not to look too sad and pathetic? I needn't have worried. When I neared the bookshop I could see that there were at least two dozen people queued up outside with still over half an hour until I was 'on', so to speak.

'There you are, Gemma. We thought you'd got lost.' Carmen, my awesome agent, bustled up to steer me away from the main entrance towards the side door of the shop. 'Best go in this way. It keeps the excitement bubbling if they don't see you until we're ready to rock.'

* * * * *

I threw a surreptitious glance at my watch. One fifteen. Another quarter of an hour to go. The timing had been perfect; only four people still waited patiently in the queue with their copies of '*Cosmic Legacy*'; the new, pristine covers gleamed under the shop lights. The two hours had flown by. I was delighted – and to be honest, a bit shocked – at how many copies of the book I'd sold and my hand ached from holding the pen, signing book after book for a seemingly endless queue of purchasers. Writer's cramp didn't begin to describe it, although I wasn't going to complain about it; it was a good problem to have and I was enjoying myself immensely. The people I'd met had all been so knowledgeable about '*The Skull Inheritance*'. My confidence was flying sky-high and my ego had lapped up every moment, every positive and enthusiastic comment.

'Would you dedicate it to me, please? Alina.' My eyes met those of the young girl standing at the table and suddenly I was filled with the same weird sense of recognition that had swept through me when I had encountered Sophie Montsegur earlier. Only this time, the sensation was a hundred times stronger. My heart was thudding fit to leap out of my chest.

I definitely didn't know her. I was absolutely certain that I had never met her before. She was young, maybe eighteen or nineteen, and tiny, barely five feet tall with such a delicate frame that she looked like a fragile china doll. Amber-gold eyes, heavily lined with black make-up, looked across at me out of a pale, almost white face framed with shoulder-length, raven-black air that flashed purple and indigo where the light caught it.

'Alina,' she repeated. 'A-L-I-N-A.' Spelling it out.

'That's you?'

She nodded.

With difficulty I shook the feeling off and wrote on the fly leaf: *'For Alina, who is here to accomplish a great good.'* God only knows where that had come from, or what it meant! 'Thank you for coming, Alina. And thank you for buying my book.' I said, adding my signature.

'No, thank you.' Tears brimmed on her thickly mascara'd lashes. 'At last I know why I'm here. I begged for a sign and I got one. From you. You confirmed it.' She'd lost me! How had I given her a sign? Before I could ask, she spoke again. 'I've always known I was here, that I'd been born for a particular purpose, only I could never work out what it was. Not until I read *'The Skull Inheritance'*. That's when all the pieces dropped into place.'

'I don't understand…' The sentence died on my lips. Shock, and not a small element of fear, had silenced me.

He was half-hidden by a rank of low bookshelves but it was definitely him. I'd have recognised him anywhere. Jürgens Brinkmann. Mr Shiny Shoes. How long had he been there? Not long, I was certain of that. More importantly, why was he here? Our eyes locked and a flash of irritation swept across his blunt features. He hadn't wanted me to see him. Hastily, he turned away.

Alina! With Mr Shiny Shoes' unexpected – and unwelcome – reappearance, I'd momentarily forgotten about her. I turned back to ask what she had meant.

'She left.' A middle-aged woman stood there holding out a book. 'It's a birthday present for my daughter, Jennifer.' The book slid across the polished tabletop. 'She's a huge fan of yours, Mrs Mason. She's read '*The Skull Inheritance*' at least three times already. Would you write something nice for her? She'd be thrilled.'

It was only by force of will that I stopped my gaze from returning to Mr Shiny Shoes and focussed on my customer, opening the book to the flyleaf and penning a short message. 'I hope you'll enjoy this one as much as '*The Skull Inheritance*'. Wishing you a happy birthday, Jennifer. Best wishes, Gemma Mason.'

As I handed it back, smiling my thanks, I threw a glance over her shoulder. Mr Shiny Shoes had vanished. My smile deepened. In his place, someone else was making his way towards me through the busy store. Joe. He had promised me a late lunch after my stint here had finished and had arrived bang on time to keep that promise.

I signed the last book as he reached my table. 'Hi, superstar. How's it gone?'

'Fabulous.' I hugged him. 'Except…'

'What? What's up, Gems?'

'Mr Shiny Shoes was here. I spotted him a few minutes ago. He's gone now.'

'Back in a tick.' Joe raced out of the shop.

'Gemma, congratulations.' Carmen bustled up. 'You're probably shattered so we won't talk now. I'll call you in the week. Go and have yourself a well-deserved lunch.'

'Thanks for everything, Carmen. Yes, let's talk in a couple of days.' I stood up and stretched. 'I'll say goodbye to the staff and then I'll be off.'

I was on my way out of the door when Joe returned.

'No sign of him,' he said. 'There are a lot of people out enjoying the day and it would have been easy for him to melt into the crowds.' He put his arm around my shoulders and gave me a squeeze. 'I suggest we don't let it put even the tiniest downer on your day. Come on, let's get to our table and you can tell me all about your triumphant entry onto the London literary scene.'

I couldn't help but giggle. Dear Joe. He was right. It had been – with that momentary exception – a fantastic day. Mr Shiny Shoes could wait. What I really wanted to tell him about was my curious encounters with Sophie Montsegur and Alina.

Chapter 51

It couldn't be – yet the image on my computer screen proved otherwise.

'Joe!' I yelled, goose-bumps rippling over my skin, 'Joe! You have to see this.' Footsteps raced up the stairs.

'See what?'

'Look!' I pointed at the screen.

His eyes widened in a disbelief that turned rapidly into an excitement to match mine. There, filling the display, was a photograph of a section of rough, vertically striated black rock, and in the centre of the image…

'The key symbol,' Joe breathed.

We could see every aspect of the indentation in sharp detail, its shape like an 'f' and a 'J' set at one hundred and eighty degrees to each other on a small central ring. An indentation that matched exactly the golden key hidden in my bank safety deposit box.

'He's found it,' Joe sputtered. 'He's only gone and bloody well found it.'

The enormity of the situation suddenly crashed into me.

'He's found Gileada,' I whispered, more to myself than to Joe, the implications tumbling over each other as they arose. If the black skull had been found, it was because it had allowed itself to be found, and if it had allowed itself to be found, it meant that the Skulls of Light were preparing to re-introduce themselves to humankind. To reunite and lead us forward as they had always intended. And if *that* was the case, it was because we, the human race, were ready to welcome them and allow them to guide us. Were we ready? The state of the world implied otherwise and yet… Heaven knows we needed their help. Maybe our growing determination to change things was exactly why the Skulls believed we were ready?

Joe interrupted my speculations. 'It's from van Broek.' It was more of a statement than a question.

I nodded. 'The email came in only a couple of minutes ago.'

We'd heard nothing from Pieter van Broek since the day we'd met at the long-barrow ten months earlier and, while I hadn't completely forgotten about him, as the months had passed he'd slipped further and further from the forefront of my thoughts. If I'm honest, I really hadn't expected to hear from him again, and certainly not with news like this.

I read out the email to Joe. 'Mrs Mason and Mr Cunningham, I told you I'd find it. Here is the proof. Without the key, however, I can go no further. I am certain that, now you see the truth of my story, you are as impatient as I am to set eyes on this incredible object. Will you now agree to let me have the key so that I may gain entry to the cell and recover the black skull?'

'Well?' Joe asked. 'One, are you going to admit to him that you have the key and two, are you going to let him have it?'

'I don't know.' Despite intuitively believing van Broek, I wasn't sure I was ready to trust him. And yet… 'He's found where Gileada is hidden. How could he have done that if the skull hadn't led him there? Surely it wouldn't have done so if he wasn't the person chosen to discover it?'

'What does Tim say?'

I lifted the little obsidian skull from the corner of my desk, which was now his permanent home. As soon as my fingers closed around him, I had my answer. Warmth flooded my body and Gal-Athiel's melodic tones whispered in my mind. 'You know what to do. Follow your feelings. It is time.'

'We say yes. We let him have the key.' I paused. 'I'm not willing to simply hand it over to him though. Olina entrusted it to me; she gave her life to keep it safe. I'm not prepared to let it out of our sight.'

'You're going to take it to him?'

I shook my head. 'I can't. The next month or so is packed with deadlines that I have to hit for my latest manuscript. There's no way I can disappear off, even for just a few days. Much as I'd love to, I simply can't.' I looked at him with a grin. 'But you can.'

'You're joking.'

I wasn't.

'You can't miss out on this, Gemma. It's too huge. You have to be there. You have to come too.'

He was right. It *was* huge. At the same time, buzzing though I was that one of the Skulls of Light would soon be back in the world, no. Oddly, I didn't feel the need to be there. I had a strong sense that this wasn't meant to be my adventure.

'No, Joe, this is for you, not me. Not this time.'

Two days later, I waved him goodbye as he set out on his long journey to northern Norway. There was no way he'd have got the key through any airport security so he was driving, crossing the English Channel into Belgium to travel up through Germany and into Denmark to

Copenhagen where he would catch the ferry to Norway. Hopefully without incident. The key? That was wrapped up well in couple of pillowcases and stored beneath the spare wheel in the boot.

MUU-NAN

PART 5

THE COMPANY OF GUARDIANS

Chapter 52

There were fifteen of them, successors to those first Guardians who had come here so long ago. They had spent their lifetime watching over the sacred skull Muu-Nan and the final resting place of the great queen who had called him to this place, protecting and keeping safe the secret of the underground labyrinth and the Heart of Regulus, as their predecessors had done for generations.

Now the Guardians were under the greatest threat they had ever faced; Pharaoh had learned of Muu-Nan. How, none could say. There had been whispers of strangers who had come to the City, spreading rumours and accusations, and telling stories of bloodshed and betrayal, but they were only whispers. If those strangers had indeed once been amongst them, they no longer were. They had vanished like the dawn mist on the Great River.

No matter, the damage was done. Their stories had reached Pharaoh, stories that told of a magnificent treasure unlike any the world had ever seen; a treasure of such immense power that if he held it as his own, no enemy could to stand against him. It was the treasure, the stories told, on which mighty empires had been built and with the loss of which, they had crumbled. This treasure was a skull but a skull unlike any other. It was an ancient crystal skull of limitless power. As soon as Pharaoh had learned of it, he had determined to find and possess it. His empire was already vast, stretching from the seas in the north to the Great Lake in the South, many months march apart, and was as wide as it was deep, yet it was not enough. He thirsted to rule all of the known – and the unknown – world.

He immediately ordered the Commander of the Imperial Guard to find this treasure by any and all means. His iron fist gripped even more tightly on his people. Spies – soldiers disguised as tradesmen, merchants and labourers – were sent out into the towns and villages to garner any knowledge a loose tongue might give away. Fear of his fury gave birth to suspicion of brother and neighbour alike, and they spoke to condemn in order to save their lives and those of their families. Known dissidents were arrested and questioned. Countless innocent men and women perished in his zealous quest. Nothing. The days and weeks passed with no progress and Pharaoh's obsession grew in equal measure to his frustration. It could only be a matter of time before the net closed in on those who did hold the information he sought.

He summoned his three mystics to him time and time again, demanding information. Though all were powerful men and proven, talented seers – two High Priests in his personal service, the third a sorcerer of renown from the Eastern lands – this morning, as they knelt before Pharaoh, they trembled in the face of his fury.

'My friends,' Pharaoh's voice was terrifyingly gentle and caressing, 'why can you not tell me where to find this treasure? You are the most powerful oracles in my kingdom. You have assured me that it exists and that I will possess it, so tell me. Where is it?'

'We – we do not know exactly, Highness. It is not clear.'

The volcano erupted. 'Tell me,' he thundered, his expression as black and dangerous as his voice. 'Do you think I am a fool? Do you think you can fabricate your tales to humour me? I have had my army searching my kingdom on your word and day after day they come back to me empty-handed, no further forward than before.' His staff struck the marble floor with such ferocity that it shattered the tile beneath, his anger a red-hot wave that hit them with such force that they threw themselves prostrate on the ground.

'Do you speak the truth? Or do you lie to save your miserable skins? Speak! Where does it lie? You!' He pushed the tip of the staff hard against the first mystic's neck, pinning him to the ground. 'Tell me.'

'Within the kingdom, your most holy Highness,' the terrified man gasped.

'Be more precise, Priest. My kingdom is vast. I could spend a lifetime searching and not cover it all.'

'I - I cannot.' He grunted in pain as the staff pressed harder. 'I do not know, Highness.'

'Not good enough, Priest. You, what do you say?' The menace in Pharaoh's voice was palpable as he towered above the next prone, shaking man.

'In... in the south, Highness. Beyond the first great water.' The man's voice wavered in fear. One wrong word and he would be lost, for the truth was that he had no idea where the skull was located or even if it was indeed in the kingdom. He could not form any connection to it at all, but Pharaoh must not know that. He had the bitter suspicion, however, that Pharaoh did know. He squeezed his eyes tightly shut and prayed to Ra for salvation.

'And you, Mystic. What do you say?' The third man was no temple priest. He was from the East, with narrow eyes and a strange pallor to his skin that contrasted strongly with the dark complexions of those around him. He, of the three that lay prone before Pharaoh, had the greatest ability to see beyond the physical and the mundane.

'Highness, the treasure is within this City.' He spoke with a confidence that contrasted starkly with the demeanour of his two companions yet was nevertheless filled with fear. Pharaoh was volatile and unpredictable; no-one could guess how he would react.

'Where?'

'I cannot see more, Highness, only that it lies within the boundaries of the City. He grunted in pain as the staff dug into his spine. 'It is protected by some form of energetic shield.'

'Do you speak the truth, Mystic? Or do you also lie to save yourself?' The menace had deepened.

'I speak the truth, Highness. I swear.'

'It is poor detail but it is the best I have yet received. A City is easier to search than a kingdom.' He gestured to the guard. 'Lock him in his quarters.' Pharaoh bent over him. 'If I find the treasure in the City, as you say, you will be richly rewarded. If not...' The words hung in the air like sword blades.

'And these two, Highness?' The soldier indicated the two unfortunate priests.

'They are no use to me. Execute them.'

* * * * *

Over the next days, the City's streets were overrun with soldiers who searched every building. No possible hiding place was left unturned. No-one was spared. Temples, houses, shops, all were pulled apart in the search for the skull. With each day that passed without its discovery

Pharaoh's fervour – and his temper – blazed more fiercely. On the eighth day, the unfortunate Eastern mystic was dragged into the main square and beheaded. Still they did not find it, and still Pharaoh did not give up the search.

Chapter 53

The breakthrough came, as so many do, by pure chance. A patrol, returning to the City at sunset, encountered two men leading a heavily laden mule away from the gates out onto the plateau. There was little unusual in that other than the timing. Why were they leaving the City at an hour when most would be returning for the night? In normal times, the soldiers would have paid them little attention, but these were not normal times. Pharaoh's obsession, and the unpleasant consequences of failure, meant that everything and anything even a little out of the ordinary was viewed as suspicious. The patrol commander, who had already experienced the lash of his Pharaoh's rage, was in no mood to hesitate. When the two men could not give a solid reason for being out with a mule laden with grain, fruit and vegetables, he immediately arrested them, dragged them back to the City and handed them over to Pharaoh's head inquisitor, Dak.

They were ordinary men, one a trader, the other a builder. Neither was particularly strong or brave or special. Nevertheless, they were dedicated to their cause and would not willingly reveal the secrets they held. But no matter how courageous and committed they were, even the strongest, bravest and most loyal could not withstand for long the horrors of Pharaoh's torture chambers. Dak's proudest boast was that none of his 'guests' had ever died before they had revealed their most precious secrets. It was, perhaps, the wisest who spoke soonest, their reward a swift death that spared them days, if not weeks, of unimaginable agony. Those few who endured spent their last days in a living hell before they inevitably broke under the brutal, if skilful, interrogation. As would the two terrified prisoners.

Pharaoh was impatient. These men had information that he wanted and he was not prepared to wait even one day to prise it from them. He sent his guards to arrest the men's families and bring them to the prison, knowing well that while a man might refuse to speak to save himself torment, no husband would keep his silence while he watched his beloved wife tortured, nor a father his child.

The plan worked. The moment the builder saw the white, panic-stricken face of his wife, pleading for mercy as their daughter, barely nine years old, was torn sobbing and screaming in terror from her arms, his tongue loosened and he told all he knew, gabbling out his secrets, words falling over words to save his family. When at last he fell silent, his broken body slumped in its chains. He had betrayed them – his friends and his beliefs, the Heart of Regulus and his Guardians. But he had had no choice if he was to save his family. He had saved them, hadn't he?

'I've told you all I know.' Uttered through split, bleeding lips, the plea came as a ragged whisper. 'Please, let them go.' Desperate, dull eyes begged.

He didn't see it until the last moment. A vicious, curve-bladed knife flashed into view and disappeared into his heart filling his chest with a flash of red-hot agony that turned a breath later to an icy cold that flooded his arms, his belly, his neck. Somewhere in the distance, he thought he heard a woman wail. The world turned dark, and a last, rasping breath rattled in his throat. The tears and screams of his wife and daughter went unheeded when rough arms seized them and dragged them to their cell. They were the family of a traitor and Pharaoh would decide their fate, death or slavery.

The second man, the trader, had no family to persuade him. He was an only child, his parents both long dead, and he had never married. Death did not come so quickly or easily to him, yet he was spared prolonged torment by the blessing of a weak heart that mercifully gave up the battle to live. It was the first time Dak had failed.

*   *   *   *   *

The builder had revealed that a group of warriors known as the Company of Guardians held a priceless treasure safe in the honeycomb of caves under the plateau on which the City and its massive monuments had been built, and that they defended the secrets of their existence and their treasure zealously. Their existence was known only to a handful outside of the sanctuary; less than half of those had ever met one. They allowed no-one close enough to learn where they went after any encounter.

His role, and that of the trader, was to provide them with supplies once a month at the waxing quarter moon. He had never seen where they had gone, he had sworn, his voice breaking and his gaze never leaving the terrified faces of his wife and daughter. Each time, he met them at a large rock at the foot of the second ridge – one or two of them, never more – and always at night, when they were quickly swallowed up by the dark shadows of the craggy terrain. Once he had tried to follow but had quickly lost them in the broken ground, he had blurted out, hoping his tormenters would go more gently with him if he volunteered more than they were asking. The dim figures of the Guardians had simply melted away into the night.

It was not the news that Pharaoh wanted to hear. The Guardians were clearly shrewd and intelligent, trusting no-one more than was necessary, even those who served them loyally. When he demanded more, Dak assured him that there had been no more to be learned. Years of experience had given the head inquisitor a sharp instinct that told him without error when his 'guest' was telling the truth and when he or she was lying or holding back. The builder, Dak vowed, had given all he had to give. The threat to his wife and child had ensured that.

Pharaoh had wanted more but maybe, just maybe, it would be enough. With the builder's confession, he now knew that the treasure was hidden under the hills, and he knew the location of the meetings with the Guardians. The entrance to the Sanctuary had to be close by. With that information, it would only be a matter of hours before the skull was in his hands.

He summoned the Captain of the Palace Guard. 'Take every man you have and scour the ridge. The entrance to the Sanctuary is there, somewhere. Find it. Find the sacred Skull for your Pharaoh and god.'

'Yes, Highness. Those who defend it?'

'Do not leave even one alive.'

'Yes, Highness.'

'And Captain...' The soldier waited. 'Don't come back until you have it. If you fail in this, you will suffer my deepest displeasure.'

'Highness.' The Captain bowed deeply.

Within the hour a thousand soldiers were pounding across the plateau towards the high ground.

Chapter 54

The young servant boy Al-Azar worked in the palace kitchens, the perfect position to hear all the gossip and grapevine news that flew about continually within the royal walls like flocks of excited sparrows. That morning, he had heard the whispers he had been dreading. They had swept through the palace like the wind – 'The prisoners have talked. Pharaoh knows where the treasure lies.' – and everyone had breathed a little easier hoping that Pharaoh's temper and its repercussions would soon ease a little. Everyone that is but Al-Azar. Fear twisted in his guts. Pharaoh's men would even now be marching towards the Sanctuary. He had to warn the Guardians, or was it already too late? Perhaps. Nevertheless, he had to try. He had to get to the Sanctuary.

The salver of luscious fruits he was carrying to the first wife slipped from his hands and crashed to the floor, spilling its colourful contents onto the white marble and staining it with their juices. 'Heart of Regulus, help me,' he prayed, turning on his heels to race back down the corridor, paying no attention to the protests of those he elbowed aside, avoiding the hands thrust out to grab him. Behind him, shouts ordered him to stop. He ignored them.

They must not catch him. Adrenalin gave his legs a speed he hadn't know he possessed and he twisted and turned through the narrow passageways of the palace's working areas until, at last, there it was – the small door that led onto the maze of alleyways outside the palace walls. The next obstacle was the sentry who stood guard outside, day and night. Al-Azar prayed that the soldier would not have yet received word of the commotion he had caused inside the palace.

Anxiously listening for footsteps on his trail, the young servant fought to slow his breathing. He had to act as if everything was normal, as if he was simply heading out on a minor errand the way he often did. He smoothed down his robe and his hair, opened the door and stepped through, smiling casually. The door was unguarded, the sentry nowhere in sight. Thanking the gods for the unexpected stroke of luck the boy set off down the alley at a steady walk. Running would only draw unwanted attention. Once outside the City walls, he would be able to move much more quickly.

* * * * *

No-one outside of the small band of Guardians knew where the entrance to the Sanctuary was located. No-one, that is, except Al-Azar. Since he had been a small child, he had spent every free hour roaming the valleys and hills surrounding the plateau and he knew them as well as he knew every contour and pock-mark on his face. Although those free hours were scarce since he had been sent to work in the palace kitchens, during the night hours that were his own he still headed out to roam. One night he had been exploring the ridge at the far end of the plateau when he had spotted two silhouettes weaving their way quickly up the slope towards him.

Al-Azar was small and wiry and as stealthy as a wild cat. He had had no problem following them unseen and unheard to where they had vanished through a narrow fissure in the rock. From that point, he had had a clear view over the plateau, the palace and massive stone monuments beyond, the three enormous pyramids clad in white limestone that glistened in the moonlight, guarded by a strange and equally enormous stone figure with the body of a lion – or perhaps a sacred cat – and the head of a long-dead Pharaoh.

He knew who the dark figures were; the Company of Guardians, sworn to protect of the Heart of Regulus, the sacred Skull that Pharaoh coveted. Through the generations, his family – his father, his grandfather, his grandfather's father, and his father before him, back down the ancestral line into forgotten times – had served them in the outside world. He had learned of it on his fourteenth name day, only a few moons earlier, and he had not yet learned what that meant for him.

That night, he had followed them inside, feeling his way hesitantly a few steps down the steep uneven passageway that was lit only by the faintest hint of moonlight filtering in from the entrance above. Of those he was following, there was no sign. No flickering flame from a torch, no footsteps. He stopped, darkness closing in around him and plucking at his skin like dead men's fingers. What was he doing? He had no light and no map. If he went any further into the blackness, it was unlikely he would ever find his way out again. Self-preservation had overridden curiosity; he had turned and clambered back out into the moonlight.

Tonight was not the time or place for fear. As he ran from the City, he prayed silently to the gods and to the Heart of Regulus to guide him and keep him safe. He was wise to pray. The lower slopes of the hillsides crawled with soldiers working their way inch by inch upwards, searching behind every boulder, in every animal burrow, at the root of every shrub and tree for a gap large enough for a man to pass. Behind them, Al-Azar crouched in the shelter of an overhanging rock and watched them comb the ground. They were still a long way from the entrance, which was way off to the right. At this speed, they wouldn't reach it for several hours.

He crept out and away into the night, circling the troops, darting from shadow to shadow, keeping low so that his silhouette would not stand out in the day-bright moonlight, his bare feet making no sound. It took him far longer than he would have wished before he finally squeezed between the rocks he remembered and found himself in total blackness. The moon had not reached the point in its journey where it would fall through the entrance as it had on that last occasion.

What now? Every step promised danger. The natural tunnel was steep, he remembered, the floor rough and covered in loose rocks. It was so dark that, he couldn't see his hand when it touched his nose. If he moved from where he was, with the entrance only two steps behind him, he would become completely disoriented and perhaps never find his way out again. What was he to do? Even if he could feel his way along the walls, who could say what waited for him beneath his feet?

He blinked and rubbed his eyes. A tiny pinprick of light was moving slowly up towards him. Had he angered the spirits of this place by coming here? Were they coming to exact their vengeance for disturbing their peace? He stood frozen, unable to move.

'It's a boy!' The gruff voice betrayed its astonishment. Though softly spoken, its authority filled the tunnel. Al-Azar woke from his trance. Two middle-aged men, strong and well-built despite their advancing years, stared down at him.

'Shhh, they might hear you.' He gestured back towards the entrance.

'Who might? Who are you? What are you doing here?'

'Pharaoh's soldiers. They're searching the ridge for the entrance to the Sanctuary.' Even in the half-light, he couldn't miss the worried look that passed between the two men.

'Who are you?' the man repeated.

'Al-Azar. I-I work in the palace... a-and for the cause of the Guardians, as does my father, and his father before him. Pharaoh captured the men who were bringing you your supplies and forced them to talk. He knows the entrance to the Sanctuary is on this ridge, though not the exact location. It's crawling with soldiers out there. They could find this entrance at any moment.'

'I want to know how *you* found it...' the second man growled. 'Oh, never mind. That's the least of our worries. Come boy, follow us.'

They led the way down the precariously steep slope so quickly that Al-Azar, agile as he was, found it hard to keep up. He stumbled and tripped across the uneven floor, edged painfully slowly sideways across perilous ledges no wider than his feet, inky blackness hiding everything outside of the pool of light cast by the torches, and making it all the more terrifying for that. The men with him knew their way unerringly and never missed a step. Without them, Al-Azar would have been hopelessly lost within seconds.

After what felt like a lifetime, the structure of the tunnel changed. The floor was now level and even, and the walls beneath his fingertips were smooth and polished. Men had made this, or at the very least had tamed the natural rock into an elegant corridor illuminated by rows of lamps, crystal and mirrors that reflected the light into every corner.

They emerged from the passage into a vast soaring amphitheatre that stretched easily two hundred paces across, with a roof so high it disappeared into the shadows, and lit from above by a thousand and more lamps whose light streamed down to fall onto the floor in waves of soft white. The walls were covered with figures – people, symbols, strange objects – that looked to be drawn in flowing, liquid gold.

All this Al-Azar barely registered. His attention had been captured firmly by the object in the centre of the amphitheatre, a stone dais bearing an enormous sarcophagus surrounded by blazing torches. Five steps led up to the dais, which had been formed from a slab of smooth white marble and was supported by nine thick legs, each intricately carved with trailing vines.

'Come, boy.'

There was no time to stare. His companions had already descended to the floor of the amphitheatre where a small group of around a dozen men and women waited, watching him uneasily.

'Who is this? Why do you bring him to the heart of the Sanctuary when none but the Guardians may enter here?' The man who stepped forward to speak was as old and as thin as a skeleton, his parchment skin stretched so tight over his skull that Al-Azar feared it would tear.

'We found him inside the entrance, Vayu. He says Pharaoh has learned that the treasure in within these caves and that his soldiers are even now searching for a way in. Much too close for comfort, it would seem.'

'Is this true?' Vayu turned to the boy, ice-blue eyes boring into his dark ones, seeking out lies and truths.

'Yes, sir. I-I came to warn you.' The boy told his story once more, the words tumbling over each other in his rush. 'There are at least a thousand of them. They were already moving up the hillside when I slipped past them. They could have found the entrance and be inside the hill by now.'

'They'll never find us in this labyrinth.' A stocky, bearded man spoke up. 'Even if they do, we can defend this place against any attack.'

'Possibly, but for how long?' Vayu's calm, pale gaze turned to him. 'Pharaoh is no fool. As soon as he finds the entrance, he'll know his information is correct. He'll set every last man he has on us and won't stop until he has the Heart of Regulus in his hands. We are warriors, yes, but we are only fifteen. He has an entire army to set against us. And we must face it, some of us are not as young and strong as we once were. We would fall, and do so within a very short time. If Muu-Nan stays here, sooner or later, Pharaoh will capture him. That we cannot permit. It would not only be our lives and honour that we would forfeit should that come to pass.'

'Then what?' A third man spoke up. Although he appeared still young, he was stooped and bald-headed resembling a scholar far more than a warrior. 'Do we flee? If so, where would we go? Pharaoh would have no difficulty in hunting us down and slaughtering us without mercy. And what of the Queen?' He gestured towards the stone sarcophagus.

'We must leave her.' Though the old man's eyes were damp with tears, his voice was strong. 'She will understand. She brought the Heart of Regulus here to safeguard him. His safety will still be her priority in death.'

'We can't all go.' Every head turned towards the scholarly Guardian. 'If we do, the soldiers will know that Muu-Nan is no longer here and will hunt us down. I propose that only two or three leave, taking Muu-Nan to safety. The rest of us will remain here and fight, fulfilling our pledge to protect the Queen and the Heart of Regulus. It will provide a diversion, giving those who go a greater chance of success, and we will know that we have not abandoned our vows.'

A low murmur rippled through the gathering, hushing when Vayu spoke.

'It is a wise plan. If we stay and fight, it is likely that Pharaoh's men will believe that they have taken us by surprise and that the skull must still be somewhere in these tunnels. After all, why else would we be here fighting instead of fleeing? Mikos, Daan. Take Muu-Nan and the boy and go. Now! Travel light. Take only that which you will need to sustain you over the next day or so.' He clasped the men's hands, unable to hide his emotions, letting the tears fall onto his papery cheeks. He had known these men for nearly a lifetime. He would not see them again.

'Farewell, my friends. It has been my honour. May the gods and the blessing of the Queen go with you. Now go. Hurry!'

'Come.' The man, Mikos, one of the two who had brought Al-Azar down into this place, seized his arm. 'While I cannot promise that you will live if you come with us, I can guarantee that if you stay here, you'll die before the day is over.'

Daan, a thickset man whose pale skin was sprinkled with brown speckles, and with a shock of unruly orange hair, a peculiar colouring that Al-Azar had never encountered before, stepped down from the dais wrapping a heavy, roughly spherical object in a length of cream linen. He met the eyes of the gathered group for a long momentin a silent goodbye. After centuries, the Company of Guardians was at an end. Abruptly, Mikos turned and seized a torch, thrusting another into Al-Azar's hand.

'We have to move fast, boy. Keep up.'

Daan was already hurrying away, his flaming light held high. They sprinted to catch up, leaving the vastness of the lamplit amphitheatre to plunge into the dark maze of tunnels beyond.

Chapter 55

A chink of light pierced the gloom of the tunnel.

'That's our way out,' Daan pointed.

Al-Azar had no idea where they were, though he was certain that they were in a different place to where he had entered the underground world. This time, there had been no steep ascent, as he so clearly remembered from before.

The sun was high. It had to be long past noon, he guessed from the slanting rays. Dust motes danced in the golden light. Daan moved forward, flattening himself against the rough wall as he glanced out, only to pull back sharply.

'Three soldiers. Coming up the hill.'

'What are they doing here?' Mikos murmured. 'We're a long way from the ridge. They can't be searching here, not yet.'

Daan risked another look, keeping well to the shadows at the edge of the opening. 'My guess is that it's a regular patrol returning to the City. They don't appear to be poking around.' He listened; in the half-light, Al-Azar caught a smile forming on his face. 'No, they're not looking for us. They're discussing the joys of bedding their wives. They probably don't even know about the search. Yet.'

They waited in silence for the soldiers to pass. The footsteps and the voices grew louder then faded to nothing as the soldiers rounded the bluff and disappeared.

'Move.' Mikos' heavy hand shoved Al-Azar forward after Daan. 'They may not have been searching for us. There's no guarantee the next patrol won't be.'

The wiry boy slipped easily through the crack, not so his two companions. Wide of shoulder and deep of chest, they were uncomfortably large for the small opening and had to squeeze painfully through, scouring skin from shoulders and torso as they did so. Neither man even grunted with the pain.

Outside, Al-Azar was surprised to discover that he did not recognise the landscape. He had roamed the hills and ridges far and wide since he was a small child but this was new to him. He had little time to think about it. Daan's hand on his shoulder pushed him flat to the ground behind a group of scrubby shrubs out of sight of any watching eyes, while his other raised to his lips warning him not to speak. Around them, all was quiet with no hint of the swarm of troops searching desperately for the entrance to the Sanctuary only a short distance away.

Mikos placed his lips to Daan's ear. 'I had imagined they would have found their way in by now,' he breathed.

'Muu-Nan and the Queen are with us.' Daan lifted his head slightly to scan the landscape ahead of them. 'We can't assume they can continue to protect us, though. We have to put as much distance between us and Pharaoh as we can, as quickly as we can.'

'Where do we go?' Al-Azar stared at the two men. They would know, wouldn't they?

'Away from here,' Mikos growled. 'After that, who can say?' He turned to Daan. 'West?'

'West,' Daan agreed.

Crouching low to the scrubby ground and using what vegetation there was for cover, they crept down the slope to the shallow open valley floor. Here, cover was even sparser. They slipped from boulder to tree to hollow, all senses on high alert, scanning the high ground in all directions before moving on, until they crested the top of the next ridge and dropped out of sight of the sharp eyes of any look-out who was surveying the terrain from the hills they had just left. The sun was going down when they heard the faint blast of a distant horn. Mikos halted and stared back.

'They've found it. The entrance. May the gods help them.'

'Will they find the Sanctuary?' Would it be possible in that subterranean honeycomb, Al-Azar wondered?

'Eventually,' Daan muttered, his pale skin flushed red. 'Many will perish in the tunnels but there are so many of them that some must inevitably find their goal eventually. Our brothers' and sisters' fate is sealed as they knew it would be.' He drew his hand across his face and straightened his shoulders. 'Mourning them will not save us. We must carry on. When Pharaoh discovers that his prize has slipped through his fingers, the search will intensify and his ferocity will grow. We are not safe until we have put his Kingdom far behind us.'

'Where will we go?'

'That remains to be seen. We will know when it is right for us to know. The Heart of Regulus will guide our steps.'

Night fell rapidly and completely, the way it always did in this land, and they had little choice but to stop. Going on would risk life and limb, for tonight the moon was giving them little help, lost behind a bank of heavy storm clouds that was thickening on the horizon. Blindly they stumbled over unseen obstacles, peering into shadows only a fraction darker than the ground in search of shelter. When the storm broke, as it soon would if the looming skies spoke truthfully, they would be soaked in seconds. To be caught in the open when the weather vented its anger was an experience none of them wanted.

Chapter 56

Of the thousand of Pharaoh's men who entered the caves, little over a third of them came out again. They were caught in a treacherous, deceptive labyrinth that hid traps and pitfalls at every step, a maze of tunnels leading off tunnels leading off tunnels. Several companies of men, despite their best precautions, became hopelessly and irretrievably lost, unable to find their way back. Condemned to wander in circles until they dropped from exhaustion, thirst and hunger, they would breathe their last in an unforgiving underground tomb. Others succumbed to natural hazards; chasms that slit open the ground, unseen until it was too late, the unfortunate soldiers plunging into their stygian depths; raging underground rivers; poisonous gases. Still more died at the hands of long-dead engineers and the fiendishly clever booby-traps they had installed to keep this hiding place impenetrable.

Of those who did reach the Sanctuary, many more fell beneath the weapons of the Guardians. Pharaoh's men were brave, skilled, and disciplined yet they were outwitted by the thirteen who stood against them. This was the Guardians' realm and they knew it intimately by light or by darkness, moving quickly and expertly around the amphitheatre, now cloaked in the utter blackness of this subterranean world where every lamp had been extinguished long before the soldiers burst in. The invaders fell like lambs to the slaughter under the Guardians' relentless attack. In the end though, despite the Guardians' courage and commitment, there could be only one outcome for they were hopelessly outnumbered. Thirteen against six hundred. Nevertheless, by the time the last one fell, her blood staining the polished floor ruby crimson in the flickering light of the few torches that the victorious intruders had relit, the bodies of more than two hundred of Pharaoh's soldiers littered the floor of the amphitheatre.

The captain stepped forward, clutching his upper arm that streamed blood from a deep wound through his fingers.

'Find it!' he bellowed. Those under his command who could still stand hurried to obey, relighting the lamps at the perimeter of the space, searching in every possible crevice and shadowy corner. It was a huge task in a huge area.

His legs leaden from loss of blood, the captain climbed the steps to the dais. The man who lay dead there was not of this land. He had a full head of coarse orange-gold hair sprinkled with grey, and a thick covering of hair of the same colour concealed the lower half of his face. As for his skin... The captain peered more closely at the short, sturdy limbs that protruded grotesquely from beneath his robes. Where they were not covered in the bright red of his blood, the skin was pale, like milk, sprinkled with a rash of brown dots and bristling with hair, the same colour as that on his face and head. He wasn't a young man, perhaps in the early years of his fourth decade. From what unknown land had he come here, the captain wondered?

He limped to the sarcophagus. Would that be the most likely hiding place for the treasure or was it too obvious? To his surprise, the stone casket was open, the massive lid that lay on the ground on the far side glinting in the torchlight. He examined it more closely. It was richly decorated with gold and precious jewels worth a kings' ransom, but not the sacred Skull that Pharaoh coveted. Still, it would make a worthy addition to the palace treasure rooms.

He turned his attention back to the sarcophagus; shocked, he took a rapid couple of steps back, stumbling over the orange-haired Guardian's corpse and nearly losing his balance. Inside the casket lay the body of a woman, or rather her mummy, so perfectly preserved that the linen bandages that bound her were as white as the day they had been woven. The wrappings outlined a shapely silhouette, the golden mask that covered her face of such delicate beauty that he failed to stifle a gasp of wonder. It was as if her face had been brushed with gold leaf, every feature finely and carefully moulded to reproduce that of the woman she had been. No, not just a woman, he recognised. A queen. She had to have been, given the richness of her burial trappings. Who was she and why did she lie here in this underground chamber in an open casket?

He shook his head to break the spell. The skull, that was all he was interested in, and it wasn't here. There was nothing here but the embalmed body of an unknown queen.

* * * * *

Hours later, the amphitheatre had been searched thoroughly; he had even sent his men clambering up the walls to the highest ledges. They had found nothing. It had to be here somewhere. Why else would the Guardians have fought so ferociously? The captain scowled, his temper as dark as his surroundings. The wound in his arm, though no longer bleeding so profusely, was a constant torment, his head thick and fogged from loss of blood. Wearily, he glanced across at the sarcophagus – and straightened. What if...?

'You,' he bawled at the nearest soldier, 'take two men and strip the body in the casket. Check if the skull has been hidden under the wrappings.'

Desecrating an embalmed body was a sacrilege punishable by death under the law of the kingdom. Given their captain's current mood, however, none of the three men dared to object. He would just as likely strike them down himself for disobeying orders. Reluctantly, they lifted the body from its resting place. The gold mask came off first, set aside for Pharaoh's treasure rooms. Next, hesitantly, fearful that he was bringing a curse down upon their heads, one slid his knife from his belt, sliced through the bandages that covered the face of the corpse and warily pulled them away.

He stumbled backwards, his eyes wild, his face the colour of the bandages he had just removed, his mouth working without sound. The face that stared back at him from the casket was as fresh and alive as it had been in life. Her full lips were slightly parted in a half smile, as if she was only asleep and dreaming of a lover. A curtain of silver hair reached to her waist and long raven black eyelashes rested on cheeks as soft as rose petals. Blue cheeks. The mummy's skin was a blue as the purest lapis lazuli. What demon was this? What sorcery was this? Whatever the magic, it could not be maintained. In front of their eyes, the rose petal cheeks dried and withered, sinking back onto the bones as brown and taut as old parchment, and the silken lashes grew brittle over the hollows of what had been her eye sockets. Beside the captain, someone retched. It was only iron self-control that prevented him doing the same.

'Search the body.' His voice came out tight and hoarse. 'It has to be here somewhere.'

A short while later, he dropped down heavily onto the steps. It wasn't here. The desiccated corpse had been torn apart in their search and given them nothing. The Guardians had tricked them, calling their bluff even as they sacrificed themselves. Pharaoh's fury would be unrestrained and it would be he, the Captain of the Palace Guard, who would feel its full force. He was under no illusion that he would live to see the sun rise the following morning.

Chapter 57

The three fugitives huddled together in the narrow cleft in the hillside. They had found this shelter, inadequate as it was, only just in time. It had turned bitterly cold, the gathering storm pushing before it a brisk, chill wind that cut through to their bones. Overhead, clouds had stolen over the stars, turning the sky from soft black velvet to a dull, light-sucking slate. The fugitives had put a good distance between themselves and the ridge. Would it be enough? None of them felt easy. Pharaoh would not give up his search, not when he had come so close. He would soon realise that the Guardians had somehow been forewarned and the skull carried away to safety. They would be hunted down relentlessly with a handsome price on their heads. Declared traitors, capture would not lead to a quick, merciful death for any of them.

From under half-closed lids, Al-Azar studied his companions. They seemed unaffected by the weariness that had claimed him, and had only stopped because of the imminent storm. He, on the other hand, had never felt so tired, even after his habitual long hours of servitude in the palace. His legs would not have taken him one step further had all the ghouls of the underworld been at his heels. He had been awake for two full days now and despite the cold and discomfort, he was soon snoring in the rear-most part of their small hideout.

The first flash of lightning pierced the rocky chink to its furthermost point, illuminating the drawn face of the slumbering Al-Azar. He merely stirred and grunted, the crash of the resultant thunderclap failing to wake him from his deathlike sleep. His companions exchanged glances. He was still only a boy, fourteen or fifteen years at the most, and he was no soldier. He would slow them down and greatly reduce their chances of success. Yet they could not – would not – leave him behind, not when he had risked everything to warn them.

* * * * *

The storm blew in with all the furies the gods could call on. The wind howled to wake the dead and the thunder shook the ground under their feet. Torrents of rain fell from the sky, racing down the hillsides in ever-widening rivers.

The two Guardians took turns to stand watch all through the cold, wet night, leaving Al-Azar to sleep. The better rested he was, the easier the following day would be for all of them. Deep into the darkest hours, Mirek roused Daan from his dreams for his watch, though to be fair Daan had scarcely slept an hour in the chaos of the storm raging around their refuge.

'All quiet. No sign of Pharaoh's troops. Not that I'd expect anyone to be out on a night like...' He tailed off. Daan was staring wide-eyed over his shoulder towards the entrance.

Mirek whirled around, expecting to see armed soldiers blocking their escape. He was wrong. Stunned, terrified, he stumbled and fell to his knees, his legs refusing to hold him, scrabbling backwards on all fours until he came up against cold solid rock. Daan was beside him, breathing heavily, his knife in his hand.

In the entrance to the tiny, shallow cave, filling it completely, stood an enormous male lion. His shoulder stood as high as Mirek's and the glowing halo of his thick mane reached more than an arm's length across – and he was watching them intently.

Behind them in the cave, Al-Azar stirred, opened his eyes, and let out a yell. Abject fear danced with wonder on his face. Never before had he seen a beast such as this. While the lions of the palace menageries were magnificent creatures to be sure, the one standing before them now dwarfed them all. He blinked, wondering if the night was playing tricks on his eyes. This majestic creature was white, as pure a white as the marble that graced so much of the palace, not the rich, tawny gold of those in the royal household. And it glowed, as if lit from within.

Mirek's hand edged slowly towards his sword, to be stopped by a low growl that rumbled around the cave like the thunder that still echoed across the hill tops.

'Lay down your weapons. I do not come to harm you. I am here to guide you.'

While their ears heard only a deep-throated growl, to their bewilderment, they understood perfectly. The snow-white lion was speaking to them.

'W-what do you wish of us?' After a long silence, Daan managed to stammer out the question they were all thinking.

'Where do you take the skull you carry?'

The Guardians exchanged glances. 'We have no skull,' Mirek stated firmly.

'Do not pretend.' The roar shook the ground beneath their feet. 'You have in your possession Muu-Nan, Skull of Arcturus, Heart of Regulus. He who was brought back to this land generations ago. I know this to be true, so I ask again. Where do you take him?'

'We have no plan,' Daan admitted. 'Our only aim was – is – to keep it out of Pharaoh's hands. More than that, we have not yet determined. Events have happened too quickly to allow for considered thought. Perhaps it would be best to take it overseas, to the west.'

'Muu-Nan must remain here among these great monuments he helped to build.' The rumbling paused. 'There is a place that awaits him. You must take it there.'

Al-Azar pushed forward, inexplicably no longer afraid of the mighty lion. 'Who are you? Why should we trust you?'

'I am Rasalus of Regulus. My ancestors were present when the sacred skull Muu-Nan was created in the temples of Arcturus, far from this world. They brought him here and we have watched over him ever since. Many times we have feared for his safety. Never until now was the danger so pressing.'

'Far from this world?' The boy had heard. He studied the night sky above their heads, now star-studded black velvet once more. 'You are not of ours?'

'My people travelled a vast distance to bring our gift of Muu-Nan to you.' Al-Azar had the weird sensation that Rasalus was smiling. 'Long ago. We have returned many times since. I was here when the great stone lion was raised on the plateau and Muu-Nan placed in its head. I come now to help you to keep him safe and undiscovered for the next thousand generations.'

'What do you wish us to do?' Mirek was on his knees, his head bowed.

'In the Great Pyramid, close to the apex, is a small compartment, created for this purpose when the pyramid was built.' Another pause, longer this time. When the lion spoke again, the men heard a warning in his words. 'It will ask much of you, demand all your courage and resourcefulness. The recess is all but impossible to reach, located at the top of a narrow ventilation shaft behind a thin veneer of stone. You must take the skull to the Great Pyramid, place it in this compartment, then leave this land immediately. The skull's whereabouts must forever remain your secret.'

'So, all we have to do is to find a way to gain access to the Great Pyramid, without arousing any suspicion in the guards, priests, architects or masons and without them seeing the skull – which we will be carrying with us – climb all the way up a tiny vertical shaft to the apex to an 'all but impossible to reach' spot, hide the skull and escape – and do all of that without being seen or caught. No problem.' Mirek's sarcasm was biting. 'Just how do you suggest we do it?'

'It will require all your strength, agility and ingenuity, it is true. Nevertheless, you can succeed. We will help you.'

'We?'

'I have not come alone.' Again, the three sensed that amusement mingled with the urgency in the Rasalus' words. 'You must make your plans without delay. Pharaoh will not rest in his search and it will not be long before his men reach this hillside.'

Daan swept up his sword. 'We will do as you ask.' He turned to the Al-Azar. 'Take the sack of food and the water and run. Get as far away from here as you can, as quickly as you can.'

'I'm coming with you.' Al-Azar stood firm.

'You have shown great courage but you are no warrior, boy. You cannot return to the City. You will not be safe there. Your absence will have been noted and you will be under suspicion. They will be searching for you. Head north, to the sea and the great cities of the coast. Come Mirek, we have work to do.'

'I'm not going anywhere except with you.' Al-Azar studied the two strongly built men staring down at him in surprise. 'Which of you will climb the shaft? Your shoulders are too wide, your legs too long. You would be stuck fast as soon as you started to climb. I'm the only one who can do it.'

Mirek considered the small, wiry boy-man who glared at him. 'He has a point.'

'He isn't strong enough. I do not question his courage but he'd never make it.'

'Muu-Nan cannot shrink the width of your shoulders nor shorten your legs.' Rasalus growled. 'He can, however, give strength when needed. The boy goes with you. You have need of him.'

'It appears the task is yours, boy.' Mirek clapped him on the shoulder. 'Now all we have to do is come up with a way to get past the guards into the Great Pyramid and hide the skull without being discovered. Oh, and get back out again.'

'We will ensure their attention is elsewhere when you need it to be.' The huge snow-white beast bent its fore-knees and lowered its massive haloed head in a deep bow. 'You have our eternal thanks. We will be with you.'

The glow around him flared so brightly they had to turn their heads to avoid its blinding radiance. When they turned back, Rasalus was gone.

* * * * *

It was easier than they expected to gain entry to the City. A merchant, crossing the plain beyond its wall, willingly sold them tunics and hooded cloaks – and asked no questions – in return for a blood red ruby the size of his thumbnail that Daan produced from his knife sheath. Al-Azar's eyes grew as huge as the merchant's when he saw the jewel glinting in the sunlight.

Daan and Mikos buried their distinctive attire deep in the sandy soil, dragging a large boulder over the spot so that no dog or other scavenger could unearth it. No man carrying a weapon was permitted to enter the City without lengthy questioning, and they had had no choice but to leave theirs behind, wrapped in sackcloth and oiled hide and left hanging from the rope of an unused well in a thicket close to the City gates in case they needed to retrieve them in a hurry. If the bundles were discovered, good fortune – and Muu-Nan's blessing – would have indeed abandoned them.

* * * * *

'Keep your eyes down, boy. It would be bad luck indeed if we ran into someone who recognised you but better safe than sorry.' Mikos pulled the hood further down over Al-Azar's face until only his chin remained visible. 'Let us do the talking.'

Sandwiched between the two Guardians, Al-Azar approached the City gates convinced that the sentries would hear his heart thumping loud enough to wake the dead and see his hands shaking. Daan rested an encouraging hand on his shoulder.

'Stay strong, boy,' he whispered. 'We're nearly there.'

Chapter 58

Al-Azar peered up at the massive bulk of stone that towered above him, sharp and clean against the clear deep blue of the mid-afternoon sky. He had always known these pyramids, had lived in their shadow his whole life. They, and the giant pharaoh-headed cat that watched over them, dominated both the plateau and the City. Never though had he been so near. This close, no more than fifty paces distant, they filled his field of vision in a soaring barricade of glistening white limestone. His palms were clammy, his heart racing. This was it. If he was caught... No, he couldn't let his thoughts head off down that road.

Pharaoh was making changes inside the pyramid. Old passageways and chambers were being filled in and new ones created. It was dangerous work and many men had already died, crushed by massive slabs of stone that had dropped unexpectedly when the architect had miscalculated, or fallen prey to the wily defences of the original, long-dead builders. Mirek and Daan had easily got themselves hired as labourers. The foreman had taken one look at their muscled limbs and signed them up immediately. He had simply glanced scornfully at Al-Azar and sent him on his way. Refusing to be defeated, the boy had persevered and finally been hired as a messenger to the second architect, Al-Akuhar, running errands for him all day long. That had been three days ago.

'What's in the bag?'

Al-Azar looked at the sentry with what he hoped was a superior expression, praying his face wouldn't betray his fear. 'Stelas for Al-Akuhar,' he replied. 'Carrying sacred spells for the protection of the Gods' chamber.'

'Show me.'

'He gave orders that no-one but himself was to view them.'

'Do you defy me, boy?'

'No, sir. I'm only carrying out my orders. I dare not disobey the second architect. I do not disrespect you when I say that I fear his anger more than yours.'

The sentry hesitated. Al-Akuhar's wrath was well-known to be fierce and often brutal.

'The second architect, you say?'

Al-Azar nodded.

'In that case, you may continue.'

The boy hurried to the gaping mouth of the pyramid's entrance and stumbled inside, praying his legs would hold out. They were shaking under him, threatening to land him face first on the stony ground. That had been too close.

The clang of hammers on chisels and the shouts of the overseers echoed through the wavering torchlight at the far end the passageway. That was where Al-Akuhar was overseeing progress. It wasn't where Al-Azar was going. The heavy sack containing the supposed stelas banged against his thigh, a powerful reminder of what he was here to do. He glanced behind. No-one was in sight. Before his courage failed him, he darted off into a side tunnel that branched off at ninety degrees to the main corridor and climbed steeply to a small cubbyhole located at the bottom of the shaft. Daan had explored it the previous day.

There was no light here, only the thick, all-encompassing black of a tomb. The boy made his way slowly, feeling his way by brushing his fingertips along the wall until it turned another ninety degrees into the tiny room that was lit by a single lamp. Daan and Mirek were waiting for him.

'Hurry, boy. What kept you? We haven't got long.'

It was easy for them to scold. They hadn't had to smuggle the skull in, dodging the sentries and their questions. Scowling, he lowered the bag to the floor.

'Where is it?' he asked.

Mirek raised a finger. In the ceiling, a tiny opening taunted him, darker even than the passageway he had just negotiated. Black against blackness. His courage faltered. It was even narrower than he had anticipated, barely wider than his shoulders. He looked at it doubtfully.

'I... I don't think I can do this,' he stuttered.

'You have to.' Daan had taken his shoulders. 'You are the only one who can.'

'We are with you.' The echo of Rasalus' words whispered through the stale air.

It was true, he was the only one who could do this. He reached into the hide bag and drew out a linen pouch holding a roughly spherical object: Muu-Nan. Even though every second was critical, he could not resist unwrapping it. The skull glittered darkly in the weak light. Al-Azar's palms began to tingle, the vibrations moving up his arms until his whole body quivered.

'He has awoken.' Daan spoke in hushed tones, filled with reverence and awe. 'Never before in the memory of the Guardians has that been so.'

'He has returned to his rightful place,' whispered Mirek. 'The scripts tell as much.'

For a long time – too long – the three of them sat silently in the presence of the glittering skull, allowing his energy to pulse through their bodies, healing and strengthening every cell. They could have been there a moment, or a day, they could not have said. Time had ceased to exist.

None of them wanted to break the spell and yet break it they had to. His limbs as sluggish as if he was swimming through river mud, Mirek picked up the skull, wrapped it in its linen pouch once more and handed it to Al-Azar.

'Go now,' he ordered, laying an encouraging hand on the boy's shoulder.

Al-Azar hung the heavy bag around his neck, placed his foot in Daan's interlocked fingers and pushed up into the shaft. With the skull safely held, his arms and legs were free to climb. Even so, it weighed heavily, making every move a challenge. If he moved suddenly, the bag swung like a pendulum, threatening to send him plunging downwards – and if he fell, there was nothing to stop him until he crashed onto the floor below, killing himself if he was lucky. Delivering him – and the skull – into the hands of Pharaoh's soldiers if he was not.

*   *   *   *   *

Progress was painfully, tortuously slow. The shaft walls had been built from smooth, close-fitting blocks with few hand or foot-holds and he climbed solely with the strength of his legs and back, his knees and lower legs pushed against one wall, his spine pressed tight to the other. Inching up fraction by tiny fraction until his shins, toes and shoulders were raw and bleeding. How much further would he have to climb? He rested for a moment, straining against the stone, his knees and back wedging him in place, every muscle screaming its protest. Far below, the tiny square of light taunted him.

He rested his head back against the cool stone and looked up. Above – and not very far above – a sprinkling of silver dust glittered across a square of deep dark indigo, a scant shade paler than the surrounding black. It was a second or two before he realised what he was looking at. The night sky. Night had fallen. How long had he been climbing? He had entered the pyramid towards noon, which meant they had been in here for the remainder of the day and a good part of the night.

Al-Azar was exhausted and almost at the end of his strength. He closed his eyes, willing his body to obey, remembering Rasalus' promise that Muu-Nan would help him. Well, if ever he needed the skull's help, it was now.

No sooner had the thought formed than warmth trickled into his aching, bleeding body, seeping from the stone that surrounded him into flesh, into bone. As the warmth came, it chased out fatigue and it chased out pain. The pouch around his neck pulsed like a heartbeat where it rested on his chest. The skull. It had to be the skull, just as Rasalus had told them. Why now and not before? Had Muu-Nan simply been waiting for him to ask? It didn't matter. The help had come and just in time.

'Thank you,' he murmured.

He opened his eyes, closed them, fearing he was hallucinating, and opened them again. No, he hadn't imagined it, it was still there. Level with his nose, a circle glowed silver-gold on the surface of the stone block. It hadn't been there before, he was sure of it. Was this the sign that he had found the compartment? Wedging himself even more firmly into the shaft, he brushed the symbol with his fingertips. Nothing. He pressed harder. Still nothing. What did he have to do?

It turned out he didn't have to do anything. The pouch around his neck started to emit a low light, radiating through the tightly woven cloth onto the wall. Muu-Nan had once again burst into life. The symbol flared and in front of the boy's incredulous gaze, the stone dissolved, revealing a small niche barely two handspans square.

With the dead weight of the skull dangling from his neck, there was no room to manoeuvre. If Al-Azar's muscles had been shrieking in protest before, it was nothing to the strain they were now under despite Muu-Nan's inflow of strength. He needed both hands to lift the skull into the niche, which shifted the delicate balance on his back and shoulders, and he held himself steady by the pressure on his knees and spine alone. Every tiny movement pushed them closer to their limits.

At last it was done. Radiance surged from the skull. Mist seeped into the alcove, surrounding it, thickening and solidifying, cloaking it in stone. The symbol had vanished. There was no longer any sign that this piece of stone was different to the thousands of others that made up this immense monument. Drained, hurting, Al-Azar began the long, slow, body-numbing descent back to his companions.

*   *   *   *   *

Footsteps echoed in the tunnel, rapidly approaching the dim cubbyhole where the two Guardians waited for the boy to return.

'The light!' Daan snuffed out the lamp's meagre flame and plunged the tiny room into the blackest night. From above, a faint shuffling and laboured breathing betrayed Al-Azar's descent.

'Stay still, boy,' Mikos hissed. 'Soldiers.' Had the boy heard? It seemed so, for the sounds stopped.

The two Guardians held their breath, waiting for their inevitable discovery. They had nowhere to run but maybe – if his strength held out and he could stay wedged in the shaft for long enough – the boy would escape discovery. The two warriors waited calmly, in their hands the short knives they had smuggled in beneath their tunics. The precise rectangle of the access tunnel entrance stood out clearly now. Torchlight. The soldiers were almost on them. Mikos and Daan were ready. They would die by their own hand before they let themselves be taken.

An ear-shattering roar blasted through the small room, echoing through the chambers and passageways of the vast pyramid as if a never-ending thunderclap had been captured and released within its confines. On and on it boomed, shaking the foundations of the huge edifice and hurling the two men to their knees. Above them, in the shaft, Al-Azar could only brace himself as well as he was able and pray that he wouldn't fall.

The thunder died away, replaced now by the clamour of three hundred men yelling in fear and confusion, and running feet pounding the flagstone floors. From the passageway, footsteps echoed again, this time racing away from the chamber towards the pyramid's main entrance. It was only a brief respite in the uproar. Again it came, reverberating through the massive stone blocks of the pyramid, vibrating through the bellies and bones of all who heard it.

'Come on.' Daan scrabbled for the lamp, relighting it quickly with a flint he kept in his belt. 'It's in uproar out there. No-one will be paying any attention to us.'

'What about the boy?' Mikos glanced upwards.

'I'm here.' Ashen-faced, exhausted, Al-Azar dropped from the shaft, landing heavily on legs that had no strength left. 'What is that?'

'I have no idea.' Mikos took hold of the boy's arm, steadying him. 'But whatever it is, it's helping us. No-one is going to bother about us when they've got that to think about.'

At the exit to the main corridor they paused to peer out cautiously. Their wariness was unnecessary. The passageway was filled with men running headlong towards the daylight, some terrified, others curious. None of them so much as glanced at the three figures standing at the side of the corridor; they were all in too much of a hurry to leave the shaking mountain of stone that surrounded them. Mikos, Daan and Al-Azar slipped unnoticed into the crowd of masons, labourers, architects and priests, running with them – only to pull up sharply as they emerged into dazzling daylight to avoid crashing into the huge crowd that had gathered, wild-eyed and disbelieving.

On the stone-paved terrace directly in front of the pyramid, six enormous lions faced them. At the front was a huge male, a pride leader in his prime, his powerful muscles rippling under an alabaster coat. Two sleek, powerful females of the same colour flanked his haunches and behind them stood a further three males, their manes rippling in dazzling incandescent haloes. Each stood as tall as a man to the shoulder, their coats molten white gold under the glaring sun. Eyes as blue as the noonday sky radiated absolute power and command. Huge fangs glistened menacingly and from their throats came the thunder that filled the air. The crowd cowered as the six mighty beasts opened their jaws once more to let forth a roar that shook the ground they stood on and set the leaves of nearby trees shaking as if an earthquake had hit. Mesmerised by the spectacle, no-one could tear their gaze away from the terrifying, magnificent beasts. None but Daan.

'Mikos.' The Guardian nudged his companion, waking him from the spell. 'Come on.' He looked around. 'Where's the boy?' Al-Azar wasn't with them.

'There.' A small, slight figure had slipped out of the pyramid's entrance, and was racing towards and then around its furthest corner, into the shadows and out of sight. A quick backward glance confirmed that the crowd was still firmly captured in the lions' thrall. Backing slowly away, the two Guardians turned and bolted after Al-Azar. No-one saw them leave.

Within moments of the two men disappearing around the corner of the monument and out of sight of anyone on the terrace, the roars fell away. The silhouettes of the lions softened, became less solid, less real, than they had only seconds before, growing ever more insubstantial until, at some moment, though precisely when none of those watching could have said, they dissolved into the air, leaving no trace that they had ever been there.

PRESENT DAY: SOMEWHERE IN NORTHERN NORWAY

JOE

Chapter 59

Bloody hell! That was one heck of a journey. Four days since I said goodbye to Gemma back in England and most of the time since spent behind the wheel, fourteen hours of it today. I was hungry and I was knackered. My back ached, my shoulders ached, my legs ached, and my head ached. And somebody had been sandpapering my eyeballs. I was ready to sleep for a week.

It was a few minutes after eleven in the evening and I had just arrived in Narvik in the far north of Norway. Tomorrow, Pieter van Broek would meet me here and together we would drive to the site where the black skull was hidden. I dragged my backpack – in which I'd safely stowed the golden key – from the passenger seat and trudged into the hotel. I'd already texted van Broek to let him know I'd arrived, and I was signing the hotel register when a ping from my phone signalled his OK. Ten minutes later, with the black-out blinds in my room blocking out the almost continual daylight, I pulled the duvet up to my chin, snuggled down into the soft pillow, and zonked out.

The shrill ring of the room's phone dragged me grudgingly from a deep and dreamless sleep.

'Hello?' I sounded as dopey as I felt.

'Mr Cunningham? This is Reception. There is a Mr van Broek here to see you.'

Van Broek? Instantly my drowsiness evaporated. What the hell time was it? With fingers still clumsy with sleep I fumbled for my phone. Quarter past nine. I'd overslept.

'Tell him I'll be down in five,' I called down the phone, diving into my clothes. I grabbed the backpack and tore down the stairs.

In Reception, van Broek was pacing restlessly up and down the foyer, no doubt as impatient to be off as I was. Now that I had slept off my brain-deadening fatigue, the reality of the situation had caught up with me and I was fizzing with excitement. We were about to head out to the place where, if van Broek was right – and the photo he had sent Gemma seemed to be compelling proof that he was – we would use an ancient golden key to open a secret entrance to a secret cave where we would find one of the sacred Skulls of Light. Within hours, we would have taken Gileada from his millennia-old hiding place and brought him back out into the world. It was going to be one hell of a day. (Note to self: If only I'd known then just what a hell of a day it was going to be!)

'Have you got everything you need?' Van Broek eyed my sweatshirt and trainers doubtfully.

'My coat and trek boots are in my car. I'll grab them on the way out.'

'And the...?'

I nodded, patting the backpack.

'Then let's go.' He indicated a battered blue Land Rover Discovery. 'She's old and she looks a bit rough,' he admitted, 'but she's as reliable as they come.'

My heart was already beating faster, my skin tingling. This was the stuff of an Indiana Jones movie and here I was, ordinary old Joe Cunningham, in the middle of it. I grinned at van Broek, seeing in his eyes the same poorly hidden excitement that he no doubt saw in mine. He grinned back, pale eyes flashing behind the thick lenses of his spectacles.

*   *   *   *   *

The roads were virtually empty of traffic and the few sparsely dotted houses and villages we passed were quiet and sleepy. Van Broek said little as we drove through the magnificent landscape to a soundtrack of classical music from the radio. It suited me. I was too busy being blown away by the scenery to want to chat. I couldn't take my eyes off it. Steep, densely wooded hills, and meadows vibrant with wildflowers descended to winding rivers that chuckled along the valley floors while above, drifts of clouds wandered lazily across the sparkling blue sky. It was hard to imagine that within a few short months, all of it would be buried under feet of snow. Hard to imagine, that is, until we stopped for a break and I stepped out of the heated vehicle into a stiff breeze that carried with it a distinct polar chill. It was a sharp reminder that we were well inside the Arctic Circle.

'Here, Mr Cunningham.' Van Broek handed me a pack of sandwiches and a mug of steaming hot coffee he'd just poured from a vacuum flask, dragging my attention away from the majesty of the world that surrounded me. 'May I see it? The key?'

Why not? He'd see it soon enough anyway. I pulled the small, well-wrapped package from my bag and laid it on top of a wide, flat-topped boulder, freeing it from the layers of bubble-wrap.

'It's Joe,' I said, stepping back so he could see. 'Not Mr Cunningham.'

'So you must call me Pieter,' he replied, without taking his eyes off the key that shone like fire in the bright sunlight. Even from a couple of paces away, I could feel the power coming out of it.

'Owww!' He leapt back, shaking out his hand. 'It gave me an electric shock!' He reached out again, more cautiously this time, brushing it lightly with his fingertips, lost for words. 'I have been dreaming of this for so long,' he murmured at last, 'and now to see it, to touch it.' He looked at me and tears glistened momentarily on his lashes. 'It's real. It's all real.' There was no greed or hunger in his expression, simply wonder and elation. 'Let's go find Gileada,' he beamed.

We'd been travelling for about four hours when we turned off the metalled road onto a dirt track that led off into the hills. For another hour, we drove through the same flower-filled meadows and pine forests that had kept us company for most of the morning. Here, the sturdy Land Rover came into its own, pitching and lurching along a rough – often virtually non-existent – track covered in large, jagged rocks and up and down impossible inclines. How on earth had he ever found his way here? I held the question back, leaving him to focus on negotiating the challenging terrain without pitching us into a gulley.

We came out of the gloom of a dense pine forest onto a wide, flat plateau littered with sharp stones and broken here and there by huge outcrops of dull, black rock. Pieter stopped the car and pointed to the far end.

'There. The tall cliff in the distance. That's where the black skull is.' His hands were trembling, his face flushed.

Disbelief, hope, fear, excitement – all took a turn. In the end, excitement won. 'Well what the hell are we waiting for?' I whooped, 'Let's go!'

Grinning from ear to ear, Pieter threw the car into gear and pressed the accelerator to the floor. The engine roared and the Land Rover sped forward towards the wall of black rock – and Gileada.

Chapter 60

'Here. This is the place.' Pieter pointed at the cliff face. Sure enough, there in the rock I could make out the trace of an impression that matched exactly the shape of the key. The key that was lying, heavy, in my hand. I passed it to him and held my breath as he offered it up. It fit perfectly. And… Nothing. Not a damn thing. No secret doors opened. No solid rock evaporated before our eyes. Not so much as a hairline appeared in the rock face.

'This has to be it.' Disappointment and bewilderment cracked his words. He tried again. Still nothing. 'Why doesn't it work? It has to work. This *is* the place and this *is* the key.' He glared at the black rock, willing it to obey. He tried a third time and for a third time the rock stayed as solid and unbroken as it had been when we arrived.

He slumped down, his back against the cliff. 'What have we missed, Joe? What have we missed?' He turned back to the rock, studying it in detail.

'Pieter.' He wasn't listening. 'Pieter!' Within seconds my elation had turned to confusion. Another second and that confusion erupted into fear when something hard and round and small was pressed painfully into my back between my shoulder blades. Something that felt frighteningly like the barrel of a gun.

'Don't move,' a voice hissed, followed more loudly by, 'Open it!'

Shaken from his disappointment by an unfamiliar voice, Pieter at last looked up. His eyes widened and the colour drained from his face.

'I -I can't,' he stammered. 'It doesn't work.'

'You're lying.' A different voice. There were two of them. At least two.

'No, I'm not. It doesn't open. It should do but it doesn't. Look.' Again he offered up the key. Again, nothing happened.

'You try.' The first man, the one pushing a gun into my back, who I'll call Thug One from now on, shoved me forward with such force that I tripped and fell into Pieter. With a sleight of hand that would make any decent illusionist jealous, he slipped something heavy and bulky into my pocket with one hand as he passed me the key with the other. Thug One grabbed his arm and yanked him away.

Holding my breath, I brought the key up to the rock. Whereas five minutes before I had wanted nothing more than for a section of the cliff face to slide back and reveal the black skull, now I prayed it wouldn't. These goons could not – must not – get their filthy hands on Gileada.

I pressed the key into the indentation. Seconds passed. Nothing changed.

'If you're playing games with us…'

'Honest to God, I'm not. How could I? I have no idea how this works or what's meant to happen.'

'Give it to me.' Shoving me aside, Thug Two snatched the key from my hand and slammed it against the rock. He had no more success than Pieter and I.

'Friggin' useless piece of shit!' he yelled, hurling the precious relic across the plateau. 'Has to be another fake, same as ours.'

Another fake? These gorillas must have a key too, another one that hadn't worked. Where had they got it? My blood ran cold as understanding dawned. It had been these two who had broken in to Olina Gjerde's laboratory and stolen the replica in error, believing it to be the genuine article, and killed her and her colleague, Dr Mackintosh. These thoughts raced through my mind in less than a couple of seconds, chased by an equally unpleasant certainty. These men wouldn't leave any loose ends here either – the loose ends that were Pieter and me. There was no way they were going to let us leave here alive.

Pieter's expression revealed that he had reached the same conclusion. We had to get away, but how? It was a few more seconds before it registered that his eyes were flicking quickly to my coat pocket and away again. The same pocket he'd slipped something into earlier. A gun? I'd never fired a gun in my life but right now, I was sure as hell ready to start. Slowly, watching the two thugs carefully in case they looked my way, I slid my hand in. There was the grip. It had to be a gun – except that, as far I knew, a gun didn't have a bulky rectangular barrel. A Taser. Pieter had passed me a Taser. What in God's name was he planning? I didn't have to wait long to find out.

He picked his moment well. With lightning speed that surprised me as much as anything else he did that day, he whirled, yelling 'NOW!' and with a perfectly timed blow knocked the pistol from his captor's hand, following it up with a powerful, lung-emptying kick to the stomach that sent the man retching and gasping to the floor.

Thug Two was nearest me and (I hoped!) unarmed. At Pieter's sudden assault on his partner he froze for a split second. I took my chance. I pulled the Taser from my pocket and as he turned to take me down, I fired, hitting him squarely in the chest.

'Run!' yelled Pieter, scrambling for the Land Rover. I started to follow then changed direction.

'Joe! Come on! They won't stay down forever.'

No, they wouldn't but no way was I leaving without the key. Neither of the two thugs noticed what I was doing. They weren't in a fit state to do so. The one Pieter had tackled was groaning, semi-conscious, on the ground. The other was fully conscious but only of the pain still wracking through his body from the Taser hit. I scooped up the key and sprinted for the car, zipping it into the front of my coat.

'The key,' I panted as I leapt in. 'Had to get the key.'

Pieter slapped his hand to his forehead. 'How did I forget *that*? Good move. Now hang on.' He flung the car into gear and floored the accelerator, sending the Land Rover bouncing over the rough ground so violently that I was convinced my teeth would be shaken from my head.

'Where did you learn those moves?' I asked between the jolts.

'Karate. Brown belt. It was a long time ago. Wasn't sure I still had it.'

'Well, I'm bloody glad you did.' I turned to look through the rear window. The two men were back on their feet, staggering towards a dark green Nissan pick-up parked a few hundred yards from the location where we believed the entrance to be, tucked behind a fold in the rock and only now visible to us. How did we not see it when we approached? We must have driven in at a different angle. It was the only reason I could think of.

'They're after us.' The dark vehicle was moving, careening across the plateau.

Pieter gritted his teeth, concentrating totally on negotiating the numerous hazards that littered the track ahead. Colliding with any of them would wreck the Land Rover and leave us at the mercy of our pursuers.

* * * * *

'Damn it!' I shook my head to clear my vision. We had just pitched into a deep rut on my side of the track and my head had collided hard with the door pillar.

'Sorry,' Pieter barked, his eyes glued to the ground ahead. 'Didn't see that one. How are we doing?'

I shot a glance behind. 'They're not gaining yet.' There was a limit as to how fast any vehicle could travel over this ground. We were at that limit and so were the men on our tail.

'They'll make it up when we reach the road proper. That Nissan has a lot more horsepower than this old girl. She hasn't got the speed she used to have.' His knuckles were white on the wheel as he pushed the Land Rover as hard as he could.

'There's the road.' I pointed to where a ribbon of tarmac crossed the track, about a quarter of a mile away. Another quick look over my shoulder brought bad news.

'They've got a lot closer. What the…?' The man in the passenger seat was half out of the window, his arm in the air. Crack! I ducked instinctively as something whistled past the car. Not close. Still, too close for comfort.

'The bastards are shooting at us,' I yelled. On this rough terrain, taking an accurate aim was near impossible. Once we reached the road however…

'Hang on!'

I reacted barely in time to Pieter's warning, gripping the dashboard with one hand and the door handle with the other. The Discovery lurched and skidded, tyres screaming, as he flung the wheel to the left, dragging us off the track and onto the hard, smooth surface of the road. This guy could drive! Even so, our would-be murderers were closing on us by the second and on this surface, they'd quickly be on our tailgate. A resounding clang of a bullet hitting the rear bodywork left us in no doubt of their intentions. As if we didn't already know!

Pieter drove like a man possessed, throwing the heavy vehicle around the bends and hurtling down the hills. We were running for our lives and time was running out for us. We'd left the open meadows behind and were tearing through thick, dark pine forests, only a narrow strip of blue sky visible above us. The road twisted and turned, which had the advantage of blocking us from the view of our pursuers. The downside was that we couldn't see them either, so we had no idea of how quickly they were gaining on us. Our one – desperate and very slim – hope was that we would come to some village or town with a police station, on the assumption that they wouldn't do anything in full view of any witnesses. Of course, they could simply wait for us to leave and take us out then. These deserted roads often didn't see a car for hours, if not days.

Ahead, the road was opening up a little. The trees were sparser, clear areas of bracken-dotted heathland stretched back from the verge for several hundred feet and the road ran straight.

'They're almost on us.' Pieter's eyes flicked from road to rear view mirror and back again. I turned to look. Not one hundred yards behind us was the Nissan. I swear I could see the driver grinning triumphantly.

'Oh shit! We're not going to make it!' The panic in Pieter's voice spun me back to stare through the windscreen. The road ahead had vanished – or rather it had unexpectedly swung sharply down and back on itself in a hairpin, unsighted until we were virtually on top of it. We were going too fast. Pieter was right. We wouldn't make it. His face set, he wrestled with the wheel, braking as hard as he dared without sending us into what would be a fatal skid, tyres searching for grip and failing to find it. It was no good. We weren't slowing, or turning, quickly enough.

'We're going over,' he yelled, yanking the wheel straight. 'We have to hit this nose first if we're to stand any chance at all. If we go over sideways, we'll barrel roll.' He was virtually standing on the brakes, using all his strength to keep the car moving in a straight line.

For a heartbeat, nothing but blue sky filled the windscreen. A moment later, the front pitched forward with a stomach-churning lurch, revealing a terrifyingly steep hillside that plunged down to the edge of the forest way below, and suddenly we were hurtling down over rocks and through the shrubs and bracken towards that line of thickly set pines. Pieter was still wrestling with the wheel to keep us as straight as possible as the Discovery jolted and bucked, the brakes useless.

'Jump!' he yelled.

'WHAT?' Had he lost it?

'If we hit those trees, we're dead. Jump. NOW!' He was unbuckling his seat belt as he spoke. 'It's our only chance.'

Yes, he was crazy. He was also right. I fumbled with my belt, pulling on the release, and kicked open the door. The world outside was a blur, rushing past at a terrifying speed. I hesitated.

'Go. NOW!' he yelled.

I went, hitting the ground hard, somersaulting downwards unable to slow my momentum, only stopping when I crashed into the tangled branches of a low-growing shrub where I lay unable to move and gasping for breath. The fall had knocked all the air from my lungs and my ankle hurt like hell but to my amazement, I was still alive. Far below, I heard the Land Rover continue its crashing descent until, with a final drawn-out screech of torn metal and branches, the peace of the valley returned.

Chapter 61

Voices, up by the side of the road. Voices that I half recognised, drifting down to where I lay dazed and only half conscious. I didn't move a muscle, praying they wouldn't notice me.

'Do we go down and finish them?' That was Thug Two.

'No, leave 'em.'

'What if they're not dead?'

'They soon will be. There's a storm coming in. They won't last long out here in the open when it does. By the time anyone finds them, it'll be too late.'

'What about any investigation?'

'It's an accident. They were driving too fast and went off the road. Happens all the time.' He chuckled. 'Which means no-one will be looking for us. Nice and clean.'

Car doors slammed, an engine revved and the Nissan drove off. Pieter and I were alone out here in the middle of nowhere with no prospect of help. And a storm was coming in? I stared up at the sky. The unbroken blue of only a few minutes before was now alive with dark, racing clouds. The thug was right. He was also right that we wouldn't survive it. The already chill wind was now carrying an iciness that hadn't been there earlier and it was gathering strength, cutting through my padded parka as if it was no more than a thin cotton shirt.

Pieter. Was he alive? I had to find him. I pushed myself up, wriggling to pull free of the shrub's spiky grip. In the effort, my already throbbing ankle caught on a rock, exploding in pain. My body surrendered, a wave of blackness engulfed me, and I passed out.

I don't know how long I was unconscious. I don't think it was for long. Even so, when I came to, I was shivering violently with cold. My teeth were chattering so hard I thought they'd crack, and I'd lost feeling in my fingers and toes, so I tucked my hands under my arms to warm them up. It didn't help. It was *so* cold. The wind was whistling like a banshee and the sky was now lead-grey and menacing.

I had to find Pieter. I struggled to my feet and tested my ankle. It hurt like hell but if I gritted my teeth, it would hold. Just about. I scanned the hillside. Where was he? He'd gone out of the driver's door, which meant he had to be somewhere to my right – if he'd got out. I pushed that possibility from my mind, the prospect of being alone out here being one I didn't want to contemplate. Limping painfully, I shuffled across the rough, tree-stump and rock-strewn ground.

There, about fifty yards away. I hurried over as fast as my ankle would let me to where he was sprawled across a clump of bracken. He wasn't dead but he was out cold with a lump the size of a satsuma on his temple that was already turning purple and oozed blood where the skin had split.

'Pieter, wake up.' He stirred, groaned, and drifted off again. 'Pieter. We've to get out of here.' Where though? I hoped inspiration would strike once we were back up on the road. Or maybe the black skull would help? 'Pieter.' I shook him. It was no good. He wasn't waking up any time soon.

I looked up at the road, only about a hundred feet above us, although it might as well have been ten thousand. I couldn't carry him up there. To be honest, I doubted I'd make it myself. My ankle had carried me, protesting, this far; now it had had enough. It crumpled beneath me and I landed hard on the ground. No, it wasn't going to take me any further, at least for a while. Oddly enough, right now I was OK with that. An unexpected euphoria was stealing through me, soothing my worries. It didn't matter any longer. We'd stay here. It was nice here. It was peaceful and I needed to rest. I was sleepy. So, *so* sleepy. I'd stopped shivering. In fact, for the first time since I'd taken that flying leap from the car, I felt warm. I'd have a little sleep and when I woke up, I'd figure out how to get us out of here. There was no rush. Sleep. Yes, that's what I needed. I curled up, closed my eyes and let it claim me.

GEMMA, 5

Chapter 62

'It begins.' Regus, the man I now knew to be my husband here in this Atlantean incarnation, stood in front of me, his deep brown eyes filled with apprehension and determination, meeting mine.

Once again, I had been transported to another world, a world of fragrant blossoms, birdsong, and tinkling water falling from a hundred elegant fountains. With a sigh, I moved to him, melting against his body, feeling his arms encircle me, strong and reassuring.

'Yes,' I replied, my head resting against his chest, his white silken robe soft on my skin, his breath warm on my hair. 'It begins.'

Not one moment of discord disturbed the tranquillity of these gardens. It was an illusion. In the air that surrounded us, embracing us in its gentle warmth, and in the chill that I sensed tiptoeing around the edges of my soul, cruel winds of change – of destruction and misery – were rising. Each time I was brought back here into this unfamiliar world and this unfamiliar body, I sensed it more strongly. The peaceful, heart-centred way of life that had held sway here in Atlantis for so many generations was coming to an abrupt end and there was no longer anything anyone could do to stop it. That opportunity had long since passed. The waves of fear and suspicion that stood neighbour against neighbour, created and fuelled by the Shadow Chasers, had grown too strong.

What was happening here? Who was I really? Was I this woman, Haa'nu, senior Priestess of Yo'tlàn's Pyramid Temple and one of the four architects of a desperate plan to smuggle the Skulls of Light to safety? Or was I the woman I'd always believed myself to be, Gemma Mason, a divorced mother and author in twenty-first century England, a time and place so far removed from here as to feel in another world? Each time I found myself in these tranquil gardens the lines became more blurred.

'Haa'nu?' This was who I was today. Here. Now. Gemma was a long way away. I stirred from my thoughts and raised my head, looking into the face of the man who held me. He bent and kissed me tenderly and in that kiss was all the love in the universe. 'We must go,' he murmured against my lips. 'Omar will be waiting.'

More blurred lines. Regus was tall, a good head taller than me, well-built with a mane of chestnut brown hair that that fell to his shoulders and was starting to streak silver at the temples. Yet when looked into those deep, warm eyes, I saw Joe behind them. Blond, slender Joe with his hazel eyes and ready smile. Just as I was, at times, Haa'nu, I was also beginning to understand that Joe and Regus were the same, in different times and different worlds. Yet I didn't feel for Joe the all-consuming love that overflowed from me for this man, my husband Regus. I didn't understand any of it, not really.

'Come.' Arms around each other's waist, we left the quiet sanctuary of the gardens for the Temple chamber to join Omar and, over the course of next days, speak with those who the Skulls had chosen to be their guardians.

* * * * *

The room was sparsely furnished and simply decorated. A bare stone floor and pale cream walls reflected the shafts of white-gold morning sunlight that poured in through the floor to ceiling windows on the far wall, giving an air of peace and serenity. Today, and over the next two days, that peace would be tested. Twelve of the Temple's priests and priestesses would make their way one at a time through the wide corridors to this place, none knowing why they had been summoned to this innermost of sanctums.

Regus sat on my left, with Oolan on his left. On my right was Omar. The tension in the room and within each of us was palpable. We were about to send those men and women on a mission that would demand that they leave behind everything and everyone they had ever known. Much would be asked of them, more than we could ever have foreseen. As for the four of us? We were under no illusion. We would be asked to sacrifice as much.

A sharp, confident knock on the thick oak door signalled the arrival of the first of our visitors. It was time. Regus' hand found mine beneath the cover of the table as Omar stood, his power flowing around him in an almost visible cloak.

'Come,' he commanded.

The door swung slowly open and the first of the new Guardians stepped over the threshold.

* * * * *

I opened my eyes. Moonlight filtered through a crack in the curtains, illuminating the familiar silhouette of the maidenhair fern on my windowsill, and in the distance an owl hooted softly. The light, airy Temple room had vanished. I was back in my bed, in my own room, in my own life. For now, at least. I was in no doubt that before too long I would return to Atlantis and the Pyramid Temple.

At the edges of my mind, fingers of unease prodded for my attention, calling me from the tranquillity of that far-off life. What were they trying to tell me? Coming like a slap across the face, I remembered. Joe! Yesterday morning he and Pieter had set out to recover Gileada and since then I hadn't heard from him. My voicemails remained unanswered and he hadn't yet returned to his hotel where I'd left several messages at the Reception desk. I grabbed my phone from the bedside table and checked again. Still nothing.

Where are you, Joe? Are you and Pieter OK? Although worrying wouldn't help, with no word from them to reassure me, I couldn't help feeling concerned.

'Gileada,' I whispered into the night. 'Keep them safe, please.' Had he heard? I had no way of knowing, and the harsh truth was that there was nothing I could do now but wait and trust.

I turned over and snuggled down under the duvet, searching for the peace that had enveloped me on my return from the Pyramid Temple. Against all my expectations, I drifted into sleep and with its soothing blanket settling over me, they came. The Skulls of Light. Circling on the threshold of my consciousness: ice-clear quartz, soft purple amethyst, fierce red jasper, night-black obsidian and so many more. Keeping their distance. Elusive in their presence. When I turned to look at them, they slipped away, dancing in and out of my half-slumbering dreams.

Returning.

Clearer.

The black skull, Gileada; sea blue Gal-Athiel; Gor-Kual; Maat-Su; Khalia; Muu-Nan. And this time, misty and indistinct, dancing on the edge of my awareness and tantalising in its mystery, was the promise of another, of the seventh skull. Only time would tell what this one would share.

THE SKULLS OF LIGHT WILL RETURN…

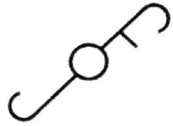

CHARACTER LIST & CATCH-UP NOTES

THE SKULLS OF LIGHT:

Thirteen powerful 'crystal' skulls created over 250,000 years ago by highly evolved and benevolent races from across the galaxies and brought by them to Earth to watch over and guide the evolution of humankind.

The Skulls were brought together in the ancient civilisation of Atlantis until the rise of the Shadow Chasers, a regime who sought to possess the Skulls' power for themselves. Temple priests fled the continent with the Skulls, taking them to safety and hiding them until humankind was ready to accept them once again.

(Note: I put the word crystal in inverted commas here because these skulls are not made solely of crystal as most people understand it. Crystal skull in this context refers to any skull created from a natural stone or mineral such as obsidian, jasper, or jade as well as quartz.)

Gileada: Introduced in Book I, Lost Legacy. The first skull that makes contact with Gemma.

A black obsidian skull originating in the star system of Eleusia in the far reaches of the Andromeda galaxy.

Current location believed to be in northern Europe on the Norway/Sweden border

Gal-Athiel: Introduced in Book I, Lost Legacy.

Also known as the 'Voice of the Mother.'

A blue obsidian skull originating in the star system of Theta.

Current location believed to be in the deserts of the South West USA.

Has a strong and ongoing connection with Gemma.

Gor-Kual: Introduced in Book II, The Red Skull of Aldebaran.

A red jasper skull originating in the star system of Aldebaran in the Taurus constellation.

Current location believed to be in eastern North Africa.

Maat-Su: Introduced in Book III, Daughter of the Gods.

Also known as the 'Daughter of the Gods'.

A lapis lazuli skull originating in the star system of Valkan in the constellation of Corvus in the (very!) distant Antennae galaxies.

Current location believed to be beneath the Giza plateau.

Khalia: Introduced in Book IV, Khalia's Tomb.

A green jade skull originating in the Pleiades.

Current location believed to be the south of France.

GEMMA'S STORY:

Gemma Mason: Englishwoman in her 40's living in present day Wiltshire in England. The black skull, Gileada, first appears to Gemma in her dreams. Compelled to write the skull's story in the form of novels – and subsequently those of the other Skulls of Light as they connect with her – she rebuilds her life as a successful author. As she does, she is drawn further and further into an unfamiliar and dangerous world.

Joe Cunningham: Former work colleague of Gemma's who has a life-long fascination with the 'crystal' skulls. Following his redundancy and months' long disappearance, he returns with a firm purpose to discover all he can about these skulls. He and Gemma have become good friends and allies as together they navigate this unknown road.

Pieter van Broek: Dutch historian/archaeologist, introduced at the end of Book IV. He claims to have discovered the location of Gileada, the black skull.

Callum Davis: Maverick archaeologist working outside the mainstream system and shunned by it for his views. He is driven to track down the Skulls of Light. Initially a friend of Joe, after he is introduced to Gemma she accompanies him to the deserts of Arizona to search for the blue skull, Gal-Athiel.

Duncan: Friend of Joe. Duncan has a flat full of 'crystal' skulls and an encyclopaedic knowledge of them. It is Duncan who first takes Gemma on a meditation journey to understand what the skulls are all about. He is also an highly skilled hacker.

D.I. Chamberlain: Police detective inspector, introduced in Book IV. Gemma and Joe suspect that he has some form of hidden agenda.

Cathy: Long-time friend of Gemma. She is down to earth, supports Gemma completely, and is also highly psychic. She uses her talents when necessary to help Joe and Gemma.

Olina Gjerde: Norwegian scientist and Assistant Head Archaeologist at the Norwegian University of Science & Technology. She contacts Gemma after archaeologists discover a strange gold artefact in a river in northern Norway.

Jürgens Brinkmann: Suspected Dark One who has turned up at Gemma's book signings and appears to be watching her.

ATLANTIS:

Omar: High priest and most senior temple elder; initiator and leader of the skull rescue plan.

Haa'nu: High priestess and temple elder in the Pyramid Temple of Yo'tlàn in Atlantis and one of the four architects of the plan to smuggle the Skulls of Light out of the Temple to keep them from the grasp of the Shadow Chasers. Gemma's Atlantean incarnation.

Regus: one of the four senior priests and temple elders, and co-architect of the plan. Joe's Atlantean incarnation.

Oolan: High priest and temple elder, the last of the four architects of the plan.

OTHER:

The Skull Chamber: Situated in the Pyramid Temple in Yo'tlàn, capital city of Atlantis and home to the thirteen Skulls of Light. The Pyramid Temple is the spiritual and administrative hub of the Atlantean continent and is overseen by the Priests and Priestesses of the Light who are in turn guided by the Skulls of Light, and from whom the Skulls' guardians are chosen.

SPOILER ALERT

It's been a while since Heart of Regulus (Book V) and if your memory needs a refresh as much as mine did when I started writing Call of the Ancients, read on. Likewise, if you are a new reader and would like some background. I have concentrated solely on Gemma's story as the skull stories pretty much stand alone.

Heart of Regulus ended with Gemma's good friend Joe lying unconscious on a bleak hillside after he and Pieter van Broek were driven off the road. Joe was in northern Norway with van Broek in search if the black obsidian skull, Gileada, where they were attacked by two unknown men also looking for the skull. Unable to join the search, Gemma had stayed in England, unaware of what was happening.

Van Broek had contacted them a few days earlier with evidence that he really had discovered Gileada's hiding place and, wanting to stay as untraceable as possible, Joe drove up through Europe to meet him, carrying the golden key that would unseal the entrance.

Earlier in the year, Gemma survived an attack on her life only because Joe, who shares her home, rushed to her rescue, inadvertently killing her assailant as he fought him off. Not knowing what else to do, they called D I

Chamberlain who had investigated the murder of their friend, the maverick archaeologist Callum Davis. Chamberlain raised their suspicions when he spirited away the evidence as if nothing had happened and left them a signet ring bearing a symbol identical to the shape of the golden key.

While Joe is away, Gemma once again finds herself transported to the gardens of the Pyramid Temple in Atlantis, inhabiting the body of the High Priestess Haa'nu and witnessing the unfolding of the Skulls' rescue.

LOST LEGACY

THE SKULLS OF LIGHT, BOOK I

Chapter 1

The huge discus-shaped craft hovered silently above the forest canopy, an incongruous visitor in a virgin landscape as yet unshaped by man. The elegant curves of its dark silvery hull, flashing blue and violet as it reflected the sun's rays, cast over the land below a glowering shadow that deepened further the already dense gloom of the forest floor.

The ship had travelled here from way beyond Earth's solar system, its origins in the distant star systems of the galaxy, bringing with it gifts of a value and importance that Earth had never received before and never would again. Earth's nascent human race was being given a helping hand, one that would open the door to the evolution of its consciousness and the achievement of its full potential. It would be nurtured, protected, and guided. At first from a distance, a subtle energetic influence would lightly touch and, when the time was right, awaken the latent skills and abilities that would otherwise remain undiscovered and unused. This loving, benevolent and guiding hand would set humanity on its path to true understanding and lead it gently forwards.

Far below the spacecraft, a small party battled its way through the fetid humidity and dense, clutching undergrowth of the jungle. Vines and creepers, some swollen as thick as a man's waist in the dripping warmth, hung in tangled, impenetrable curtains. The group was making slow, energy-sapping progress, besieged by biting insects, while the moisture-laden air robbed every breath of oxygen. There was no trail for them to follow; they had no choice but to hack out each hard-won step of the way through vegetation that even their toughened knives, honed to a razor edge that no Earth-found metal could ever hold, struggled to conquer. They had descended to the surface at the nearest possible point to their destination, which was hidden deep in the trees, and they did not have far to travel – a few miles at most – but in these difficult conditions it would be almost a day's punishing trek.

It was a disparate and exotic looking group of males and females, drawn from each of the races involved in the ambitious operation that had brought them here. Tall slender Pleiadians, golden-haired Thetans and bronze-skinned Sirians trekked side by side with short, squat Metulians, small, delicate-boned Eleusians, and the strange childlike forms of the Arcturans. At the head of the group, two powerfully built males from the Alpha Centauri system opened up the path, wielding their huge machetes like machines. Yet others followed on behind. They carried with them a small square box of a dull grey metal, inscribed with strange symbols. This box was the last of thirteen and held the final element of the precious cargo that had travelled from the stars. All the others had already been set in their chosen places, concealed securely within the protective embrace of the Earth.

Their objective was a small gully that sliced through the hillside, so well camouflaged by the vegetation that the Alpha-Centaureans did not see it until they were right on top of it, and only narrowly missed plunging headlong. It was not deep, barely thirty feet at most, and its floor was pleasantly cool after the heat of the trek. At the gully head, a small waterfall tumbled prettily over moss-covered rocks, its stream gushing through a narrow channel at the far end where the slope of the hill descended to meet it. One by one the party climbed down and quenched their thirst in the fresh, pure water.

Behind the waterfall, a narrow crack pierced the wall of moisture-drenched grey rock and opened out into a deep recess a little further inside. This was where the treasure would remain until the time was right to bring it into direct contact with the human race.

One of the taller males stepped forward. He was slender with blond, almost white hair that hung like silk to below his shoulders; his moustache and beard were of the same colour. From beneath pale eyebrows, intelligent, vividly blue eyes looked out on the world. This was Artem, elected leader of the Galactic Council. In his hand lay an odd-looking key made of pure gold. It was the length of his palm and had arms shaped like an 'f' and a 'j' that were attached at one hundred and eighty degrees to each other from a small centre circle. A brief nod was the signal for the box to be brought to him. It had no visible catch or lock but as he pressed the key into a indentation on the side of the box that matched the it exactly, there was a faint click and the top slid open. Reaching inside, he drew out the carved skull that it held. This was the priceless gift that the people of the stars had brought to the Earth and its infant race.

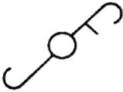

www.dkhenderson.com

Other books by this author
(Fiction)
Heel Lead

(Non-Fiction)
Forgotten Wings
Starspeak, Vols 1 & 2

ABOUT D. K. HENDERSON

Author & storyteller. Eternal spiritual adventurer, teacher & mentor; energy healer & channel. Coffee guzzler and chocolate muncher.

D.K. (otherwise known as Dawn) Henderson lives and writes in the mystical, magical landscape of Wiltshire, England, surrounded by the ancient & mysterious stone circles of Stonehenge and Avebury. If you can't find her snuggled up on the sofa with her notepad and pen, writing her next novel fuelled by a bottomless supply of coffee and chocolate digestives, she'll be wandering the ancient down-lands that inspire her writing.

Contact the author through her website at www.dkhenderson.com/contact

or email: mail@dkhenderson.com

www.dkhenderson.com

ISBN: 978-0-9934125-7-8

Printed in Great Britain
by Amazon